A Clare James Art Adventure
SOUL STAIN

———•‡•———

Soul Snare

Soul Stain

Soul Charade
coming 2016

———•‡•———

A Clare James Art Adventure
SOUL STAIN

Jasmine—
So nice to meet you!
I hope you enjoy it!
Blessings!
Charlene

Charlene M. Yoder
NUM 6:24-26

CHARLENE YODER

SOUL STAIN
copyright 2015 Charlene Yoder

Information on purchasing this series is available at www.charleneyoder.com

All Rights Reserved.
No part of this book may be reproduced, scanned, or distributed in any printed or electronic form without permission.

Author's photo by Alyssa Shrock Photography. Used by permission.
alyssashrock.com

This is a work of fiction and any resemblance to real people, living or dead, is coincidental.

Scriptures taken from THE HOLY BIBLE, NEW INTERNATIONAL VERSION®, NIV® Copyright © 1973, 1978, 1984, 2011 by Biblica, Inc.® Used by permission. All rights reserved worldwide.

Any people depicted in stock imagery provided by Thinkstock are models, and such images are being used for illustrative purposes only.
Certain stock imagery licensing purchased. © Thinkstock.

Because of the dynamic nature of the Internet, any web addresses or links contained in this book may have been changed since publication and may no longer be valid.

This book was written for God to use and
dedicated to my daughter, Adie.
*The song in your heart
is an example for me.*

He saved us,

not because of righteous things we had done,

but because of his mercy.

He saved us

through the washing of rebirth and renewal

by the Holy Spirit,

whom he poured out on us generously

through Jesus Christ our Savior,

so that,

having been justified by his grace,

we might become heirs

having the hope of eternal life.

Titus 3:5-7

Chapter One

How was I going to be able to keep this dog quiet? They were going to hear us and I had no idea how violent these people were. If they hadn't come back when they had, I'd have been out of there with the little pain–in–the–neck and come back later with Toby and the cops. Instead, it was turning into a bigger rescue mission then I anticipated now that I was a damsel in distress.

I heard the second car door slam outside, so I gave one final grunt and stretched under the dusty armoire as far as I could. I caught Reginald by a hind leg and pulled him out, squirming and snapping at me from his dust-bunny beard. Cradling him like a baby, I dove into the coat closet across the hall. I could hear keys jingling in the front door. Two men laughed with horse play as they passed the closet or they would have heard Reginald's pouty whining.

I desperately clawed at my pocket for the treats I'd brought in case he gave me trouble, which was more than likely. He was a clean cut little pug with a creamy coat and a chocolate colored face that reeled you in with a blink of his big brown eyes. Before you could help yourself you were cooing and saying, what a big, stuffy name for such a teeny weeny sweetie.

And then it passed.

You realized you should have said, what a sweetie of a name for such a manipulative little barracuda. He just wouldn't cooperate with me. Ever.

Oh Lord, make him understand I need him to behave or we're toast. I thought as I shoved all the treats in his greedy mouth at once. His hot doggy breath, mixed with kibble, came back at me, to tickling my nose. I swallowed a sneeze and gasped for air. *At least his crunching and sniffling in the dark were quieter than his whining and sassing.* Despite my optimism, I still couldn't hear what the men in the hall were saying over his wheezing.

Knowing this wouldn't hold him for long, I shifted him to my left arm and patted around on the floor beneath where I was squatting while the voices in the hallway moved away from us. The unevenness beneath my sandals appeared to be a pile of shoes emitting an unpleasant odor I didn't recognize. I tugged on one, but it resisted. I grabbed another by the heel and pulled harder. In the dark, they seemed to be all tangled up. Reginald was shoving his nose insistently at my pocket attempting to squirm his entire body in after the smell of treats. Trying to balance his little twisting form in the dark, I desperately clamped onto the neck of a boot. I had to get one free for Reginald to wrestle with before he chewed my pants off.

The boot was upright and I slipped my fingers around its neck. But for some reason, it felt more solid than the others had. I slowly slid my fingers up its smooth length in the dark until I hit material. Also solid. The leg continued up. As I patted at the knee in disbelief, I tipped my head back slowly, choking on the scream lodged in my throat. Reginald had frozen on my arm as well, as if he too had just noticed we weren't alone in the closet.

Oh God.

A gurgle erupted out of my throat, but a hand clamped over my mouth from behind me and an arm slipped over my head and brushed the door open a hair's width to allow a single sliver of light to spill in. Every muscle in my body tensed as I squeezed Reginald in terror.

And then my mind registered Key's tan Polynesian features floating over me. He had a finger placed to his lips and I sagged back against his legs in relief. He took his hand off my mouth and leaned over closer to scoop Reginald out of my noodle arms. The tiny guy nestled against Key's broad chest and licked his face with sheer delight. Sheer *quiet* delight. Only Key could master that feat.

Outside the closet the gruff male voices had returned and they had grown agitated.

"Don't tell me that rat has escaped again. He's got to be around here somewhere."

"It's *not* my fault this time, Red." A nasal voice whined. "I checked all the doors and windows before we left. He's hiding somewhere. It's a trick. He's trying to get me in trouble. He's not a nice puppy, you know. It's creepy. He's like a tiny, angry old man. Just like the guy we rescued him from, Red."

"How many times do I have to tell you we didn't rescue him from anyone? Look, you knucklehead, just get his food out. He always comes running for grub, little hog dog."

In panic, I looked up at Key. His eyes met mine and he shook his head slightly. Reginald was sleeping like a baby in his arms.

How'd he managed that? I tried not to chuckle. Relief was making me giddy. At least if the two guys out there found me now, I had a feisty guard pug and a connected Hawaiian tagger with me.

I shivered, thinking of how I'd met Key.

It had all started with a wild hair our design teacher had gotten over our final project. She wanted us to do a piece in the opposite of our personal style and it had to be something we'd never done before. Even with the new media and new style, it still had to represent our artistic viewpoint. It was the most ridiculous thing I'd ever heard. But I needed to knock it out of the park, so to speak, to keep my scholarship. And for two weeks I gnawed on the problem, but my idea tank had been as empty as a bear's tummy waking up from hibernation.

With the deadline looming, I'd gone to my closet to assess the situation. Art supplies cost an arm and a leg and I didn't have any money left to buy my way out of this with a fancy piece of charcoal. Rolled against the back wall behind my clothes was a spare square of movie screen. A theater had closed in our small town and my high school art teacher had secured enough white screen to use as backdrops in theater productions for all time. Since I had done so much volunteer painting, she had given me a scrap the size of a shower curtain as a memento.

In desperation, I pulled it out and spread it on the floor of my dorm room. It had to look like me, but be the opposite of my style. Hmmm. I quickly sketched a line drawing of my face, chin to forehead, with a yellow high lighter a friend had left in my room while studying some kind of microbiology.

Now normally I'm a realist down to the core. From drapery patterns to strappy sandals, I avoid anything abstract like the plague. I like a good story, but abhor science fiction. I am fascinated with techniques that make drawn and painted art look like photographs, but not quite. And my rock stars were Rembrandt and Caravaggio and John Singer Sargent. So this assignment was about what I *wasn't*.

I took all the left over ink, paint, glue, and weird supplies – stuff on the class list to buy but we'd never used – and dumped them all on the yellow outline of my unsmiling face. I didn't have much of a visual vocabulary of what I disliked to compare it to. I was leery of smearing or blending it too much in case I made it into something I liked. As I debated with myself about what to do, the materials took over and did it for me. The paint thinner reacted with the ink and the salt ate out the watercolor. The oil pastel shavings melted in the rubbing alcohol puddles and the willow charcoal dissolved into the Elmer's glue. I cracked open a window to the snowy cold and the rush of December air pushed the chemical smell from the room, leaving me light headed. When I turned back around from the slap of icy air I knew it was done. It fit the perimeters of the assignment and I hated it.

It had taken all night for the sloppy scene to set up enough for me to roll it up without total disaster. At the crack of dawn I'd shoved it through the teacher's office door drop-slot in one long tube. Praying I wouldn't fail I went back to my room to pack for Christmas break.

To my surprise, I was called to the dean's office before my carpool left campus for the drive home.

"Soooo, apparently you slipped under the fence without anyone noticing. How coy of you." The dean tapped his fingertips together while bracing his elbows on his chair arms and surveying me over his glasses. "Probably because you had to miss your entrance portfolio interviews when you had the German measles. I read your file. Something about the epidemic last year that hit the Midwest when the Amish spread it. No vaccinations. Those Amish. Can't tell if that's genius or crazy. Have they ever done an Amish Opera? Now that's an idea. Anyway, I understand you were born the year there was a bad batch of vaccinations, so you got the measles. Tough break."

Where is he going with this? Amish Opera? My entrance interview? That painting has cooked my goose. I'm being expelled. Or losing my scholarship. Lord, what am I going to do? My mind raced, trying to brace me for what was coming next.

"Martin tells me we have the next undiscovered art phenom here. Like when they found Jackson Pollock. Splatter. Splatter. Like anyone else couldn't make splatter art." He frowned and bit his lip. "Personally I favor the music department. What can I say? I was a music major. No money there though. Not everyone is a Carrie Underwood, so here I am behind this desk. That Amish Opera could be my break through, though. I could take the medieval one that no one seems to think is production worthy and —" Bright-eyed, he had paused in his inspired ramblings and focused his eyes on me. "But ho hum enough about that because it's congratulations to you today!"

He sat forward in his chair and shuffled the papers on his desk. "Martin wants you in his class immediately. It's a senior level oil painting class, but you're ready, or so he says. Here! It says we've replaced poor classic English in your schedule for when you return after the break, so report to Martin's painters in its place. Well, that's all. Happy Holidays. Keep my opera under your hat and close the door when go, will you? I owe you one." His wink only added to the surreal situation as I backed from the room in shock.

And that's how I met Key. That first day of painting with the seniors had been terrifying. I'd arrived early and tried to blend, but they all seemed like giants and it took an eternity for the professor to arrive. Everyone had clapped when Key came through the double swinging doors in a round off-spin-flip kind of maneuver. Like an acrobat, he landed in the middle of the students sitting around on metal stools and leaning on paint carts. He was five inches shorter than me and with a smile that split his face and closed his eyes. I was relieved everyone was focused on him. And then his entrance was interrupted by a hissing voice in my ear.

"Hey, Fresh Meat, you're in the wrong class. This is *senior* painting." Everyone's attention had swiveled to me as a pot head with three foot dread locks leered too far toward me on his stool. I'd sidestepped him and he'd sprawled on the waxed linoleum floor with a squishy thud. The room exploded in jeers and snickers.

As if on cue Martin had glided in with a cigar in one hand and a mug in the other. I hoped my face didn't show how scared I'd felt as our eyes met. He had smirked and cleared his throat. The room fell instantly quiet.

"No touch-y or fail-y." He wagged his cigar in my direction as cat calls and whistles rained down on my head. Holding his mug up over his head, he'd silenced them again. Setting the cup on the work bench, he licked his finger and selected the top sheet of paper off a stack. He held it out to me. Swallowing my intimidation, I'd forced my legs to walk around the stinky lecher now sitting cross legged on the floor and take the paper from Martin. Scanning it, I realized it was a supply list. Picking up his coffee again, he motioned to the door with his head. I nodded woodenly and turned to go. He'd put his cigar in his mouth and swatted my behind as I passed him.

Clearing the studio's swinging doors without looking back, I'd sank down on a bench in the hall to gulp in deep breaths and try not to cry with embarrassment. It was a den of wolves in there. I hated it before I'd even started.

I was prining (pray/whining) to God about my sad lot in life when the door had swung silently open next to me. I had swiftly straightened up, swiping a palm over my wet checks and bracing for the next attack. The compact acrobat sat next to me like a breeze.

"Little one, you have been given something to say. Do not fear saying it the way you were meant to. When my mother and I moved from Hawaii to Chicago, I too thought I would shrivel under the power of others. But I knew I had been given something to say, so I whispered it at first. Then I spoke what I was given to say. And finally I shouted what I was given to say. And each time I said it, someone listened. Someone heard. That is why I will keep saying it no matter where else I am or what else is being said. Do you understand?"

My eyes were wide and I had forgotten to blink. I nodded. It was like when the gospel was being spread.

"They call me Key. My family name is Kalean-kei.

"Nice to meet you, Key. I'm Clare. Clare James. And there's nothing going on, I mean with Professor –"

He held up his hand and stopped my stammering. "I know. You are a white lily. Young and fresh. Do not let them daunt you. Be brave, Lily. And keep your face turned toward the sun."

He stood up then and slipped back into the studio like a stream of smoke.

When I'd come back from the store with my supplies, the three hour class was still going. I set my packages on the bench by the door and leaned against the jam to watch them through the crack. I was a timid country mouse observing a room full of orangutans.

While searching for an art school, I had learned quickly that there were two camps in art world. Multiple piercings, colored hair, and dark clothing gained you admittance to the fine art tribe. On the other hand, the graphic arts clan tried to set themselves apart with a careful balance between creativity and geek-chic. Binders color coordinated to outfits and expensive markers in brief cases were accentuated with a lot of bow ties, vintage eyeglasses, and handmade jewelry. I was a dyed in the wool graphics advocate and if truth be told, the fine artists secretly scared me. I had chosen a liberal arts school with a strong art program on purpose. I wanted only a percentage of strangeness to deal with as opposed to being immersed in it. And now here I was in my worst case scenario. A naive freshman graphic art major advanced into a class of seasoned senior fine artists as if I was one of them. How long would it be before they sniffed me out? I was an imposter.

Praying for a way to make this work, I stood spying on them through the crack in the door. And there was Key again. His legs were wrapped around a beam spanning the metal, faux warehouse ceiling in the studio. He was spray painting upside down on a white canvas unfurled from the sky light. He deftly switched cans out of the pockets in his trouser legs as he added highlights and shadows to his work. It was a rolling sea of symbols and swirls cascading down from the sky. Out of the center of it all, a ginormous white lily bloomed.

I jumped back from the door jamb, my face hot with the bloom of bashful blush. He was clearly the big city graffiti artist everyone was whispering about on campus.

And he was painting a lily, the metaphorical me!

RATTLE, SHAKE, RATTLE.

RATTLE, SHAKE, RATTLE.

I was snapped back to the stuffy closet where I was kneeling in the dark. The racket from the dog food tin being vigorously shaken outside the door was like nails on a chalkboard. Up and down the hall the noise marched as the man tried to coax Reginald out with an awkward falsetto.

"Here Doggie, Doggie, Doggie. Nice Doggie. Come on Reggie. Here boy. Here Doggie, Doggie, Doggie. Time to eat."

I squinted up nervously at Reginald in the dark. He had stretched and yawned in Key's arms at the onset of the clamor. But then he settled back down with his chin on his paws in Key's elbow. His eyes were closed the entire time. He was a magazine shoot for innocence and tranquility. As I squinted at him in the dark, his hind leg twitched and a stink bomb enveloped the closet. *Oh no!* I silently gagged. *Dog farts are the worst. You can't get away from them fast enough.*

Only we couldn't get away at all because the caterwauling was still going on out in the hall.

"Come on little Reggie." RATTLE, SHAKE, RATTLE. "Don't get me in trouble with Red again." RATTLE, RATTLE. "Here, Doggie, Doggie, Doggie." SHAKE, SHAKE. "Come on, come out, Reggie. It's our little secret I fed you all them boiled eggs so you're not hungry now."

Reginald's hind leg twitched again in his sleep and a small tooting noise announced it wasn't a secret anymore. My eyes were watering and I buried my nose as deep as I could into the elbow of my sweater sleeve. I looked up at Key. He was a statue holding a dog. His eyes were closed and his lips were stretched in a tight grimace. Reginald slept on like a baby — a gassy baby who ate boiled eggs like they were going out of style. His stub of a tail wagged every once in a while with happy dreams.

Toot. Toot. Toot.

I gasped and hunkered lower to the floor, pressing my mouth against the crack in the door as my thoughts raced. *Air! Fresh air! It's a miracle. And not the only one today. How is Reginald not hearing that man and all that food racket?*

It didn't matter a moment later, because things were changing in the hall. My eyes were now close enough to the crack I could see the two men facing each other by the front door.

"You let him out again, didn't you, Coop?"

"No, Red, honest. He must have slipped out when we left. Or maybe he's in our gear."

"Well, get out there and catch him. We can't let some college kid see him again."

"I know, I know, Red. Just don't blame me, okay?"

"Blame you?" Red slapped him upside of the head. "Who should I blame then? It's either you or me."

Coop slumped toward the front door and Red turned around. He had a shot gun nestled in his elbow. I involuntarily drew back in the dark.

"I'm waiting here till they call with instructions."

I heard the click of the front door as Coop went out to search for the pug.

How are we going to get out of here, Lord? My thoughts flip-flopped back and forth between prayer and panic. *And how long till Reginald wakes up and gives us away with his noisy yipping? I'm going to die with a Polynesian gang member and a stolen dog in a closet full of methane. And I haven't even gotten a chance to decide if I love Toby yet!*

Toot. Toot. Toot.

🐙 Chapter Two

"Are you Clare James?"

Startled I turned around on the edge of the rocky outcropping where I had been balancing, almost dropping my shoes and socks into the waiting water. As far as my eyes could see, only tanned men and women were around me casting nets into the hungry sea. My parents were a little further up the rocky terrain resting on the edge of a beached fishing boat. Their pants were rolled up and they'd spread their shoes and socks on the bottom of the overturned boat.

Now I'm hearing things. It had to be sea noises and sleep deprivation. I thought. Living out of hostels and trains half the summer had been both exhilarating and exhausting. *That couldn't have been my name.*

I turned my face into the sun and sucked in a deep breath of salty sea air. Salty *Adriatic* Sea air to be exact. I could pinch myself for being on the coast of Italy in yet another idyllic scene from the pages of my books at home.

A sea gull screamed at me in Italian as a chilly wave licked my white toes. I had a farmer's tan for sure this summer. We had been on the road traveling for nearly three months and I hadn't had time nor opportunity to work on evening out my torso. My deep brown forearms, calves, and face were way ahead of the game, separated by a distinct pale line on my body wherever a sleeve or pant leg fell.

"Well, you don't look much like I remember, but are you Clare James?" The voice came again and I whipped around this time hard enough to lose my balance and topple into the sea. Before my head went under I saw on an outcropping next to mine a slip of a girl, who looked vaguely familiar, bent over an artist working on a painting. I hadn't paid the painter much heed because they were everywhere in Italy and this one had been no different. An Asian girl with a backpack hunkered over a collapsible easel, fighting the wind to paint.

As my head broke back through the icy rough water, I gave a hearty scream. I was not much of a swimmer and I was weighed down by my gear and heavy clothes. I clubbed at the water with my hands full of shoes and socks. I couldn't let go of them. I needed them to hike back off the treacherous beach to the train station. I could feel the freezing water beginning to paralyze me and my hair kept swirling into my nose and mouth.

As quickly as that I was between the devil and deep blue sea. Literally. "God, help me!" I cried out frantically in a burst of underwater bubbles as I went under again.

I fought to surface one last time and miraculously multiple helping hands yanked me out of the frigid water sputtering like a cat who'd accidently tumbled into an aquarium. I coughed hard and lay back on the stone slab where I'd been standing dry only moments before. I could hear my parent's calls as they ran up the sea shore. Broken English and Italian from the locals standing around me made a noise like wind chimes tinkling in the fresh breezes that played tag around the rocks.

The bright ball of sun overhead shining blindingly in my eyes was momentarily blocked. "*You* must be Clare James," a female voice said triumphantly.

I continued to sputter and sat up, wiping the wet mats of curly hair out of my hazel eyes.

"What do you want?" I rasped out with a shiver as the fishermen, seeing I was okay, melted back to their work. I haphazardly tossed a few fingers in the air to thank them.

"Are you all right? Did you slip? What happened?" My parents were both breathless as they tugged at my drenched coat front.

I waved them away. "I'm okay. Fine. Fine. Yeah, slipped. Now I'm soaked. Ugh. And it's colder out here then what it seems. What a mess." I rubbed my frosty fingers together trying warm them.

"We'd better get to the station. It's almost time for our train and you can change there. We can pick up a touristy t-shirt and hopefully some shorts since everything in your pack is probably wet too." My mom said as my dad helped me off the slippery outcropping. I quickly sat down again on a patch of sand with wobbly knees.

"Are you sure you're okay?" My dad asked with concern in his voice.

I nodded as I stretched all my arms and legs and took another deep breath. The wave of weakness began to subside as the sun returned the color my face.

"Yeah, just wet as a quilt on wash day." I rang the ice water out of my socks before wrestling them onto my frozen feet.

As we picked our way up the jagged beach toward the road the girl trailed along behind us like a dolphin following a rowboat.

Shaking my head in a doggish attempt to get the water out of my ears, I paused in our exit. "Who did you say you were again?"

She bounced to my side, "Well, that's just it. I hope you remember me. I'm Sammy. Sammy Sullivan. That's short for Samantha Sullivan, but everyone calls me Sammy." She stuck her hand out for a shake.

"How did you find me?" I was trying to place how I knew her

snappy brown eyes, a bit wide apart, and her loads of wavy chestnut hair. She might be said to look a little like me, so perhaps that was all. I was an artist and faces painted themselves in my mind, whether I wanted them there or not. It had been a long summer and an even longer semester studying in London before this trip, so my brain was on sensory overload.

Sure she looks like me. I thought. *Right now that long haired fat guy sorting fish over there could look like me too. Whoa, my heart's still racing. I nearly drowned. Thanks, God for sending help. I've seen too far many faces lately to separate them all out here.*

"Are you sure you're okay?" She asked hesitantly, snapping me out of my reflections.

"I do feel rather steamy with all these wet clothes and the sun kicking in. I need to be sure and drink water." I reminded myself as I cracked open the bottle I had buttoned in a jacket pocket. "But why are you looking for me? How do I know you?" I took a long swig.

Dad and mom took a water break too. I could feel their worried eyes like invisible probes inspecting my face for signs of trauma. I smiled at them.

"Well," Sammy shifted from one foot to the other. "It's the kind of story I needed to tell you in person. So I asked my roommate to ask your roommate if she knew where you were. They're neighbors in Chicago. Jackie used to babysit her. Anyway, Jackie had just talked to you and you told her where you were supposed to be at today and my roommate told me and I've just been here combing the beaches ever since. I figured you'd come here at least once before you left. I mean it's amazing, right?"

Jackie was my college roommate back in the States and I had talked to her yesterday about filing our housing paperwork for the fall since I would be back from studying abroad.

So that part of her story checks out. But how'd she get here so fast? Like a bunny rabbit with a dynamite carrot. I chuckled at my own wild idiom and I chugged some more water.

Brindisi was a stinky port town on the toe of the boot shape of Italy and we had only come here to catch a ferry over to Greece. We had waited in a ticket line for several hours only to discover the ferry offered a twenty-four hour ride on an open ship's deck in what was predicted to be stormy weather for the next week or two. Unanimously my parents and I had voted to skip Greece. We were too tired for that leg of the trip and a connecting train up to Rome could put us on our way home instead. It was a no brainer. After weeks of traveling, home sounded like a honey pot to a hungry bear.

With some time to kill before we boarded our sleeper car back across Europe, we ventured out to look around a little.

Our look proved to be very little. Brindisi wasn't made for tourists. The town was polluted with trash on every surface and the men hanging about doorways did nothing but stare at us as we walked passed. Probably because we were women without head coverings. This far to the East, the guidebook said it could get problematic pretty fast if we didn't stick to populated areas when exploring. Safety in numbers also meant access to food and restrooms. Of course the later term I use loosely about the vast cement bathrooms with no stalls and only holes in the floor to squat over. On a side note, I had been happier than a squirrel with a cheek full of nuts we carried our own rolls of toilet paper.

By mutual consensus, we didn't want to miss the next train out of there and we had only stopped at the coast for a cleansing peek at the water. The beach had proved to be a quiet place to reflect over our trip thus far as we shucked our shoes and wandered along the sandy shore. Before I heard my name being called, I had been staring out to sea asking God if I would regret skipping Greece. I might never have another opportunity like this in my lifetime.

However, thus far my only regret was walking too far out on those slippery rocks.

"Okay, well, you found me and you have my attention, walk and talk, Sammy. Walk and talk. I don't want to miss the next train. Sounds like you're from back home."

"I am. I just finished freshmen year. I've been here studying painting for the past month. Well, not here, here." She waved at the ground and glanced around as we scaled another rock between us and the road like mountain goats. "I'm not particularly fond of this area. I've been staying in Venice and Rome mostly. I've been working on my technique for a commission."

"Oh, are you a part of that group at school? The one Clare is in?" My mom smiled at Sammy and gave her a hand as she jumped down from the rock.

"Thank you. Yes. I'm in the Commission Club. I know they don't usually let in freshmen, but with your seat vacant last semester, they gave me a charity job. I'm not too proud to admit it, I needed the work to stay in school and I made myself a bit of a nuisance to get it." She jumped a puddle. "Actually for this fall and spring too."

The Commission Club had been started by poor art students back in the forties to create artwork ordered by patrons in whatever style they wanted at whatever price they would donate. The students who formed it only let the best students in and they only let in a few so that they fostered a reputation for quality pieces, both originals and replicas. Fifty years later, it was an institution on campus and students competed every year for the spots graduating seniors left open. I had been invited, without having to apply, my sophomore year.

Most of the jobs were mantle portraits of the various wealthy patrons who supported the college. While I was studying abroad in London, if a needy student qualified, or there were too many jobs, an alternate could be named. Apparently Sammy was my alternate.

"Wait a minute, if you don't mind my asking, how can you afford to be here? This backpacking stuff is the cheap way to go, but it's still not cheap." My dad shook his head and waved his bottle of water.

He had a point. I'd taken the money my grandmother had given me to see Europe and budgeted it so that all three of us could back pack across the continent. It wasn't glamorous, but it let my parents see Europe too. Something they probably could never have afforded while they were still young enough to survive it.

"Actually, the client sent me here." Sammy looked embarrassed. "The commission wasn't going too well. I think I might have sold myself a little too strongly. I mean, I thought the piece looked okay just to begin with. It's a portrait, and they start out rough, you now? But my client didn't agree. Suddenly I found myself enrolled in a summer painting class here in Italy." She waved her arms around her. "And it's been *amazing*! I've learned so much. And it's all paid for, as part of the commission."

"Wow." I raised my eyebrows at her. "That's a great donation. Most of the time they're adequate, but not very generous. The committee tries to screen them, but they still insist on only taking donations, not setting fees, so we're stuck with whatever they offer. And the work experience too, of course." I added.

"Yeah, I know." Sammy spread her arms out as we walked. "I couldn't believe they were donating three semesters of tuition. And then, on top of it they sent me here. It's been a dream come true. Until yesterday." Her arms dropped and her shoulders sagged.

We had entered the train station and my dad was haggling with a woman in a stall for a tacky pink I-heart-Brindisi shirt and some black sweat pants. *Ugh! At least they're dry.* I thought as I turned my attention back to Sammy.

"What happened yesterday?"

She sank onto a bench as the bounce deflated the rest of the way out of her. "I got a phone call from the states my mom was in a bad car accident."

"Oh, no, you poor dear," My mom sank down next to her and put an arm around her shoulders.

"I've got to leave here in about an hour on a puddle jumper so I can catch an international flight out of Rome for South Dakota. She's still in the critical care unit and there's a lot of burn damage so I don't know if, I just don't know if..."

She was choking and I automatically bent and hugged her before I thought about being soaking wet. I drew back but in a vice like grip, she grasped my hand with both of hers as if I could pull her from the stream of fear engulfing her.

"I *had* to find you, Clare, before I left Italy. You're the *only* one that can help me. The *only* one on the earth and if you say no, I'm lost, just lost." She sagged back against the bench and closed her eyes.

I looked down at her anguish and realized I was leaving a

puddle of water where I was standing. A puddle of sea water that is. Snapping out of my empathy daze, I shifted my weight on squishy soles and took action.

"Sammy, I'm so sorry! Let's pray for your mom first then you can tell me how I can help. We need God to ease her pain and comfort your fear and worry." My mom took my other hand and we bowed our heads in the dirty, bustling train station and asked for healing and divine guidance. At amen, I took a deep breath and brushed the tears from my face, opening my eyes. My dad joined us with a small bag of clothes. A train whistle hollered in the distance.

"I'm so sorry this is happening, Sammy, but if I'm going to help you, you've got to talk like the wind. Our train is coming and your plane has got to be leaving soon."

She nodded, blowing her nose on a scrap of paper left on the bench. "Thanks, Clare. I have to ask you for a huge favor. I'm headed home for this semester to help my dad take care of my little brother. But my portrait commission has a strict deadline and it's going to be impossible for me to finish it. It has to be presented at the Sulferson Christmas party. The subject's crazy sitting schedule makes it impossible for me to fly in and do it on weekends. And photos are out too. I've asked. They won't let me work from home. I've tried every which way to make it work. But my biggest problem is if I don't complete the commission, I've got to pay back the cost of this trip and last semester's tuition without even getting a degree. I'll be flipping burgers for the rest of my life!"

I exchanged glances with my parents. Surely the situation wasn't as dire as all that. As if she knew I was skeptical, she continued.

"I've talked to the man himself and there's no grace. He'll only accept an alternate artist to finish the painting. But not just any artist. It has to be one who's been to Italy, of all things. I know I can't get the portrait done by the deadline. I need, no, I'm asking, no, I'm *begging* you to finish this commission for me. You have the experience, you're in Italy, and everyone knows you have a heart."

She released my hand and held up her palm toward me as she finished explaining her predicament.

"I know, I know, I know. I can't guarantee you'll get paid at all. I don't know what they'll do about the next two semester's tuition but if they'll give it to you, you're welcome to it. He said it was negotiable, depending on the end result. And I'll do anything you say, anything I can. *Anything!* Just please don't make me choose between my future and my family!"

❦ Chapter Three

Sprawling on the floor under my open window, I lay still, watching the curtains billow out overhead. The hot gasping breath of summer was giving way to the buffeting breezes of fall in Illinois. It was my favorite time of year. Any open window could catch a steady breeze unpolluted by the sound of a fan. Even as a kid, surrounded by cows and corn fields, I envisioned a billowing curtain as a beach towel floating out over exotic sands, or a hot air balloon lifting with a whoosh, or a sail unfurrowing with a snap. Without hesitation those winds had blown my imagination on many a gentle journey, putting my decisions and problems in perspective, like whispers from God.

Today the wind was from the North and the way it started flipping the curtains like butterfly wings reminded me of my room in London. I had been propped up in bed while my broken bones mended with only the drapes, tossed by a flirty breeze, to keep me company. I'd pinned bits of stationery to them from notes my friends had given me.

I now kept those precious scraps of paper in a small carved box under my desk. Kind words always helped me reel in the drama and focus on God whenever I thought I was between a rock and hard place.

Rolling over, I pulled the box toward me and fished out the card on top. I never tired of reading it.

Dearest Clare, John 15:13 says, "Greater love has no one than this, that he lay down his life for his friends." Thank you for the risk you took that day in the gallery when you told us about Christ as you explained the picture of Salome with John the Baptist's head. I know how important your scholarship is to you completing an education that could impact what you do with your life and I appreciate that you put it all on the line for the people in that show room. I could have reacted differently and thrown you out of the class with an incomplete. But instead, your love changed my heart and saved my life and I will never forget it. For no other friend has shown me greater love. In Christ, Penelope

Penelope had been the most horrible and the absolute dearest teacher I'd ever had all rolled into one. When I met her, she was a cynical assistant for the Courtald's art history professor I had been assigned. She did all the professor's teaching and all her model boyfriend's homework.

Worst of all, as if the Boston Tea Party were yesterday, her British heart strongly resented Americans. Her prejudice spilled into every class lecture as she berated Toby and I, the only two yanks in her group, with tales of imminent failure.

Despite my anxieties, I had seized an opportunity to present a painting for class with the love of Christ. And shockingly, her stern heart had melted. From that point on, she had become a whole different person, a whole different teacher. She became a couch, a mentor, and a sister – a sister in Christ.

"Hey!" Jacquelyn, my roommate, strolled into the room and dumped a stack of books on her bed, a cascade of straight blonde hair falling into her blue eyes. "Why can't I be an art major and day dream all day without this weight lifting kit? My mantra should be – Pre-med, what was I thinking?"

I sat up and threw a pillow at her. She dodged it with a laugh as she pulled her shimmering hair off her plump face and into a pony tail in front of her dresser mirror.

"*You* were thinking about all those sick little kids you're going to help and *I* wasn't daydreaming. I was mustering up courage. I have to call and make an appointment to start to finish Sammy Sullivan's portrait commission."

"Oh, that's right. You were talking about that when we were moving in. Whoa, that's not like you to put something off. We've been here like three weeks. What's up?" She wrinkled her freckled nose at me.

"Sammy's client sounds tougher then boiled owl. I'm kinda worried this project will be a bigger bite then I can chew," I said.

Jackie paused to look at me with her hands on her hips.

I sighed. We both knew that wasn't the whole problem. "I guess I just want to enjoy being normal for a little bit before someone obligates me to board the train to crazy town again, you know?" It was a rhetorical question, but I saw her nod as she sorted her books, listening to me process my thoughts out loud.

I eased my back against the wall under the window and let the undulating curtains brush the top of my head. "After what happened in London all I planned on this year was humdrum classes, fun senior show work, and hanging out at church with you guys. Showing Toby around campus was the spiciest thing I was hoping for." I ducked my head to hide a grin and then looked up with a frown. "And so far it's all been nice and bland, even Toby."

Jackie laughed. "You're the one keeping him at arm's length. He'd jump at a chance to have an actual date with you. Like the Fall Dance. He keeps hinting."

"Yeah, I know." I looked down at my hands resting limply on my lap. "I feel like we came back from London together and everyone thinks we're getting married or something. It wasn't like that over there."

"So what was it like?" She leaned forward, her elbows propping up her chin on the bed. "Cause you never really talk about Toby there. It was you and Simon, wasn't it?"

She was smirking, but I ignored her teasing and thought seriously about it. "Simon might be the closest thing to my ideal man I've ever come across. I mean, I loved how I could talk to him about the other side, you know, the supernatural. And it felt great when he challenged me to use the talents God gave me. I learned so much from him." I paused after I said that. I wanted to experience God as fearlessly as Simon did and being around him taught me so much. It edified my spirit, he would say. *But being with him was more like being with my favorite teacher, or a big brother I wanted to grow up and be just like. Not how I imagined it would be to fall in love*, I reflected privately. *Like the second verse of the beginning of the Song of Songs, 'Let him kiss me with the kisses of his mouth — for your love is more delightful than wine.' Ah, not so much with Simon.*

"Here's the thing, Jackie. I chased after God and it got really intense. And while I'm resting a little here, I still crave that feeling of getting closer to God. I don't want to get all wrapped up in love and make decisions about what job I take after graduation based on someone else's geography. I'm God hunting and I'm not sure Toby is after that same rush."

Before she could respond I added. "And his hair cut."

"What?" She half laughed as she sputtered out the word.

"Yeah, it's driving me crazy. It doesn't look like him! I feel like I don't know him. Which makes me sad. He was such a good friend in London. I mean I could tell him anything. And there was this boy-girl tension between us. I felt breathless around him. Maybe it was just the adrenaline of survival. And I enjoyed the sparing about God a lot. You know what they say, the thrill of the chase or whatever." I twisted a hank of hair between my fingers as I watched the curtains billow almost straight out from the wall over my head as the wind gusted.

I waited for its whistle to ebb before speaking again. "It's like starting over with a whole other person. Only this time his glasses are bigger than the Hubble telescope lens."

Jackie laughed. "Oh, Clare, you're always so dramatic. Those glasses he wears are fake. They're just a prop. He wears them to look smart, which he thinks you'll like better."

"You're kidding! He does not." I tossed a football shaped pillow at her from beside me on the floor. "He knows I loved the little wire rims he wore in England. He found them at a Civil War reenactment with his dad."

She had snagged the football out of the air. "I told him to cut it out, but he's insecure about how popular you are since you've been back. He's new here and he's feeling like a third wheel. Plus I think the new look is him trying to be a changed person now that he's a Christian, you know?"

"Well, that's a horse of different color. I guess it explains some of his bizarre behavior. And you'd know more about it since you've been chatting with him so much lately."

She tossed the football pillow back at me. "I am here studying in the room when he comes by and he's lonely. He's cute, so a lot of girls talk to him and he doesn't want to give you the wrong impression. For some reason, he thinks he's into you."

I ignored her jab as I thought about what else she'd said. I had moved to my bed, where I sat with my elbows locked behind me, swinging my legs over the side. "I understand what you're saying about turning over a new leaf, but some things about him, like between us, weren't a part of his old life. I mean, like he used to always have a roll of Smarties in his pocket in London. He was always giving them to me. I don't know where he got them because I rarely see them around here anymore, let alone London. But it was our thing there. I have all the notes he left with them when he stopped by the flat and I wasn't home." I sighed. "So many things are *different* now. With everything."

She looked startled. "With me too?"

"Nah, you're still dependable as a pocket watch." I grinned. "A book in your hand everywhere from the bathroom to the lunch line. You were even studying while you were vacuuming out your car yesterday!"

She laughed. "It was just that one time. I'm paranoid about getting it dirty and you know I can't afford to let my grades falter." Her voice went up high and then sunk back down to a normal octave. "I almost wish my parents had waited to get it for me until after graduation. From medical school, that is. I tempted to go places and wash it all the time." Her woeful expression collapsed into a mischievous smile. "Don't be jealous! I love it, but I still love you more!"

Her playful banter made me laugh too. Her parents had given her the sleek, champagne-colored convertible for her twenty-first birthday over the summer. I think they figured she'd never actually have time to zip around in such a fun car and get into any serious trouble, so they spoiled her. We had managed to get the top down in the last few weeks of smoldering August weather despite her rigorous study schedule. All too soon the first snow would be here and we'd have to winterize the car and put socks on under our flip flops.

I pulled my snack stash, a cardboard box covered with stamps, off my head board shelf and tossed a homemade rice crispy square at her. She automatically caught it without looking up from the book she had ducked into as our conversation wound down.

Since my freshmen year, my mom had sent me a box of homemade treats every week I was away at school. Everyone who lived near me had reaped the benefits, so I wasn't surprised when several heads immediately popped in our open door.

"Did I just hear a care package open?" Marcella from upstairs sauntered into our room.

"I heard it even if you're not sure you did!" Simone quipped as she shoved past her. Giggling, they both copped a squat by the open windows.

I noticed Wendy, the new girl in the house, keying in to her room across the hall and I leaned forward to wave at her through our open door. "Hey, want a snack?"

She ignored me and quickly disappeared, closing her door behind her with a sharp click. I frowned. *Maybe she didn't hear me. But still, everyone props their doors open when they're home except Wendy and Sillo.*

We did it to circulate the air and add to the comradery of the house. It was easier to stick your head in to ask if anyone wanted to go in on a pizza, or a car pool to the movies, or compare lecture notes. Since our room was right by the front foyer, Jackie and I had a lot of visitors coming and going. And we liked it that way. But it might not be everyone's cup of tea.

"That box opening is like a bell for Pavlov's dogs," Marcella said, licking her lips with an exaggerated silly face. I tossed both girls a big square speckled with M&M's. Marcella waved an arm toward the brown parcel on my bed.

"My mouth starts watering every time I hear the rustling of paper and the scrape of cardboard. You've ruined me forever working at the entry level mail room positions I'm going to have to take to get into a big firm. I'll be drooling all over the packages! And don't even get me started on the smell of duct tape." She leaned over and took a big bite out of Simone's square.

"Hey!" Simone raised her treat over her head and punched Marcella's arm with her other hand. "Stay back. I have a ring of keys and I know how to use them!"

Simone was the house RA, the resident assistant, or the Sheriff, as we called her. Having a single room and a break on tuition were a few of the perks for taking on extra responsibilities. She had the master keys so whether you accidently locked yourself out or your roommate purposely locked you out, she was 9-1-1.

Her pre-vet major required a big heart for animals and that transferred over to her house. Everyone loved her. Her sassy wash-and-wear haircut created a perfect frame of blond hair to accent her attractive almond-shaped green eyes. She loved to regale us with tales of rich ranchers from her internship who took her number in case they needed a vet who made house calls for all the sick baby animals of the world.

Somehow, though, despite her love of the dramatic and all its attention, she always found her way back to Rupert, a local policeman. They had met while he was at the academy. He had doggedly dated her through thick and thin. His recent promotion to the horse patrol had delighted her to no end and it seemed they might finally get married. I was happy for them. They were one of those couples God had made for each other and you knew it as soon as you met them, whether they did or not.

Simone motioned give-me with the fingers of one hand. "Come on girl, you know I need more."

"Oh, sorry, is Rupert coming by?" I winged another one at her and she nodded.

"Gotta keep my very-tall-very-dark-and-very-handsome African Prince happy." We all giggled.

"Sure thing, Mrs. Sheriff." I tossed her a second one as the front doorbell rang and she snagged the treat out of the air. Rupert was over six feet tall and could probably pack away my whole box in one sitting. She smiled a thanks at me for sharing two with him. Her mouth was full of marshmallow and crispy, so she just pointed toward the front of the house, before bolting from our doorway with a wave.

"Hey, have you guys noticed anything going on across the hall?" I nodded toward the door and lowered my voice. "Wendy and Sillo never prop their door. Wendy just came home and closed it without as much as a by-your-leave. I haven't even seen Sillo since I got back."

"How long were you gone, anyway?" Marcella waved a tan

hand at me from the floor. "Don't you remember that's the way Sillo and Berry always were? Even if Sillo is a fairly normal Wicken, she always had Berry's nonsense to put up with. Those anthropology majors are a breed of their own." She shook her head without a hair of her tomboyish cut moving out of place and took a moment to chew and swallow another bite before she went on. "I dated an anthropology major once until he wanted me to meet his parents at a mud dinner. I kid you not, it's just like it sounds — with face paint and squatting in the mud. Kooky!" She paused to eat some more.

I jumped as she spoke again into the silent pause her last statement had created as we munched and pictured a miry soiree. "He was nice enough, but I couldn't see myself doing Christmas for the rest of my life in swill." Marcella leaned against our door jam and trailed her fingers over the SPAM cans decorating our entrance. "Man, maybe Sillo won't let Wendy prop the door, you know? Roommate wars can be vicious."

"Yeah, I guess." I chewed thoughtfully for a minute before I spoke again. "But you do realize that Wickens are into pagan stuff and things like witches, don't you? I mean, it seems like this harmless trend to worship nature, but there's a whole lot more to it than that."

Marcella rolled her brown eyes. "It's 1993, Clare. It's not like we have Salem witch trials anymore. Or need for superstitions or magic tricks. We're a lot more educated then they were back then."

"Maybe that's the problem," I muttered at the same old song

and dance I kept running into around campus. Since I'd come back from London I'd begun to notice how fashionable it was to pick and choose parts of the Bible to follow, saying the rest was outdated, or a suggestion. Those teachings had always been there. I'd realized I was the one who'd changed enough to see them for what they were.

"Look, Marcella, it doesn't matter what year it is, the Bible is God's *living* word. It's a powerful collection of things he wants us to know. Some of it is obvious and some of it needs to be decoded or worked out, no, revealed, that's it, that's the word I want. It's alive so it can *reveal* to each of us what we need to know as we need to know it. Individually. Only we have to actually read it for it to work with the Holy Spirit."

Marcella looked at me blankly. "So you're going all nun on me and telling me to read my Bible? Except," Here she raised her eyebrows skeptically. "You think it's alive or something?"

"Yes, yes!" I felt the blood coursing faster through my veins as my excitement at talking about God ignited.

"And," She was speaking slowly, as if to a child. "You think it has a special message for me that no one else but me can, ah, decode?"

"Yes, I do. In Hebrews 4:12 it tells us, 'For the word of God is living and active. Sharper than any double-edged sword, it penetrates even to dividing soul and spirit, joints and marrow; it judges the thoughts and attitudes of the heart.'

"I've found this to be true, Marcella. Each time I read the scriptures, I notice new details in them that make sense like they never did before. Why don't you see for yourself?" I slid open a drawer in my desk and selected a small black Bible off the stack inside. I kept them, like Simon, to pass out when someone needed one. She accepted the book between two fingers like it was a going to bite her.

I glanced at Jackie. She was hidden behind her textbook. One of the new things I'd noticed while reading the scriptures was all the references to magic as rebellion against God. Consequently, I felt convicted about not using the word magic casually in conversation. My experiences overseas had shown me that the supernatural did exist and there were two sides warring against each other. I didn't want the lines between the two to blur anymore in my life and make me an ineffective Christian.

I'd shared what I was learning with Jackie the last time she'd gushed about the Magic Kingdom. I asked her to consider the stories we'd both grown up with. "Even if we ignore the word magic, what are we supposed to do with all the spells in stories like Cinderella?"

"Well, the witch is clearly the bad guy. No little girl is going to want to be her. We want to be Cinderella!" Jackie had protested.

"I'll give you that." I had spoken honestly. "Except, Cinderella still participates in magic arts with another being called her fairy godmother who suddenly appears and comes to her rescue. How many girls want to be her? There's this whole culture of good witches that tries to peddle the notion it's okay to fix the problem on your own with good magic. But the Bible doesn't say only some magic is bad. It's all the same thing. I mean, Cinderella and this being called a fairy godmother use magic to make a pumpkin a carriage and manipulate Cinderella's future instead of asking God for help and accepting his salvation. What if Cinderella shared the love of Christ with her step-sisters and they got saved? Was the prince a Christian? Was that God's will for her life?"

Jackie had sat there looking lost. "I never heard such ideas. What makes you think – no – why would that even happen?" She stammered around. "It's just for fun. Come on, the moral of the story is good triumphing over evil. You know? You're getting too deep. And, well, and maybe the fairy godmother is supposed to represent God rescuing her." Before I could respond, her face had gotten a sick look on it. "Otherwise, you're saying her fairy godmother is like the devil or a demon or something." Her voice had trailed off

"Well, Jack, something I've learned the hard way is just because we think something is good doesn't make it God. God doesn't use spells. It's contrary to how he'd instructed us to behave in the Bible. A house divided against itself cannot stand. However, it does tell us that Satan will deceive us anyway he can, even by looking pretty. So how is this story, interwoven with magic, constructive? Especially for *children*."

"Well, it didn't hurt us and we both grew up hearing magical stories," she shot back.

"How can you be so sure?' I asked with a faraway voice as I started twisting a lock of hair around my fingers. I was thinking about that idea hard. "I mean, Jackie, how many people have we healed of blindness or fed with a few loaves and fish or saved from Hell? I can count that number on one hand. Is God using us as much as he could?"

I dropped the piece of hair I was twisting and our eyes had locked across the room.

"You mean like bringing people back from the dead?" She whispered.

"Yah. Can you imagine what kind of doctor you'd be doing that all day?"

She uttered a weak laugh. "That's ridiculous. A silly children's book isn't stopping me from doing that all day."

"Then what is?" I'd thrown the challenge out into the room.

"Magic is only pretend. Everyone knows that. Stop trying to make my favorite things ugly." She had avoided my question and started to get defensive so I knew it was time to change the subject.

In the end, Jackie couldn't let go of the magic of magic. She liked the make believe and glitter it clothed itself in. I had left this verse on her desk: *Do not conform to the pattern of this world, but be transformed by the renewing of your mind. Then you will be able to test and approve what God's will is—his good, pleasing and perfect will. Romans 12:2*

I saw it across the room tacked to the bulletin board over her desk. It helped me focus what I had to say now to the thin marketing major eating marshmallow squares under my window. "Look, Marcella, I know you are an intelligent woman who believes God exists. Your first step is to accept God wants to have a personal relationship with you. He knows who you are. He even knows how many hairs you have on your head."

"He does not!" She looked startled.

"It says so in the Bible, Matthew ten, thirty." She looked at the black book resting on her knee as I continued. "He loves you so much he sent his only son to die in your place. He gave you the Holy Spirit and the Bible to help. If you start with that, you can find the truth for yourself."

I moved over and sat next to her under the undulating polyester panels the University issued for curtains. "I've been finding things in here I never heard before since I got back from England. Take magic for instance." I ignored the sound of a big breath being sucked in from behind Jackie's book and plowed on. "It's on the tip of my tongue to talk about because I've been wrestling with how our society views it. How often do we say, 'Oh it was a magical experience' when we have a good time? Or we exclaim, 'That was magic' when something happens we can't readily explain?

"I was raised with a blind eye toward magic. I was taught it was not real and God is all powerful. And I do believe God is all powerful, but the more I read, the more I'm finding magic isn't just a figment of our imagination.

"Among other places, I've found evidence of magic in Exodus 7:10." I flipped through the pages of my Bible on my desk. "Here, it says, 'So Moses and Aaron went to Pharaoh and did just as the Lord commanded. Aaron threw his staff down in front of Pharaoh and his officials, and it became a snake. Pharaoh then summoned wise men and sorcerers, and the Egyptian magicians also did the same things by their secret arts: Each one threw down his staff and it became a snake. But Aaron's staff swallowed up their staffs.'

"God doesn't want us to waste our time trying to duplicate what he can do by chasing after magic so we feel in control or empowered. This rebellion separates us from his perfect will for us. He wants us to trust in him and rely on him to save us like he did with Moses and the Israelites.

"I'm noticing multiple instances like this where magic practiced by sorcerers and witches is defeated by God. And not because it doesn't exist, but because God is more powerful.

"To help us avoid this trap set by Satan to separate us from God and make us unproductive, God specifically tells us in Deuteronomy eighteen, verses ten and eleven, 'Let no one be found among you who sacrifices their son or daughter in the fire, who practices divination or sorcery, interprets omens, engages in witchcraft, or casts spells, or who is a medium or spiritist or who consults the dead.'

Paul in Galatians chapter five says in verses nineteen to twenty-one, 'The acts of the flesh are obvious: sexual immorality, impurity and debauchery; idolatry and witchcraft; hatred, discord, jealousy, fits of rage, selfish ambition, dissensions, factions and envy; drunkenness, orgies, and the like. I warn you, as I did before, that those who live like this will not inherit the kingdom of God.'

"Marcella, your Catholic school training taught you the Ten Commandments and they say not to have other gods or commit murder or lie, stuff like that, right?"

She nodded.

"My point in reading these verses is to show the Bible tells us not to envy or lie or murder, and most people agree those things are pretty obvious not to do. So if we aren't doing them, why are we so accepting of witchcraft? We are picking and choosing what to obey. How did witchcraft become a harmless practice from the past to be ignored or even taught to our children as play? Something I've learned is whether we know why or not, God has a reason for *everything* he asks of us, not just some things."

"Hmmph," Marcella cleared her throat. "So you're saying if I read this book, it will say things to me that I need when I need them?"

I wasn't sure if she'd heard anything else I'd said. But did it matter as long as she was reading the Bible?

We all lifted an arm as Rupert and Simone walked past munching their treats.

"That's what she's saying," Jackie piped up from behind her textbook. Marcella opened the front cover of the Bible I'd handed her.

"So, has anyone mentioned seeing Sillo this year?" I circled the subject like a dog at a rabbit hole.

Jackie lowered her book. "Hey, cut it out, Clare. I know what you're doing. You're trying to get distracted by something else so you can ignore your painting job. I'm sure Sillo is not looking to be converted from Wicken. Do what you're always saying; take the bull by the horns and call about the job. Stewing over it isn't going to make it less of a nightmare, which I'm sure it's not. You've done plenty of these before. Wealthy people are always a bit eccentric, but they always love what you do. It's going to be – OH, whew!" Jackie cut herself off and waved a hand in front of her face. "Close that window! The wind is shifting." She pinched her nose and her voice came out squished. "Good old Sulferson Silks. Somehow I always forget how bad it is over the summer at home and then I have to get used to it all over again every fall. If that's even possible."

"Ugh," Marcella waved a hand in front of her face. "I better go shut mine upstairs!" She jumped to her feet and sprinted up the stairs two at time, taking the little black book with her. We could hear her thud all the way to the upstairs landing.

The sickeningly sweet burnt odor tickled my nose as I stepped through the billowing curtains to close the window. I stretched up and straightened the lambrequin. Jackie was right about my hesitation. I needed to stop dragging my feet and get the commission out of the way. And go out with Toby. And pray for Sillo.

I leaned on the sill and pressed my face against the cool glass. The sky was a tint of cerulean blue and stretched on for miles and miles, as far as the eye could see across hundreds of acres of flat corn fields. I loved that kind of view. The hill our house sat on was surrounded by a ring of city, but beyond that was farmland. And the only thing that broke the horizon was the Sulferson Silks factory silhouette. Taller than anything else on this side of town, the tan factory rose up and spewed massive billows of pure white steam and smoke hundreds of feet high into the cloudless sky. Cooked corn. Ethanol. Stuff to use to make other stuff.

Like something called high fructose corn syrup. I'd read the posters in town. This new ingredient was going to replace sugar in all processed foods. It would help preserve them longer and cost a fraction of what sugar production did. I didn't know anything about it beyond that. The posters were for jobs. Sulferson Silks wanted new factory workers for this wave of the future. This seriously stinky wave of the future.

I tried to keep my breathing shallow through my mouth to limit the smell. It was a difficult odor to assimilate. It made your mouth water like something amazing was cooking, but at the same time it made your stomach turn. I watched the piles of white steam stack up in graceful mountains and slowly float away from the top of the factory's massive chimney stacks.

"Thanks, Jack, for piping up with Marcella." I gave procrastination one last stab. "I know I've done these paintings before. I just haven't done one for forty thousand dollars that someone else started and messed up so bad they had to be sent to Italy. Leaping Lizards! Sure I was in Italy as a tourist, but I wasn't there getting *trained*."

Jackie sighed. "She needs to know Jesus whether or not she's as radical as you've gotten. Not that I'm saying that's bad or anything." She looked over her book and down her nose at me. "And nice try, but you'll get no sympathy here. You can paint rings around everyone on campus. Go. Meet your subject. Find out the sitting schedule. See Sammy's work. If it's that bad, start over. Remember – the fake miniature you did in England was in Scotland Yard with them testing the fake hair in the back because you're sooo bad at painting that they thought it was all real. Case closed." Her sarcasm went a long way to cheer me up.

She sat up on her bed next to a stack of books almost as tall as she was and threw an arm around them. "Meanwhile, if you need me, I'll be here with a few people I met at the library, getting to know them a whole lot better." She extended her arm and held out the phone receiver with an exaggerated winked.

Before I could give myself time to think, I took the phone from her and punched in the number Sammy had scrawled on a crumpled street flyer at the Brindisi train station. I'd looked at it so many times before I had it memorized.

A woman answered and identified herself as Curtis Sulferson's assistant. She immediately knew who I was and said she'd send a car around to pick me up that afternoon. I shouldn't have been so leery. Clearly Curtis Sulferson had other staff who would be around, a car to give me lift, and maybe he even had pets. While he was massively rich, he was still a person and this was a simple painting task. I squared my shoulders as I replaced the receiver. A girl's quality of life depended on me getting this piece done and done on deadline. It was better to be done early and have a lemonade then procrastinate like the hare and get beaten by a tortoise.

"Where you headed, Indiana James?" Toby's teasing voice cut through my thoughts as I skipped down the front stairs of our house dorm. He was coming up our sidewalk.

"I was going to leave a backpack somewhere *just because I*

can." I stuck out my tongue and crossed my eyes. He threw back his head and laughed. That's how we had met, during a bomb evacuation my books had caused at the library. London was on high alert for unattended parcels because of the IRA bombings. The police would come and confiscate anything left out. They would blow it to smithereens in case it was an explosive device left by terrorists.

    I giggled. I did enjoy being snarky with him. I snuck a look at his profile out of the corner of my eye. I was still seeing him in my head with the crew cut he had in London. It surprised me every time I saw him now because he looked so different. He'd grown his hair out over the summer and the shaggy blond hanks brushed his shoulders. The long strands he brushed out of his eyes made them darker and less sparkly.

    In London I had admired his small wire-rimmed antique frames. He had proudly shared how he and his dad had found them at a Civil War Reenactment and had lenses fitted to them. I didn't think he'd ever part with them, but they must have gotten broken because now he wore thick black modern frames, giving him an exaggerated bookish manner like a character in a sitcom.

    The new look still got him lots of attention from the girls who turned to look as we passed wherever we went. I sighed. He didn't look unattractive. I just missed him somehow. I wistfully pictured the guy who had written the notes I'd put up on my curtain bulletin board. I loved his handwriting. I'd kept the tiny letters in neat rows blocking out his one-liners and put them in my wooden treasure box.

Peace, Toby.

God Bless, Toby.

Here with an ear, Toby.

He'd left them with a roll of Smarties at the flat when I wasn't home. After three months of not being able to talk over the summer while I backpacked from country to country with my parents, I was disappointed he didn't greet me with any Smarties. I'd have settled for a single roll tossed at me with his play-boyish grin when we saw each other our first day back on campus. I mean in my romantic heart a bouquet of flowers somehow woven out of Smarties as I came off the plane would have sealed the deal for me, but I guess that was too Hollywood. Either way, I guess Smarties were not as significant to us as I thought they were.

We had become friends while we were in London out of necessity. We had lived in the same building and he had asked me to help him with his essay writing. I'd agreed on the condition he attend church with me. Surprisingly enough he had. And our friendship had fostered his return to his faith.

He had transferred to my University when we came back from London because he wasn't living the way he wanted to with his college friends. I agreed starting over with a new community who understood the choices he was making as a Christian was a smart move.

Now, that I was back home, though, we didn't need our friendship out of necessity any more so at times it felt forced to me. He wasn't someone I'd normally hang out with.

"You're hilarious, Clare! Let's find a roof top and talk, like we used to, you know?" He caught my hand as we walked around the house toward the parking lot behind it.

"That sounds like fun, but I have a ride actually." We rounded the corner of the house and he dropped my hand like a hot potato.

"You've got to be kidding me, Clare! A limo? Here? After all those limos led to all that hullaballoo in London? How do you keep getting picked up by limos?"

I laughed. "Hullaballoo? That word is straight out of my dictionary." He blushed. "Look," I softened my tone. "The limos weren't the problem, Toby and you know it. I'm going to find out about Sammy's commission at the Sulferson Estate. They sent it because I don't have a car." His disappointment made me regret I couldn't take him along. "Try not to be so down in the dumps. I'll call you when I get back or you can hang out in our room. Jackie's there."

He waved forlornly as the limo lumbered out of the dirt and stone lot behind the house and merged into traffic, leaving him in a cloud of dust.

Only a few people in town could afford such a generous

donation for a student painting, even one from the Commission Club. Curtis Sulferson was obviously one of the few mega wealthy people who lived near enough to send a limo for me. As the car slide through town I contemplated what I had learned up to this point about the job. The current owner of Sulferson Silks, Curtis Sulferson, had to be in his nineties. Why did he want a formal portrait painted now? He didn't have any family living and he had never married. Hmmmm. The portrait must be for some milestone apparently to be unveiled at this year's Christmas party. Maybe a girlfriend or a fiancé? Kind of odd, but I guess it was never too late to find love.

I had been distracted one day at the library when I'd come across a photo of Curtis Sulferson cutting a ribbon at a shop downtown twenty years ago. He had looked old then. I was supposed to be researching image resources for my senior exhibit pieces, but I'd ended up ferreting out old Sulferson newspaper articles on microfiche.

The viewing machine had an annoying squeak, but it was easy to scroll through pages and pages of past newspapers on a tiny roll of film. I was grateful for this modern invention so I didn't have to sort through boxes and boxes of dusty, disintegrating newsprint. I had learned quite a bit about the family history, even if I didn't get many thumbnail sketches done that afternoon.

Curtis' father had owned a small mercantile on the east coast. As big department stores started to put the little specialty shops out of business, he'd moved his family to the Midwest where the stores were still little. He started Sulferson Silks in the late 1800's when he realized there was an exploding market for starch to smooth the new department store shirts. The starch came from corn and there was nothing but space to grow corn in the middle of Illinois. He took what he'd saved from his small country store and paid the farmers to plant their fields with corn. He hired their sons to build and run his factory. As families grew and services were needed, more people came and the town, Sulferson Springs, formed. Over time Sulferson bought as much of the land as he could and his factory continued to expand, providing a resource not found in many other places. The Sulferson's made millions. Several other masters of industry had moved into the area and a University was birthed. Hence, I was here getting my degree and a second generation Sulferson was hiring an art student to paint a pricey portrait. I wish I'd had time to ask Sammy more details about what I was painting. Maybe it was an architectural portrait, like of his fancy house.

I'd seen a picture of the sleek, modern Sulferson Estate built on a cliff over hanging the river. I couldn't help but compare it to the centuries old Wellington Manor. That had been where I was going in my last limo ride.

While I had been traveling, I had called my friend, Lizbeth, from a pay phone in the South of France to see how she was doing. We had decided to meet at her adopted family home in England, the

Wellington Manor, one last time before my parents and I caught our flight back to the States.

I had been surprised Simon and his family came. And even more so that Lord Wellington had made time in his important political schedule to host us. Lots of affectionate back slapping and sniffles went all around, especially among the parents. It was a sight for sore eyes as scruffy American backpackers exchanged hugs with tribal royalty in flamboyant robes. A proper English host in a tuxedo escorting a young girl with the grey eyes and wide smile of a princess three centuries smiled and shook hands.

It was what heaven's reunions will be like. Unlikely on earth and beautiful beyond our narrow mind's scope, I thought, blinking back a few emotional tears as I focused my eyes on the corn fields zinging by the window. I smiled as I remembered my parents' discussion about the evening on the long flight home.

"Lord Wellington would be perfect narrating an Agatha Christie movie on PBS, wouldn't he?" My dad grinned mischievously across the aisle seat at me. We were in first class because our fancy friends had upgraded our tickets. We'd spent the first hour exploring the bathrooms, the small sitting room, and the way the seats made into sleeping compartments. We were amazed at how they fit so much luxury in such tight spaces, making it all clean and fresh smelling. It was astonishing to our sensibilities after two months of dirty hostels and crook-in-your-neck train travel.

"Or he could be the voice narrating Simon's story when the movie comes out," my mom contributed.

"Oh, yeah, I could see that," I said. "But who's going to play me?" They laughed.

"I've been thinking about Lizbeth." My mom's tone turned serious, making her sound like a mom. "And I don't mean who's going to play her in the movie! You two." She grinned and shook her head at us before we could add our two cents. "No, I'm afraid she's not going to be happy in that big house all by herself playing piano and working weekends when young people should be out having fun. She's taking classes, I know, but she doesn't have a friend like you to visit. It takes a while to make new friends." A worried frown creased her brow. Lizbeth had moved to England to work on recording an album of her adopted grandfather's classical music compositions and she had taken a position as a weekend museum director to help rotate staff so they could have time with their families on Sundays to attend church together. She had been able to transfer to Oxford to finish her senior year and earn her degree.

"Well, she's leading a Bible study in Simon's new church." I volunteered the information she told me before I'd left. "She said she's been enjoying hanging out with some of the young adults she's been helping make sense of the whole thing. You know with their pastor and church leaders being arrested and stuff." I chuckled. "She even said she liked talking with Langland. At least she knows what she's getting into there."

"Oh, is he the one who drives really crazy and depending on how the girls in the car react he decides to date them or not?" My mom smiled.

"Yep, that's him. But seriously, don't worry about her, Mom. Remember Penelope, my TA? She moved out of London, but she's in a village not far from the Manor doing restoration work on another manor. She and Lizbeth went to a country fair thing they call a fate. And Lizbeth's been over to Mrs. Corning's house to meet her daughter and husband. You know, the woman who helped us find the real miniature? Jumping Jehoshaphat, Lizbeth always has more friends than anyone else I know! She'll be fine, Mom. She can talk to a sheep and make a conversation." I yawned.

"I'm looking forward to getting some serious sleep myself. It should be nice sailing through the air all night on this bird." My dad stretched back in his seat half made into a bed already. "So, is Simon's dad like a king or what? All that royalty stuff confuses me."

"Well, royal titles are no picnic for any of us, dear, but the way I understand it –" My mom paused to sip from a glass of orange juice. "His oldest brother is king, so he's a member of the royal family. He has to live in England in case someone tried to overthrow his family. He has thirteen brothers and sisters and he's number eight. So seven siblings would have to be assassinated. He's their contingency plan in case that happens. You know, not all your eggs in one basket. But he's not likely to ever be king. He and his wife have lived in England and been a part of British society since before Simon was born. It's been well over twenty years and they've grown to love it." She waved and hand and settled back into her seat. "They only wear those amazing clothes for special occasions, not every day. Wasn't that nice of them to wear them for our dinner? They were all so nice. I expected them to be stuffy and hard to talk to. I guess manners are one thing and loving Jesus together makes them a whole other matter."

My dad nodded. "I know what you mean. I have to say I was glad Simon told us his whole story. The undercover work, what being shot felt like, and what he saw when he was in a coma. That guy is something else! Now he's preaching every night of the week and teaching all those people. Wow! I feel for his parents, though. I just can't imagine having my child in a coma for six weeks." Dad leaned forward and patted my knee. I smiled sleepily at him.

"Well, God took care of all of us. I know we've talked it to oblivion and beyond during our trip, but thank you guys for listening. And how about the food? Have you ever been to a meal like that?" For me, the most unnerving part of the whole evening had been the dinner with sixteen courses and a servant for each of us to cut our meat and keep our glasses full after every sip.

"The closest I've ever come to a meal like that before was that girl I went to college with, Candy something. Remember her wedding?" She turned to my dad, who nodded.

"Yes," he said. "But still, her thing wasn't any sixteen courses. Or someone cutting your food for you. I didn't know what to do while they were doing it. It was strange. Nothing I'd want every day. I like to do for myself. Dress myself, feed myself, drive myself, you know?"

We hit a rut in the road and I realized I had been sitting on the edge of my seat day dreaming as the limo I was now in slowed down. I took a deep breath and relaxed back against the seat as the driver maneuvered the vehicle off the main road and into a driveway alongside the house in the picture I'd seen. We circled around and then looped under it.

That was pretty cool. I thought in admiration.

The driver parked beneath a piece of the house that created a carport area with the river bank dropping away on one side of us and the grand double doors standing there in the shadow on the other.

Lord, thank you for this opportunity and forgive me for dragging my feet. Help me do a great job so the people are happy and Sammy is free. Please be with her family and continue to help her mother recover. Give me courage for this. Love you. Amen. I said the prayer quickly in my head as the driver came around and opened my door. I noticed the air smelled fresh here. Not like the burnt sweet smell of cooking corn we gagged over on campus.

Can he buy clean air at his house? He could afford it, but was it actually possible? Nah, no one can buy clean air. It's gotta be the way the wind blows along the river. I thought to myself as I stepped out of the car onto the polished cement. One of the front doors swung open and a pleasant faced woman wearing a brown business suit came forward and held out her hand.

"Welcome, Clare. I'm Muriel, Mr. Sulferson's assistant. We spoke on the phone. It's so nice to meet you. Mr. Sulferson is impressed with your *moxie*, as he puts it. He followed all the news from London. It was quite a splash."

"Oh! But my part in it wasn't made public. I mean, how could he know about that?" I didn't contain my surprise.

"Mr. Sulferson never misses anything that can affect the economy. Things that shake up the world can shake up the need for ethanol, of course. He makes it his business to know about the movers and shakers." She smiled kindly and turned back to the house.

I followed her down the length of a marbled hall and into a room with a breath taking view of the river.

"Please wait here, Clare. Mr. Sulferson will be with you momentarily."

"Thank you, Muriel." I said.

When the door closed behind her, I spun in a slow circle. To the left of the room entrance a wall of windows stretched out for what seemed a mile of overlooking the river. It joined a wall of books. As you continued to turn, your back was to the river and you faced a massive desk.

But it was the art installation behind the desk that stopped my rotation. The entire wall was covered by a mosaic of SPAM cans like what I looked at every day. I'd never eaten SPAM in my life, but I had an installation by this same artist. And it could mean only one thing.

My mind drifted back to about three weeks ago, when I'd returned to campus for my senior year after studying and traveling abroad. I had my key and was going to prop the door open to move in my stuff, only I couldn't find my door. I'd found where my apartment door should have been, but instead of the familiar wood door we'd always had, tins of SPAM were stacked end to end in a kaleidoscope of color worthy of Andy Warhol himself.

I had burst out laughing and dropped the arm load of plants and bathroom towels I'd been toting down the hall. I knew what this meant.

"Key, you're back! After two years! Key, where are you?" I had spun around in time to see him vault over the back of the couch in the foyer and somersault into the hall to land sitting at my feet with his arms as wide open as the smile on his round brown face.

His landing had been punctuated by Toby Fir bursting through the front door. Toby had strolled across the foyer in a few steps. He had scooped me up and twirled me around the hall before depositing me back in front of Key with a dizzy smile.

"Toby! Oh goodness!" I had thrown an arm around each of them and squeezed before stepping away. "Welcome back to school, guys!"

"We were in London together, but where are *you* back from?" Toby had extended a hand to Key, who had quickly taken it in a two handed shake.

"Chicago. I had to drop out my senior year two years ago. Family troubles. But my mother always wanted me to have a college degree, even if I was planning to be a graffiti artist. So, I'm back to complete my credits and graduate. With Clare, or Lily, as I always called her."

"Yippee!" I had tossed my hands in the air and twirled about on my own steam.

"I see." Toby had looked uncertain, like he didn't see at all.

"Relax, man, she's a little sister to me." I smiled remembering Key's mischievous grin. He had turned his ball cap backwards on his short dark hair, and doffed Toby on the shoulder.

Toby had grinned back and shook his head. "What's up with the SPAM?" He pointed toward where my door should have been.

Key waved a hand toward it like it was nothing. "Hawaiian delicacy to certain palates, trash to the average person." He shrugged and smiled. "But, to the discerning eye, it's art with a message." He hooked his thumbs in his belt loops and leaned a shoulder confidently against the wall, surveying us through half closed eye slits. "I'm staking my claim. Marking my territory. Offering my protection."

By then I had moved to the place where the door should have been, running my fingers over the bolted cans, trying to figure it out before I had to ask. Where was my apartment opening?

I hadn't gotten very far when Jacqueline had slammed through the house's front door with such force it smacked against the wall behind it and the window in it shivered with shock.

My roommate ran across the foyer and threw her arms around me. We squealed with glee like girls will who are best friends and haven't seen each other for almost a year. And then the squealing stopped and she parked herself in front of our door.

"You've got to be kidding me. How do we get in? You art people are nuts! But I have missed a little nuts in my life, I have to admit." She stepped forward and yanked on the can where the door knob should have been. I had winched and thrown up an arm expecting them to all come crashing down on our heads, but the can swung out on a hinge and revealed the door lock. She bent forward and inserted her key. The wall of SPAM tins swung silently out toward us to reveal the same design on the inside as well. The art installation had engulfed our door and it worked perfectly once you found the can the lock was behind.

"Do you think we'll get our housing deposit back?" She had whispered, in awe.

"You've been tagged!" Key had shrieked behind us making us all jump. Then he had vanished like the vapor from a bag of microwave popcorn.

I remember stepping into the apartment and breathing deeply. It was good to be back in the States and good to be back at school and good to be back in the same apartment. On the days when the Sulferson Silk smell wasn't blowing downwind, that is.

I opened my eyes. I was still standing in a client's office with a wall of SPAM confronting me. I shook my head to clear away the memories, but one clung like a cobweb. Hawaiian delicacy, trash, or a message. A staked claim. A marked territory. An offering of protection. I squinted at the cans. So what protection was Key extending to Curtis Sulferson?

✸ Chapter Four

The wall of SPAM cans in the Sulferson study silently swung in half and I stifled an involuntary scream. A bald man in a black turtle neck motored through the gap in a souped up wheel chair and the wall swung shut. He circled around the desk and came to stop in front of me. My heart was still racing and I felt rather breathless from his unexpected entry.

A woven grey blanket spilled off his legs and landed on my feet. His gnarled hands released the controls and grasped at the air in front of him.

"My blanket. My blanket. I always forget to strap it on and I'm always going too fast when I stop. Anything that's not tied down goes sailing," he said in an irritated raspy voice.

I bent and scooped the soft throw off the hard wood floor and spread it gently on his lap, using the activity to slow my breathing down. He smoothed the blanket under his age-spotted, lumpy fingers. Then he turned his bright blue eyes back to me.

"Thank you. You must be Miss James. Taking down a plot to over throw a government while sporting a broken foot is my kind of person." He extended a hand and we shook.

"It's nice to meet you, Sir. Just in the right place at the right time, I assure you. No special skills on my part. This is an amazing home you have here. The view from this room alone is astounding. And such interesting art." I gestured toward the wall of SPAM, hoping for clue as why Key did it for him.

He shrugged. "I select things to have in my home which remind me of important events. Obviously I've been around for a few decades, almost a century now. Whoowee! You should see the pieces I have for hallmarks in my life back in the early days." He chuckled. "I even like some of that steam punk stuff they have now days. Reminds me of it all mushed together." He chuckled again.

"But back to the matter at hand. You sell yourself short, young woman. Clearly you can paint like an old master. You did Cosway proud when you copied his miniature from the 1700's and started that whole ball of wax rolling. I'm hoping your work is powerful enough to stop a Union riot I think I'm going to have on my hands about Christmas time. When I read about the events in London, and I know, I know, I had to pull a few strings to get those files from Interpol, but when I read that, I knew I must have you paint for me in Sammy's place."

He leaned over and pressed an intercom button on the side of the desk.

"Muriel, where's Reginald? I expected him to be here by now. I want Miss James to meet him."

I frowned. My research did not reveal that Curtis Sulferson had a son. Or even a nephew. Was this the portrait I was painting and not Mr. Sulferson's? Making kids sit still for hours was no picnic. I should know by now never to assume anything. Why hadn't I thought to ask Sammy?

"Sorry, Sir. Right away." Muriel hesitated. "It's just. Well."

"Is he hiding again, Muriel?" Curtis Sulferson frowned.

There was a loud sneeze over the intercom making us both flinch. Then Muriel said sheepishly, "Yes, Sir. The new sitter had to leave early for something her father needed and I thought I could watch him for just a few minutes until Janice came."

Mr. Sulferson chuckled. "Mischievous little scamp. Very well, when you find him, we will be in the North wing."

"Thank you, Sir." She sniffled and the intercom clicked off.

"Walk with me, it relaxes me to roll." He beckoned to me as his chair glided noiselessly across the room and through another hidden door in the bookcase. Intrigued, I high-tailed it across the room to keep up.

"Poor Sammy, she tried. She would have been okay, I think, if her mother hadn't had that unfortunate accident. I hope she knows this couldn't be helped."

"She might, Sir, but I'm sorry, I don't. I've been rather unsettled about taking over this commission. Now that I'm here, I want some answers. I mean you seem to understand Sammy's situation and you seem like a nice enough guy, so why couldn't you work something out with her? If we are going to work together, I have to know. Who exactly am I painting? And why is the deadline so set in stone?"

I abruptly stopped in the glass tunnel we were moving through. I had barely taken in my surroundings as I confronted him like an angry little terrier. Now I glanced down and swung my hand out on reflex to balance myself from falling. The river was turbulently teaming forty feet beneath my feet. We looked like we were floating in space.

He smiled and continued to roll. "Quite prodigious for just a balcony overlooking the water, wouldn't you say? The first time you see it, I know, it's difficult to comprehend where you are and *how* you are, really. Everyone has the same reaction. The synthetic material this observation tunnel is made from is being tested at NASA. It has amazing properties for expanding and contracting in the heat and cold, unlike glass as we know it. And the best part is, it's not mined from the earth, or made from peanuts like plastics. No it's from corn. Sweet, delicious corn." He continued rolling as if nothing had happened as I followed along behind like a cat walking across a frozen pond.

"I will answer all your questions, I assure you." His chair did a one eighty in front of me and I froze. He looked at me with piercing eyes the same color as the sky behind him as he rolled backwards down the narrowing invisible tunnel.

"I want you to paint this portrait for me. I want you to be comfortable. I want to pay you. And I want everything to stay just as it is, as it has for almost a hundred years. Trust me, there's nothing I want more."

"You have got to be kidding me." I stormed through our SPAM door and collapsed with an exasperated sigh on my bed in the middle of the room. Maintenance was behind and they hadn't stacked our beds back into bunks yet. I actually didn't mind. I was just grateful to have a bed at all since they had taken it out of the room during a bunk shortage while I was abroad. And for now it lent itself well to dramatic entrances.

"What, what is it?" Jackie jerked awake from the pile of books she had fallen asleep on while reading. She batted at a stream of drool hanging off her chin.

"Yeah, that. Exactly. You hit the nail on the head." I swiped a Kleenex off the dresser by my bed and sprang up to toss it at her. "Drool is what I have to deal with. Expensive, solid gold drool."

"What are you talking about, Clare? Did you see Mr. Sulferson? Is he scary? How was Sammy's underpainting?"

"One thing at a time." I held up my hands in front of me as if to stop the tide of curiosity. "First, I'm not painting his portrait. I'm painting his *dog's* portrait."

"What?" She sat up startled, knocking a cascade of books off the bed. "You've got to be kidding." An impish grin began to play around the corners of her mouth.

"No, no, I'm not. Sammy was getting three semesters of tuition and a lavish trip to Italy for a painting of a pooch!"

She laughed. "Well, that should be easier than painting the guy's portrait, shouldn't it?"

"Oh, you would think so. But imagine getting a dog to sit for a painting. A dog I didn't even get to meet because he was playing hide and seek with Sulferson's assistant the whole time I was there. And as you might have guessed, no photos can be taken of him for security purposes and copy rights and all that. Like I'm going to peddle a bootleg shot of him pooping to *Horse and Hound* or something!" I ranted. "And he has a specific schedule of activities each day, so there are only the weirdest times he can sit for me." I paused. "That's actually a pretty good pun." We both giggled.

"This is crazy. Do go on," she said.

"Well, apparently this dog is richer then the Queen of Sheba and the hottest thing since sliced bread." I gripped the window sill and leaned forward on locked elbows, my body rigid with consternation as I looked out without seeing. "He's won a bunch of championships for his breed. He's part of a bloodline the Sulferson family has owned for decades. Their family brought them over from Europe on the boat kind of thing. And each dog has been immortalized with a painted portrait. There's a whole gallery of them at the big house."

I pushed off from the sill and waved my arms to punctuate my words as I paced around my bed. "The batty criteria for this whole thing was established when they actually had some real money. The dog care became his mother's project. Personally, I think she figured out a way to stick it to the men in the family who were controlling everything at the time. You know, the vote, the factory jobs, their arranged marriages and their money. Women from that time period were clever and tired of sitting around just looking pretty." Jackie was nodding with me as I talked. "Anyway, each successor has to have his portrait painted from a live sitting for his eighth birthday party. That's this December for this dog."

"What, why his eighth birthday? What happens then?" She

leaned forward with wide eyes.

"Then the dog's guardian gets another piece of the Sulferson pie released to him out of the trust where the fortune is tied up. Apparently the money is wrapped around these dogs as a way to spread it out and make sure someone in the family always cares for them. See, like for every full blooded heir he has, more money released. Every eight years he lives, more money released. When he retires and a new dog takes his place as the family show hound, more money. Capiche? It's the craziest thing I've ever heard."

"Yeah, but doesn't Mr. Sulferson have tons of his own money? Why does he need the trust money from the family fortune?"

"He's overextended, as these millionaires always are." We both rolled our eyes at the ceiling. "Some research projects. Top Secret corn stuff."

"Of course," Jackie quipped. "So he needs the painting to get the cash to save whatever. Why doesn't he just rewrite the trust save himself? He's the only one left. Or why can't he just have any old painting done for the family wall of dog fame? Who's to know?"

I laughed. "I wish it was that simple." I turned around and leaned my back and an elbow on the window sill as I relaxed. I had asked Sulferson the same questions.

"For your first solution to the problem, the trust is handled by a board of directors who have its power of attorney in their hands. He never married and so there's no kids or grandkids fulfilling the rules of the trust, so it's gone to the dogs. Ha. Ha. Literally." We laughed a minute at that one.

"His sisters and mother were killed in an explosion at the factory years ago when they were on a visit to research working conditions for women. As women's rights issues heated up, so did their demands for equal treatment in factory labor conditions. The explosion left Curtis as sole heir and apparently there are provisions for that too. Like the old saying goes, don't put your eggs all in one basket.

"Apparently Sulferson's father thought Curtis was a spend thrift when it came to corn inventions. Since they differed on their approach to corn research, the father made sure Curtis couldn't access all the money at once as a safe guard for the family and his factory legacy. So he's stuck with this trust and a bunch of little baskets. He has to follow the rules or all the money is donated to a dog habitat or retirement home or whatever.

"Now the second solution you suggested is in my wheelhouse. Why doesn't he just get a cheap knock off of any old dog? Well, he was sort of trying that with Sammy. Once he realized he needed the money for sure, he didn't have time to hire a credentialed portrait painter. Which isn't one of the rules. But apparently she confessed she was out of her depth and that's when his herd of lawyers pointed out the money is only released if the panel that selects the members of the American Portrait Painters

Association and the current judges serving for the AKC vote the piece to be an accurate rendition of Reginald.

"Which is the part I'm freaking out about. I'm not even old enough to apply to be a member of such a prestigious organization in the art world! I mean the American Portrait Painters Association? You have to be over thirty and living off the income you make from portrait painting and pass this jury application process of your work by these judges.

"And don't even get me started about dog judges. Who knows what they want? I don't know anything about dog pedigrees. Golly! Sammy sure dodged a bullet and I think it's headed straight for my head!"

"Wow," Jackie interjected when I paused for breath. "You really did get all the dirt. Sulferson apparently doesn't mind sharing with you."

"Yeah, he's all impressed by my escapades in England. Plus he was stalling to give his staff time to find Reginald. What a name. It's short for The Honorable Goldfish Marked Reginald Winnyfeld Kampindiner Clarance Pepper the third."

"With a dog like that, each one of those names must have a story attached to it. What's the deal-e-o? Lay it on me, nothing can sound too outrageous after all that." Jackie had closed her book and was sucking on a lollipop from her candy stash in the jar by her bed.

"I don't know. Sulferson got an important call and I had to say goodbye." I could see she was clearly disappointed. I was curious too, but I could always find out the next time I went. "It really doesn't matter to the portrait. Although 'Goldfish Marked' might signify some spot somewhere shaped like a fish."

"Well," Jackie stretched and yawned, "it's not like Sulferson's going to be destitute in the street if he doesn't get his money released with your portrait of his dog. I mean, how bad can it be? Loose a few extra houses and cars?" Jackie slid off the bed and picked up the books that had fallen. "Wanna get some pizza?"

I pushed off from the antique window pane I had been leaning on. The windows of the converted turn-of-the-century mansion we lived in seemed small now compared to the glass tunnel at the Sulferson house.

"No, that's okay. I need to get to work on my senior stuff. I have to make the most of my time. See, it is more than just a rich guy with an eccentric request. Now that some investments went bad, he needs the money to improve work conditions at Sulferson Silks. Things have been neglected at the factory and there's been no wage increases for five years. A strike is imminent if he doesn't do something by Christmas. Something drastic.

"And a strike means this city is going to get ripped apart at the seams. People are not only going to go hungry, but there will be riots and scabs." I wrung my hands. "He's pretty shaken up by it all because the last big controversy was when women started working on the factory floor and his mother and sisters all died in that freak explosion no one ever explained. He believes it was a protestor's bomb and that's another reason I'm endeared to him. I can't seem to get away from the whole London-bomb thing."

I shook my head trying to clear the cobwebs. "Jackie, no matter how ridiculous that dog provision is his family stuck him with, it could be life or death if I can't paint a satisfactory portrait."

❧ Chapter Five

It was early evening and I heard the front doorbell as I wandered slowly down the basement steps to sit on the bottom rung and wait for the dim bulbs to brighten.

Probably the pizza guy. I thought, pushing with my sandal at a brittle, gray leaf that looked like it had been there since the house was built.

Jackie and I lived in an academic house on the edge of campus. You had to keep a GPA of at least a three point eight and have sophomore status to get in. After our freshmen year, it was a no brainer. We loved how much homier the house was compared to the massive dorms that rose fifteen stories in the sky and housed thirty people on a floor. Thirty girls all sharing one bathroom was no picnic without ants, let me tell you.

Our house was a two story sprawling estate from back in the day when the wealthier executives of Sulferson Silks had stately homes build along Main Street. As the town grew up and became a city, its main drag changed demographics. Houses like this had been willed to the University which converted them into multiple two person rooms with a bathroom attached to most. Our house had eight double rooms between the two floors and a single room in the small attic.

The basement was a little moist and had no windows, a typical tornado shelter in the Midwest. The housing department stored a collection of outdoor campus Christmas decorations down there, but rather than be distracting, I thought they made the place festive. Christmas was my favorite time of year. After a good mopping and a little shuffling, I managed to fit an easel, stool, and paint cart down there for late night work. Simone had given me her RA key.

It was only Wednesday. I saved my pizza money for the weekends. The canteen was open with sandwiches until eleven, so even if I didn't make it over to the cafeteria before meal service ended, I could still eat off my meal card which was loaded at the beginning of each semester with more than enough scholarship money.

I was tired even though I hadn't had classes that day. After three years of college, I knew how to play the scheduling game. I only had classes on Tuesdays and Thursdays. Granted, they were long Tuesdays and Thursdays, but I was free the other five days of the week, so it was worth it. Wednesdays were hardest though, giving me barely enough time to recover from Tuesday before Thursday came.

In the brightening raw light of the naked basement bulbs, I studied the painting on my easel.

I think my idea should have enough substance to make a show. It also demonstrates my technical ability. I hugged my knees trying to avoid being honest with myself. *I really like some of the pieces a lot.* I ran my hand thought my hair. *Okay, just not all of them.* My stomach felt uneasy, and I knew that meant I wasn't satisfied. I sighed. I was on the edge of being bored already. *It's never a good sign when a coon dog decides to chase cars after he tracks his first coon. Is it too late to start over, Lord?*

I nervously swallowed a gulp of Sulferson's burning corn smell in the stuffy basement. From my stairwell vantage point, I studied each piece I had already painted searching for a niggling sensation in my spirit, a yah or nay from God. It was hard to describe hearing the voice of God, but it is a settling over your spirit and then peace and you just know. A knowing that comes from inside somewhere, but not from your own brain.

Ok, I've tried and this is a disaster. I'm ready for whatever you've got for me. What do you want me to say, Lord? I asked him in my head.

I had started the year planning to do a show of pieces in sets. Each set was going to be of one subject over time, telling a story about that subject through the symbols or clues in the paintings. I had filled a sketch book with lifespan thumbnails of different people I thought might work on the train rides across Europe. I had daydreamed for hours while watching the countryside roll by of what clues I might use for each time period of their lives. When I got back, I'd started with a self-portrait set, now leaning over against the wall between the bagged foyer Christmas tree and the boxes holding the manger scene for the house's front lawn. I didn't intend to give anyone the answers to the riddles in the paintings, but they were loaded with meaning, especially to me.

The first canvas held an image of a baby about three months old sitting up on a giant rabbit that was crouched on all fours. She was in a velvety soft dress wearing a tiny cowgirl hat and smiling. She was so little she slouched against the back of the couch. A toy boat with a plastic grasshopper and bee lay beside her on the cushion. Among other things, behind the couch hung a photo of a vast, placid lake.

The piece spoke about how I was born to ride off into the sunset pursing my next adventure like the men and woman in the Bible: building arks where it didn't rain, eating locust and honey, and walking on water. The painting was in a sepia tone giving it the cast of an old Polaroid photo. These were popular around the time I was born.

The second painting had a little girl, with two big pony tails looking squarely at the viewer. She was grinning from ear to ear with not one of the top or bottom front teeth in her mouth. Her hands were slippery with butter as she clenched at an ear of corn. Scattered across the table cloth were various items like a cross pendant, a cluster of purple grapes, and some broken crackers. There was an enormous wave on the lake behind her and the sky was dark with thunderheads.

I had accepted Jesus as my personal savior when I was eight. I had been raised in a strict Brethren Church that children were to be seen and not heard and so I waited for three Sundays for children to be invited to come to the front of the church when the adults were talking about how Jesus died to save us. But each Sunday, the pastor didn't mention children, so I waited politely while my younger brothers scribbled on bulletins under the wooden pews or made faces at the little girl behind us. Finally, the pastor said this would be the last Sunday for his series.

When I think about it I can still feel the same surge of determination that overtook me that morning. Nothing was going to keep me from asking Jesus to live in my heart, even if it meant being punished. With all the courage I had, I slipped out of the pew and walked to the front of the packed church. I was terrified and elated at the same time.

The church was overtaken by a hiss of whispers that grew louder into voices. About the time I thought my knees would buckle and I'd pass out from the suspense of what they were going to do to me, the clapping started. I turned and saw the front row of swimming faces were all smiling. I looked back up at the pastor and he was smiling too. Behind him a blinding beam of sunlight spilled in through the stained glass window and I was standing in a pool of light. I did a twirl and curtsied. The pastor's wife hugged me in a gush of perfume and then my parents were standing on each side of me holding my hands while the pastor spoke a blessing to me. Over my shoulder, I looked all the way back at my two little brothers sitting in the empty pew by themselves. They looked small and stiff and a little scared. Did I look like that from up here? I remembered thinking I surely wouldn't look like that anymore. With Jesus in my heart, I knew my face must be glowing.

I wrapped my arms around my body and hugged myself where I sat on the basement steps. I loved thinking about that day. Whenever I looked at this painting, it came back to me. From that day forward I was always determined to do my best for Jesus no matter what curve ball life threw at me. I also remembered everyone talking about my stubbornness to eat corn on the cob after relinquishing my four front teeth. It reminded me of that day too and so I used it as a metaphor for my testimony. The painting style was cast in the high contrast, color saturated photo developing of the eighties. It was my favorite piece of the three.

I was standing next to a column at St. Paul's Cathedral in London in the third work of the series. Bits of a rubbing that Lizbeth had made in the church were scattered at my feet, which were clad in my threadbare shoes with the secret compartment in the sole. I had a paintbrush clenched in my teeth I and carrying a backpack full of Bibles spilling out and cascading down the steps.

Among the things I learned during my time in London, I found it was most important to know what you stand for before you are tested. That way you can stand your ground when the devil comes with his schemes. I felt like I had found my voice from God to talk about him while I was there. I knew I could draw and paint before I went, but I confirmed to myself when I draw and paint about him, people get the message.

Appropriately to the story, the piece was done with thick brush strokes of heavy paint in rich, dark colors like a piece would be that had been painted several centuries ago and was hanging in a museum.

Resting my elbows on the step behind me, I leaned back and squinted at each painting in the triptych. Intriguingly, the portraits had to all resemble each other at different ages so that the viewer knew it was the same person. As I surveyed them, the basic facial structure seemed the same to my eye.

I had planned to do around six people in sets like this. Maybe three who had successful lives and three who had crashed and burned? Who was next? I pulled out my sketchbook and flipped through the pages.

Hmmm. Jezebel? Absalom? Famous ancient villains, or . . . I'm a contemporary person. Should they all be? I could do Ailish. I shivered as I pictured her waving a gun on our rooftop in London. *I'm not sure I want to work on that one at all. I wonder if Mr. Sulferson has had a good life.*

Clearly his father thought their descendants either needed to procreate or appreciate their mother's famous dogs. *Awkward.* Came to my mind.

"What're you doing, James?" The basement door thunked open and I leaped off the steps in a start, flipping my sketchbook somewhere into a pile of wreaths.

"You scared me half silly!" I had a hand over my heart as Toby clamored down the unfinished wooden stairs.

"Sorry, Babe." He grinned and pecked me on the check. I rolled my eyes to the floor shyly and stuffed my hands in my back pockets. He threw his arms out toward the haphazardly arranged paintings amid the Christmas finery.

"I just wanted to check on you, but these are great!" He said with enthusiasm as he reached into the stacked wreaths and fishing out my sketchbook. "Jackie let me in and told me you were down here. Hope you don't mind. What does Umber think? Man, you're far. No wonder I've been seeing you less and less around campus." He let out a long low whistle.

Before I could answer, his words continued. "You're making me think maybe I made a mistake declaring computer graphics for my show. I mean, it's a whole new tool to learn in like seven months. And the sign out sheets are ridiculously full. They've had to open the lab for twenty-four hours now."

"Oh, wow. I hadn't heard that." It didn't surprise me, though. Closing them from midnight to eight in the morning cut off a lot of work time. I painted all night sometimes, why couldn't you compute all night? Or whatever it was called.

As art majors, one of our graduation requirements was to produce a body of work consisting of at least a dozen pieces for a senior exhibit. We were each assigned a gallery in the University Conference Center and a week to display the fruits of our labors. We could select either our first or secondary art media concentration to create our show from. We met with a faculty advisor weekly who evaluated our progress and reported to the graduation committee. As graphics majors, our mentor was Jerry Umber.

I wanted to make a living off of art, so I had opted to major in the commercial side of things. My other choices were fine art, which meant eking out a living selling paintings to people to hang in their bathrooms, or teaching, which meant loads of other people's art being produced instead of my own.

I wasn't in love with computers, though, or the look of what they produced, so I'd chose my secondary area of drawing to base my exhibit on. I'd been second guessing my major too. The field was changing overnight. I was going to have this degree, but I wasn't sure what it was going to equip me to do. Right now everyone was gaga about computer graphics. But how fast could the industry catch up and would it last or was it another fad?

"So, I won't be the only one slipping away at all hours to work now." I said.

"Yeah, looks that way. I have to get a move on or I'm toast. Do you want to get some grub before my next lab time? That weird smell in the air is kind of turning my stomach."

"Oh that. Cheer up. It takes a while to get used to it, then you *almost* don't notice it."

He laughed. "I know what you're saying. My mom is a perfumer and she is always coming home smelling of strange odors which she demands our opinions of. You kind of get used to most of them, but every once in a while, one really slaps you in the face and you can't get past it."

"That's wild." I looked at Toby in the harsh light of the basement bulbs, distracted momentarily from my work. "I had no idea your mom made perfumes. Not a lot of people have that job."

"Yah, it's definitely a specialty boutique thing. She started doing it when I was in elementary school. It was her hobby. Always been an interesting tidbit to toss out there when conversation lags, though."

"Was our conversation lagging?" I raised an eye brow.

"Oh, no, that's not what I meant, James," he said sheepishly.

I decided to let him off the hook and change the subject. "Did Jackie spill the beans about my commission? It's a dog."

"She did not. Hmmm. That's unexpected. How was Sammy's work?"

"Oh that," I waved a hand. "It looked fine, but I had no basis of comparison since the dog was hiding from the staff and never came out to see me. I mean, it's a nice under drawing, but is that what that dog looks like? You know? I won't know what I'm dealing with until our first sitting Saturday morning. Something had to be wrong with it, the painting I mean, or he wouldn't have panicked and sent her to Italy to learn to paint."

"What breed is it?"

"You know, I never asked. I mean Sammy's cartoon suggested a poodle with an unusual haircut. I guess I was just assuming a show dog would be something fancy."

"No way! Those can be the funniest looking dogs. Is it a toy or a standard?"

"That could make a difference to getting the joke." We both jumped at the new voice behind us on the stairs.

"Can I see Sammy's cartoon? I'm usually pretty good at riddles. What's a toy or a standard mean?" Sillo's roommate, the new girl, was draping herself awkwardly down the stairs like she was trying to be sophisticated or something but it wasn't working with her gangly limbs and dirty white t-shirt.

"What?" Toby was confused.

I laughed. "No, Wendy, not a cartoon like a comic in the newspaper. A cartoon like in painting. The drawn outline of a subject that a painter starts with. Our word for a funny drawing in the newspaper comes from the old Italian word for an under drawing because they are both simple outline drawings. Painters use it all the time when referring to what they do to start a painting. I'm painting a dog for a client. So the cartoon is an outline of that dog's body type, which could be a poodle. Toys and Standards are two types of poodles. But, hey, Wendy, this is Toby, Toby Fir, Wendy Gallonte. She lives across the hall from Jackie and me."

Wendy clumped down the stairs the rest of the way to shake Toby's hand. "I just transferred here. I'm an artist too."

"Yeah, I was hoping so with that shirt, or else you were just a Clare groupie." Toby pointed at her splattered T-shirt. I had changed before coming to the basement into an old paint shirt and cutoff jeans. No sense destroying good clothes with stray paint marks.

Wendy was wearing a similar outfit, even down to my red flip flops.

"Where'd you transfer from, Wendy? Your senior year is a tough time to do it, don't I know. I'm a transfer too. Lot of credits to hassle." Toby was good at drawing people out. I hadn't even thought of that.

"I was at Washington State. It can be pretty dreary up there." She stood looking at us with a toothy smile, her short, curly hair messily framing her bright green eyes. She had a scattering of freckles and was a head taller than me.

We stood a moment, waiting for something else to come, but she offered no further explanation.

"Okay, well, what's your major?" Toby tried to start the conversation again.

"Oh, one of those things, graphic design or something like that."

"Ours too." I chimed in. "Do you have to do a senior show too or are you graduating with us?"

"Yes," she said with gusto and then turned her back on us to do a slow stroll around the crowded basement. Toby and I glanced at each other. Sometimes it was hard to get to know new people. You didn't know where they were coming from. Put in context, her stilted behavior might be perfectly acceptable. Of course we had been here over three weeks and I'd only seen her drift in and out of the house mixer the first week and hadn't encountered her anywhere since.

.cceptable or up to something?

She has to be in at least one of my classes. How am I missing her? Surely I haven't been that self-absorbed. Again.

It reminded me of when I met Paul. I'd been in that miserable painting class of seniors thinking I was the only freshmen the whole first quarter. In all fairness I kept my head down and tried to work hard, so I didn't look anyone else in the eye. I didn't want to draw attention to myself and after the first day Martin had basically ignored me. Then quarterly critiques came.

My first semester art classes had run critiques like a kindergarten show and tell. The student in the spot light told what he or she did to accomplish the task assigned. Then the floor was opened up to the other students to make comments. Lastly, the professor summed up what was both good and bad about the piece before it was turned in to be graded.

I should have guessed Martin's critiques were not like that at all. He skipped into the room with a big smile splitting his scraggly beard and mustache and kicked the doorstops loose from the oversized studio doors. As they glided silently shut, he turned and taped a piece of paper to the back of one, all the while balancing his cup of coffee in one hand and his cigar in the other like a movie director.

Strolling over to the nearest easel, he stood with his back to us surveying a painting by Lucy Lugley through his thick black glasses. He was wearing corduroys with a worn seat and a stripped dress shirt that had seen better days. I held my breath, wondering what he would say and trying not to inhale the heady cigar smoke that burned my throat. This was a smoke free building and there was enough paint thinner in the studio to blaze for a month. We were not off to a good start with this character.

The painting he had paused in front of was layers of colors in a waterfall with a figure sort of growing out of it. And maybe an animal. It didn't matter at that point because before I could work it out, Martin threw his cup of coffee on it. The room gasped. The girl who had painted it stepped forward involuntarily with her hands out in front of her as if to stop him and then she let her arms drop to her sides. The painting was in oil, so it wasn't dry. The hot coffee beaded on top of the oil, then slowly began to melt it. I wouldn't have thought it would affect the paint, but it must have been the heat. Or it wasn't coffee at all. As the thinly applied colors began to run around the stubborn thick layers and drip onto the floor, Martin threw his cup in the trash can nearby and took a long drag on his cigar. Abruptly he spun around to face us.

"Anything I put my hand on becomes mine and will not count toward your quota." He glanced back at the migrating painting. "Ah, now it's brilliant. Too bad for you. It will go in my show at the end of the year. I usually have enough works of incompetence that I've salvaged to make a hale and hearty exhibit." He laughed in the silent room of eighteen people and took another drag on his cigar.

"You all should have heard how this works by now, but in case my reputation hasn't proceeded me, or at least for my darling freshmen..." His voice trailed off as he blew a kiss at me and then, to my surprise, one at the easel next to me. I felt like a deer in the headlights and beyond glancing over and seeing a short, thick guy with charcoal dusting his square jaw, it didn't totally sink in he'd been there all along and he was a freshmen too.

Martin was still talking. "It's simple. Your grade has two parts, a *quality* grade and a *quantity* grade. I first evaluate the paintings on quality. If the painting is acceptable, it has to receive a grade higher than a C to be counted toward the quantity portion of the total. The square footage scale for quantity grades is on the door."

He pounded out his cigar on a student's palette cart next to him and pulled a long dramatic paint rag from his back pocket. Dipping it into the brush jar full of turpentine next to his smoldering cigar, he bent and scooped up another of Lucy's painting leaning against the bottom of the easel catching drips of coffee. With a few strokes he wiped it clean of the damp and uncured oil painting on it. Discarding it on the floor, he selected another work and wiped it off too. When he was done, she had a dozen blank, turpentine soaked canvases scattered about on the floor at the base of her easel.

"Such a good example for the freshmen to see. I'm so glad you volunteered to go first, Ms. Lugley. Now clean this mess up.

That's really all you're good for, someone's maid." He stood over her as she scampered on all fours to gather the ruined paintings into a stack. She leaned them back against her easel foot and tried to wipe up the coffee and sticky turpentine off the floor with an old towel from her cart. The knees of her jeans were soaked. She was trying unsuccessfully not to cry.

"So for the thick headed ones," Martin's loud voice made me jump, "this means that none of Ms. Lugley's works were good enough to even get a grade. Oh, go ahead and let it out, Ms. Lugley. Cry. Cry and be humiliated. You should be after this presentation. Currently Ms. Lugley's score is an incomplete in quality and a zero in quantity for her quarterly marks. And she will need to stretch another canvas because this one is mine." He unscrewed the easel claw at the top that was securing the painting he had tossed coffee on and opening one of the massive classroom doors, winged it out into the hall. As he turned back from the door, he began rolling up his sleeves, and I knew in the pit of my stomach that this wasn't going to be good.

I looked at my paintings. I wasn't ready to say goodbye to them yet. I felt something brush my sleeve and I automatically clenched the paper the guy next to me passed. Glancing down I saw he had sketched a caricature of Martin with wild hair and rolled up sleeves wiping off the Mona Lisa. He'd printed in block letters: GENIUS MEETS IGNORANCE BY PAUL GERBILKAHN, THE OTHER

WHITE MEAT. I felt my eyes widen with the hilarity and naughtiness of it. I turned my head slightly and smiled ever so small at him. And that was how I'd met Paul, the other freshmen, an ally I'd been accidently ignoring for three months.

"Seems like you're going to run out of room down here," Toby's observation snapped me out of my daydream.

"What is this place, anyway?" Wendy waved her arms over her head enthusiastically, but she didn't clear the low ceiling beams. Her hands slapped them with jarring force and a cloud of dust ungracefully enveloped her. She hunched her shoulders in a coughing fit.

"Oh, ouch there, Tiger. You okay?" Toby stepped forward as if to help, but there was nothing to do. She had dust bunnies all over her tangled ringlets. It was hard not to laugh. What was she thinking?

She nodded at him and waved him away, coughing and clearing her throat.

"Sorry, I didn't do a great job sweeping the cobwebs and stuff out of the ceiling." I padded her on the back gently. She held up a finger at me to compose herself, so I continued, "No one was using the basement and I like to paint late into the night. My roommate, Jackie, has massive pre-med studies, so this gives me a place I go without disturbing her work or her sleep. Plus sometimes I work in oils, which can be seriously stinky." I fanned a hand in front of my face. "There's a side door leading to where we park that I can crack if I need to."

Wendy was brushing at her hair with her fingers and didn't seem to be listening to me anymore. I tried a different approach to get her attention. "Do you go to church? You are welcome to come with us on Sunday. I've asked your roommate Sillo before, but she's not interested. Hopefully she's cutting you some slack as a new girl. Anyway, Jackie and I, have you met Jackie? Jacquelyn Voss? Well, we walk across the intersection to the church you can see from our porch. There's a free meal Monday nights for any student too." I've found the best way to gauge someone was to play the church card.

"Okay," she said, "sounds nice. I don't know what to do with myself here. I was so busy before I came here, you know, what with being student body president and director of the choir and all." She stood there shaking her head gently.

I wasn't sure how to take her. Was she being sarcastic? She couldn't carry a conversation, let alone an election or a tune.

"Well, then it's settled." Toby spoke up in the strained silence. "We'll all go together this weekend. And don't worry, there's lots of stuff to keep you as busy as you want to be on this campus. So," he rubbed his hands together. "We were just heading to the Union to grab a bite, wanna come?"

I nodded. "Yah, there's bound to be some people there I can introduce you to."

"Sure, but can you guys tell me what's up with that smell? The one in the air that seems like a bakery of old socks?" She made a face and clamored back up the stairs ahead of us like a new colt on spindly legs. I smiled. She was just a little zany. I was sorry I hadn't spoken to her sooner.

❧ Chapter Six

Class today was one long demonstration on how computers were the future of animation.

Yawn.

First we watched a video about the history of illustrating motion or the illusion of movement. It started with cave paintings, believe it or not. The artists who did the Paleolithic cave paintings of hunting scenes made animals with multiple legs drawn over each other to suggest running.

Of course, I thought, *it could have been the guy didn't like the first leg he drew and erasers hadn't been invented yet so he just drew over the top of his first attempt several times before becoming frustrated and* moving on to the next attempt. And as a side note, why weren't the people running too? Apparently our cave artist was happy with how they looked so he hadn't redrawn them six times. Ha, put that in your pipe and smoke it.

Amusing myself by refuting the theories presented to us, I considered the next example in the motion time line. There was a pot that survived from over five thousand years ago. That in itself was quite a feat. Then there were the five scenes of a goat on the pot to consider. In each scene, the goat appeared to be jumping up in different positions to eat some leaves from a tree. *That's supposed to be the first movie? A goat eating?* I thought it was more likely it was a practice pot. A lot of times I'd try out a few different compositions on a scrap of what I was working on before I committed to the final design. If the pot had survived that long, it wasn't likely it was in everyday use like regular pots. Perhaps it was lopsided or too thick. The artist used it to practice how he wanted the goat to look on his final piece and then dumped the pot in the trash when he had what he wanted. Buried in layers of garbage, the unused pot remained whole until it was found centuries later. The actual show piece pot with one goat scene on it had been completed, sold, used, and broken in the hustle and bustle of a busy house hold.

Now they're saying the guy was some kind of creative genius, making the first motion picture suggestion. Clearly these people are not practicing artists. I shifted in my seat and tried not to day dream with sarcasm as the film proceeded to explain what was now possible in a bunch of technical terms. I realized everyone around me was starting to sketch to alleviate boredom.

I wondered what it would be like to take all of our doodles and string them together in an animation. I glanced over at Ethan's paper on my left and was surprised to see a buffalo bucking off a mailman in a cascade of envelopes. On my right, Ceci was mounding piles and piles of flowers made from little circles like she was raking leaves on a fall day. Beside her, Grace had started a row of comic strips. At the table across from me, Bart's pen was deftly making row after row of little soldiers. Morgan and Caroline's scribbles on a shared scrap looked like a litter of kittens. I couldn't quite see Sarah's paper.

My own note pad had a dark cave opening with a bunch of circle stones and an angel figure piled high with wing shapes. I had sketched the tomb Jesus was buried in after he was crucified. An angel had rolled the stone off the tomb entrance to let everyone see he had risen. I was trying to suggest motion, but it didn't make sense to put a stone in multiple places in one drawing and expect it to be interpreted as one stone. The angel looked like I couldn't draw a wing and didn't have an eraser. The early attempts at motion, if that's what they were, made it obvious why people had kept trying to figure out new ways to portray verbs on 2D surfaces.

Our teacher, who liked to be called Prof Bob, rose from his

seat and flipped on the lights. "Okay, people, we all know how an animation is produced. An artist has to draw each tiny shift during a scene. Raising an arm to wave goodbye could take twenty frames of the same scene with only the arm moved up and out a sliver at a time. Everything else in the scene must be duplicated but not changed for each scene or frame. Once the scene and all its frames are done, they get strung together and played back quickly to give the illusion the arm is being raised to wave goodbye."

Prof Bob sighed. "Fine as all this progress sounds, computers mean a changing job market for us. A computer can take your first scene, perhaps a middle scene, and then your end scene and draw all the scenes in between for you. Imagine. You will only need to draw three frames instead of the twenty originally needed. The computer program will connect them with the other seventeen."

It was sobering to think of all the artists put out of work. A guy and a computer could draw what once took a building full of people to produce. And in a lot less time, I'd wager. We crowded around the professor's monitor to watch him open something he called a program.

There was a shortage of trained professors who knew how to be a technician as well as an artist and a teacher. Such a rare bird was like having one person be the pilot, co-pilot, flight attendant, and mechanic on an international flight. The promise of such a person and a lab had been there when I was a freshmen.

Now, three years later, I had come back from abroad to find the old janitor's closet in the basement of the art building emptied out and painted. They had filled it with tables and chairs and cords and wires and big boxes with little flashing lights and whirring and buzzing noises. And a jolly little man, who was known as Prof Bob, was our rare bird.

I took notes as best I could, but it was tricky to know when he was tapping something on the keyboard and when he was clicking a little car on a cord to move a blinking line called a cursor across the screen in front of us. He called the little car a mouse. I suppose they thought it looked like one with the cord being the tail, but it was too much a round furless blob of cold plastic for me to think of as a mouse.

Inventors and their goofy names. I was momentarily distracted by my own thoughts. *There's no way 'mouse' will stick. Like that guy, Celeb Bradham first calling Pepsi Brad's drink. Can't imagine what would have happened if he hadn't renamed it Pepsi-Cola after the digestive enzyme pepsin in his recipe. Booyah! Much better.*

Our first assignment had been to master control of the mouse by drawing a landscape starting with a blank screen. We were required to save and print the file. It was hard to understand the terms Prof Bob was using when no file cabinet was in the room and printing didn't mean the opposite of cursive.

I remember struggling with the mouse tool and my fingers

aching afterwards. I'd managed to pull off a vineyard with a woman standing in front hoisting a jug up onto her shoulders. In my head I pretended it was Martha fussing over the meal when Jesus visited their home in Luke 10:38-42.

As Jesus and his disciples were traveling, they came to a village where a woman named Martha opened her home for them to stay. She had a sister, Mary, who sat at the Lord's feet listening to what he said. But Martha was distracted by all the preparations for their visitors. She asked Jesus, "Lord, don't you care that my sister has left me to do the work by myself? Tell her to help me!"

"Martha, Martha," he answered, "you are worried and upset about many things, but few things are needed—or indeed only one. Mary has chosen what is better, and it will not be taken away from her."

During the critique I posed the question to the class, "Are you a Mary or a Martha?" I'd boldly continued on my tangent. "I've been thinking about it a lot lately. If I imagine Jesus is here on campus lounging under an oak in the quad I don't hesitate to say I would be there hanging on every word He was saying in a very Mary-esque way.

"But then I have to reevaluate the context for us. At that time he had not died and risen back to life. They only had him with them for those moments he was visiting. We, on the other hand, are currently on the other side of that. He is with us all the time. Once we accept Jesus as our savior, we have access twenty-four seven. So am a Martha with the necessities of daily life keeping me from him or am I a Mary, hanging out with him all the time? I fear I have created a self-portrait with this simple landscape exercise." I gestured at the letter size piece of paper clipped to the dry erase board in our classroom. "And somehow, while this invention seems as if it will cost us less time working and allow us more time to worship, I fear that may not be the case either. Normally I would sketch a scene like this in about thirty minutes. This eight by ten took me four hours!" The room erupted with laughter. "Yeah, that's what I thought too. Somewhere in this learning curve, I suspect the integrity of fine art skills may be lost to progress. And I don't see how the art world will ever let that happen. Just saying."

I sat down amid an eruption of applause like a rock star. Almost everyone was glad I was back from Europe. The new computer professor, however, looked startled. By now all the regular teachers on campus knew me and my frequent Biblical references to make my points. I'd forgotten he might not be as receptive. But he had made no direct comment about my work after my presentation. When last week's demo was over, our assignment had been to manipulate a photo using the digital camera and scanner technology to input images.

"Your challenge," Prof Bob said, "is to create a portrait explaining whether you are a Mary or a Martha at the technology party the world is currently having. That's a wrap guys and gals. I'll be playing in my office on my brand new computer named after my favorite fruit if you need me."

Is he making fun of me or is he for real? It was my turn to be startled by his assignment. *Guess it doesn't matter.* I realized as I left the building. Either way, people will be contemplating how they relate to Jesus.

As I entered our house after class, I heard voices floating out of our room. "Since Clare isn't back yet, can you help me? I'm trying to remember how to find that thing she said about my hair. In the Bible. You know. Matthew ten, thirty she said. You know how to find things in the Bible, don't you?"

"Oh, okay. Sure," Jackie said. I paused in the foyer to utter a prayer. *This is great. Jackie's helping Marcella use the Bible I gave her, Lord. Please help them.* I didn't want to interrupt, so I lingered outside the room.

"The name at the beginning is a book in the Bible. You can find it in the table of contents. So we are looking for Matthew. It's in the new testament at the back of the book." There was the rustle of pages. "Once you get to the book, then the chapters are referenced by the number before the colon. So we want chapter ten. The verses are the numbers after the colon and they are the small numbers inside the chapters. See here. Number thirty."

"Wow, and it does say that." Marcella's voice changed as she read from the page. "And even the very hairs of your head are all numbered." She paused a minute. "Thanks, Jackie. I kind of remembered how the Bible is set up from Catholic school, but they pretty much read us everything. I never had to look for myself. I think I'm going to read more. Do you read every day? What's God told you?" I was as eager as Marcella was to hear what Jackie said.

There was an uncomfortable pause. "Well, Marcella, I should read every day, it's just that right now with so much reading for my studies, I don't have time or energy left over to read the Bible a lot. I know what most of it says and I believe all of it. I go to church and I pray. I'm just kind of on hold from helping people till I get through medical school, then I'll be doing it right and left. I mean, I know God wants me to be a doctor."

"No kidding, he told you to be a doctor? That would be so cool to know what you are supposed to do and just do it. That's what I want. Thanks, Jackie." I sidestepped Marcella as she charged out of the room full of excitement.

"Hey, Clare! I'm coming to Monday meal, don't leave without me, okay?"

"Sure, we'll be glad to have you, Marcella." I walked into our room and sank down on the bed. I was tired.

"Thanks for forcing me into being an evangelist." I could tell by her tone Jackie wasn't happy with me. "I haven't got time for all this drama."

"What are you talking about?" I asked.

"You breeze in here like a super hero telling everyone what they should be doing for God. They all fall all over themselves to be like you. Only you run off to who knows where and I'm left to answer all their questions and I've got studying to do."

"Uh, okay. I was in class and that took like two minutes of your time. You should be thrilled Marcella is seeking out God. Come on, Jackie, I didn't come up with how we are supposed to share our faith – that was God's plan. He commanded us to go and tell everyone about it. It's our first priority. Is that why you're really upset? You've been really busy and have drifted out of God's presence? We all have those times, Jack."

She tossed a book across the room and I jumped when it hit the floor with a loud slap. "It's not just that," she declared as she shifted forward on her bed. "You're always so sure since you've been back. So committed to all this wild stuff like people coming back from the dead and spirits and stuff. I wasn't raised that way. We don't need all that in my quiet little suburb. I'm alright. I'm a good girl."

Before I could respond, she threw another text book against the wall. "But I'm scared, Clare! If I'm going to be a doctor, I'm going to be dealing with life and death. People are going to be asking me what's going to happen to them or their children or their loved ones and I'm going to have to tell them the truth. Without Jesus they are going to Hell. What if I can't do it? I don't think I can do this. I mean, what about supernatural healing? What about magic? What about the number on this hair? Or this one? Do they renumber themselves now that that one is gone?" She was plucking hair out of her head and flinching with each strand she waved at me.

"Jackie. Jack! Stop it." I moved across the room and wrapped my arms around her. She had started to cry and I realized the things I'd been talking about since coming back really had been working on her heart.

"I never meant for any of my experiences or my own questions to scare you or make you feel guilty. I'm looking for answers and I trust you, so I share a lot with you. Something I do know, though, is God loves us more than anything." I rocked her gently as her sobbing quieted.

"Everything okay in here?" Simone stuck her head in the door with a worried expression.

"Yah, Simone, thanks." Jackie straightened up and fished a Kleenex out of the box by her bed. "I guess you'd say I'm having a crisis of faith. Clare makes me feel so lost. Like I don't know anything about God. And I thought I was all set."

Simone came in and sat down on my bed facing us, the worried expression in her eyes relaxing. "Hey, I hear you. She's a challenge to all of us. We love you, though, Clare." She winked at me. "Look, Jackie, in all fairness I don't think any of us knows everything there is to know about God. We are all seeking his face, though.

"Look, we all have lots to learn, all of us." I was praying in my head like crazy for what to say to them. "But everything we need is in the Bible or in our hearts with the Holy Spirit. Acts one, eight says so." I reached over and grabbed my worn Bible off my desk, quickly turning the pages. "Here, it says, 'But you will receive power when the Holy Spirit comes on you; and you will be my witnesses in Jerusalem, and in all Judea and Samaria, and to the ends of the earth.' We have power guys and we're supposed to share the gospel."

"I know, I know, I need to read my Bible and then I won't be scared by the things you talk about that I can't figure out." Jackie hugged her pillow and curled up on her end of the bed. "I'm just soooo tired of reading."

"Well, what about an audio Bible?" Simone asked.

"Hey, yeah!" I jumped up off Jackie's bed. "We could listen every night before bed."

Jackie began to smile. "I'd like that."

"Glad to be of service. The bill will be in the mail." Simone got up to go with a mischievous grin. We laughed. "Tell you what, you guys can share mine. It's like thirty cassette tapes, so it's not like I'll be using them all every night. I listen before I go to sleep too. It's something Rupert has me doing since I've been worried about him with all the strike talk from the townies over the factory conditions."

***

I had gone back to the Bible and looked up all the references to Mary and Martha for my computer graphics assignment. When I turned to the one in John, chapter twelve, I started reading at the beginning of the chapter and trailed off in thought by verse eight.

Six days before the Passover, Jesus came to Bethany, where Lazarus lived, whom Jesus had raised from the dead. Here a dinner was given in Jesus' honor. Martha served, while Lazarus was among those reclining at the table with him. Then Mary took about a pint of pure nard, an expensive perfume; she poured it on Jesus' feet and wiped his feet with her hair. And the house was filled with fragrance.

But one of his disciples, Judas Iscariot, who was later to betray him, objected, "Why wasn't this perfume sold and the money given to the poor? It was worth a year's wages." He did not say this because he cared about the poor but because he was a thief; as keeper of the money bag, he used to help himself to what was put into it.

"Leave her alone," Jesus replied. "It was intended that she should save this perfume for the day of my burial. You will always have the poor among you, but you will not always have me."

Hmmm. So do I feel like hanging on every word about computers? Honestly, no. I think to this technology party, as Prof Bob calls it, I'm actually a Martha. I'd rather keep art happening as art and let the new guy, the computer, join us, but not make that medium my sole priority. So how do I show that?!? I had puzzled over it most of the week before coming up with a simple composition to present.

Using the self-timer on the digital camera with a tripod, I had taken some shots of myself sitting at my easel painting in the house basement. Then I had grabbed the bottle of pancake syrup I'd gotten at Walgreens out of my bag. Walgreens was in easy walking distance, so it supplied most of what we used in our personal lives.

Setting the camera to take a series of shots in a row on the timer, I stood pouring the syrup over a box I'd pulled from the dumpster behind the drug store that was about the size of a computer monitor. At my appointment in the lab I plugged a cord into the camera and then into the computer and transferred the photos over to my monitor. I weeded through them and selected my favorites. Then I snapped some shots of the computer next to me in the lab and transferred them over too.

Next, I laid a comic book I'd borrowed from a friend on the scanner bed. With a flash of light and a slow mechanical grinding, a spread of tiny boxed images with speaking bubbles popped up on my screen. I laid a row of sharpened pencils on the scanner and watched them materialize on the screen. Then I set to work cutting and pasting.

I used the structure of the comic book page and the thinking bubbles to create a narrative of me sitting at my easel with a thought bubble imaging myself pouring nard over a computer monitor. I replaced the box with syrup dripping down its side in my photo with the monitor I'd snapped a pic of. I shook my head to clear the image from my thoughts in the next frame. Then I sat at my easel and pictured myself drawing with giant pencils. I shook that image away too.

In the final scene, I'm painting on a self-portrait of a self-portrait like Norman Rockwell's composition in a nod I was making to traditional illustration. Behind me, the lab was smoking from pools of sticky liquid shorting out the computers. I smirked at the idea of those white cubes being reverenced with expensive perfume. They were just a tool. And one I didn't prefer even though the assignment made me think about Mary and Martha somewhat differently. We could apply their behaviors and attitudes to anything in our lives and compare it to how we were treating Jesus.

As I left class I felt good about my work. The critique of our Mary and Martha pieces had gone well and Prof Bob had seemed amused by the various explanations students presented for the computer generated compositions. We had used print outs and met in the more comfortable design studio upstairs.

I sighed as I descended the stairs to get back to the computer lab. *How can they expect us to thrive like this? Must be the sunlight isn't good for the computers or something. Although, there probably isn't any* other space available. I don't imagine a lab was ever part of the building plan. I shifted my back pack to the other shoulder. *The only good thing about it is the Sulferson Silk smell doesn't seem to make it down here. Frankly, though, I'd settle for a desk in the front hall with all those big windows even if I had to smell it.*

Our assignment this week was to create a ten second animated clip. Apparently it was going to take longer than ten seconds to make. We had three weeks. I'd signed up for lab time directly after class so I could still keep everything school related on Tuesdays and Thursdays if at all possible. A fantastic three hour block had been open on the fastest computer because everyone else was usually too dazed from the lectures to want to see another computer again for a while.

Everyone except for me and the twins that is.

Jayden and Kayden Chung graduated last year so they were auditing computer classes this year. They needed access to the expensive computer animation programs the University's lab grant had gotten. It was rumored that somehow they had managed to secure unpaid internships at a local unpublicized facility that Pixar frequently handpicked artists from.

For decades, everyone in graphic design thought Disney was the golden ticket for a long and prosperous art career. It was known around campus though, that the Chung brothers believed a new group of companies, like Pixar, were going to rival the Disney

Dynasty if it didn't swallow them first.

The technology we were learning could even the playing field. Small companies wouldn't need to hire giant animating teams. And it would eliminate the need for actors, sets, and all the crews and staff that went with them. Soon one or two guys in a windowless lab could create everything we watched. And Jay and Kay wanted to be those guys.

They were definitely a couple of computer Marys.

Kay flipped on the lights and we dropped our bags on the empty chairs by the door. The three of us stood surveying the room a moment. Now that no students and hyper-excited professors were steaming up the place with their simpering about new things, it was empty and sterile. The stark white room with white equipment and tangles of white cords emitted a low hum. The faux wood paneled tables and gray metal folding chairs were the only color. It was the least creative room in the entire school.

"Wow, would somebody at least hang up a *picture* of a window in here?" I said. The guys laughed, but the chuckle died in my throat as Martin strolled through the open lab door and gripped my shoulder from behind. I cringed away, but he hung on tight and stooped slightly to speak into my ear.

"So nice you made it back in one piece, my darling protégé. Don't you know if you cross over to the dark side with these people, when they rule the world, there won't be any windows in any buildings anymore? They will burn the art and the supplies that made it in giant heaps on campuses across the country. All that will be left is what is inside that pretty little head of yours, locked away in a lab like this."

I tried to sidestep away again, but he moved with me. His voice barely above a whisper.

"Don't be foolish, Clare. Come back to my painting class where you will be treasured for the gift you are. Listen to me. I can make you famous beyond your wildest dreams. Everyone on earth will know your name. You must return to my class. I moved it so it's during the opening you have in your schedule on Tuesdays and Thursdays. I promise not to take your literature classes away from you again. I know my mistakes of the past and I am ready to start over." He released my shoulder and his hand trailed under my hair and across the back of my neck. As he turned to slink out, the faculty phone mounted on the wall rang and he answered it.

"It's for you," he sneered as he pointed at Kay and dropped the receiver so it hung like a bird swinging by one long leg against the wall.

We were all frozen like statues. Martin hesitated, then shook his head. "No it can't be," he muttered to himself. "It can't be her. Why would she be calling *him*?" He glanced over at Kay and then turned toward me. Using two fingers, he pointed at his eyes and then at me. Repeating the gesture, to emphasis he would be watching me, he backed out of the room and the door clicked shut.

The three of us stood there staring at the back of the door for a long minute until the shivers hit me. Kay snapped into action and grabbed the swaying phone receiver.

"Ugh, is it just me, or is that man half crazy?" I wrapped my arms around my body to steady myself.

Jay was nodding in agreement as he quickly stepped forward to slide the bolt into place on the inside.

"Sorry we didn't do that sooner James." Jay put a hand on my shoulder and gently piloted me into a chair. I put my hand over his and squeezed. "It's okay. I'm glad I wasn't by myself, though. Mental note to keep an eye out for Martin so I don't get cornered."

"Yah, lucky you, the jelly doughnut flavor of the month." Kay had hung up the phone and chuckled at his own joke.

Jay waved his nonsense away impatiently. "Seriously, James, if he corners you by yourself, remind him the place is crawling with cameras. It won't stop him from saying gross things, but he won't touch you." Jay pointed at the monitor by the computer lab door. It was one of the many security measures installed since the new lab arrived.

This particular monitor was linked to a camera in the hall. All students registered for a computer class had a key to the lab. With the schedule of students who were supposed to be there posted on the door in case someone forgot their key, we could see outside if anyone knocked unexpectedly. If they weren't on the list, they weren't allowed in and we were supposed to press a silent alarm. This was standard now across the country after several campus labs had been robbed. No one had been apprehended yet.

My eyes lingered on the shiny new monitor in front of me and skimmed the pizza policy posted on the wall next to it. PIZZA CAN BE A PORTAL TO OUR LAB AND ENDANGER YOU! It screamed a warning in capital letters. Nothing sounded too ridiculous after the paranoia I encountered in London over unattended books and bags suspected of harboring terrorist bombs.

Pizza, a main stable of lab rats, wasn't forbidden. The sign reminded us it was how the other labs were robbed and outlined protocol for getting it. First, you called a student who was not in the lab and asked him or her to order it. It had to be ordered and paid for somewhere else on campus. Your friend could then bring it to the lab door and show student ID so everyone in the room could verify a student was alone on the other side of the door. Supposedly even if some of us didn't know him or her, we could check their ID. How we were supposed to know if it was fake or not was beyond me. So far I'd personally known everyone who had borne the bounty.

The lab was always busy, though, so it wasn't like you were ever a lone target. It felt like a clubhouse to me. The long hours and frustrations bonded us like nothing else could. We were in this together, even risking our lives to order pizza was a group effort.

And when Prof Bob spent too long at the neighborhood bar and grill and didn't want to wake his kids, he'd drop in too. He always wanted to sleep it off on the hard tile floor, but the students were like vultures, picking his groggy brain for as long as they could keep him awake. It was rather a comical zoo the later it got on any given day.

"Hey, James, we got Wendy bringing the pizza tonight." Jay swung into his seat and pressed the power button on his computer.

I was startled. "Wendy? As in Wendy Gallonte? How do you guys know her?"

"From class. You know her too, don't you?" Kay was waiting for his machine to finish starting. It took forever. My screen was still blank.

"Yah, I know her because she lives across from me, but I've never seen her in class." Now I was starting to feel bad. I was being too self-absorbed. I needed to make her feel welcome.

"Well maybe not. She usually comes at the end. She's afraid of crowds," Kay said.

"No, no, that's not it. She's afraid to leave her room. Agoraphobic or something." Jay contradicted him.

"Well, if she's afraid to leave her room, how's she bringing us pizza?" She had eaten with Toby and I the other night at the cafeteria. Both out of her room and in a crowd. This raised my suspicions of her again. Why was she really skipping classes?

They shrugged at the same time while they were both staring at their monitors.

"Look, what do we know? She's kind of hard to understand. Like she doesn't really talk to you when she's talking to you. Know what I mean?" Jay's voice drifted off as his computer screen lit up and he was absorbed into the tiny world in the box.

I nodded even though he wasn't looking. I did know what he meant. I was probably being too suspicious after my adventures abroad. But something else was nagging at me now. "Hey, I thought only faculty and security had this phone number. Who called you *here*?" I asked Kay. He pretended to ignore me for a long minute but when he glanced sideways at me, I was looking directly at him. He sighed. "It's kind of complicated. It was my girlfriend. I'm dating an older woman."

"Oh, really?" I leaned back in my chair. "You're dating a professor? Someone Martin knows?"

He looked at his hands. "I don't know, maybe. What difference does it make? I'm over twenty-one. I can date who I want."

The conversation ended as Kay's monitor hummed to life and he turned a cold shoulder toward me. The only noises in the room as my monitor lit up were the click of the keyboards and an occasional squeak from a folding chair.

Left to my own thoughts, I swiped at the back of my neck with my free hand while I maneuvered the mouse through its maze of commands. I could still feel Martin's rough fingers brushing my skin. The little darting cursor on the screen skittered about, trying to help me shake off his coffee-soaked whisper, hissing in my ear. The smell of his hot breath mingled with his cigar tainted clothes still burned in my nostrils. Why did he want me in his class? I hadn't seen Martin since I'd gotten back. It had been a relief to hear he had stepped down as chairman and was only teaching his senior painting classes.

As I listened to the click of the mouse under my hand, I felt my stomach turn. I hugged my body with a free arm as a smoldering coal of anger ignited in my belly. I hadn't felt that uncomfortable burn in the pit of my gut since I'd been back. It hadn't taken much, though, just a few words from him and the scars from the scalding I'd gotten in his class were back in a wave of confusion, anxiety, and resentment. My soul felt trampled and dirty, stained with the hurt from his cruel words and humiliation. I would have plenty of time for my thoughts to crowd in on my class notes in this mental petri dish of solitary work. I looked at the clock. Hours to go.

Well, it doesn't matter what he's done to the schedule, I'll never take another class from him again. I don't agree with his methods or his beliefs. I thought defiantly.

He had lectured time and again, like a swallow berating you for coming too near her nest, that depression was the only path to making truly great art. The dregs of the soul were like the coffee grounds of creativity, he said, over and over. One must focus on the worst things in life, the injustices and the grief, or be eternally a fail. The evidence he cited always appalled me, but I had held my tongue. He insisted all great artists ended up killing themselves because to be great was to be depressed.

Clearly he hadn't reached that stage in his own art because he was still breathing. *Who starts this nonsense?* I fumed as I punched keys. He had always bullied students in the name of making great art. And then he randomly took their art and hung it in his office or gave it to his friends. It was supposed to be a great honor, so no one said anything. My mom had warned me about professor theft. She had lost one of her favorite pieces to a professor in college.

I had waited for him to even hint at taking one of my works and I was ready to scream bloody murder. I'd kept careful records and photos the whole time I worked on my pieces in his classes. But he was a crafty fox and hadn't stolen any of my pieces. Yet.

I huffed out loud in the quiet lab. I doubted he had painted anything himself in the last twenty years. What a con - a reflection in a mud puddle compared to the real thing. An illusion of the thing God meant art to be.

My mind groped around for the words to explain what that would be like. *Art should inspires others to achieve the same feeling the artist did while making the piece.* My mouse hand paused as I closed my eyes and let experiences wash over me. Like when you tip your head back and look at a thousand stars in the night sky. Or the warm sticky juice of a ripe nectarine running down your chin in the middle of an orchard buzzing with bees. Art should excite your five senses, not just manipulate your emotions. What about the shimmer of a dragonfly wing brushing your cheek with a buzz by your ear in the blinding sunshine? Or how your breathing feels in your body after running to greet a loved one in an airport? What about the colors your soul turns when you converse with God? He made the rainbow and gave it to us as a gift and a promise. He mentions the color green right off in the Bible. Who were assembled to make the temple where God was worshipped? Artisans, of course. Creating is a loving act of worship recognizing our own miraculous creation. If I'd learned nothing else from looking at all the interiors of the cathedrals across Europe, I had learned that. We could only aspire to feel like God when he made those things, but wasn't it worth it to at least try?

  I felt a stir in my torso, and realized I had been sitting with my eyes closed. It wasn't my stomach growling. I wasn't hungry. It was my spirit groaning to make a connection, but I couldn't quite. Something was in my way. It was like waking up from a dream and almost remembering it, but you couldn't see it clearly. I had seen something different in my heart. I looked around the room for someone to tell but the guys were ignoring me as they worked.

  I turned on my creaking folding chair and stretched back

behind me to the pile of backpacks. Digging mine out, I fished through it and pulled out my tattered Bible. It flopped open in my hands to the marker for my daily devotional I had read that morning.

He saved us, not because of righteous things we had done, but because of his mercy. He saved us through the washing of rebirth and renewal by the Holy Spirit, whom he poured out on us generously through Jesus Christ our Savior, so that, having been justified by his grace, we might become heirs having the hope of eternal life. Titus 3:5-7

The words flowed over me and relaxed my troubled heart like a salve. I was on a path to be used by God. He washed me of my sins and saved me. But a niggling thought accompanied the hurts in my gut. What about the sins of others? What about what they had done to me? I knew I was instructed to forgive them and let God punish them. Revenge was not a healthy thing and it wasn't ours to take. God would deal with Martin. I pushed the hurts back and read on, soon absorbed again in the passages explaining the mystery of God's love for us.

Two hours passed quickly in the sterile box and the door buzzer made us all jump. Kay checked the monitor and opened the door to let Wendy pass through carrying a large pizza box eliciting mouthwatering smells. Carmichael's double crust, double cheese, cheddar and Canadian bacon pizza was the best thing on the planet. I didn't know if they ever sold any other combination. Or if the rumors were true that they were a money laundering front. Either way, their pizza was the best thing I'd ever eaten.

"Hey, Wendy, thanks so much for doing this for us. You okay?" I asked her quickly. She seemed fine for an agoraphobic.

"Yah, sure. It was a little creepy walking across campus this time of night with a pizza. I thought I might get ambushed by hungry students." She laughed. "But all went smoothly."

"How much do I owe?" I closed the floppy Bible and slid it into my backpack to dig for my money.

Jay waved me away. "Our treat tonight. Welcome back, James!"

Kay smirked. "Yeah, I'm half afraid to work in the lab when you do. Are the stories true?" They settled back in their side-by-side chairs with their square slices. The anticipation on their duplicate faces made me feel like I had double vision. Wendy peeled a piece out of the open box for herself and sat cross legged on the waxed linoleum floor.

"Look, you guys, I don't know what everyone is saying, but it was a real situation." I selected a slice for myself. It was the only place I knew that cut the round pizza into squares instead of triangles.

The boys wiggled with excitement and I had to laugh. The door buzzer sounded and we all started.

"It's Prof Bob, should we let him in?" Jay joked.

"I can hear you through the door, Jay. I'll use my key if you don't. And next time I'll key in and freak you out without asking!" He gruffed from the hall. Prof Bob was a short man with a black goatee and neat dress pants. He had two little girls and a sweet wife we all adored.

"You're in time for pizza, sir," Kay waved his slice at Bob as he stomped through the door and surveyed the room.

"Everything okay tonight, guys?"

We nodded. "Clare was about to give us the unabridged version of what happened in London," Jay said around a mouthful.

"By all means, don't let me stop you. I love a good yarn." Bob was smiling as he grabbed an index card size wedge of pizza with his stubby fingers and sat on a folding chair by the wall.

"It doesn't seem real now that I'm back." I paused to eat another bite and collect my thoughts. *This is getting harder to tell every time someone requests it. I should just write up what happened and pass it out for people to read.* I shrugged. "It didn't seem too real while it was happening, though, either." When I concluded the tale they clapped despite their handfuls of pizza. I stood and mock curtsied.

"We should make a full length animated movie out of that!" Kay said.

"We'd be too late." Prof Bob was wiping his hands on his pants.
"It's already been done or at least nearly done."

"Not Clare's story," Kay grumbled in a low voice.

Jay chimed in over him. "I've heard the one about to be released was stolen during one of the lab break-ins, but it's so top secret, no one knows which lab had it."

"No way, a whole two hour movie? On one of those?" Wendy's eyes were big as she gestured toward the tables of computers and cords.

"It'd be easy to take. Those files can be compressed onto little pieces of metal as thick as a sheet of paper and vanish into thin air before you know it." Jay waved his hands in front of his eyes. We all looked at Prof Bob.

He guffawed. "All I know is that whatever lab or company does release it first will literally roll in the dough. And get all the grants. *That's* a piece of art you should be forging, and fast, James."

"Forging? If there's no time to create an original, there's no time to create a forgery. Besides, it's a race, not a question of pedigree for value. Why not just come out with an original movie first? It's about who's first, right?" I was skeptical about anything coming from the computers being art anyway, much less valuable enough to steal or forge. Why not press the command and letter C keys and make a copy?

"It is about who's first, Miss James." Prof Bob crossed his arms and stretched his legs out in front of him to cross his ankles. His folding chair groaned. "We don't have time now to write all the original code. A movie is done or almost done in some lab somewhere in this country. It either has to be destroyed and stopped to buy more time for everyone else or copied and stolen to end everyone else's time."

"Well, if you know anything about James, Sir, you know she would classify those moves as sin, so we need another solution to get a piece of the pie." Jay scratched his head and frowned. I was surprised he knew so much about what I'd think. He was speaking again. "What if it's not very good? I mean, it could be an amazing feat of technology and be poorly written. Maybe it could be discredited." Jay winked at me. I tilted my head and raised my eye brows at him.

"I think by the time the awe wears off and everyone figures out it's plotless, the money will already be made and the splash will have already happened. Perhaps Miss James could find the stolen movie and return credit to its rightful owner. That would be within your moral compass, wouldn't it?" He looked at me.

"And we could be the heroes that saved the first computer animated movie, even if we didn't get to make it!" Wendy shouted and pointed to the ceiling like it was a huge ah ha moment.

I looked from one to the other of them suspiciously. "This conversation is like an orchestrated dance. What are you trying to tell me? Do you guys have some inside information?" I was still studying their faces, looking for a clue to their agenda.

"No, No, No."

"Well maybe. What if someone wanted to return it and not

get into trouble?"

"No, we're not supposed to say." Kay and Jay cut each other off, but I was watching Prof Bob. He hadn't moved a muscle, hiding his expression behind his beard.

"Seriously, guys? You're old enough to know what to do if you have the movie and you want to turn it in." I wasn't sure what they were implying or if I even cared. They were always in their own little world and I wasn't going to be baited into looking for a lost movie I didn't even know if I supported. I turned to Wendy and smiled, determined to at least make an effort to get to know her.

"So, Wendy, since you're next on this computer, what's your idea for the ten seconds?" I took a big bite of another slice of pizza giving her a chance to talk.

"Oh, oh," She looked flustered. "That's right. My movie. Well, I thought I'd make a volcano erupting with an airplane flying out of it and some ballet dancers on the beach in front of it with some fireworks and maybe an elephant or," her voice trailed off in midsentence. The guys were shaking their heads.

"Too much. Way too much. Keep it simple," Kay spoke around another mouth full of cheese and meat. The pizza never seemed to run out.

"Yah, just the volcano with the airplane would be plenty," Jay said. "I can help you after we get done eating. Hey, why are you guys dressed the same?" He gestured down and I looked at my clothes –

leather sandals, ripped up jeans, and a University sweatshirt. I looked at Wendy. She was wearing the same sweatshirt. With her jeans and sandals, we matched.

I wasn't used to the brand new burgundy Jeep Grand Cherokee in the house parking lot belonging to me. Or at least I was the one holding the keys in the unseasonably warm sunshine. It was another perk of the Sulferson Commission. They were loaning it to me so they didn't have to keep sending a car around.

I'd come out to see how dirty it looked. I was in a quandary about washing it. Was I supposed to, or would the chauffeur do take care of it the next time I was there to paint? If I was responsible for it, then this was a perfect day to clean it for free at the house. The weather was warm enough to make it a pleasant task and Jackie would let me use her supplies.

As I contemplated my liability, the back door of our house swung open and hit the outside wall with a thunk.

"Oh, excuse me. I didn't mean to do that," Jackie called as she wrestled a large trash bag out to the dumpster in our parking lot. I ran over to help her close the dumpster door flap.

"Thanks!" She brushed her hands together as if to dislodge dust. "You know how everybody dumps their pizza boxes in the foyer trash can instead of out here. I can't stand all the stink in the hall after the weekend!" She said with venom.

"Yah, the smell does drift into our room like a skunk marking his territory."

She laughed. "Gosh, it's nice out here. Wanna pull a Ferris?"

"Are you serious? Don't you need to study?" I looked at her in surprise.

"I do, but it'll all be there when I get back." She spun around in a circle. "What I don't always have are the elements for a perfect day to play hooky." She continued to spin, waving her arms as she elaborated. "It's all here, my best roommate home, a sunshiny day in October, a sassy attention-getting convertible and," she paused for dramatic effect, "a twenty." She pulled a green bill out of her pocket and waved it in front of my face.

"Grandma Money!" I clapped my hands together like a toddler.

"Grandma Money." She confirmed with a nod. "Came in the mail this morning."

"I'm in." I swung open the passenger door of her car as she pressed the little button on her fob. I slipped the jeep keys in my pocket as the top of her car slide silently backward. I would figure out the washing issue next time I was at the Sulferson place. It wasn't a priority now that a day to do brainless activities like Ferris Bueller in that movie was on the table. And with grandma money, no less. The nickname we used for extra cash didn't mean it necessarily come from your grandmother, but in Jackie's case it always did. Her grandma randomly sent her surprise twenty dollar bills and we started calling any unexpected windfall of cash "grandma money."

She squealed the tires as we left the parking lot and I grabbed at the edges of my t-shirt to keep the air whipping around the car from hiking it up my torso and over my chest as we tore down the interstate to the outskirts of town. I leaned my head back on the rest and let the eighty-mile-an-hour wind swirl my hair around my face into a visor of invisibility. The air smelled of fresh cut grass and dried leaves. The sun was warm on my arms and the top of my thighs. The seatbelt gently slapped my shoulder as if trying to get my attention, but I ignored it. Everything was perfect.

At a stop light a new pickup truck full of frat boys paused next to us so they could hoot and whistle. We waved and giggled. The driver revved the engine. Jackie let them race off ahead of us as she turned down a side street to cut through an alley.

"So where are we going?" I asked now that the car was going slower and the wind wasn't so possessive.

"I accidently brought dad's golf clubs back with me in the trunk." She gave me sidelong look with a sly grin.

I nodded and grinned back as my eyes met hers in the rear view mirror.

She maneuvered the car into a slot at the drive-in root beer stand and we ordered triple-decker sundaes to-go from the girl on roller skates. I balanced both our urns of ice cream as Jackie drove out of town and found a nice vantage point overlooking the lake that pooled next to the Sulferson Silks factory.

She backed the car off the road toward the water and we discarded our sandals to climb over the seats. Our ice cream was melting quickly so we settled cross legged on the warm trunk of the car and shoveled it in like astronauts having their last meal before a mission. We were quiet, eating and watching the clouds mingle with the puffs of white factory smoke to form shapes that vaguely resembled things – an elephant, a pair of scissors, an angel. The parade of objects was as endless as the sky stretching away from us in an arch across the earth.

A light breeze was blowing against our backs and pushing the sickly scented smoke away from us and back at the factory making it. Finishing my ice cream, I tossed the oversized plastic cup and spoon into the back seat and slide off the sleek car burying my bare toes in the sand that bordered the water's edge.

"What do you think being in true love feels like?" I tossed the question out there haphazardly.

"The opposite of being in true hate." Jackie responded without seeming to think about it.

"That's too obvious." But I thought about her answer a minute. "I do have a dislike for Martin that burns in the pit of my stomach, but I can't say what I feel for Toby has near that intensity. I guess that answers my question. I'm not falling in love with him." I kicked at the sand.

"You sound disappointed, maybe that should figure into the equation." Jackie slid off the trunk and popped it open. We worked together to pull out the bag of clubs, the bucket of balls, and the old x-ray blanket she had gotten from her dentist when he retired it for a newer one.

"Look, maybe you need to think about the five love languages and see which one you are so you know if you're expressing love or not." Jackie leaned her back against the car and surveyed the water with squinting eyes.

"Go on," I said, closing the trunk and hoisting the heavy blanket up on the trunk lid.

"Well, we had a speaker talking about bed side manner for doctors." Jackie turned to help me unfold the blanket and smooth it out. "She was explaining how each person expresses and receives love in one of five different ways. It stuck in my head because it was so different than anything I've heard before, but it makes total sense. Like one of the languages is appropriate physical touch and that's totally my dad. He gives everybody a hug, all the time, coming or going." She rolled her eyes and bent to pick up the bag of clubs. Her voice was muffled. "Gift receiving is another one."

I paused with the bucket of balls in hand. "Yeah, but

everybody gives presents, what's that supposed to mean?"

"No, some people feel loved when they receive gifts and a lot of times we express love the way we like to receive love. Look at your mom."

"My mom? What?" I was startled.

"Yah, I bet she feels loved when she gets gifts so that's how she expresses love too. I mean, she sends you homemade snacks every week. You know she loves you before she even says it. Everyone thinks she loves you more than their moms love them, but she just knows how to express it better. That's what knowing about the languages of love can help us with. We can confirm we are loved by the people around us and we know how to express our love to the people around us so they actually hear us, so to speak."

"Wow, I never thought about any of that. I just thought everyone told each other they loved them. So, what are the other languages?" I asked.

"Let's see." She paused and looked up at the sky as if reading a note in the clouds. "We've talked about receiving gifts and physical touch already. The other three are quality time, acts of service, and words of affirmation." She counted them off her fingers. "The words of affirmation aren't only saying, I love you. Words of praise and appreciation can affirm a person too. Quality time is pretty self-explanatory and acts of service is just doing things for others. Like when my mom does my laundry and folds it all and repacks it when I come home. She makes all my favorite meals too. She's telling me she loves me. That's her primary love language.

"So you could be falling in love with Toby, but since it's a romantic love, you don't know yet how you feel it or express it. I don't know, just a thought. Ball." She held out her hand. She had climbed up on the trunk and shucked a club from the bag at her feet. I stretched up and placed a golf ball in her hand. She dropped it in front of her and delivered a smooth swing with the iron. The ball sailed in an arch and plopped into the water without a splash.

She could be right, but either way, what language did I speak?

I called Muriel on Sunday afternoon after I got back from church to confirm my appointment for Reginald's first sitting. I was a prepared as I'd ever be. I had purchased another canvas in case I ran into problems with Sammy Sullivan's cartoon. Plus, I had read up on the expectations of the judging panel from their membership qualifications in back issues of *Illustrator* magazine. It was a tough crowd of experts who'd painted presidents and movie stars for tens of thousands of dollars. They claimed they could distinguish if a subject was painted from life or photographs or the imagination.

Hmmm, is that even possible? I didn't know how one even began to differentiate such variances. *Surely they know what's at stake here and they will be fair and generous. It's not like I'm auditioning for their organization. Although they probably figure that's my next move. And if I survive this, it's not a bad one.*

Muriel met me at the front door again and escorted me through to the dog wing of the house. I could hear him before I saw him. Reginald was barking and snorting.

"He's playing with his dog walker. They're back from a nice long stroll. Reginald should be worn down a little to help him sit quietly for a few hours."

"Do you think he can? I mean sit for two hours?"

"He did for Sammy. I think Wendy can stay with him to see how it goes this time."

Wendy? My mind was suddenly reeling. *She can't mean Wendy Gallonte.*

❄ Chapter Seven

I was right on Muriel's heels as we entered Reginald's sitting room so when she stopped abruptly to sneeze, I ran smack dab into her.

"Oh, excuse me!" I said quickly. "I'm so sorry!"

She sniffled and brushed the disheveled hair from her eyes. "No, I'm sorry. I stopped too quickly. I don't know what comes over me in this room. I always sneeze when I walk in. I should have let you go first."

Wendy Gallonte's head of messy black curls popped up over the back of the couch.

"I had a friend who sneezed whenever she walked outside."

She volunteered. "Must have had something to do with going from dark to light or light to dark. I'm not sure which."

"How do you do it, Wendy?" I asked in amazement as she stood up, brushing her pants off. "You're everywhere!" In my surprise at seeing her here, I vaguely registered our tan pants matched. And she had on a red shirt too.

"Oh, Clare, how fortunate we already know each other. It will make it a more relaxed atmosphere for Reggie." Wendy said. Ignoring my perplexed comments she cupped her hand in front of her mouth and leaned over toward me to whisper. "Dogs can sense tension and whatnot, you know."

"Okay. Well, does he require we wear the same colors too?" I gestured toward her clothes.

"I need to look professional and be comfortable when I'm on a job. I mean, we were playing hide and seek when you came in. Can you imagine me doing so in Muriel's skirt getup?" Wendy snatched a Kleenex out of the box on a shelf and waved it at Muriel, who was trying to sniffle quietly. "I noticed your clothes were perfect for that, so I asked Jackie where you shop. Kind of crackers we picked the same thing to wear today!"

"Yeah, well, okay. I'm going to set up over here where the light is good." Who was this polished young woman? Wendy didn't appear to be an agoraphobic *or* a clueless computer student. She was able to explain away her suspicious stalker tendencies without even thinking about it. And this confident young woman was hardly the victim of an extreme roommate like Sillo. *There is more to her then meets the eye.* I thought. *Nothing about this job is what it seems.*

"I'll probably do some thumbnails while he's moving around." I said. "Then in a little while we can begin a more formal sitting and see how he does holding a pose."

As I moved about positioning the easel, I noticed I lacked the usual first sitting jitters.

Must be since it's a dog. Not a person with a mouthful of questions. I speculated to myself. *He won't care that I'm going to do a bunch of quick sketches first to learn about him. And that they are called thumbnails because they are smaller than the piece but not actually the size of my thumbnail.* I rolled my eyes, reminded of my last client. *He's not going to demand to see the piece every five minutes and want his wrinkles reduced and his freckles painted out. This should be a piece of cake.*

I turned at Muriel's second violent sneeze and took the canvas out of her arms.

Ah, Sammy's painting. The mystery is finally over. I flipped it around in anticipation.

Muriel scurried for the door before I could thank her and I glanced down at the underpainting.

Oh, no! Is this the same dog? I looked up to call her back, but she was gone. I was confused.

"*That* is Reginald and not his stunt double or anything, right?" I asked Wendy, pointing to the tiny pug bouncing past me. I set Sammy's canvas on the easel and stepped back to compare. *What on earth was she looking at? Her underpainting isn't even close to a pug.* I thought in mild panic.

Wendy scooped Reginald off the couch and held him toward me for inspection. When I didn't move, she grew tired and tucked him under her arm so they could both come around and take a peek at the canvas I was standing in front of.

"Ok-ayyyy, now I see why they shipped her off to Italy," Wendy chuckled.

"You mean you weren't here last summer when she started? Ouch! You just nipped me. He just bit me." I pointed accusingly at Reginald who cuddled in Wendy's arms with an innocent expression. My elbow started to throb. I rubbed it, feeling attacked.

"He likes to get a person's attention that way. But no, back to your earlier question, I took the job a few weeks ago when I came here for classes. Curtis, I mean Mr. Sulferson, and my dad are old friends. Way back." She waved a hand to show just how far back and knocked a jar of dog treats off a pedestal beside us.

She released the squirming Reginald and scooped up the ceramic jar where it had landed on a dog pillow. "Thank the Lord it didn't shatter. Poor Reggie would have been on his last nerve and a nervous pug is hard to restrain, you know?"

"No I don't," I snapped, still massaging my elbow. It burned from his hard pinch. I turned back to my bag and retrieved some paints and a canvas pad. Stalking to a stool off to the side, I hopped up to perch like an uncomfortable crane. Reginald had left Wendy's adoring arms and was rolling on his back in the sunshine with a ball. Until I got situated. Then he dove under an end table and batted at a string toy with his paw from undercover.

"He's teasing you." Wendy coaxed him out with a treat and he stood perfectly posed chewing it for a few minutes. Dipping a thin round tipped brush into a paint thinner diluted squirt of burnt umber, I used it like a pencil to outline his body and flesh out his face. I got a shadow under his belly and down his back legs and he was off again, rolling under an umbrella awning made for his pleasure.

Feeling a bit like a hunter, I set the paints aside and pulled a charcoal set in sepia tones out of my bag. With the dry tools I could move about the room more freely. I crouched behind a couch with my pad and a stick of charcoal. I had a clear sight line down the left side of the room. I just needed some patience.

Sure enough, after the room became silent, he slowly nosed out from under his canapé and marched over to where Wendy was flipping through a magazine. He barked once at her and waited. I was already sketching again by the time he started to chew on her toes. Amazingly enough, Martin's inane drawing drills in Intro were now paying off. My hand and eye were quick to capture the fleeting dog's image.

I hadn't thought about Intro to Drawing in years. I recalled being seated in a circle on wooden drawing horses. They were essentially a bench to straddle with a board nailed on the end to brace your drawing pad against. Our class ringed a still life station. An old blanket, if we were blessed, sometimes covered the box it was on. Otherwise it was just cardboard and a saddle. An old leather horse saddle. We drew that saddle three times a week for three hours a class.

Every day was a different format. Sometimes there would be a drawing slide shot up on the wall. Martin would bark at us to begin. I remember the first time that happened. I looked around at everyone else. Begin what? He hadn't said what media to use, or what style to draw in or how long we had. No one was drawing. I looked up at the crumpled ballet dancer, a pile of charcoal scribbled tulle really. The projection was dim against the whitewashed wall with the lights on around the back of the drawing pit.

I had jumped when Martin suddenly barked that anyone who wasn't finished in 90 seconds would receive an F for the day. He hit the button on a stop clock he had in the room and it began thumping out the seconds in the quiet studio. People floundered about on their papers. Some drew the slide of the dancer, some drew whatever they wanted, and some focused on the dreaded saddle. The timer buzzed so loudly that several people tossed their drawing utensils in the air.

He had marched about the room collecting three drawing pads, mine among them. He tossed the pads on the back table.

"Those three students are done for the day. They completed their assignments in 'A' quality exactly as I asked you all to do." He screamed at the class about how ignorant everyone was. He abruptly had turned on me and yelled, "Well, why haven't you left the room? Go! These idiots will draw every 90 seconds until they get it right. Once they do they can go too. Until class is done. If they haven't gotten it by then, they're done, for good."

I scrambled to box up my supplies and scamper for the door with the other two students he had dismissed. The timer was already thumping out the next ninety seconds. One girl was crying.

"DRAW!"

The last standing easel by the door had a messy boy with clothes that were too big for him. He caught my arm as I slipped past him. "What did you draw?" He hissed under his breath while looking ahead at the saddle and moving his arm over the page as if he were drawing.

"I don't know. I just scribbled the saddle in charcoal because of the time crunch." I whispered back and then ran out of the room.

Four people were expelled from class that day.

It hadn't gotten much better as the semester had progressed. We pieced together that Martin wanted us to interpret the saddle the way the artist in the slide had drawn. Like if it was a loose line drawing in graphite, then we mimicked the saddle in that style. If it was a scratchy Conte Crayon sketch with no shading, we made saddles like that. We had to keep drawing until everyone in the room got something acceptable. Sometimes a slide would remain on the wall for weeks and often times we were yelled at to begin again before we had even finished. I don't know if everyone actually achieved an acceptable drawing or he got bored with his own torture.

Some days there were timed drawings. He would bark out a pencil or stick he wanted us to use on our newsprint pads and yell go. Depending on the time allotted he would then yell stop into the room's scratching pencil noise. One time we did over three hundred drawings at thirty-seconds each of the saddle in a three hour class. Every three drawings we rotated left to a new seat and a new angle. After the hundred sheets were used out of our pads, we turned them over and started on the backs. Martin wasn't done, but we were out of paper when we reached the beginning of our third hour.

"What do I do?" The girl sitting next to me whispered in panic.

I didn't know either. Some of the other students began packing up, relieved for an excuse to leave. But Martin was still shouting to begin. Two thirds of the class were too afraid of him to stop before he said we could, myself included. I looked around at the motionless students all staring at one another in panic. There was nothing else to do. I flipped the pad I sat at back over to the first drawing done in it. The student had only made a few scratch marks till thirty seconds had been up.

"Draw on top of the first ones. They aren't that good and it's all we've got." I stage whispered to the girl crying beside me. Someone was always weeping. I sighed and began to quickly make marks. My suggestion flew like wild fire around the room and the students continued to draw with gusto. Everyone was filthy with charcoal and exhausted, but our hands and eyes continued to move with a dread of the alternative.

Martin's voice had halted us. Finally. "STOP!" He leaned on the wall with his arms crossed, surveying the room.

"Clare receives an A for this quarter, which she must work to keep. The rest of you who stayed and used her idea, have a C, with the option to improve, of course. Those who chose to leave early are at F status, with doubtful opportunities to achieve much higher. Quitters have no imagination and no problem solving abilities. Please leave your pads on the back table as you go."

Some of my classmates held grudges even though it wasn't my fault he was so absolute. I had been so embarrassed. I didn't feel any safer about my A then if I'd have gotten a C. He could change it any minute, for any ridiculous reason. Everything that man did was orchestrated to destroy, not build up.

I tried to shake the humiliating memories off as I flipped to a fresh page. I could draw fast now, but at what cost?

God, please help me do this commission well. I know Martin was trying to reward me for passing his tests, but somehow it felt shameful. I was so upset for the other students. That can't be how to teach. We all just wanted to learn how to be better artists, not compete for grades. God, help me forget about it. I want to make you proud now and help Sammy and Mr. Sulferson. Give me some favor with Reginald. Help me communicate with Wendy. Instead of using the time to dwell on the unhappy past, I spent it talking to God as my pencil moved over the page.

After thirty minutes of sketching a playful dog, Reginald decided to acknowledge I was there and not cooperate any longer. Throwing back his head, he let out a throaty howl and dove at me barking furiously and nipping so hard his teeth snapped audibly.

"Ekkkkk!" I vaulted over the back of the couch, sending my pad and charcoal sticks flying as he charged straight at me. He tore down one side of the couch I perched on and then lapped it, barking in an angry voice. Stopping at my charcoal, he took a hearty mouthful and bit down, cracking them all in half before spitting them out with a sneeze and a snort.

"Hey, those are mine, you little grouch!" I yelled. He just glared at me from where he stood on top of my sketch pad of drawings. Lifting his leg, he began to pee.

"Oh, my," Wendy said as she closed her magazine and stood.

"That is not good behavior, Little Mister. Stop that right now. No treats the rest of the day." She scooped him up and headed to the wall of equipment across the room. He bared his teeth at me and yipped sassily. I pulled my lips back and showed my teeth to him behind Wendy's back.

Pressing some buttons, she started some slow big band music. Instantly, 'Little Mister' froze in her arms. She deposited him on a covered footstool in front of the easel.

I hesitated where I was hanging on the back of the couch like a parakeet.

Whoa! I couldn't believe it. *How long will this last? Is this honestly all it takes, some music?*

Moving in slow motion so as not to disturb him, I crept off the couch. He remained like a statue.

"Is he okay?" I mouthed in a whisper masked by the music.

She nodded with a grin and waved at the easel with a flourish before pulling a sponge out of a drawer to attack the urine puddle my sketches were in. I tiptoed across the room and realized I had been holding my breath. With a big sigh I tilted my head back slightly to survey the work Sammy had done before me. Frankly, her under drawing was terrible. Besides being ill proportioned, it was so faint and uncertain that I could easily paint over it with a ground color and work into the wet paint with my own lines. At least she hadn't damaged the canvas or made piles of uneven paint to work around.

I had decided before hand to go with a local landscape behind Reginald. It would harken back to a turn of the century scene with smooth hills and delicate little trees in the distance. A tiny replica of the factory would chug a few white billows into the clouds. It would be classical for the judges, yet symbolic. I thought it would give dignity to the piece too, although I wasn't sure Reginald deserved that now.

He stood like a statue for two hours while the same song repeated over and over on the room's sound system. I recognized it was *Unforgettable* and that made me smile while I worked. Reginald yawned daintily and stretched a front leg and I knew that was my queue to stop. Wendy clicked the music off and snapped a lease on Reginald's collar. He hopped off the stool.

"That seemed to go well," Wendy smiled uncertainly at me.

I smiled back. "Yes, it did. Thanks for the song. That's a secret worth gold."

She laughed. "That's his show piece. They play that during competitions when the dogs are being inspected. He thinks he's on display. He loves to show off for a crowd." She affectionately scratched behind his ears and he nuzzled her hand.

"Why aren't you painting his portrait?"

She rotated her shoulders up and down in a shrug. "Cause I haven't been to Italy."

"No really, you're a family friend and an artist too." I called after her as she followed Reginald out the side door.

She waved at the canvas. "Cause I couldn't do that." And she was gone, drug off by an obnoxious little dog pulling for all he was worth on his leash. And he was worth a lot.

❄ Chapter Eight

"Come on Paul, just once. It's senior year and your last chance. Come with us. You need a break from this place."

Everyone knew Paul lived in the University painting studio. At first we all thought it was because he was supposed to be this impassioned Michelangelo type who ate, slept, and drank art. He had to do something dramatic to survive in Martin's world. And Martin seemed to get a kick out of it. He left him alone for the most part after that first semester.

Later, we all suspected Paul was homeless and for some reason didn't get financial aid to cover his dorm fees. Once people figured it out, they offered him help, but he only took an occasional meal or shirt. He had a sleeping bag neatly rolled under his paint palette cart and a little bag of personal items stowed with his canvas in the tall thin locker we all were assigned for paintings. He showered in the campus gym and attended events like all the other students did.

I couldn't believe it was senior year and he'd just about pulled it off. Four years living in a classroom. It had to be some kind of record. Even over summer, he had a job on the campus mowing crew and the staff let him into the building to sleep at night.

"I'm not going to eat a free meal that's not really free." Paul had stopped painting to speak gently to me. "You guys are like a time share. I have to listen to the sales pitch on religion and then I'll get to enjoy a feast. You've only been gone a few months, Clare. I'm still an atheist and I'm not going to posture."

It was Monday night and I'd stopped by the painting studio to invite him yet again to Monday Meals at the church.

I looked down at my shoes in disappointment and swallowed a lump in my throat. I'd tried everything I could think of to share God's love with Paul.

He spoke again in almost a whisper. "I will admit while you were gone, it was an empty feeling to not have you stop by and invite me on Mondays. If I had known how, I might even have prayed for your safe return." My head shot up in surprise. He set down his hand palette and brush and dug around on the second shelf of his cart.

"Ah, here it is. I drew you one every Monday as if I'd seen you." He held out a little stack of papers the size of a deck of playing cards.

I smiled and accepted the gift. The little squares of paper had a faint odor about them. It was kind of like the Sulferson Silk smell, but more sour. I was momentarily distracted and brought them up to my nose. *Whew, remind me to never do that again.* I thought as I jerked them away from my face.

Paul was watching me curiously. "You smell it too, don't you?"

"Yah, what is it?" I asked.

He shrugged. "I have no idea. When I came back after a long weekend out of town, all my stuff smelled like that. I got the impression someone had been going through my things, probably right after spraying on some cologne and it rubbed off their hands & arms. I haven't run into anybody who stinks like that, though, so I don't know who it was, or if I'm just being paranoid. I washed everything good, but I guess the paper didn't air out completely. Sorry."

"It's not bad if I don't sniff it directly." I shuffled through the hand sized sketches, smiling now and then as his irony tickled me. Paul was known for his tiny comics. I still had all of them he'd given me when we'd taken painting together. I frowned. I didn't recall any of them having this tart herb smell. It sort of reminded me of Indiana in late summer, weeding in the garden near harvest time in the humidity.

Overlooking the odd odor, I reflected on this collection of Paul's comics. While skillfully drawn, they were more of the Napoleon figure of Martin. I wanted to get past this chapter in my life. Didn't he want to too? I slipped them into my pocket and focused back on the reason I came to see him.

"Look Paul, I'm here in person and I'm inviting you now. What if I told you there was no speech. Eat with us. Like you are coming to my house for dinner. We made it tonight, Jackie and me."

He scratched his shaggy head. "Even if you stop the preacher from talking about it, Clare, you'll still have a nifty story to tell about crossing the street or using a fork to make us all consider Jesus and his teachings."

"But that shouldn't bother a dyed-in-the-wool atheist like yourself. Or are you starting to wonder if I'm right?"

"Maybe. I don't know, Clare. I've always been content alone. I've always been happy knowing this was it. Until last semester when I missed you inviting me and telling me about Christ. I'm just not totally satisfied anymore. That's all. Nothing else has changed. There is still no god and no place to go when we die."

He said maybe! My thoughts raced. *Oh, God, it's an opening. What do I say? What do I do? I don't want him to slam the door shut again. Soften his heart and help him. He's not content without you anymore!*

I was holding my breath and realized I was getting light

headed. I opened my mouth to speak, but with his back to me while he painted, he spoke first.

"Fine, the silent treatment worked. I'm coming tonight. But you have to still come and invite me next week, deal?"

The church basement was full and I was glad the ovens were too. The smells of fresh bread baking, Italian sauces & herbs brewing, and cucumbers being chopped for salad mingled with the familiar pungency of waxed linoleum and bleach based cleaning supplies. I was happy it drowned out the spoiled smell that the Sulferson Silk smoke stack spewed into the sky all day and night as we took the basement stairs downward two at a time. The sun still set late as summer gave a few last kicks, so bright light streamed in from the small, high windows rimming the large underground room full of tables and chairs and laughter.

Jackie was already in the kitchen when I arrived with Paul, Wendy, and some of the other girls from our house. Edna and the other widows who usually hosted us were on a mission's trip to Mexico. They had all always wanted to go, but nearly canceled the trip when it finally came about because by then the Monday Meals had taken off with a roar.

"Our mission is here, with you girls. We are being used to

bless others at a time when we all thought we were useless to anyone, including God." Edna had hugged us as they shared what had been transpiring. Of course Jackie and I couldn't let them miss any opportunity God laid on their hearts. And he had laid this one on ours. So, we had been cooking in the basement on and off all day to cover for them. The ingredients had all been donated and delivered for us by other church members. We only needed to add the labor of love.

"Smells good," Paul shied away from the large kitchen knife that Jackie was dicing cucumbers with and shook her free hand.

"Thanks. Good to see you again, Paul. Would you mind washing your hands there and helping me toss these salads? It's all I have left to do and as you saw out there," She gestured with the large knife. "The natives are restless."

Paul shied away from the knife again and turned to flip the knobs on the sink. Jackie blushed. I noticed Wendy, who was matching my outfit again, hadn't come in the kitchen with us.

"It's okay, Paul, she's pre-med. She practically has her license to wave around a big knife." I made myself chime in merrily. Everyone in the kitchen laughed at my joke.

Jackie was a sweet heart. She knew how to make people feel at home. Even though Paul looked sloppy with miss matched clothes and wild hair, she included him in the meal preparations without a cringe. His nails were broken and paint stained, but so were mine. It came with the territory. He had a tooth actually missing off to one side of his smile and his eyes were red rimmed. A charcoal smear decorated one side of his face, but otherwise he appeared and smelled clean. I tossed a tea towel at him to dry his hands on and gestured to his cheek. He grinned because he knew exactly what I meant.

"It's everywhere. I can't ever seem to get it all off. I guess I'm marked as an artist." He grimaced and swiped his cheek clean before clumsily tossing the towel back at me. I ducked and snagged it from the air to hang over the oven door with one hand while I loaded ramekins of parmesan cheese, salt, pepper, salad dressing and butter onto trays for each table.

"Are we about ready?" I asked Jackie as I finished, brushing my hands together to shake off a few random crumbs.

"Yes!" She and Paul enthusiastically slam dunked handfuls of cucumbers into the last two salad bowls.

We all started as the door to the outside banged open and a frantic middle aged man rushed in. "Where's Pastor Rick? I've been calling, but I can't reach him. Is Pastor Rick here?"

Paul stepped in front of Jackie, but I smiled and moved forward. "Hey, Travis. Pastor Rick is in Mexico, remember?" I knew Travis from the church office. He coordinated help for people around town when someone had a baby or was laid off.

"Awww. I totally forgot! But all this food is perfect! I need supper for a couple dozen men at the half way house across town. Their power is out and they are on lock down tonight because of the protest mob at the factory. The sheriff didn't want reforming prisoners in the mix, you know?"

"Travis, this food is for the students, can't you get take out or pizzas?" Jackie had sidestepped Paul.

"It's not in the budget. We're running that place on a shoe string."

I looked at the steaming bowls and platters of food. A few dozen didn't sound like that many. We could spare part of our food. And the helpers here didn't need to eat if there wasn't enough.

"Look, let's share guys, it's what we do it for, isn't it?"

"But you girls worked so hard and there won't be enough for all those students out there. There's got to be at least fifty." Paul's protest sounded stern.

Jackie was shaking her head. "We don't have time to argue. Everyone is hungry. I'll give up my plate if I have to. Let's give it to God and get everyone fed, like the loaves and fishes. If it happened once, it can happen again." She winked at me across the counter and I nodded at her unexpected support for a miracle. "Travis, will you pray for enough food?"

"Why, sure!" Travis eagerly stepped forward offering his hands. Jackie and I and two other girls from the house joined him. Paul shook his head no and slunk back to the darkened stairs leading out of the basement.

"Dear Jesus, thank you for this food you have given us. We trust you. You knew we would face this situation and we come to you with it. Just like you fed the huge crowd in the Bible with two loaves and five fish, we ask you to feed these men and women tonight. Bless our meal and multiply it. Bless the hands that prepared it and the willing hearts that shared it. Amen."

Our circle dissolved and we quickly began spreading foil over the bowls and trays on the counter.

"That's it?" Paul shouted, bringing the happy rustle of our preparations to a halt as everyone looked at him. "That's supposed to feed everyone? If it were that simple I wouldn't have gone hungry for years!" He slammed a fist down on the counter and looked around at each startled face with a furious frown.

"What did you expect? Fireworks and angel horns blowing?" I rolled my eyes and turned back to loading hot bread chunks into a cloth bag. "We'll know soon enough if you are right and there isn't enough or if we were right and there is a God who provided enough."

With a murmur, the kitchen sprang to life again and soon Travis was gone and half the bowls and platters were left on the prep counter.

"Let's get this party started! You go give the devotional and the house girls and I will set the trays out." Jackie offered me a high five. I slapped her hand with gusto. "This feels amazing," she whispered as we passed.

"Not quite for everybody." I rolled my eyes at Paul who hadn't left yet, but was a huffy cloud in the corner. Jackie nodded and then shooed him from the kitchen with the wave of her knife as she put it in the sink. He trailed me out to the dining area like a lost and defensive puppy.

"Hi! Hello!" I raised my voice above the crowd. "Can I have your attention, please?" The room quieted and all eyes turned to me.

"I'm Clare James and that is Jackie Voss back there by the food. On behalf of Edna, Pastor Rick, and the ladies who normally host this meal, we want to thank you for coming out tonight. Welcome to our first timers, including my friend, Paul." I swung an arm at him and the room clapped and hooted.

"All right, all right. Usually Pastor Rick takes fifteen or twenty minutes to talk to us about the Word, but tonight he and the ladies are in Mexico cooking for orphans, so you have me. And I'll tell you, the only way I could get Paul to come out tonight was to promise there would be no sales pitch he had to listen to in order to eat dinner. I want him to know that Christianity is not a time share situation. No, loving Christ and being loved by Christ is a full time, twenty-four, seven experience with full access.

"So please make Paul and the rest of our visitors feel welcome and loved as you guys chew the fat together. Now I'm going to bless the food and then if you'll form a line to the right, Jackie can serve you the main course and the sides and fixings will be on your tables by the time you return courtesy of Lisa, Trisha, Gaby, and Rachel."

I paused while the room clapped and whistled. As it quieted I began.

"Dear Lord, thank you for this time together. Bless the food and the hands that provided and prepared it. Multiply it and the blessings we receive from it. Bless our fellowship tonight and bless Edna, Pastor Rick, and the ladies in Mexico. Please protect them, provide for them, and use them. Thank you for loving us first without us having to ask. In Jesus' name, Amen."

As the room erupted again in conversation and movement toward the food, Paul looked tired and disappointed.

"That's it? Love? And you ask him to protect those people? How do you know he will? You didn't do anything for him in return for his protection."

"First," I put my hands on my hips. "You were the one lonely and crying in your paints. I asked a room full of people to love you. That should knock your socks off."

"Oh!" He looked hesitantly around the room.

"Secondly, you have a very worldly view of God for not believing he exists. It *is* as simple as asking for his help. We trust him because we know he loved us first. We can't do anything big enough or amazing enough to pacify Him anyway. If we could, he wouldn't be much of a God, would he?

"And before you ask," I held up my hand at his open mouth, "we know He loves us because he has given us free will. We have the choice to trust Him or not. He doesn't control us or stop us. He lets us pick. How much love would it take for you to allow your children to choose to be with you or to go and live with your worst enemy who offers them candy for all their meals? You would do everything you could to get them to stay with you. Everything but offer them something that would hurt them, like candy for every meal. It would be painful to offer that much love and have them reject it."

Before he could reply, a group of guys joined us to shake his hand and pull him up to the front of the food line. They piled his plate high even though he protested that there wouldn't be enough food for everyone. They slapped his back and swarmed him over to a table with them. My work here, for the moment, was done.

I stuck my head into the kitchen, pleased it didn't look like any of the food had been used yet. "How are we doing, Gang?"

Gaby looked up from a tray of lasagna she was cutting. "Oh, Clare, it doesn't seem to be going down at all! God is providing for the students and the men!"

"Hey, Beautiful, going my way?" Toby slipped an arm across my shoulders and pulled me from the kitchen door. I laughed.

"I might be if those two plates of lasagna over there are for us. I am seriously ready to grab a root and growl after the day I've had."

"You know it, Clare." He steered me over to a table off to the side of the room and pulled a folding chair out for me. I sank down on the cool metal seat feeling like an honored guest. I had food to eat that shouldn't really be there. God was amazing.

"How have you been doing on your animation's storyline?" Toby asked around a hunk of bread. I smiled at him and took a sip of iced tea before answering him.

"It's done. I've dipped my toe into the pond and demonstrated I know how to use the basics of the program. That's all I need. I'm not going to go into this stuff for a career. I don't like doing it."

He was shaking his head. "Not what I was asking and you know it."

I looked down at my salad and stabbed a tomato with my fork. "Lazarus."

"I knew it. Did you scan in a picture of Simon's face for the guy Jesus brought back from the dead too?" He sounded exasperated.

"No. Like I told you before. I'm not obsessed with Simon. I have no plans to rush over to England and marry him." I realized my voice was rising as I was getting irritated. Several people at the next table had turned to look at us.

I continued in a lower voice and leaned closer across the

table toward Toby. "Look, you were there too. You know it really happened. It was life and death there for a lot of people. Especially if those bombs had been detonated."

I could feel a little worry frown between my eyes and I swallowed hard. I stared at the carpet past where his knee jutted out from under the little card table. As it began to blur, I blinked extra fast.

"What I mean is," I whispered, "sometimes I get a little freaked out the next part of his bigger plan is going to take people I care about away earlier then I'm expecting. So that story helps me remember how big God really is.

"Otherwise I find I just don't want to do anything but lay on the floor and watch the curtains blow in the breeze. There's a part of me that knows I can trust him no matter what. But sometimes, sometimes that part is very quiet. Like when I have the nightmares. At least they're only once in a while now."

"Clare, you're still having nightmares? I didn't know. I'm sorry. I feel so helpless." He placed his warm hand over mine on the table and squeezed my fingers. "I wasn't there when you needed me. And now all I do is act jealous of Simon. No wonder I'm not your first choice to hang out with. But you have to believe me. I do miss you. Miss us."

I stopped my pity party and looked into his light blue eyes, sad and full of hurt.

"Toby, Toby, Toby, this isn't fun for either of us. We need to change this up right now." I felt the old spunk coursing back through my veins. "First off, how about we meet for breakfast and do our morning devotionals together. We can talk Bible stuff then."

His eyes brightened a little. "And I can call you every night and we can see how our devotionals applied to our day, because you know how God creates an echo of his themes through the day or week."

"I like that." I nodded. "And we can pray together to end the day."

"Or at least close to the end of the day," he agreed. "The hours are only going to get longer as we get closer to deadlines. Look, I'm in. Let's do it. 6:30 am? I'll stop by and walk you to Break Fast Grotto, okay?"

"You betcha!" We fist bumped and exploded our fingers to seal the deal. It always made me giggle to do that.

Paul's shadow blanketed our table. "Okay, now that you two are done playing patty cake over here, tell me the story about the fish and stuff, because we had way more food then we even needed and no one left. I'm kind of weirded out." He hunkered down on the floor in the corner in a much humbler mood and a crowd of non-art majors honed in to the conversation like flies to honey.

"Oh and add to that what you two were talking about earlier, you know, the animation graphic art major thing." He waved a hand at us as if to dismiss his eavesdropping. "I'm not in the class, obviously, but that movie race is all everyone in the whole building talks about. Well, that and super hero Clare. It must be a letdown to come back here to the corn fields and the Sulferson stink. Gone are the days when a fine art major painting a professor's car is the biggest talk of the town."

"What? Did someone ask for an auto body job? Done overnight?" Key pushed his way through the circle of students around our table as everyone laughed. He squatted next to Paul. "Hey, how you doing, man?" They shook hands and slapped each other on the back.

"I didn't take you for this kind of shindig." Paul was surprised.

"Oh, I'm supposed to be Hawaiian religion all the way, hundreds of gods and the waves and the wind too. I come here for sweet little Edna. Too bad you can't meet her. She's like the perfect gramma. You have to come back when she's here. But I will be honest, dude, the free food is where it's at. Best on the mainland. If you can't get your momma's SPAM Musubi then get Edna's fried chicken, or lasagna, or pork chops marinated--"

"Okay, Okay, I get it." Paul rubbed his belly. "I get it. I'm stuffed. Which I can't explain." He looked pointedly at me.

"What?" Key looked confused.

"I was in the kitchen before dinner and this guy comes in with some hard luck story and these chicks give away half the food. They pray about it and everyone here eats and there's still a pan left in there. How is that possible? They keep talking about some story with fish." Paul grunted.

"They just made too much food to begin with, you mean?" Key lowered himself the rest of the way to the floor and crossed his legs to sit next to Paul.

"No," Paul was adamant. "I saw it with my own eyes. There was food, but not tons. And then they gave away half of it. Pans of it. There is no way this could happen. There is no god, let alone your tons of gods. It's some kind of trick. They tricked me into coming tonight so they could do this. Something to do with fish and bread."

I took Paul's hand to calm his rising agitation. "There's no need to get angry, Paul. I will tell you the story right now. Jesus was teaching his disciples to trust him and rely on God's provision. There was a crowd of people far out in the country listening to him and no one had any food. Jesus took five fish and two loaves of bread and prayed over them and broke them into pieces and kept breaking off pieces and the disciples passed out the food and over 5,000 people were fed that day. And bonus – there was like twelve baskets of food left over. We asked God to do the same thing for us and he did. Since he made the food to begin with, why not ask the source for more with faith he will provide it?"

Paul shook his head like a bull getting ready to charge and Key reached up from the floor to shake Toby's hand and change the subject.

"How you doing, man? Haven't seen you much in the fine art end of the building."

"Yeah, I know, I've been buried in that new computer lab. It's getting old fast. But what were you talking about earlier, an auto body job?" Toby asked.

"Oh, man, that's right. The dude doesn't know." Key pointed a finger and a thumb at Toby as he stood up with a swagger, posturing. "Look, *I* don't know anything about who did that so somebody else better tell the story."

Paul snapped out of his fit and a sparkle entered his eyes. He lifted two fingers to his forehead in a salute. "It was a thing of beauty, my man. See, Toby, back when Clare and I were freshmen, this guy was a senior and we were all in Martin's painting class. Now you've never had Martin, so it might be hard for you to picture, but this guy fixes everything so you'll fail."

Paul explained Martin's grading system. "But to guys like say our friend Key here, that's not really the worst part. You see, them it's about respect and territory and sending a message. Most of us have to come up with something to inspire us or something we want to say when we make art. When Key lifts his hand to make a stroke on something, it's already more than just a mark practically before he starts. The lives of his Hawaiian family and the lives of his gang family in Chicago are all affected by any stray mark he makes, whether in this world or the nether world he believes exists.

"And someone like Key is used to working large, Toby, with spray paint, air brush, that kind of thing. So a guy like him once stretched a series of huge canvases, like eight foot by eight foot and bigger. He worked across all of them at once in one big scene. And he hung a full roll of canvas down from the rafters in the painting studio. I'll never forget that. The one hanging from the ceiling. It was a tidal wave full of gorgeous fish all whirl pooling around a white lily. Huge, like the size of a city bus, only hanging vertical down from the ceiling.

"So it's the first critique of the year and Martin is wiping people's work down, throwing turpentine or coffee or something on stuff. You know it's all oils, so it's still wet at this point. Martin's worked himself up a right good sweat destroying everything we got because he's saying it's not acceptable for his quality standards and so it also doesn't count for his quantity quota.

"Of course, our friend, who resembles Key here, had enough square footage in the first week for his quantity grade like twice over. Martin saves him for nearly last and considers his work for about thirty seconds longer then he did anyone else's. Personally I think he was stymied on how best to destroy it because it was spray paint. It was already dry and he couldn't wipe it off." Paul paused to take a swig out of his glass of ice tea. You could have heard a pin drop in the church basement as the whole room now listened to him recount the famous campus legend.

"Cool as a cucumber, Martin strolls over to the edge of the hanging tarp and pulls out his cigar lighter."

There was a gasp around our table and Paul nodded.

"Yeah, and I mean like the room evacuated in ten seconds. It's all paint thinner in there. It's going to go up like a roman candle see."

"No way," Toby said as his chair plunked down on all four legs and he leaned forward in anticipation.

"Yes, I was there." I confirmed it. "Most of us were out of the room before he lit it. But Key, I mean the guy like Key, stood his ground when Martin set it on fire. We could smell the smoke in the hall."

"Hey, who's telling this story?" Paul kidded.

I smiled at him. "And a fine job you're doing too."

"I remember that day." Someone from the back of the room chirped up. "All those fire trucks shut that side of campus down and there wasn't a show in the performing arts center that night. We knew there was a fire, but we didn't know all that happened."

"What a lunatic. And he wasn't fired?" Someone else asked.

"Ha, no, not Martin." Paul took his narrative over again. "Key's banner dissolved in seconds but with just enough smoke to activate the sprinkler system in the studio. There was more water damage than anything. It warped all our freshly stretched canvases. See, when canvas dries, it shrinks. It's a trick to tighten up a loose canvas. But with too much water, they split and splintered the wooden stretchers. Janitors sopped up the puddles and I helped. We added soap and gave that filthy room a good scrubbing. They replaced a few old canvas lockers and cupboards and it was like new in there. Like it never happened."

"Except it did and we bore the stains on canvases and our hearts." Key said in a low voice.

I nodded. I knew what he was talking about. Martin hadn't come for Paul and me that day. His reign of terror had ended with Key. He would save us for another time. But that didn't reduce the humiliation and anger over what had happened to everyone else. I hadn't thought about those emotions in a while. It seemed like it had all happened a long time ago. I still felt a spot of dread and dislike for that man that I knew I needed to get over.

"So where does the car come in?" Toby asked.

"Wait a minute, wait a minute, are we talking about that painted beetle on campus? Don't tell me that has something to do with this." Another student exclaimed. The big basement rippled with excitement.

"Yeah, that would be Martin's car all right." Paul slapped Key on the back with pride. "See, he was lucky to still have his life. You don't mess with professional gang taggers. Just saying if there was one in the room it would be wise to respect the work. You might flunk him, but you don't destroy his work."

Key just smiled without saying a word.

"See, when Martin came out the next morning bright and early to drive into campus, he found a certain graffiti artist had painted his classic Volkswagen bug from tip to toe with a magnificent woman after what you Christian guys would delicately call the fashion of Eve." Paul and Key exchanged glances and started to laugh.

"Course, the jokes on us, really," Key sobered. "The old dictator fell in love with her charm and left her there like a trophy for his wickedness."

The room was silent. Only Paul continued to chuckle.

"That's it?" Toby sounded disappointed. "He didn't do anything about it?"

"What could he do? We all *knew* who did it, but he had no proof. Plus he'd have to show the student's damaged canvas to document his style. That would mean admitting what he'd done in order to even start pointing a finger. No, he just owned it. Drove the car and acted like nothing happened." Paul snickered.

"And I never saw him after that because I had to drop out for a family emergency. Martin probably thought I was hiding from him and he'd won. He's so self-centered. He misses the bigger picture." Key shook his head.

I was exasperated by this story taking over our night at the church. Our one night to share with Paul. Of course, at one time, after it all went down, I thought Martin had gotten what he deserved. I had wanted revenge and vandalism to satisfy my earthly need for a definition of justice. It felt good to laugh at Martin's misfortune. Until now. The whole thing was just sin causing sin.

That's what mom always meant by two wrongs don't make a right. Yeah, it seems obvious now, but I never thought about it like this. Perspective. Hmmm. We're supposed to be sharing what God's doing in our lives, not extolling the rebellious vandalism of hurt people. How do I get the conversation back on track, Lord?

"Look guys," I spoke up out of my thoughts. "I've been thinking about all this again. Paul and I were placed in a difficult situation and the teacher, not to mention the other students had been merciless to us.

"So when Key welcomed me and called me a white Lily, it meant a lot. I know I inspired him to paint the banner Martin burned." Key reached over and squeezed my hand. I smiled. "I wish Lily would have stuck as my nickname over Wholesome, but it is what it is."

There was a murmur throughout the room.

"Yah, yah, for those who didn't make the connection, I rolled off the turnip truck, naïve and with a lot of idioms-"

I was interrupted by a plethora of voices.

"Fly in the ointment."

"Don't count your chickens before they hatch."

"A skunk smells his own hole first."

"Slower than molasses in January."

"We love you, Wholesome!"

"Yes, yes. Thank you." I rolled my eyes. This stuff never died. "But what I wanted to point out," I continued, "what I'm still struggling with myself, is that we aren't wired to respond to situations like this one in a good way. We immediately want to get back at the person who hurt us. It burns us. I mean, literally, I can feel a burning anger at what Martin did. Injustice. Destruction of things we created and cared about. Paintings that were difficult to share with others for fear of rejection, much less humiliation.

"It's like Key said, a stain. I feel like my soul is water spotted and marked with charcoal and burn marks and I know that some time has passed and I need to work on forgiveness which will get that stuff off me. I know it's not going to be good for me to keep it, but I'm not ready yet to let it go. That's where I'm at, so don't think I'm here to wrap it all up in a neat bow and not do the work personally.

"And, believe it or not, I do have a solution for the way we are to treat these situations in the future. Check this out, it even fits in with our theme tonight." I pulled my hand from Key's to flip through the Bible on the table. I could tell Paul and Key were listening despite themselves.

"Ah here it is in Matthew, for those of you looking too, it's chapter five, down at verse forty-three I think I'll go to verse forty eight. Okay.

"You have heard that it was said, 'Love your neighbor and hate your enemy.' But I tell you, love your enemies and pray for those who persecute you, that you may be children of your Father in heaven. He causes his sun to rise on the evil and the good, and sends rain on the righteous and the unrighteous. If you love those who love you, what reward will you get? Are not even the tax collectors doing that? And if you greet only your own people, what are you doing more than others? Do not even pagans do that? Be perfect, therefore, as your heavenly Father is perfect."

I closed the book and the crowded room was full of a heavy silence.

Key broke it first. "Whoa, man, that's some major challenge." He paused to find his thoughts and then spoke again slowly. "I like it because it's saying do the unexpected. Everybody seeks revenge. Be the bigger person and just love the guy. But I think it's impossible. I mean a god can do it, he's perfect, like it says, but we can't be perfect, so how do we do it? It's too hard to expect us to."

"I don't believe there are any gods." Paul spoke up. "So I don't have to be perfect. I think this is all we have, so revenge is warranted."

Key shook his head. "You still believing that ignorance, Paul? How can you look at the ocean and not know someone made it?"

"I've never been to the ocean." Paul said.

"Hmmm. Christmas break, you and me, man. Hawaii. We are surfing. You are going to meet your maker." He chuckled.

"Look," Toby said, "even if you discount God's existence, Paul, how does a cycle of revenge make sense? Someone hurts you, you hurt them, and they hurt you. It's that old feud mentality that the Hatfields and Macoys are so famous for. We would all live in hate and kill each other off."

"What difference does it make if we do it ourselves or we just wait for this God to do it for us? If there is a God, what does he care about us? He doesn't know what we need. He's way up there somewhere," Paul waved an arm over his head, "and we're way down here, suffering." Paul sounded defensive, and I realized we were getting closer to the root of why he was angry with God.

God, help us love Paul. I don't think this conversation is helping. At least I don't think so. Help Paul and Key and the others in the room hear from you tonight. Whatever is stopping up their spiritual ears, unclog it, Jesus. Here we go . . .

"Hey, Paul, would it be okay if I changed the subject? I want to share about my animation." I leaned forward entreating him. He waved a hand and nodded, relaxing his back against the wall. He was visibly relieved.

"Something you said reminded me of the story I was depicting. You see, Jesus is God but he was also part man so he could be a part of what is happening to us and live a life here like we do. He even had a friend die of an illness. His name was Lazarus. My animation shows a the end of the story.

"I know what she's talking about. Here, can I read it, Clare?" A guy named Wayne, who kept pushing his glasses up on his nose, was already riffling through his Bible.

"Sure, be my guest." I smiled at Toby and whispered. "When he's done, I want to know what your animation is about."

He nodded as Wayne began reading the events in John chapter eleven, verses one through forty-four.

"Now a man named Lazarus was sick. He was from Bethany, the village of Mary and her sister Martha. So the sisters sent word to Jesus, "Lord, the one you love is sick."

When he heard this, Jesus said, "This sickness will not end in death. No, it is for God's glory so that God's Son may be glorified through it."

Now Jesus loved Martha and her sister and Lazarus. So when he heard that Lazarus was sick, he stayed where he was two more days, and then he said to his disciples, "Let us go back to Judea."

"But Rabbi," they said, "a short while ago the Jews there tried to stone you, and yet you are going back?"

Jesus answered, "Are there not twelve hours of daylight? Anyone who walks in the daytime will not stumble, for they see by this world's light. It is when a person walks at night that they stumble, for they have no light."

After he had said this, he went on to tell them, "Our friend Lazarus has fallen asleep; but I am going there to wake him up."

His disciples replied, "Lord, if he sleeps, he will get better." Jesus had been speaking of his death, but his disciples thought he meant natural sleep.

So then he told them plainly, "Lazarus is dead, and for your sake I am glad I was not there, so that you may believe. But let us go to him."

On his arrival, Jesus found that Lazarus had already been in the tomb for four days. Now Bethany was less than two miles from Jerusalem, and many Jews had come to Martha and Mary to comfort them in the loss of their brother. When Martha heard that Jesus was coming, she went out to meet him, but Mary stayed at home.

"Lord," Martha said to Jesus, "if you had been here, my brother would not have died. But I know that even now God will give you whatever you ask."

Jesus said to her, "Your brother will rise again."

Martha answered, "I know he will rise again in the resurrection at the last day."

Jesus said to her, "I am the resurrection and the life. The one who believes in me will live, even though they die; and whoever lives by believing in me will never die. Do you believe this?"

"Yes, Lord," she replied, "I believe that you are the Messiah, the Son of God, who is to come into the world."

After she had said this, she went back and called her sister Mary aside. "The Teacher is here," she said, "and is asking for you." When Mary heard this, she got up quickly and went to him. Now Jesus had not yet entered the village, but was still at the place where Martha had met him. When the Jews who had been with Mary in the house, comforting her, noticed how quickly she got up and went out, they followed her, supposing she was going to the tomb to mourn there.

When Mary reached the place where Jesus was and saw him, she fell at his feet and said, "Lord, if you had been here, my brother would not have died."

When Jesus saw her weeping, and the Jews who had come along with her also weeping, he was deeply moved in spirit and troubled. "Where have you laid him?" he asked.

"Come and see, Lord," they replied.

Jesus wept.

Then the Jews said, "See how he loved him!"

But some of them said, "Could not he who opened the eyes of the blind man have kept this man from dying?"

Jesus, once more deeply moved, came to the tomb. It was a cave with a stone laid across the entrance. "Take away the stone," he said.

"But, Lord," said Martha, the sister of the dead man, "by this time there is a bad odor, for he has been there four days."

Then Jesus said, "Did I not tell you that if you believe, you will see the glory of God?"

So they took away the stone. Then Jesus looked up and said, "Father, I thank you that you have heard me. I knew that you always hear me, but I said this for the benefit of the people standing here, that they may believe that you sent me."

When he had said this, Jesus called in a loud voice, "Lazarus, come out!" The dead man came out, his hands and feet wrapped with strips of linen, and a cloth around his face.

Jesus said to them, "Take off the grave clothes and let him go."

Wayne lowered his Bible and again the room was quiet with the expectation of something.

And then Toby delivered it.

"I've shaken the hand of a man who came back from the dead after six weeks," he said. The room exploded. Everyone was talking over everyone else.

Paul looked startled. Key was just sitting there cross legged, his eyes narrowed to two slits in his round face as he thought.

"Quiet everybody. Quiet! Okay, Toby, spill it," Wayne said, pushing his glasses up on his nose.

"I can't believe you guys haven't shared about Simon sooner." Jackie was done in the kitchen and she and the other girls who lived in our house came out and joined us. Jackie had a tray of ice teas for our table where all the main talking was coming from. Toby took a big swig of his and the room became deafeningly silent as he began to talk again.

"Simon Berg is a rich English guy our age who was working undercover with Scotland Yard to catch a gang of thieves. As the leaders of this massive church in London, they used it to cover their tracks and provide them with targets. Simon told me, while he was undercover he started to see the whole crime spree from a different viewpoint. The average church members were as much victims as the people who had been physically burglarized. You see, he believed that everyone in the church had been spiritually burglarized." The room murmured. Toby ignored them as he continued.

"With a membership of over 2,000 people, Simon didn't want the church to be dissolved and everyone cut adrift when the ring was broken up. He prayed about it day and night before he was shot by one of the gang members trying to kidnap our Clare here over a miniature painting she was protecting. Simon lost a lot of blood on the rooftop before help came. They had to put him on machines to help him breathe and make his heart pump. He was considered dead by the doctors. It was only his vast fortune and well-connected family that kept his body alive for six weeks. His family and friends were praying and fasting for him the whole time."

Someone cut into Toby's narrative with skepticism. "Really?

Then they just pulled the plugs out of the wall and he sat up, ready to go?"

"I saw it with my own eyes." I contributed.

"But that's highly unlikely," Jackie was frowning. "We just did a chapter on comas and stuff and even if someone does 'wake up' after a long episode, they can't talk or use their muscles and stuff. Everything has been dormant. It takes a while for the body to catch up or even retrain itself."

"I was there, in the room, when he came back, Jackie." I didn't want to pick a fight, but I had to testify. "He opened his eyes, sat up, and started peeling off tubes and stuff. He wanted to know if he was too late to preach on Sunday. The doctors were amazed. More than one said it was inexplicable."

"My Dad and I went to see him before we left London." Toby continued his narrative, nodding. "I wanted to talk to him for myself. I wanted to know what it was like. Had he been to heaven? Did he talk to God?" Toby paused and the whole room leaned in toward him. I felt like I couldn't breathe. I could see it all happening again in my mind. I jumped as several students couldn't stand the suspense and shouted,

"What did he say?"

"Did he really see something?"

Toby stretched back and put his hands behind his head, locking his elbows in a comfortable pose. He loved having the crowd eating out of his hand. I smiled at him as he began to speak again like he was reading a letter to them, "Simon is the kind of person who knows who he is and what he wants. And he makes you feel like everything is possible. Have you ever met someone like that? My dad instantly liked him and we sat down under a tree in a park with like ants and everything and he told us that he wouldn't change anything that had happened to him."

Toby swiftly leaned forward and the room gasped at the intensity of his next words. "From the second the bullet hit his body and knocked him backwards, he said he saw his body from a distance. He said he didn't believe he was in heaven because he knew the whole time he was coming back to his body. He spent his time in a garden with Jesus asking him every question he could think of and learning from him personally what he would be doing and how to lead that big church. He also got to talk to a brother who had died young and his grandfather, neither of whom he'd met on earth. His grandfather told him to obey God whatever the consequences because the rewards were far greater than we could ever know. And just a side note here, his grandfather was king of some African country and when he converted to Christianity, he had to fight like witch doctors and stuff. He had crazy details about his grandfather's reign after he woke up that his parents were stunned he knew."

"He said that while it seemed like he'd only been there a few hours, he knew when it was time to leave that he had been there much longer. He knew what Jackie was talking about, that normally coma patients wake up gradually and encounter all kinds of problems in the process. It's never like the movies. But he also knew that as part of his story, his miracle for the earth to see was that he would be an exception to every rule.

"He knew his first sermon and he knew his second and third sermons. He knew the number of people wanting to hear what had happened to him would surge the numbers of the church and he would add additional services.

"He knew the faces of the people who were to lead small groups that would answer questions and teach accurate Biblical doctrine. He said as soon as he got out of the hospital, he was stopping people he recognized from his visions from on the street. He said it was crazy to walk to up to someone and be like hello, I'm Simon and I recognize you from when I was dead. You're supposed to help me. But he said they were all saying things like they had dreamed about him personally talking to them.

A flood of supernatural miracles have washed over London. People are looking for answers instead of just whining over their questions. And God is answering. God is real, Paul, and he is big." Toby's excited voice tailed off and then the room filled back up like a wading pool with the noise of human chatter.

No one left until about an hour later when Wayne stood up. "Look, this has been one of the best Monday Meals I've ever been to, but I have a ton of homework. I want to know before I go, though, what story you animated, Toby, for your computer class. I'm obviously not going to be in your class this week to find out."

"Me either."

"I want to know too."

"Do we have time to read it?"

"Tell us more, Toby."

Toby held up a hand to quiet the crowd. "Thanks, guys. I love your enthusiasm. You may not believe it, but without us knowing it, I animated Lazarus for my ten second movie too. The same story as Clare." He shrugged sheepishly. "I wasn't in the hospital when Simon woke up, but it was still the most impacting thing I've ever experienced in my life."

"Well, what can I say? Great minds think alike!" I squeezed Toby's hand and we stood up to go.

"They sure do, Wholesome. Remember that when I pick you up for the Fall Dance." Toby whispered in my ear.

Chapter Nine

"Psst, Wholesome, over here."

I had been contemplating what to wear to the Fall Dance. The whisper snapped me out of my daydream. I looked around. Nothing but polished old linoleum floors shining in the florescent lights. I was in the basement about to ring the buzzer to go into the computer lab. While my animation was done, we had to watch a certain number of tutorials showing us how to achieve different effects within the programs we were using.

"Psst, over here, Wholesome. Don't buzz them yet."

"We've got something to show you."

"We'll show you something over here."

I squinted behind me. Only two people I knew talked like that.

"Where are you guys? What's going on?"

A nondescript door swung open down the hall. As I got closer, I saw that was labeled as a Janitor's closet. I walked around the open door and peeked inside the darkened room. It was a Janitor's supply closet, alright, full of boxes of toilet paper and mops. I took a double take. It looked like the back wall was a jar. There was enough space there to walk through.

"It's okay, these guys are always doing this to people," a feminine giggle came from a dark corner. It sounded like Kara, Jay's girlfriend.

"Come on back, Clare. It's one of the entrances to the old catacombs under the building that the convention center uses when the stage puts on productions. Lots of entrances and trap doors for props and sets and the actors. There's even an intercom system. That's what the guys used to talk to you from down in the catacombs after they sent me up to show you the way.

"It's a shame these tunnels and stalls and dressing rooms all underground aren't used very much anymore. They really only tap about a third of its potential nowadays. No live horses and scores of dancers." The girlish silhouette was shaking her head as she pushed the wall open a little wider and walked through. "Once their grant goes through and the computer screens and monitors are set up in the convention center, they won't use them at all. All the backdrops and special casting will be computer produced. That'll put another batch of artist's out of work."

It *was* Kara. I had fallen into step with her as she led me deeper into the cool dark tunnels. She was holding a flashlight to illuminate our way.

"I knew it! I knew those guys knew more then they let on." I socked my fist into my hand as I walked. Kara's grin never wavered in the half light. I settled down out of my triumph. "I've heard of these passages. I thought they were just a myth. I suppose the theatre majors know all about them. Probably Trixie does," I mumbled under my breath about my friend who had stayed in London to work in theater after our semester was done. "But no one in our classes knows about them, though."

"Well, that's not entirely correct." She giggled again. "You do know us." She flung open a door and I peeked in timidly.

"This looks like a living room," I said with some disappointment as I surveyed the couches and lamps and throw rugs.

Kara giggled again and pulled a lever in the wall. The floor we were standing on begin to move!

"Whoa, I did not wake up expecting this to happen today. Is this really happening? Maybe you should pinch me."

The wall in front of us twisted to the left and our patch of floor swiveled around until we were facing where we'd just been.

When the floor stopped moving, I lowered my arms to my sides and slowly turned to look behind me. Now, instead of the door we'd just come through being behind us, a large warehouse looking room stretched out in a glow of florescent lights. And computer monitors. This was an underground lab.

"How did this get down here?" I was staggered by the idea of such a large room full of expensive equipment right underneath the little lab we were all crammed in to upstairs. I don't know which was more disconcerting, the fact that this lab was here to begin with, or that periodically on the blank wall, a mock window hung with a lush faux view of the outdoors.

Creepy and creepier. I just mentioned the blank walls to these guys last week in the lab upstairs. Did they do those windows? Or is someone eavesdropping on us in there?

I shivered, despite the perfect temperature. The air was fresh smelling too. No underground staleness or Sulferson Silk scorched corn odor. There didn't seem to be anyone in it either. Then two white panels swung around and I realized they were the high backs of the desk chairs. Jay and Kay were sitting there grinning like two Cheshire cats, their computer monitors displaying footage of the upstairs hall outside the lab where I'd just been. Kara pushed on another white panel and it rotated to reveal a seat. She plopped down and gestured to the one beside her.

A large white screen was slowly lowering over one wall.

"Would you like popcorn?" Kay said in a stage whisper.

"Well, why not. It doesn't look like I'm going to make my lab time upstairs today," I said with a shrug as I shoved the panel of the seat next to Kara and collapsed on the chair it revealed.

"Wow, I wouldn't have expected these to be this comfortable." I offered to the quiet room.

"I know, right?" The voice next to me made me jump. There I was assuming again that no one else was in the room. Every one of those panels was a seat and probably held someone nestled in working.

"Hey, don't I know you?" the girl typing beside me in a storm of clicking keys asked.

Before I could answer, she answered herself. "Yeah, probably. I'm Kelly Splint. I graduated a few years ago. I might have been a senior when you were a freshmen." She glanced over from the screen. "They are recruiting from as far back as ten years for this lab. After that you're just too old to blend in on campus, to sustain the kind of hours we do, or to want to use the technology, I guess. Hey, nice job on the windows. It really livened up the place after weeks of just blank white walls underground." She grinned with a lift of her shoulder at me, all the while never slowing the flow of typing what looked like gibberish on the screen in front of her.

"What are you doing?"

"Shhhhhhhh," echoed through the room and someone passed

me a bucket of popcorn as the lights began to dim.

"What is she doing?" I turned and whispered to Kara.

"Code. She's writing instructions in computer language. Just watch, they're ready now."

The lights had faded all the way down. A small pinpoint of activity had appeared in the middle of the giant screen that was now lowered all the way to the floor. I settled back in my cushy chair and smelled the popcorn. It smelled all right. I was leery of accepting food from strangers after some criminals in London tried to brainwash me with hallucinogenic tea. This popcorn, though, smelled irresistible. I popped a kernel in my mouth and it melted in a delicious burst of butter and salt.

Fantastic. I bet Toby is going to wish he'd come with me to the lab after all today.

And then I forgot all about eating the popcorn.

The next morning when Toby knocked on my door for breakfast, I was conflicted. They'd asked me not to tell anyone about the lab. But it was Toby's thing. He was into it far more then I was. Just because of his father's connections in the graphic design world, though, he wasn't vetted to know about the underground lab's existence. Should I keep secrets from him?

This lab was a contender in the race with a variety of other private labs and university grant labs to launch the first full-length, animated, feature film created entirely with computers. Not surprising a quagmire of technological espionage swirled around the main players. Even Jayden and Kayden, interns for the company that had built it, had only joined the underground lab two weeks ago.

And oddly enough, it would even have been in competition with the small lab upstairs, if that lab had the man power or numbers to compete on such a level, which it did not. Hence, the University's board allowed the underground lab to be built in exchange for some of its accolades should it launch first. And of course, the University would inherit the lab facility once the race was won by someone and the need for deep secrecy was over.

I was now reluctantly involved because of what I'd shared with Jay and Kay over some pizza the other night. London was still getting me into spots I didn't want to be in. And that semester didn't really qualify me to do anything about a stolen movie reel. After watching their film trailer I had learned the rumors about a movie theft weren't just rumors. The files had been stolen from their satellite lab in the series of events that had caused the pizza man ban. They wanted me to come up with a way to catch the thieves because while they were recreating the film as fast as they could, they couldn't reproduce the whole thing in time to launch first.

It was overwhelming and I'd left as quickly as I could. Which was why I had to go back today to get the particulars. I was going to insist they clear Toby too. While he had been casual with his relationships in the past, one thing he had always been, even before he knew Jesus as his personal savior, was honest. He had been willing to marry a girl he thought was pregnant with his child. And then the baby wasn't his and he decided he needed Jesus in his life. He might have other faults, but he was honest. He wouldn't have stolen their movie and I needed his help.

I sighed. *I just want to relax in our basement and paint. Or draw. That's what I'll have to talk to him about until they clear him.*

"Hey Toby. Before we go to breakfast, can I show you my idea for the next series I'm working on?"

"Sure! I'd love to see it. I was up half the night staring at a computer screen and I could use a break. You know you always inspire me, Clare."

That's nice, Toby, but who's supposed to inspire me? I felt sarcastic toward his puppy dog pandering. I avoided his eyes and ushered him into the house. It was quiet but I thought I heard the door across the hall from our SPAM barricade click shut as we walked past. That was Wendy's room. I frowned.

Is she spying on what I'm wearing today? She's gotta be. That's the only way she can keep showing up in what I have on without having a camera or like a spy hole in our room, which is impossible because she lives across the hall.

Toby draped his arm around my shoulders as we walked down the hall to the back of the house. I leaned into his side and wrapped my arm around his back. His aftershave smelled intoxicating. Surprised, I took another deep breath and smiled. I shouldn't be so hard on him. I did like hanging out with him.

Well, who cares if Wendy comes to class today in a pair of dark jeans, a white T, and a long sleeve pale blue button shirt? She doesn't have any Jesus Cruisers.

I wiggled my toes in my sandals as I walked. The campus slag for Birkenstocks always amused me. I glanced up through my eyelashes at Toby's chin and long Roman nose, pleasantly distracted from Wendy's eccentricities for the moment. He wasn't wearing those silly glasses today.

I shook my head and cleared my throat as we broke apart so I could unlock the basement door. "I decided to do the next set in graphite. I was able to use that roll of drawing paper I've had forever in my closet. This way I can cut the drawings to any size and shape I want. I taped my first slice of paper on an old board I found behind the Menard's in a dumpster. It's been so handy to have that Jeep from the Sulferson commission. Anyway, I can brace the drawings on my easel so I can reach the top of the big ones. It wou—OH NO!"

"Wow, this isn't good." Toby stepped past me and quickly lapped the basement poking at the piles of decorations. "Nobody here. Whoever did this seems to be gone."

Frozen, I hadn't moved off the stairs. Someone had lined up my four finished canvases with my drawing board and spray painted red slashes and the words *KNOW-IT-ALL-CHRISTIAN* across them.

"We need to report this immediately. I'll go up and call security. This is not cool." He paused on the stairs as he passed me and caught my hand, which drew my eyes to his earnest face. "I'm so sorry this happened. Are you really okay? It looks like spray paint. We can probably get it off the paintings and you only had the beginnings of one drawing, so it won't set you back too far. I'll be right back, okay?"

I nodded.

Sinking down on the stairs I hugged my knees. I wasn't that worried about the paintings. It was a nuisance that I had to repair them when they were done, but what really hurt was that someone would destroy something dear to me because I'd shared Christ with them. I was only trying to share love with them. They just had to say no, not attack me.

It reminded me of a time in London when I was canvasing with a friend named Niema. There was a girl sitting on a bench waiting for the tube. I could see her in my mind as clear as if I'd met her yesterday. She had short blond hair and a pleasant face. I remember my palms had been sweating and I was afraid I was going to throw up on her.

"Excuse me, do you have the time?"

"Why yes." She looked at her wrist. "It's 7:30, but don't you have a watch on?"

I looked down at my wrist. Sure enough, there it was. I laughed.

"I guess I'm so nervous about telling people about this new church I've been attending, I totally forgot I had a watch. I've been trying to talk to someone for an hour so my friend will be happy that I at least tried."

"Really? Is that your friend over there?" She gestured toward Niema who was talking so fast to a couple by the staircase that she looked like she was blasting back their eyelids.

"Yeah." I grinned. "Look, there's a lot of great young people and social events and I've been taking all my flat mates there. I've been attending there since I got here from the States."

"Really? Where are you from in the States?
"Indiana and no, nothing to do with Indiana Jones. It's just a movie they made with the name of the state. Nothing to do with me."

She laughed. "So where does this church meet?"

I handed her a business sized card with the church information on it.

"In the largest movie theater in the country, of course on Sunday's its -"

She didn't let me finish the sentence before she ripped the card in half, threw it in my face and spit on me. She side-stepped me and jumped on the tube that had just arrived.

"No thanks, Freak!" She called before the doors closed behind her.

I remember feeling stunned like I did now. It was so unexpected. It made a wave of doubt and embarrassment wash over me like nothing I'd ever experienced. And that wave tried to crash over my head now as I coward on the stairs feeling let down by everything around me.

"Aw, man, that's terrible." Jackie had tiptoed down the stairs to peek at the vandalism. "Toby told me what happened. He's using our phone to call security. I'm so sorry, Clare." She crouched down next to me on the steps and put her arm around me. I leaned my head on her shoulder and sighed.

"Who do you think it was? I've been sitting here trying to get past the offense of it all, but I'm still so stunned. I know what it says in Matthew 5:11-12, "Blessed are you when people insult you, persecute you and falsely say all kinds of evil against you because of me. Rejoice and be glad, because great is your reward in heaven, for in the same way they persecuted the prophets who were before you.

"But it just floors me that someone is so mad at me for being a Christian. I mean I pushed Paul to come to Monday Meals but I can't see him ever doing this. He'd tell me to go play in the street, not destroy my work."

"Maybe they're not necessarily mad, maybe they're jealous."

Jackie squeezed my shoulders with her arm. "I mean you have fabulous friends, mad art skills, and famous connections to Scotland Yard. Who wouldn't be jealous? *I'm* even a little jealous." She rocked me side to side teasingly trying to ease my mood, but I was only half listening to the last part.

"Yeah, you're right. This could be to throw me off of my game. It's like you said, I'm involved in a lot of stuff right now. Last night, I didn't even get to tell you about this top secret lab under--"

"Hello, Security. Man in the house. Security." A radio squawked and we heard the stomp of boots as two people came in the back door of the house.

"Opps." Jackie jumped up. "I left Toby in our room and he can't leave unescorted. I'll be right back. I'll tell them where you're at." She took the steps two at time and disappeared at the top. I stood up on the stairs and forced my legs to move down the creaking worn slabs of wood. I stopped on the last one. There was an odd smell in the musty basement. Clearly the air was heavy with the chemical twang of the spray paint, but this whiff was different. I couldn't quite place it. It was sort of flowery, but kind of salty somehow. Where had I smelled that before? I shook my head as the impression left. I was distracted by the thought of security interviews.

How much should I tell them about my suspicions? Does campus security know about the underground lab and the stolen files? Surely they have to. I mean just because I found out about it last night. . . Is that a coincidence? Is this to warn me off? I had too much to work out in the sixty seconds before Security arrived.

What if it isn't about the lab at all? My enemies, let's see. Jealousy could have bitten anybody. Probably even Toby. Especially if he found out about me getting into the lab without him. Nah. He wasn't that way. So who do I know that doesn't like Jesus? Well, that's a herd of random people, including Sillo, who lives in my own house.

What clues do I have? A funky smell and the medium itself: spray paint. Key's media of choice. Both he and Paul had all sorts of questions at the last Monday Meal. But this isn't his style. This is just sloppy hand writing, all caps full of loops. Even the capitol A is made from one big loop. More like a lower case cursive L if you ask me. And those angry slashes, definitely not Key. Besides, I'm under his protection, right? The SPAM cans. So is Curtis Sulferson. What about someone at the Sulferson Factory? Who benefits if I don't finish Reginald's portrait on time?

"Miss? Hello? Are you Clare James?" Two middle aged men dressed in navy blue descended the stair well behind me interrupting myself interrogation. I stepped off the bottom step on to the basement floor so they could come down too.

"Yes, Sir."

"Are you alone?"

I frowned, slightly apprehensive and edged toward the basement door leading to the outside. "As far as I know."

"Oh, no need to worry, Miss James." The other guard jumped in. "We're here to protect you. Name's Bert, Miss. Bert Jennings." He held out his campus ID badge on a rope around his neck and I could see the tiny picture looked like him.

Big deal, I could forge that. Is this part of a plot larger than some jealous student vandalism or random religious persecution? Who would be this elaborate, though? Well, both the underground lab and Sulferson probably have the money. Where is Toby? And Jackie? The guard was still talking.

"And this is Bud, Bud Winter. It's a real honor to meet you Miss, it is."

"Enough small talk, Bert. Miss James, we have to go. Now. Let's take the outside door right there out to our truck. We have to take you back to headquarters. There is an alert on your name. Local law enforcement and the FBI have already been called. And here in the Midwest to boot."

"Yeah, Bud, the *Bible belt*."

"Enough with you and your Bible, Bert. Just unsnap your holster and let's all move to the truck. We've told your friends to stay inside. Back up is coming. We are following protocol as first on the scene."

Kidnappers wouldn't have to go to this elaborate of scheme to snatch me, sadly enough. And there is a watch on my name in case anyone hassles me about London. I forgot about that. Maybe Toby shouldn't have called security. This seems a bit overkill for spray paint on my art. Would someone from an international ring of forgers do this? I doubt it.

Bud had move around me to exit the basement first. As he reached forward with his key the door glided open and listed to the side like a broken sailboat in a draining bathtub. He turned back to me with a frown.

"This isn't left open all the time like this, is it?"

"No, sir. I always check it when I'm down here by myself."

He nodded. "Ok, wait here a minute for my signal."

Once he cleared our path and we were out of the building and in the truck, I heard sirens coming in droves. A helicopter buzzed our SUV and the radio sputtered to life.

"We got you in our sights, truck eighty-seven. Confirm Picasso's daughter is on board."

"Oh, like how is *that* a code name?" I interrupted. "Every fourth grader in the world should know Picasso is an artist and since I'm a young girl, who else might we be transporting? I think we're sitting ducks, Boys."

"She's right, Bud. Maybe we shouldn't answer." Bert was clearly my man.

The radio sputtered again. "Confirm Picasso's daughter is in route. Truck eighty-seven, confirm."

Bud shook his head at us and clicked the button on the side

of the speaker. "Picasso's daughter thinks you gave away her location with such an obvious code name. I'm doing my job here, but I tend to agree."

"There, you two happy now?" Bud hooked the mike back on the side of the radio.

"Copy that truck eighty-seven." The static gurgle of the radio made the speaker sound like he was chuckling, but it was hard to tell.

As Bud accelerated out into traffic, we were flanked by two patrol cars with flashing lights and the helicopter hovering over us sent a swirl of leaves across our dash. Bert indicated I should lay down across the back seat. As I ducked, I looked back to see a forensics van and a pile of cars surrounding our house. Toby and Jackie were on the front porch with an officer. The other girls who hadn't left for class yet were being herded out the back door. We sped away too fast for me to tell if Wendy was among them. And what she was wearing.

🕸 Chapter Ten

The guard at the front door inspected Key's ID and said something into his walkie talkie. The wind must have changed, because while the air in my room was light and smelled faintly of the dry turning leaves outside, the hallway was a stuffy cloud of Sulferson Silk stench.

"It really is okay." I called from my room door. "I phoned him five minutes ago to come over."

"Just stay inside, please, Miss, until we clear him." The policeman at my door flattened his hand and moved it up and down at me. I guess if he killed me while we were working on repairing the damage to my pieces they would have a thorough record of who he was. I tried not to roll my eyes as I pulled my head back into our room and closed the door.

Jackie had gone home for the weekend to be with her family and since I wasn't allowed to leave campus yet, for my own safety, of course, my parents had come down as soon as they had heard about the rigmarole the painting vandalism had caused.

And, crazy as it all sounded, the front door guards even inspected my parents ID's like they were suspicious characters. Even after I'd yelled down the hall, "It's my parents. If they wanted to vandalize my paintings, they wouldn't be working so hard to help put me through college."

My parents were as harmless as a tall glass of lemonade on a hot summer day. Clearly all American and helpful. Not part of an international forgery ring run by an IRA terrorist who committed treason in England. Nor a strike at a factory five hours from their home over corn. Nor did they know anything about computers, much less how to steal a file from one.

"Do you think we can be of much help in the basement?" My dad asked from the row of potted plants on our window sills. He had been trimming and fertilizing them for us. I noticed he was sucking on something. "Sure, if you share your candy." I grinned like the kid I still partially was.

"Oh, aren't these yours?" He held out a handful of Smarties from a roll in his pocket. "I must have swiped them off of Jackie's desk by mistake. I'll have to get her some more."

I frowned. Toby must be passing them out again, but I was the one they were special to. Or so I had thought. I guess all this happening at the same time as the Fall Dance made it clear I couldn't go with him and he was starting to move on. But it wasn't my fault I was suspended from school activities until this was all cleared up. I was surprised at my disappointment. I refocused on my dad's concerned face. I cleared my throat to get a normal sounding voice back.

"Oh, don't worry about it. We share food all the time. She won't care. But back to your question -- there are actually four paintings. So once Key shows us how to lift the spray paint off of them we can each work on one and get done four times as fast, if you want to help."

"Oh, do you want us doing such delicate work on your masterpieces, dear?" My mom was sitting in the window seat reading a book. *She* was eating Smarties too. Was this some kind of conspiracy? I swallowed hard and blinked my eyes before answering her.

"Well, let's see what we have to do first, then we can decide. But really, anything is better then what they look like now."

There was a knock at the door. "Ah, Miss James? Can you hear me? You have a visitor that's been cleared."

"You know," I said aside to my parents, "I don't think they

know how to open my sculpture. If someone does get through all the undercover cops outside and in through these windows, the guards in the hall will be trapped outside by a barricade of SPAM."

We laughed as I swung the door open. Expecting to see Key I jumped back as Wendy came charging in.

"It's not comfortable here anymore with all these policemen everywhere. When are they leaving, Clare? Why did you bring them all here? Can't you tell them to go now?" She was extremely agitated. And dressed in a yellow sweater and tan capris with sandals just like I was.

"I see you got some new sandals," I said pointing at her feet.

She ignored my comment and my parents and pointed at a drawing tacked to my bulletin board over my desk.

"You are not allowed to have any images of Reginald outside of the house. You have to give that to me right now!" Her voice was high pitched nearing hysteria.

"Wendy, relax, that's not Reginald. It's a pug I've been drawing at the pound. I've been studying the body and coat of this particular breed. How the fur flows over the body, where the whorls are, you know. This sketch is of an unclaimed stray they've named Icing. She looks like she was licking the chocolate icing out of the bottom of a frosting container and got her face all dark brown. It's splotchy around the edges in her markings, see? Like smeared icing. That's not like Reginald at all, Wendy. He has a smooth line between his face mask and his body color. I respect rules. I know there's a lot at stake here."

"Oh." She looked cross.

"Look, I'm sorry about the police, but it's not my fault that someone broke into our basement. We are all at risk until they figure out who it was and why they did it. If it was a prank, then we need the person who did it to come forward so they know it's nothing worse."

"Yeah, a prank. That has to be what it was. What else would it be?"

There was a knock on the wall of SPAM again. "Ah, Miss James. You have another visitor cleared, but someone has to come out first."

"Oh brother, now I'm a museum of glass with a limited capacity." My parents both laughed, but Wendy swung the door open and brushed past Key, who was waiting outside with an officer.

"Hey, Key, thanks for coming. Sorry for the twenty questions to get in. We're all coming out, officer. I imagine Wendy is going back to her room across the hall and the four of us are going down to the basement. Key, this is my mom and dad, mom and dad, this is Key, the artist of our front door sculpture."

The cop at the door rolled his eyes behind Key's back and spoke into his walkie talkie. I frowned at him. Wendy had marched across the hall and disappeared into her room with a slam of her door. Silently our escort led the way and we all trooped down to the scene of the crime. The paintings had been arranged against a bare wall in a different order so the letters didn't spell anything. The basement had been emptied of all the Christmas clutter. My drawing board and easel contraption stood lonely against the stark white wall. My paint cart sat crooked next to them like a ship's dingy trailing it. The place smelled of chemicals and lacked even a speck of dust anywhere, including the ceiling.

"Wow, this is totally not how I'm used to it."

"Good or bad?" My mom asked.

"I don't know. Before it had all this character with old Christmas decorations stacked everywhere and some old chairs to sit on and bad lighting. Now it's just sterile and it smells. And they must have changed about a hundred light bulbs because it was never this bright before. Well, I suppose we should open the door to air out the chemicals we'll be using on the spray paint and that can help with the bleach smell in here too. So, Key, obviously, here's the damage." I talked fast, like one run on sentence, trying to not freak out.

"Before you start, Key, do you mind if we pray?" My dad stepped off the stairs and extended a hand. Key shook it and nodded. The police officer moved to the outside door where they had escorted me out just days before and unlocked it, propping it open with a large rock. He squatted against the jam in a beam of sunlight and remained there, unmoving. We bowed our heads where we stood.

"Dear Lord, thank you for today and this sunshine to brighten our spirits. Thank you for your protection and guidance. We ask forgiveness over our sins. Please bless the kids as they work on cleaning Clare's paintings. We don't know who did this or why this was done, Lord, but we ask that now you can use it for your glory. We ask for direction in finding out who did this so that no one is harmed. We ask that you speak to the vandal's heart and that if this really isn't a misdirection and someone is upset over how we live our lives for you, help them know who you really are and your love for them so they can make a true decision for their eternity. In Jesus' Name we pray, Amen."

Opening my eyes after the prayer made the basement seem even more white and stark. I watched as Key pulled a fishing tackle box out of his heavy coat before shrugging it off and tossing it onto the stairway. He shucked his mittens and they followed suit.

"I know there's only the beginning of a nip in the air for fall right now, but I'm Hawaiian and it doesn't matter how many years I'm in the cold, I just can't get used to any of it." He explained to my parents.

"Oh, yeah? Hawaii, you say." My dad hunkered down next to Key on his knees over the first painting and they were soon lost in conversation about cactus and succulents on the islands. Key opened his box and displayed a variety of small bottles, tubes, and round cakes. As they chatted and laughed, Key mixed an elixir of herbs and chemicals and applied small amounts to the surface of the canvas with Q-tips. They came away bright red, saturated with spray paint.

Slowly he graduated to cotton balls and continued to remove the spray gently off the top layer of the painting. Eventually, as we all watched what he was doing, he handed the painting and the cotton ball in his hand to my dad and moved to the next painting leaning against the wall. As that one responded to the treatment, he handed it off to me and began to work on the third painting. Once he saw that it too would release the offending red off the top layer without damaging the work under it, he gently showed my mom the direction of his strokes and she began working on the third painting. That freed him up to pull the fourth painting onto his lap as he sat on the floor with his back against the basement wall next to where I was working.

"You and your family know I didn't do this, don't you, Clare?" He asked in a low voice, looking up from his work with a pained expression.

"Of course, Key. When the FBI questioned me about you because of your spray paint pieces and stuff, I told them flat out it wasn't you. You would come to me directly if I pushed you too hard about something I believed. You would never do this because you know--" I swallowed a throat full of tears. "You know what it is like to have someone destroy your work and humiliate you. You know how personal it is. You would never do this to me. Just like I would never do this to you. We are friends, right? I mean I thought I was under the protection of the SPAM, right?"

He chuckled and I saw there were tears in his eyes too. "Yes, we are friends. I thank you, Lily. I too know this pain that someone has tried to inflict on you and I am going to find out who did this."

He paused to swirl around a clear solution in the jar he had borrowed out of the recycle bin as we'd come down the stairs.

I looked at the ugly red welts of paint across the rich thick brush strokes that I knew by heart. When you make something, you are intimate with it. You know every stitch, every nail, and every stroke. I was reminded of how God, our creator, knows us like that. I recited Matthew ten, twenty-nine through thirty-one in my head.

'Are not two sparrows sold for a penny? Yet not one of them will fall to the ground outside your Father's care. And even the very hairs of your head are all numbered. So don't be afraid; you are worth more than many sparrows.'

God made us and loves us and has to watch us destroy ourselves and wreck his creation every day. How hard is that? But it's the only way we can have free will. And we are under his care if we just accept his help. Help me know Lord. Help me fix these paintings. Thanks for Key's knowledge.

I concentrated on the canvas across my lap and the Q-tip I

was welding until my thoughts crowded in again.

Was this specific revenge against me because I'm a Christian or because they are jealous like Jackie said? Or was this a bunny trail to distract me from the bigger picture?

My commission was the other thing attacking my work could jeopardize. In which case, it wasn't about me at all, but about Sammy or the factory and the town or even Curtis Sulferson personally.

Attacking an artist's work should make the artist angry, but not necessarily stop them. Unless the artist had been abused by a person of authority destroying the work in the past. Then it could dredge up all sorts of memories. The reason for attacking me this way has to stem from someone knowing how Martin treats us all. It would be a safe bet that I harbored unforgiveness toward Martin and his abuse because we all did. Destroying my work was likely to seriously upset me. But did they realize how close they were to the truth? To my guilt over not forgiving him? I hate him, even though I'm not supposed to, Jesus. You want us to forgive, but I can't. And not just for me, for what he does to everyone. It's too much, too unfair. Not right. I paused a minute in my mental rant.

Not right. Hmmmm. That's what Martin had said about the computers making art. Could he have stolen the movie? To sabotage a technological advancement? He wouldn't know enough about computers to take it. He'd have to black mail a student. Time out, this is getting good. What had Kelly Splint said? 'Nah, you must have come after me. They are recruiting from as far back as ten years for this lab.'

Who was working in the underground lab and *had taken a painting class from Martin? Only those who had majored in graphic design would have done both. You didn't have to take computer art to graduate, but you had to take painting to meet graduation requirements.*

Martin!

Martin has to be the connection. He's crazier than a hoot owl. I need proof now. I'll nail him to the wall once and for all.

I shoved my angry, rebellious thoughts about Martin away from me. I knew that relishing my hatred was wrong, but it was hard to face the shameful past. It felt better to be outraged and wronged. I wasn't alone. And it felt so good to laugh at Martin's messed up car and never have to take a class with him again. I'd let myself enjoy it for a little while longer. But I knew I'd have to forgive him soon. Probably before I graduated and left for good.

Key interrupted my thoughts as he started speaking again.

"I have had much to think about since Monday. I have been coming to the church basement since the beginning of the year, as you know, but nothing has impacted me as much as when Toby said he shook the hand of a man who had been dead for six weeks. My family greatly prizes communication with the dead, so it caught my attention.

"That story about Jesus coming to his friend, Lazarus, showed me a deity that befriends us. He cares how we are feeling and he even expressed grief. I was surprised to hear it say he cried. I knew immediately that this was the God I have been looking for." He paused in his work and tilted his head to stare at a dark spot of spray paint.

"I have been lonely since my father died." He continued in a low voice. "We are supposed to be honored to have a deceased family member because then we can talk to them where ever we go." He paused again and I looked up into his big sad brown eyes. He swallowed and I could hear the lump in his throat. "But his passing has only given me terrible silence. I know my father loved me, so he is not ignoring me. He isn't there. And realizing it has made me see how empty we all are inside. And the deities who are supposed to coexist with us are no help. They each have an agenda to fulfill using us. We are supposed to have oneness with nature. To be as the wave and the sky. But the ones my people say made and rule over the wave and the sky don't act in oneness with anything. Their relationships are selfish, full of cheating and incest. And they demand too much sacrifice from humans to love us at all. But, your God! Wow!"

Key looked down at the canvas again to hide a surge of emotion. "Your God made the ultimate sacrifice so you didn't have to. He didn't ask you to give up a family member. He gave up his own son and made a way for us to be safe."

He stopped working again with visible excitement. "How amazing is that? You said that he did this even for me, when I don't care about him. That is a love I have never thought existed. I never heard of. It makes way more sense then what my mother believes.

"I mean, I can understand why she prays to my father and her parents. She misses them and feels empty inside too. But like me, she never gets an answer back. She is afraid to tell others because of their ridicule. She tells everyone how jolly her conversations are with all of the dead all the time, but she is lying. She thinks it is because we don't have a Kahuna anymore in our family.

"But now, since Monday, I know it is because they are just people and they are with the other dead. And I am happy and relieved. You, Clare, and Toby, you have something so simple and so pure inside your hearts. With you all the time. You pray and you are answered. That fascinates me because I think I know this God. I think I prayed to him once and he answered me."

We were quite a moment and I resisted the temptation to start talking clichés or religious lingo. Key was working something out in his head and his heart and I just needed to listen. And forget the niggling feeling about my own blemish. It was only a tiny spot of unforgiveness and it wasn't hurting anybody. It didn't matter in the grand scheme of things. It wasn't anything compared to what Key was going through.

I looked over at my parents with their heads down, hunkered over the two paintings they were cleaning. I knew they could hear our conversation in the echoing basement but Key's hushed tones suggested he wanted privacy as he spoke with me so they didn't interrupt. He started talking again.

"My brother is Christian. I have heard a lot from him but I have not listened to what he has said because I was angry we had to leave home. My mother and I moved to Chicago to escape the harassment. And she was afraid of losing her money too, when a new Kahuna is found and our family is replaced."

"I'm sorry to interrupt you, Key, but what is a Kahuna?"

He smiled. "I am so comfortable talking to you, Lily, I forget you don't know. Well, it is said that most of the islands are now Christian, but truthfully, there is a mixed religion between the old way and the new. My great, great, grandfather was a Kahuna, a position just under the king in Hawaii in the old days. Kahunas had government duties that they needed to rely on the spirits for answers to. Duties like navigating, building designs, temple work, healing, and philosophy. The position is passed down in a family and so his son, my great grandfather, became a guide for the old way. Of course, by then, he had to practice in secret because spirit consulting was outlawed in the early eighteen hundreds by the Queen who became Christian.

My great grandfather would teach and help those who wanted to find their way back to the spirits. He believed we needed to consult with our dead ancestors if we were going to survive on the islands. Terrible storms and times of poor fishing could kill an island population quickly. Listening to the guidance of the spirits could keep us safe. And he would talk to the dead for family members who needed protection or help but couldn't hear for themselves."

"So he was like a sorcerer or a fortune teller?"

"More or less, those are English words for it."

Wow, God! A real person who comes from a family of royal sorcery just like the magicians in the Bible who Pharaoh called to confront Moses and Aaron. They made snakes just like Moses did, but his snake ate theirs. Jackie needs to hear this.

I looked around the room helplessly, but since she wasn't even in town, there wasn't much I could do.

Maybe Key will share with her later. Depending on where he is going with all this. His family wasn't using God's help, so what they got from the demonic realm wasn't pretty. I have a feeling this story is heading for heartache. God, help me know what to say. Help Key unlock his heart and understand you love him.

After my earlier conversation with Jackie about the reality of magic and its evil implications, I'd memorized Deuteronomy chapter eighteen, verses nine through thirteen.

When you enter the land the Lord your God is giving you, do not learn to imitate the detestable ways of the nations there. Let no one be found among you who sacrifices their son or daughter in the fire, who practices divination or sorcery, interprets omens, engages in witchcraft, or casts spells, or who is a medium or spiritist or who consults the dead. Anyone who does these things is detestable to the Lord; because of these same detestable practices the Lord your God will drive out those nations before you. You must be blameless before the Lord your God.

I had found that having this passage on my mind had continued to convict me and point out things we all did everyday with the dark arts. It had helped me avoid temptation to join the fun when a group of girls wanted to go to a palm reader after class. It curbed my curiosity when someone started reading their horoscope in the bathroom. I left a party when they broke out the Ouija board. And I saw God's power work when I prayed during a round of light as feather and stiff as a board one night when we were having a floor slumber party. The levitation leader was mystified the girl on the floor didn't float. I was a little scared at what I'd done, so I'd just rolled over and went to sleep. The others had grown bored with the failed party trick and moved on to drinking beer they'd smuggled out of a frat party earlier that weekend.

Consequently I'd even stopped reading fortune cookies, which frankly was the hardest thing of all. It was a mini vacation to an exotic land when a carload of us would head over to the only Chinese restaurant in town. And the sweet snack at the end with the funny message inside was everyone's favorite part of the meal, including mine.

They had all laughed at me the first time I waved away my

cookie.

"You're actually serious?" Gaby had asked.

"Well, I think so. I know it's just for fun and we don't take the canned phrases inside to heart or anything, but I'm trying to eliminate everything in my life that's a hindrance to see if it makes a difference."

"A difference in what?" Gaby was curious.

"A difference in hearing God's voice. The Bible tells us to depend on God and trust him about the future. It warns us to not make light of his commands by consulting other people or other spirits. This stuff can separate us from God."

The whole table had busted out laughing.

"Let us know how that works out for you."

"It's just a cookie for crying out loud."

"These aren't real fortunes. They put the same phrases in hundreds of cookies."

"You're getting a little overboard with the dead stuff, Clare. Take a chill pill."

"Better yet, take a cookie."

Key had started talking again, pulling me from my own thoughts.

"By the time my father was old enough to take on the duties of the secret Kahuna, there was a renaissance, as the authorities called it, of the ancient practices. Things could be more out in the open. My brother, Tai, and I were taught and raised in them with classes in our school. My brother though, as the oldest of a powerful family, was supposed to take my father's place after he jumped in the great volcano."

"Wait, what? He jumped in a volcano?"

"That is a metaphor now. In the ancient times, yes, he would have. My father took a bottle of sleeping pills and kava and drifted off to a happy land when I was fifteen. It was my brother's eighteenth birthday present. He was stepping aside for my brother to become the next Kahuna."

"That's horrible," I said before I thought. Key glanced up at me.

"Well, we all knew it was going to happen our whole lives, so it wasn't like it was a surprise. It just didn't make it any easier. My brother, Tai, took it rough. He couldn't seem to make a connection to the spirit world and talk to my father like he was supposed to. He was angry that my father had killed himself instead of staying here to guide him. My mother thought maybe this anger was clouding his clairvoyance, so she took him to a counselor in the big city.

"But the counselor and his young daughter, Ruth, were Christian. They convinced him to let go of his anger, but not so he could talk to the dead, rather so he could live for eternity. It all sounded crazy when he would tell me about it. But I had heard in the crooning of many romantic songs that love makes people crazy. So, when Tai fell in love with Ruth, he went crazy too. He turned his back on his family and his duties. He became a Christian and ran away to Christian school on the mainland.

"I didn't want him to have to be the Kahuna if he didn't want to, but I didn't want him to leave us like father had either. I became angry too. Needless to say, my mother was beside herself with grief and, well, anger. She didn't want to lose her position in the community, or the money that each family paid us yearly for protection and guidance. She thought she or I could take Tai's place."

Here in the story, Key paused for a long breath as he tenderly wiped the face in the painting on his lap. I vaguely heard my dad shift from one leg to the other with a mild groan. Key looked up and I realized I had been staring at him. Our eyes locked. He was frightened and his sadness made my heart ache. I nodded to encourage him.

His voice was a whisper. "Only I couldn't hear my father or any of the dead either. Because I didn't want to."

"You didn't?" I was startled.

Neither of us were looking at what we were doing. He leaned toward me across the painting he was kneeling over.

"No, I knew it wouldn't really be my father I was talking to. When I was a little boy, I used to spy on my grandfather and him when they were speaking with the spirits for others. The spirits knew who the dead people were, but they weren't them. They were powerful, ugly, mean beings and my grandfather didn't have any control over them, they controlled *him*. I didn't want to work for them. I was scared to even talk to them. I prayed to the Christian God, your God, to protect me from them because nothing in my world seemed to stop them and the Christians I knew at school didn't have to talk to them at all. I prayed for my brother too. I didn't want him to have to do that either. I didn't know what to offer the Christian God for this help, so I told him I was sorry for what my family was doing and I didn't want to do it and I just offered him myself."

He looked down to move the cotton ball in his hand in a circular motion over the left cover of the canvas and was quiet again.

"Miss James, I'm sorry to interrupt."

We all jumped at the voice of the guard who had moved back in from his position at the back door.

"Director Pierce would like a word with you now. There's been a development in the case. We have a vehicle waiting to take you to the office she's using on campus. I'm sorry folks, only Miss James. She's not a minor, so even though you are her parents, I can't take you along."

The guard addressed my parents who had begun to stand up from the cold damp basement floor. They looked concerned.

"We'll take good care of her," the guard said with a reassuring smile as he covered the area to the door in three swift strides and stood holding it open. I stretched my stiff legs out straight under the canvas I had been working on and pushed the painting off my lap onto the floor.

"We'll have to pick this up where we left off when I get back, Key. You're staying for supper with us, right?" I wiped my hands on a soft cloth he had handed me from his kit.

He nodded and then caught my arm as I started to stand up next to him. Just above a whisper, he breathed into my ear these words. "I have never told anyone about my prayer. I have told you so you can find out for me what this Jesus wants me to do with my life. I know he talks to you. And he is protecting me. I know he is because I have never heard the voices of the dead or their messengers."

I was floored. He was a Christian and he didn't even know it.

❋ Chapter Eleven

"Hello, Miss James. We've asked you here today because we've had an anonymous tip about the vandalism that we feel is worth pursuing."

I shook FBI Director Pierce's hand and automatically took the one extended by the University President, Edward Chilling, before noticing the darkened office behind me was full to the brim of deans and board members.

"It would be an acceptable explanation for what happened and remove the need for the police presence we have turning this campus into a media circus." President Chilling was saying as my eyes focused back on his face. "Although it is a disappointing conclusion and does shed some negative press on this University's exemplary reputation."

The president lowered himself into a chair at the end of Director Pierce's desk. She also sat and gestured for me to be seated across from her, although there were no seats for the rest of the room. They merely hovered like bats at the edge of the pool of light we were in.

I shifted uncomfortably in my seat, my thoughts beginning to race. *What are they talking about now? An acceptable explanation? Disappointing conclusion? Was it the truth?*

"So, let's get right to it and hear your side of the story, Clare." Director Pierce leaned back in her chair and rested her elbows on the armrests, touching the tips of her fingers together in front of her in a summing-you-up sort of way.

My side of what story? I thought, trying not to feel defensive.

She hadn't seemed to blink as she continued. "The tip was a formal letter written to the University apologizing for the vandalism of your paintings. It took responsibility for the act, siting details we haven't released to the public." She sprang into action and snapped open a manila folder from which photos of the damaged paintings and their offensive message spilled across the smooth mahogany desk. I turned my head away from them as if they were of a mangled body. It was no less shocking for me to see.

"It corrected our press release that the paint color was red, not the blue we said. It spelled out the message, including the misspelling of Christian. The writer further alluded to the first painting propped on a wall, while the other three wrapped around a fake Christmas tree lining them up with your easel and the drawing you had started." At that there was an uncomfortable stir through the room. I frowned.

"Okay, so the vandal apologizes. Who did it and why?"

"Miss James, before we can determine the motivation for the vandalism, we have to establish the creditability of this suspect. I'm telling you all of this to tell you that this person could have done the crime."

"Or known someone who did and likes to drink and talk." I was disappointed. "Or maybe they came in to the basement through the outside door that was left unlocked after the crime on his or her way to class that morning before we found it. Really? That's your break in the case?"

"Or you. You could have written it yourself." Martin leaned forward out of the shadows with a grin the width of his face.

I didn't even try to hide my distaste for the man as I nodded toward the Director. "That makes no sense at all. Why would I have vandalized my own work?" I frowned. "That's not all, is it? What else did it say?"

Director Pierce tipped her head slightly to one side as she studied me.

What is going on here? I thought suspiciously.

The Director's chair creaked as she started talking again. "It said that the reason the perp destroyed the paintings was to draw attention to *your* senior show work. You, a master forger we all know and love, have plagiarized the four pieces you have completed and you plan to continue stealing your entire body of work. The vandal only expected to expose you as a cheat when the vandalism was investigated by campus officials. The author did not know you were on the FBI watch list and had never expected things to get so out of hand. He or she is now too frightened to come forward."

I could barely wait for her to finish before I exploded out of my seat.

"That's ridiculous! Those are my pieces. I'm not a *master forger*! I only helped a friend with one tiny miniature that any untrained eye could tell was not the real thing. And my four paintings cannot be plagiarized. They are of *me* for crying out loud!"

A storm of discussion broke out over the room and the Director waved for me to sit back down. She spoke over the hullabaloo, "People, people, you will be asked to leave if you don't settle down."

I spoke in a loud voice through the dying murmurs. "So who does the letter claim I stole my work from?"

"Well, clearly not the actual works themselves, as they are of you," President Chilling cut in before Director Pierce could speak.

Director Pierce frowned at him. "It's not a legal matter, but an ethical one. Because of the ambiguity of the accusations, it can easily be dealt with by an academic court. The University has protocol for such events. They have the power to decide if there is any action to be taken against you. We have determined, however, that the letter is legitimate and therefore, can be acted upon by the University. We have also determined, Clare," her voice softened, "you are not in any danger nor are there any terrorist activities boiling under these cool Midwestern skies. We will be around for a few weeks monitoring the Union war that seems to be developing at Sulferson Silks if you need anything, though, Clare. Anything at all."

"That's it?" I asked in disbelief. "My work is destroyed, my character and beliefs attacked, I'm drug out of my house in a helicopter, surrounded by guards and now I'm the criminal? And someone who tried to destroy my face, even a possible hate crime offender, is the frightened victim here? What is our country coming to? I'm a national hero in England. I demand you find this person and hold them accountable for what they did because what they're claiming isn't true."

Director Pierce held up her hand and rose from her seat. "I'm sorry you feel that way, Clare. At the interest of not embarrassing the University or you any further, we have decided to drop the incident. The local PD will continue to investigate this letter and the evidence found in the basement. But Clare, even if they do catch whoever wrote the letter, if I were you, I would let the vandalism charges you could press drop. I don't know anything about art, but if you are found guilty of somehow stealing this other artist's idea, you won't win anything useful from an arrest of the vandal who exposed it."

"But I didn't steal anything. I'm innocent. Someone has attacked me. Why are you believing a no name letter writer and not me?" I stood up too.

Director Pierce had circled her desk and put her hand on my shoulder. "It's up to the University now. They've had a formal complaint filed since the letter arrived and they have to investigate. You will have a chance to give your side of the story and present your work. The other artist can also present their case. Perhaps the vandal will come forward and speak about why he or she felt your work was not original. If the vandal does speak, the local PD can arrest the person and pursue charges from you if you chose. You will have to comply with whatever the University court decides is necessary in order for you to stay at this school. They will assign a security guard to shadow you in case there is more to this then we are seeing. He or she won't interfere with your life or your class work."

"This is all a huge mistake." I was shaking my head and the room was full of murmurs again.

"It's the lifespan concept we are concerned about." President

Chilling stood up to butt into the conversation.

"The what?" I was trying not to lose my patience.

"This is all a little more complicated then a campus prank, Miss James." President Chilling literally tipped his head back and looked down his nose at me. "We've had the artist who originated the lifespan concept come forward and complain about your conduct. And that artist also happens to be a professor here. One of *your* professors." The room around me gasped.

"Who in the world did that?" I was dumbfounded.

"I did." Martin stood up and walked to the President's side.

✻ Chapter Twelve

SPLAT! SPLAT!

I jumped in my seat and jerked the wheel of the jeep to the right as two eggs exploded against the driver's side window while we were turning into the Sulferson river estate driveway. It had been an action packed week since I last saw Reginald and he had a few hours in his schedule to spare for me after breakfast.

Toby and I had threaded our way through the heavy factory traffic as shifts changed. We were deep in a conversation about dreams and visions, a topic far from the fiasco the campus trial had been. Toby was planning to sketch along the river until my sitting with Reginald was done and then we were going to grab a bite to eat in town. I was glad he had offered to come this time so my security guard could have a break. So we could all have a break. And I was secretly glad he'd left his silly glasses at home today. And gotten a haircut. He looked like Toby again and that's what I needed.

"Ah! I wasn't expecting that," I panted as I swiftly corrected the wheel and clenched at my chest where my heart beat was triple timing it. Cloudy egg goo slid lazily down the window.

"I didn't see anyone. They must have come up on us fast. Or used a long range sling shot." Toby said.

As we pulled into the circle driveway under the side of the house overhang, Muriel and the driver from my first trip came out to meet us.

"They got you too. More eggs. My car got hammered when I came in earlier this morning and they attacked Ms. Gallonte's vehicle too." Muriel rang her hands. "I reported it to the police, but I doubt they even come out. A prank they said on the phone. I thought we were through with this when the unions were put off over the summer, but it looks like tempers are boiling again.

"I'm so sorry you two. Bernard will wash the jeep while you're working, Clare. Mr. Sulferson wanted me to extend an invitation to you to draw inside today, Mr. Fir. It's for your own safety and we have the most amazing views. You can walk on the water without Jesus here."

"Oh, thank you," Toby jumped out of the jeep. "I will accept the offer to draw indoors, but it's impossible to do anything without Jesus. He's right here all the time." Toby thumped his chest with a fist and swung around the back of the jeep to unload his portable easel and supplies.

That was an awesome response, Toby! I thought to myself, impressed with his quick wit.

Bernard's mouth twitched at the corners. Muriel was clearly flustered by the harassment that morning and wasn't fully listening.

"I'm sorry, Clare, I should have lead with how pleased Mr. Sulferson is with the beginning of the painting. He's usually busy with physical therapy or phone calls during the day so he seldom will visit a sitting, but he always looks at the progress."

"Oh, great! I'm glad he saw it, although it's only an underpainting." We had followed her indoors and now were making our way to the dog's suite.

"Down that hall, Mr. Fir." Muriel pointed off to the right as we walked. "You'll find a glass tunnel with lots of views."

"Sure, thanks. See you again soon, Clare." Toby waved and turned off, looking back at me over his shoulder. I smiled and waved back. A few more twists and we were in Reggie's room. He didn't appear to be in.

"Do you have everything you need?" Muriel asked as I began setting up.

"Everything but the guest of honor." I tried to be cheerful. I wasn't looking forward to this despite the fact that it got me off campus for a few hours.

"Oh. Wendy took him to our indoor gym for his walk today because of the egg attacks. He should be here shortly. And I'd rather go before that." She sniffled slightly. I nodded and she left hastily.

The paint I had applied Sunday was tacky, meaning it was sticky to the touch. This made it workable. Gently I merged paint into it, layering in depth with background vegetation. I enhanced the grass under Reginald's feet and added small flowers and rocks.

While I worked I had too much time to think. I didn't want to mull over and over last week's fiasco. I kept avoiding it in my thoughts like an ant hill in bare feet. Once my tiny subject arrived, I'd be able to concentrate on him enough to occupy that spare part of your mind that tried to work out problems.

In the quiet room with the sweeping views, I directed my thoughts to this morning's reading in my Bible, Isaiah 48:17.

This is what the Lord, your Redeemer, says: "I am the Lord your God, who teaches you what is best for you, who directs you in the way you should go."

Lord, how is this way your best for me? My show is important. I can make a statement for you in it. I've avoided questionable things, even given up fortune cookies, and this is what happens? I thought I was going to get closer to you. I thought I was going to be able to do something big for you. But I can't do anything with the University tying my hands like that. How could you let them?

Forgiveness.

Well, I guess you're going to have plenty of time to teach me about that since I'm now working with Martin as my senior show advisor. God, I can't do this, I'm going to have to quit school. Transfer somewhere else. Besides despising him, he's sleazy and he's definitely a verbal abuser and I –

Shield of Faith.

What? Look, he's going to be controlling –

Helmet of Salvation.

Breastplate of Righteousness.

It is not fair. The University found he had no merit for his claims. Clearly. Since I painted them from your inspiration, Lord. And you know I never even knew about his chicken work. I've never been to his house either. He likes to imply that he's this Casanova among college girls, but you know me. I'm waiting for marriage and I'm not going to be with someone older and married either. What if he lies again?

Belt Buckle of Truth.

Feet fitted with the readiness to spread the Gospel of Peace.

Okay, so I keep thinking about the Armor of God I learned in Sunday school years ago. But I don't think I can create with him hovering over me. He's so mean. He scares my prayers right out of me. And he won't accept any of my work about you for my show. You've got to do something miraculous and make this all change.

Forgiveness.

Well, I guess that would make a lot change.

Sword of the Spirit to extinguish the fiery arrows of Satan.

I know the Sword of the Spirit is the Word of God, your Word, God. I need a big sword for this one. And an extra helping of forgiveness, please.

It was a ludicrous suggestion that my work was inspired by a study based on a chicken. Martin had presented himself as the idea originator of the lifespan concept he developed thirty years ago while living in a chicken coop for forty days. Some grant he got. He presented three paintings. One of an egg, one of a chick, and one of a rooster that now hung in his home. As soon as he'd heard his name was mentioned in the letter, he was flattered to have inspired such a vibrant young woman like Clare James to create masterpieces. He had went on and on about how deeply troubled he was that she was unable to create original works. She clearly had not been taught beyond skills only good enough to copy others.

His words still rang in my head, bruising me wherever they landed, staining my soul with what felt like permanent gouges of humiliation, injustice and offense.

Speaking of which, President Chilling had the gall to announce he was *personally offended* when the vote unanimously went with me. He didn't bother to question the ethical validity of an anonymous letter written by a vandal. He ignored that we didn't know how that person knew about Martin's paintings in his home. He disregarded the part of my defense that questioned Martin's rights to the concept he said I copied.

I had even outlined for those who weren't art enthusiasts a quick history of Claude Monet, a French artist, famous for his series of paintings of haystacks. He had done twenty-five pieces during 1890 from the fields around where he lived. He observed the stacks during sunny and stormy weather, in the morning, in the afternoon and at dusk. He also recorded them with each seasonal change. They were worth millions of dollars today.

No, President Chilling ignored all that because he had a PR bee in his bonnet. He insisted that to help the University's Public Relations, Martin and I needed to at least work together on something. It would help stop the Clare demonstrations had popped up overnight. The conglomerate had been relieved to have an out. Martin was named my senior show mentor on the spot. They left patting themselves on the back and I left with a pat to the behind. I shivered at the memory.

Where is that dog? I said I wasn't going to think about that stuff and get all worked up. I need a subject to paint. I thought irritably.

Within an hour and a half I had about everything I wanted to do on the background worked in. I preferred to let it dry a few more days before adding additional glazes and lighter tones over the sun kissed areas. I had stalled all I could. Now I really needed a dog. I checked my watch again. Wendy was being irresponsible with the time. Reginald only had windows of availability in his schedule that worked with my class schedule and the paint curing times. I had to have an audience with him whenever I was scheduled to.

I popped my head out of the room and craned to see down the long, empty hall. There was no one around and I would be lost instantly if I ventured very far. Aimlessly, I pulled out my sketches of Reginald playing on my first visit and tried to focus on them. This was my escape time from campus. My time to not think about Martin and my senior show. To be away from the waving signs and people shouting my name. I stared at the drawings and decided I could use them to work in some shadows on his lower body and around his facial wrinkles.

I checked my watch again. It was the two hour mark and no Wendy. I was only scheduled for another hour with the dog. My eyes desperately scanned the room for a suggestion and that's when I saw a wall phone. I ran to it and picked up the receiver. No dial tone. I pressed several of the buttons but nothing happened.

"You've got to be kidding me." I plunked the receiver down and headed for the door. It was time to find someone.

The phone rang as I was leaving. I dove back across the room to answer it before it stopped.

"Hello, hello, is anybody there?"

"Ah, Miss James. I saw Reginald's line was activated and no

one was answering. I apologize for my staff. Is everything okay?" Curtis Sulferson was on the line.

"Sorry to bother you, Sir, but I needed to find out what was happening with Reginald. I've been here for two hours and Wendy never brought him in from his walk. In fact, I haven't seen anyone for that long."

"I should be the one apologizing to you, Miss James, for wasting your valuable time. Let me find out what is going on. Hang up the phone for me. I'll send someone over to you right now."

I'd barely set the receiver down and a girl with an apron and flour on her hands came running down the hall outside.

"Miss, so sorry. Can you please follow me?"

I grabbed my backpack and left the paints to follow her down the softly lit winding hall. We crossed through a sitting room and a breakfast nook and then we found Toby eating a sandwich and leaning on a glass bench in the glass tunnel over the river.

"Hey, what's up?" He looked surprise to see us.

"Can you come with us, Sir? You may bring your sandwich."

"Thanks." Toby hoisted his easel strap over his shoulder. He was already wearing his backpack.

I grabbed his free hand. "I don't know what's going on, but I think Reginald and Wendy are missing. They never showed up for our sitting."

And that's when we all heard the sirens in the distance.

Slap. Slip. Slap. Slip. Slap.

Fall was in full swing but I was still stubbornly wearing my sandals. I had switched them from my plastic flip flops to the hardy leather and cork Birkenstocks known as Jesus Cruisers around campus. Jeans, a T-shirt with a sweatshirt and a scarf or mittens would work for me until the first snow fell. Then I'd have to add some thick socks too.

Thinking about the weather and my clothes reminded me of the spiritual armor I had put on this morning. I was going to meet with Martin to discuss the progress for my senior art show and I had read through Ephesians as I ate breakfast. I was surprised how much I remembered from memorizing this passage one summer in middle school. It was Ephesians 6:10-17. And as I walked across campus, I gave myself a pep talk.

I can do this. God is with me protecting me. I will not let abuse or worldly ideals stop me from being God's girl. These verses say so: Finally, be strong in the Lord and in his mighty power. Put on the full armor of God, so that you can take your stand against the devil's schemes. For our struggle is not against flesh and blood, but against the rulers, against the authorities, against the powers of this dark world and against the spiritual forces of evil in the heavenly realms. Therefore put on the full armor of God, so that when the day of evil comes, you may be able to stand your ground, and after you have done everything, to stand. Stand firm then, with the belt of truth buckled around your waist, with the breastplate of righteousness in place, and with your feet fitted with the readiness that comes from the gospel of peace. In addition to all this, take up the shield of faith, with which you can extinguish all the flaming arrows of the evil one. Take the helmet of salvation and the sword of the Spirit, which is the word of God.

The hatred and fear when I thought of Martin left a bitter taste in my mouth. It was a chink in my armor and it was only a matter of time before the devil found it and exploited it. God couldn't patch it until I let him wash it clean with forgiveness.

I looked down at the rolled drawings under my arm. On the backs of them I had written verses to help me get through this. I had no idea what to expect so I ignored the butterflies flapping around like eagles in my stomach and focused on the words I could see on the back of the top scroll. I read as I walked.

If you, Lord, kept a record of sins, who could stand? But with you there is forgiveness, so that we can, with reverence, serve you. I wait for the Lord, my whole being waits, and in his word I put my hope. Psalms 130:3-5

Slap. Slip. Slap. Slip. Slap.

I walked over the bridge that spanned a picturesque brook in the middle of campus and brushed a red oak leaf out of my hair. The giant tree weeping its colorful tears all over the manicured lawn on both sides of the brook hardly got my attention.

Martin's words to the class my first day on campus three years ago echoed through my head trying to psych me out.

"Everything you've ever heard, read, or been taught up till now was wrong. You are impressionable new clay. An empty vessel to be shaped and filled. So we must dump out the rubbish you've started with and begin again. And if you can't or won't do this, then believe me when I say, I will smash your little clay pot and force you to start over.

"What your high school art teacher said, what your religious leader spewed, and even what your parents scolded you about is all swill in the bottom of your bucket. DUMP IT OUT!"

He'd slammed his fist on a desk and I remember jumping in my seat.

"Dump it out now and quickly. Clear your minds." The room had been dead silent for a long minute. I had been afraid to move. What were we supposed to be doing? When he spoke again, his loud voice made me jump again. I had been as skittish as a baby rabbit. Actually what I felt like this morning. Why was he so terrifying? Because I wanted to do well in class? His words continued to echo from the corridors of the past.

"From now on, everything I say is right and everything you are thinking is wrong. If you can get that, then you might graduate from here with an art degree. And one or two of you will be actual artists. Successful artists. Not art critics or teachers or gallery owners. No. You will be artists who can eat food and drive cars paid for from money made from your work. Like me. Famous when you walk down the street."

He had paused to twirl the end of his mustache and eye us like we were horses at auction. I half expected him to ask to see my teeth next.

I had tried so hard to forget those days of working to figure out what he wanted so I wouldn't be singled out and humiliated. As I walked through the brisk air, I fought the familiar dread that threatened to wash over me and choke the breath out of my lungs. I turned my drawing scrolls a little and repeated the first verse I saw in my handwriting under my breath.

What you heard from me, keep as the pattern of sound teaching, with faith and love in Christ Jesus. Guard the good deposit that was entrusted to you—guard it with the help of the Holy Spirit who lives in us. 2 Timothy 1:13-14

It wasn't on the back of any of the drawings, but I drowned out Martin's persistent voice in my head by repeating another verse I remembered that helped me to fight him from taking away what I believed in.

Start children off on the way they should go, and even when they are old they will not turn from it. Proverbs 22:6.

I shuffled through the leaf piles blocking the bridge exit and hoisted the scrolls up tighter under my arm again. They were slippery and wanted to roll away. I had time to read one more verse before I enter the convention center where the art studios were housed. I pulled an outside scroll toward me and read in the early morning light: *Bear with each other and forgive one another if any of you has a grievance against someone. Forgive as the Lord forgave you. Colossians 3:13*

Well, that about sums it up.

I grabbed the long handled door and flipped it open to the art studio's spacious and cool interior. The lights were on and the room appeared to be empty. A long waist high table stretched across the back of the room and I could see an empty easel and canvas locker with JAMES taped across it.

My new home away from home.

I started to spread my rolled up drawings out and anchor them with the empty jars lined up along one wall for brush cleaning.

"So you decided to come after all. I expected you to waste a lot of time protesting or ditching our appointments. I wouldn't have put it past you to even transfer somewhere else."

I swung around as Martin strolled in the door behind me. His tone was smug as he continued. "Oh, don't think I haven't noticed you were not in my classes. Don't think I haven't considered many times how to get you exactly where you are at right now. If you'd only been half as smart as you think you are, you could have been quite accomplished by now. As it is, you've only succeeded in being one of my greatest disappointments."

I swallowed with a dry throat. "Sir, truthfully, I have avoided you." This man made me nervous as a bull in the slaughter house pasture. "I haven't agreed with a number of your statements or methods of teaching. I have resented the way you have used me to hurt other people. I dislike you and have not shown you respect in my attitude or what I have said to others about you. I am working on forgiving you for the injustices you have inflicted on me and I ask for your forgiveness for my bad attitude. I would like us to start working together with a clean slate. And also I would appreciate it if you would respect my personal space."

I extended my hand and he shook it.

But he didn't let go. He squeezed it harder and pulled me a step closer to him. I cringed backwards as he leaned forward, the smell of his cigar breath taking the air from my mouth. Our hands, locked in a python's hug, were the only distance between our bodies.

"You won't win my favor with some rehearsed lines of baloney. I won't let you make a fool out of me! You may end up squandering your talents with your childish notions, and your religious piousness, but you won't do it on my account. I'm respected in the artistic community and I've paid my dues. I promoted you once and you spurned me. Well, not again. You *will* be my student and you will do what I say and you will give me my credit, where credit is due, every time you are interviewed whether you like it or not." He hissed angrily.

"Clare, is everything alright here?" Toby spoke calmly from the shadows by the canvas lockers. I felt Martin's hand jerk involuntarily and he released me, stepping backwards. I was pulling away from him so hard I fell when he let go of me, barely catching myself on the edge of the work table. My legs had become too weak to stand on their own. I looked down at my hands gripping the edge of the table with white knuckles and sucked in a deep breath of fresh air.

"Everything is fine here, Mr. Fir." Martin's voice was sarcastic. "You are interrupting a private student consultation and I will seek disciplinary measures against you." Martin had turned his back to us and was surveying the other end of the work table where I'd begun to spread out my drawings. He took a deep breath. "Miss James, I see you think you are too clever for me. Apparently you feel I can't use turpentine on drawing paper. Well, I'm sure you have learned all sorts of bad habits wandering about overseas like a nomad. We must start from the beginning. All this drivel you've brought is unacceptable religious propaganda."

He gathered my drawings, both rolled and flat, and tore them deftly in half, tossing them back onto the work table before dusting his hands off over them and turning to us. Toby had moved to stand beside me with his arm across my shoulders. I'd straightened up and stuck my chin out in a stubborn posture.

"I expect you to do paintings from now on. You can't present a substantial enough body of work on just paper to graduate. I want four new paintings to replace the ones you stole by this time next week. Same time, same place. Alone."

He turned to leave.

"Martin!" I didn't mean to shout it, but I was screwing up my courage like a rabbit running in front of a tiller to save a stray garden carrot.

He paused and slowly turned around to face us, drawing a cigar from his shirt pocket as I spoke.

"Those paintings were cleared by the board, so if I want to use them, I will. You know I never saw your chicken studies! I don't know who you blackmailed into vandalizing my work and you probably wrote that letter yourself because no one on campus has ever seen those old student works of yours.

"If you continue to be my advisor, Toby will be attending our meetings and you will stop touching me in any way. No more swats on the behind or hands on my shoulders. I'm not even going to so much as hand you a pencil. You will respect my personal space. If you can't keep your hands to yourself, I will file a formal complaint. And I have plenty of witnesses.

"I can't fathom why you are really doing this, but since I've filed the papers to declare my secondary area as drawing, my show must either be computer graphics or drawing, according to the policies of the department you chaired. I'm sure I can be placed with a more appropriate advisor if you only work with painters. But while I may have a few paintings to compliment my exhibit's theme, my show will feature drawings." It was almost impossible to keep the anger out of my voice.

He lit his cigar and took a long draw. He stared off into space over our heads for an extended moment before exhaling and cloaking his features behind the smoke.

"Your terms are acceptable. Return next week at this same time with three drawings. Make them ones I will like."

He turned around and walked out of the studio. The giant door silently swung closed behind him. I buried my head in Toby's shoulder and he pulled me around in a hug. We stood there as the clock ticked off several minutes and then I pulled back to look up at him.

I loved his hair cut like he wore it in England. I hugged him again with all my might.

✸ Chapter Thirteen

I had four drawings each over forty inches wide and sixty inches tall that I'd taken to my meeting with Martin. Thanks to his obnoxious attack, I now had eight drawings in various haphazard dimensions that added up to those sizes. Toby and I spread them out on the work room table and anchored their rolling edges with blocks of wood or the empty bottles. I surveyed the jagged tears unevenly cutting through the scenes I had worked especially hard on to present to Martin, my toughest critic.

"I might be able to salvage these with more tape then I need for wrapping my Christmas presents." I had hopped up on the thick wooden table and was sitting cross legged in the middle of my slaughtered drawings. My pony tail had released a big curl across my eyes and I blew it to the side. Toby was standing across the table from me, and he didn't crack a smile at my comment. He was looking at me with sincere concern. Paul, who had stirred out of his sleeping bag from the other side of the room, was standing next to him with tousled hair, rubbing his eyes.

"Seriously guys, I use tape sometimes. I mean usually it's to tape all my paper down to a hard surface to work on because I cut it off of big drawing paper rolls I order in the mail and they keep rolling up on me while I'm trying to draw." Both guys were still staring at me, blankly.

"One time I had this six foot drawing done of Henry the eighth. It was for an assignment where we had to take a famous work and do a spoof on it. You know like Duchamp's Mona Lisa with the mustache? Well, I'd copied Holbein's Henry portrait, where he's all poofed up and dressed fancy and he has his gloves in hand. But in my drawing, instead of his gloves, I put the heads of the wives and the men he'd beheaded in his crazy quest to have a son. I'd worked on it for a week straight, without sleep and when it was done, I peeled the tape off one corner and gave it a big tug, expecting it to pull up in a straight line.

"But the tape was stubborn and stuck in one spot near the bottom of the drawing. It ripped it all the way across, severing

Henry's arm and all the heads it clenched. I was instantly devastated, but too tired to get worked up. I studied it for a while and decided to frame it in two separate pieces to be hung together in a set."

Paul interrupted my story. "I remember that. It was horrendous. I was sitting down there sketching you while you worked. What?" He jabbed Toby in the ribs playfully. "Everyone here knows I've had a crush on Clare since forever. As usual, this God she loves does nothing but stand in my way of happiness, though. She won't have me because I won't love him first."

"Really, Paul? You still have a hard heart after our discussion at the Monday Meal?" I was sidetracked momentarily from my current problem solving tangent.

"I will admit, Clare, he does exist. There is God among us. But I don't believe he loves us as much as you think."

"Hunh." I grunted. "How does that even make sense? Is he a lying God? Because he says he loves us enough to die for us."

"But look, Clare, you did what he wanted. You forgave Martin and approached him humbly. He ripped up your drawings anyway. Where was God in that? I mean, why do you even have to deal with Martin? Why didn't God protect you?"

"But he did, Paul." Toby joined the conversation. "He sent me here to look for a lost brush for my roommate and I was here to step in with Clare and help her stand her ground so she wasn't abused more than she could take. She's a strong girl and she's got a great heart and God doesn't want that crushed. He's teaching her about forgiveness.

But He can't force Martin to be a nice person. God has given each of us free will. So we have to deal with people who have made poor choices to not obey God. We live on a planet full of people who have chosen to not follow God and that allows bad things to happen. How we respond to those things and how we ask God to use us in those situations is how we grow closer to God. He has the bigger picture and we do not."

I was surprised again by Toby's response. It was very insightful and it gave Paul pause to think.

"You guys are painting a picture that makes it harder and harder to stay angry at God for my life. I'm not sure I buy it yet, though, so I'm not hanging that picture on my wall, okay?"

"Fair enough. Just remember that the longer you hang onto your anger the harder it will be to let it go. It's not God who is keeping you alone." Toby placed a hand on Paul's shoulder and they faced off for a moment. I gasped at the tension that had sprung up in the air. Were they going to punch each other or hug?

Toby broke the silence, "Okay, let's get back to solving Clare's dilemma then." He dropped his arm.

Paul and I nodded. I was grateful Toby was there to challenge Paul. It was always awkward to witness to guys and I made it my policy to never get involved that way. But with Paul it had been hard.

The situation was forced on me when he kept writing me notes our freshman year.

Thanks, God, for helping me be clear about where I was coming from. I mean, we're still friends and now Toby is here to pick up where I couldn't go anymore. Now, what am I going to do with these ruined drawings, Lord?

I sighed, my chin leaning on my hands with my elbow propped on my knees.

"Well, I guess, if I don't use them to start a campfire, I'm going to have to pull a Henry on these. Paste, piece, and part these four drawings into three and hand them back at him again next week. Is that being rude? I mean, we're half way through the semester and I have a lot on my plate. He can't expect me just to sit and draw three more complete drawings in a week, can he? And barring that, I haven't the foggiest what to draw that would earn his approval anyway."

Paul ran a hand through his unruly hair. "I like that idea a lot, Clare. It's unexpected and it meets his criteria. He enjoyed destroying them, so seeing them with battle scars, so to speak, might please that weird cookie."

Toby had moved around the table and was standing behind me with a warm hand on my back. I could feel it burning through my shirt and it helped me relax.

"Since your work is all Bible stories, it could be combined in a new view from what you first expected and that will make the pieces stronger. You could splice the piece of Jonah on his back with his arms open wide laying in the whale with the cross and Christ here, like this."

He pulled the pieces side by side to demonstrate. "I was reading the other day about how the story of Jonah is the forecast for the crucifixion with Jonah being in the belly of the fish for three days like Christ in the tomb. That would take those three pieces and make one drawing. Oh, and what about this?"

He walked around the table and placed the severed drawings of Ruth and Naomi on camels next to Mary on a donkey, using three more pieces of drawings.

"Also a forecast from the Old Testament of the story of Christ coming in the New Testament." I was getting excited now as the pieces became commentaries on the Bible stories and not just illustrations of them.

"Well, I don't know the stories, but what about these two pieces that are left?" Paul held up one of Christ's hand nailed to the cross from the crucifixion drawing and one of Joseph where he was walking on the road. He had been behind Mary on the donkey, which was now a part of the Ruth and Naomi drawing. Paul moved the hand and piece of wood it was tacked to around the scene of Joseph. First he placed the wooden cross beam at the bottom of the drawing as the road Joseph was walking on.

Pondering the visual impact of it with his fingers stroking his chin, Paul moved the giant hand nailed to the board up to the clouds and turned it right and left. He playfully turned it up and set it on the road in front of Joseph like it was growing out of the ground.

"Ooo. I like that. Hold it right there." I stood up on the table to see it better.

"You know that expression, we'll cross that bridge when we come to it? Well, that's an obstacle in his life that's going to be hard. He's the step father of the savior of the world. Tough job description. I like it too." Toby nodded at the paper.

Paul stood back with his hands on his hips and looked over the pieces. "I like them because they have strong compositions and unusual images. I want to find out more about them. That means they pass the test because I'm no Bible thumper. Get your tape out, Clare. My work here is done."

We laughed as he drifted away back to his side of the studio and then out the door, probably to forage for breakfast. I sat down and swung my legs over the edge of the table to hop down. Toby stepped in front of me and looked in my eyes.

"Are you okay, seriously? That guy, Martin, he's messed up."

I smiled at him. "Yes, I am and he is. He's spread a lot of hatred and fear in his day in the name of training young artists to overcome adversity in order to create.

"But you were right, you know, God sent you to protect me

and I did what he asked. I humbled myself and I asked for forgiveness. I can't control Martin's lack of cooperation, but I can work on getting the stain he's left on my heart out. But, you don't mind coming, do you? I sort of volunteered you without asking."

He kissed me on the tip of the nose. "No worries. I'll be here every time you talk to him."

I playfully ran a hand over his newly shorn hair and he grabbed me around the waist and helped me hop off the table top. My knight in shining armor. He was always around when things got topsy-turvy.

"Your new haircut tickles me pink." I suddenly felt shy and looked down at the floor as I decided to be fully honest like Jackie suggested. "I have to say I don't miss those black frame glasses either."

"I wasn't sure you'd noticed! You didn't say anything when you picked me up the other day to go to the Sulferson House. But a little bird told me this was better."

"That Jackie! Are you sure you're okay with it?" I looked up at his grinning face and he nodded affirmative and held out a hand full of Smarties candies. I squealed with delight.

"You haven't given me Smarties since we've been back from London! Oh, I love having you back, Toby. I feel like you've been missing, but I didn't want to say anything and hurt your feelings."

"It's okay, Clare. Sometimes I don't feel like myself frankly.

I've been trying to figure out the new me. Whoever it is Christ intended me to be. I'm cleaning up my language, my thought life, and my habits. It's not easy. I guess I got carried away. I was glad when Jackie mentioned it. I've missed handing out Smarties too. They are a great ice breaker. Everyone our age remembers them from the quarter shelf at drug stores when they were kids. It's been hard making new friends without them."

I nodded as a slid a roll into my mouth. "I understand," I said. "But I'm so glad to see your face again. I have a feeling things are heating up around here faster than I can cool them down and I'm going to need these Smarties to help me out."

He laughed. "A cheeky bird in England told me once that they don't make you any smarter. Sorry."

❧ Chapter Fourteen

I hadn't been able to return to the underground lab with my barrage of security and police. I wasn't sure if they even still wanted my help after all the accusations that had been flying around. Once Martin had started the ball rolling with his plagiarism claims, campus gossip had me forging the Mona Lisa for the president and selling a faux Hope diamond on the home shopping network. It was as annoying as it was amusing. Wholesome had gone rogue and it was flipping everyone on an ear.

With my security detail over and my drawings done for my next meeting with Martin, I decided to visit the secret lab and find out what progress had been made on the stolen digital artwork. If I got involved, I was going to negotiate for lab time for Toby too. He was stuck working on his senior exhibition pieces in the middle of the night when the small campus lab was available. Despite his valiant attempts to hide it, I could tell he was getting as sapped as a marathon runner with no water.

"Hello. Hello?"

I stood outside the supply closet in the gleaming white hallway with its circa 1980 waxed school smell. I surveyed the white scuffed walls and then tipped my face up toward the pinhole camera that made one of the spots in the pattern in the white tile ceiling.

"Hi? Hey. I'm out here. I was invited to come back. I just couldn't. Hello? Anybody?"

The janitor's closet door flipped open and Jay grabbed my arm and hauled me in after him as the door closed again behind us.

"What are you doing, dude? You're going to get us all killed."

"Killed? Isn't that a bit of a strong word for computer geek retaliation?"

He grimaced. "I guess. It's just heavy here, that's all. Heavy."

"Well, I might have expected that from Kay, but you? No way."

"Look, when you come back again, IF you come back again, come right into the closet and flip this light switch here behind the TP, okay?" The back wall slid silently open and we walked through.

"From here everything is motion activated and security has

already checked to see if you're on the list, so as long as you are, doors will keep opening." He flipped on a flashlight and I saw it reflect a tiny dot on the wall by the floor every once in a while.

"Are those dots significant for us or the theater department?" I asked.

"Oh, sorry. You follow it to find the right way to grandma's living room. That's what they call it. It doesn't look anything like my grandmother's living room, though."

I smiled in the dark. What did his grandmother's living room look like?

"I wish I was there right now."

"Where?" I wasn't sure what he meant.

"Oh, *my* grandmother's living room." He had stopped in the hallway, inches from the mustard woven carpet spread out on the living room floor in front of us. He hesitated.

"You don't have to do this. You can go back up and I'll tell them you changed your mind. You can be a normal senior. It's okay, Clare. You've been through so much. You don't have to change the world."

I looked at his distorted features in the up lighting from the flashlight he held. I was in the bowels of the earth with a guide, who had a double, trying to figure out if I could help a company recover the proof they had created the closest thing I'd ever seen to real dinosaurs and talking toys. It was amazing stuff. But not as amazing as what I had to tell him first.

"Jay, before I press you for a better explanation then that for why I shouldn't step onto the spinning carpet and enter a fabulous computer art lab, I have to refute the spirit of your comment. I *do* have to change the world. And while I understand that this technology they are designing will affect the world as we know it, I know that in the long run, the very long run, it doesn't matter. I have been commissioned by Christ already to change the world. To change eternity. You see, all of this doesn't matter when we die. Knowing that you have a Savior that forgives you, loves you, and protects you, knowing you will spend eternity with him and those who have accepted him -- now that -- that is my world changing goal. Everything else that doesn't line up just doesn't matter. Do you see?"

He clicked the flashlight off and stepped onto the carpet. "I agree with you, Clare, so hop on and let's see if we can't help them with this technology that could be used to make Christian films and documentaries too. Kay and I were raised as Christians. Although our emphasis in college has been career driven, I want to marry Kara and have a family that takes the Bible seriously.

"It's just been heavy around here, though. All of it is weighing me down lately. And Kay has never actually accepted Jesus as his Savior. He thinks he is already a good person and he's saved because his family is." He hung his head and I jumped onto the carpet him as the room began to spin.

I was surprised by his personal revelations. We had been acquaintances all these years and I'd never heard him talk about his faith. Well, no sense going to the edge and not jumping in. I smiled. "You guys need to come to Monday Meals at the church on the northeast corner of campus. And bring Kara and see if you can keep Paul or Key coming if you run into either of them on the way. It's at six."

He nodded as the room stopped spinning and we stepped off the rubber ducky yellow carpet into the lab.

I guess I was expecting stuffy suit types with old green money and big body guards to explain my mission and then pressure me for a solution in a conference room that smelled of coffee and nuts while people cleared their throats in the background.

Instead, I followed Jay into an arcade and was introduced to a boy, who didn't look a hair past eleven and a dog, who responded to the funny name Gigabit. I was handed a bowl of ice cream and M&M's with whip cream and chocolate sauce dripping over the sides. I looked at Jay in confusion.

"That's right, doll face, it's me." The boy looked up from devouring his ice cream to talk with his mouth full. "You're not on Candid Camera. It's not my dad or my big brother walking out in a minute to laugh at you. I, Zach Sulferson, built this lab and plan to launch the best computer animated art anyone has ever seen in one hundred and eighty days, give or take, at the Sarasota Film festival in

Florida. Once we've blown their minds out their ear holes down South, we're on to Hollywood with a take no prisoners rally. There won't be any price too high for us to render anything they can dream up!" He took an extremely big spoonful of ice cream and aimed it at his fully open mouth.

"Excuse me, did you say Zach *Sulferson*?" I asked. "And I thought it was missing. This movie that you're going to launch. I mean I know you have five minutes recreated. I saw it last week. But you can't possibly recreate enough in time and how are you going to prove it's yours when the thieves show it and claim it's theirs? And why don't you have a backup? I'm just learning about all this stuff, but I know they always tell us to back up our stuff. And any chance I can get a friend some time to work in your lab?"

The ice cream never made it to his mouth.

"Let's see." He waved his spoon to punctuate each of his answers, sending ice cream flying in all directions.

"Yes, I did say my name is Zach *Sulferson*.

"The thieves are not going to show up with it because you're going to find it for me first.

"It wasn't backed up which is the reason why you are now told to back up everything.

"And no, your friend, Toby, can't come to my lab."

I held up my hand. "But I thought Curtis Sulferson didn't have any children."

"He didn't, Genius. His half-brother did. Curtis is half my great uncle."

"He didn't mention you. Is that one of those royal dog and all that malarkey? You didn't get me here to paint his portrait, did you?" I looked pointedly at his pug rooting around the leg of the table he was sitting at.

He laughed. The trill of his high pitched mirth reminded you, despite his rude wording and confident mannerisms, that he was still a young boy.

"Not that it's any of your business, but you're a quick study and it might play into all this somehow, so take notes." He paused dramatically. I looked around, but there was nothing to write on.

Jay grinned. "He says that all the time when something important is coming, but I don't think he wants you to actually take notes. You'll get used to it."

Zach acted as if he hadn't heard Jay as he wiped his mouth on a napkin and slid his empty bowl down to the other end of the table where it was quickly retrieved by a silent assistant. He cleared his throat.

"Gigabit is as illegitimate as my grandfather. So none of us have to sit for portraits." He squealed again at my surprised face and slapped the table with humor. "A couple of years ago, a dog walker didn't do her job and the reigning pug had mixed puppies. I found Gigabit in a sack floating down river from the big house. Mom let me keep him. The next litter the reigning dog had were priceless full breeds and that's where Reginald came from.

Just like her dog, Mrs. Sulferson, Curtis's mother, had an affair and my grandfather was the result. She wanted him to have the Sulferson name since his real father had disappeared by the time he was born. She must have known where her husband buried the bodies, so to speak, because blatant as daylights, she hired a family from the factory in this town to raise him and gave him the name Humphrey Sulferson without much fuss, only a lot of whispering.

That is until the money came into play. The way my grandpa told it before he passed this last March was that she wanted him to inherit like any of them would before it all went to the dogs." He smirked. "That still cracks me up. What a bunch of losers! People matter. Kids matter. Pets do matter, but not over people. I'm a kid and even I know that." He scoffed.

"Anyway, the rich fools all went around and around over it. The sisters, Curtis, the whole lot. Until the explosion. After that, Old Man Sulferson and Curtis didn't have much fight in them. They left us be with their name since my dad was born and wearing it by then. And they both agreed to honor Mrs. Sulferson's will to give us her Trust fund, but no Sulferson money, or headaches, really. Anyway, dear old Uncle Curtis doesn't want to even think about my existence anymore. Or my mangy dog, either." He wiggled with delight as he tossed Gigabit a cherry he had saved from the top of his sundae.

I shifted uncomfortably from one foot to another. "Okay, weird to know. Thanks for answering my questions."

To myself I thought, *which just lead to more questions. Like do your parents know you're not in school right now? And what happened to the man that Mrs. Sulferson had an affair with?*

I clasped my hands in front of me, trying not to be distracted. "So, let's get to it. Can you please explain what I'm physically looking for? I'm having a hard time wrapping my mind around this art form and what it tangibly looks like. How were all those movie files taken out of the computer boxes without trucks and a team?"

"Computer boxes? Trucks? *This* is your ace detective?" Zack jerked a thumb at me. "I mean she's cute and all, don't get me wrong, but come on, guys? What am I paying you for?"

"Hey, Zack, give her a chance. We've tried everything else. Nothing but dead ends. She's new to this stuff, that's all. But she's a quick learner, and she's an artist so she can appreciate what we're telling her about, and she was dab smack in the middle of all that stuff in London." Jay was nervous.

Zack slid around the edge of the table and I realized he was in a wheel chair.

"Yeah," He saw the surprise I was yet again unable to mask. "That's right. Take notes. Playing at the factory while my dad and mom were working there. Couldn't afford daycare or to leave this town while they were holding up our Trust fund in probate. A bin of corn fell on my legs. Never walk again. If they'd at least cut them off I could have had some of those prosthetics they're coming out with now. Great stuff. Can probably make them out of corn if Uncle Curtis gets his way. Everything will be corn based by the time he's done. But, alas, I get a chair. A chair with wheels, probably made out of corn. Thanks Uncle Curtis. Yippee."

He paused in his sarcastic tirade and blinked hard, then the emotion was gone.

"The accident finally released great grandma's money from the Sulferson grip like they'd promised. They'd held onto us as long as they could. But once the paperwork was done, my dad and mom quit and we haven't been back to that God forsaken factory since. Dad invested smart and now this boy genius has money to play with." He smiled and leaned over to scratch the dog's ears.

But you really didn't move away. You built a lab in Sulferson Springs. Should I ask him about it? I hesitated. *Did I have the job or what?*

"I do like her honest face. We can tell exactly what she's up to. What do you think, Gigabit?" He threw a treat at me and instantly I was Gigabit's new target. I automatically caught it and held it over my head.

"Sit, Gigabit," I said.

The dog sat abruptly. I bent forward and placed the treat on his nose holding his muzzle gently for a moment before slowly standing up. He didn't move a muscle, but his eyes were alert and followed my every move.

"Take it," I commanded and moved my hand in a downward motion. He flipped the tiny dog bone shape into the air over his head and snapped it gracefully out of the sky. Wagging his tail, he retreated to his master's side.

"Impressive. So you know your way around dogs." Zack swung the wheel chair around and motioned us to follow. I looked at Jay but he shrugged before falling into step with the spin of the chair.

When we got to Zack's office, he motioned me to come around and watch over his shoulder. "Be sure you take notes on this part. This is called the monitor." Zack pointed at a computer screen that looked like a television.

"I know that much," I said, trying not to sound exasperated.

He ignored me. "These have names too -- the keyboard, the mouse. Here is the tower, the brains of the whole thing." He placed a hand on the box that the monitor was connected to with a pile of wreathing cords. "Now most systems are able to have data copied onto floppies like this that save an identical backup version of your file." He waved a five inch thin piece of plastic at me as he continued.

"Data is all the numbers and symbols that the computer reads to tell it what to do. In our case, it strings together images to create our computer animated movie. Now the movie files are way too big to fit into just one of these suitcases. In order to work with this much data and store it efficiently, we developed a new form of storage. Hold up your hand." He waited. I looked at Jay and slowly raised my hand in front of my face. "Now look at your pinky. Turn your hand so you can see your nail." He paused again. He was a dramatic little kid. Must have watched a ton of cloak and dagger movies growing up in that chair.

"A laser can now write the data for an entire movie onto a chip the size of your little finger nail." He swung his chair around and looked up into our intense faces. "We were in the testing phase of this method and had only made the first copy when the data chip was stolen and our main file on the computer was erased."

"I'm clearly still learning, but can't some of those erased files be recovered? What happened?" I asked. Jay nodded.

"Usually. Unless they are erased with acid."

He shook his head at our expressions. "Whoever did this knew what they were doing. They wanted to destroy all possibility of our recovering those files or placing a claim of ownership on them."

"Don't you have a copy write or something on them?"

"No, no, see it's all top secret. We couldn't get official documentation without leaking the fact that what we were doing really exists. Even the chip the file was saved on hasn't been invented yet, so to speak. And corporate espionage is running rampant among the community right now. We couldn't, and still can't, trust anyone.

"We had used the chip for the very first time to make the first tangible copy you could hold in your hand the same night the lab was breached. We hadn't even had time to mail ourselves a copy or any of those other old school tricks." He looked tiny and his pale little face was sad as he turned his wheel chair away from us.

My heart was heavy for him. *What a load to bear to be successful for your family. He's just a kid, after all.*

"I want my movie back. Someone who worked with us did this. They think because I'm a kid they can get away with it. Well, we'll see about the bully taking *my* lunch money. I want them found and found quietly. I personally want to punish this traitor. So no authorities, okay? Find him or her and report back to me. I will make them pay and pay dearly."

Or is he just a kid?

❋ Chapter Fifteen

    I had known as soon as the woman entered the underground, piloting her three small children along in her flowing skirts, that she was begging. I had never seen vagrants in person until I'd gone to London. The streets and plat forms were spic and span of trash, but not of forgotten people.

    After she had come inside the train car doors, she had walked up and down the aisle so that we could all read the cardboard sign she carried. In neat block letters it said: *I don't speak English so I can't get a job. My husband was recently killed in our home country and we can't go back or they will kill us too. We are hungry. Please help me with your spare change.*

She had the most adorable children. Two girls and a little boy. They were dirty, but dressed in what was once well made foreign looking clothing in expensive material. No one on the train said anything to her one way or the other. Some people averted their eyes and others tossed a few pence into the oldest girl's cup.

I already had spent all the pounds I had in my pocket at the grocery store and then I had bartered with the baker for a loaf of bread in exchange for a sketch of his wife on a napkin. I rummaged through my sacks until I found a box of biscuits, or cookies as we would called them in the States. I had smiled at the little boy. He was watching what I had been doing while his mother faced the other way monitoring the new passengers entering the car. I'll never forget how he clasped his thin, little hands in front of him and smiled. His long lashes brushed his cheeks as he looked down shyly. The doors closed and the car lurched to a start. I opened the box and offered him a cookie. He took it timidly and stuffed it hungrily in his mouth. It was gone in a second. The scene had enchanted the passengers around us. Their "ahhh" noises drew his mother's attention as I handed him the box of cookies.

"Can't you read the sign? I need money." She had screamed at me as she slapped the box of cookies out of the boy's hands. The entire car had gasped. She froze at her terrible mistake.

"I'm a student. I don't have any money to spare. I drew a

sketch for my loaf of bread today. The sign says you are hungry. I was sharing what I had." I had sputtered.

"Not only that, Love, her sign says she can't speak English." A burly woman next to me said indignantly shifting in her seat.

There was an angry mutter through the car as the news of what had happened made its way to those who hadn't been looking.

"There's a constable always at the next station," someone else said. "I think you should turn those children over to someone who can feed them proper like, madam."

"Or find their real parents." Someone else shouted angrily.

The beggar had tossed her sign on a seat, and as the subway came to a grinding halt, she forced her way out the door. The children followed her silently but not before an old man scooped up the box of cookies and nestled it under the boy's arm. Then the new passengers coming on the train had blocked them from my view. I could hear yells and a bobby's whistle, though, over the noises of the people and the rumble of trains. Out the side window the crowd on the platform had parted for a moment and I saw the boy toss the box of cookies into a rubbish bin and grinning, pull a thick wallet from his sleeve.

"By golly, I can't find my wallet. Do any of you good people see it under the seats? I must have dropped it in all that excitement and it has probably been kicked. Or maybe I've forgotten it at the shop." The old man who had handed the boy the cookies was in a panic, padding his body down as he spoke.

I knelt in the quiet church letting the memories wash over me. I remembered being extremely exhausted on the train that day.

Since I had been cooped up in my flat in London with a broken leg and arm, I'd taken to spending long afternoons praying. Now that I was back home, I still found it the best way to get things done. I always prayed for that boy and those girls and the woman with them. I also lifted up the old man whose wallet had been stolen. I shook my head at the prayer list I had spread out in front of me. Names like Zach Sulferson and Wendy Gallonte were new additions.

Almost a year later, I was reminded of that exact same helpless exhaustion. Zach Sulferson was a sad little scene in his wheel chair with his long dark eye lashes brushing his ashen cheeks. But he was some kind of genius and he was probably some kind of bitter, mean little kid too. I didn't know what was in his heart. How could I?

God help me do the right things. I prayed under my breath.

Everyone was looking to me to solve their problems. Sammy wanted a painting done to save her bacon. Zack and Jay wanted me to find the missing movie and make them rich heroes for a day. And even I wanted to find who took Reginald for Mr. Sulferson and divert the rumblings in town over the factory strike. I brushed the wet patches off my cheeks from tears I had shed at the memory of the tiny boy thief.

The church where I'd come to think and pray was empty. It smelled like quiet, which to me was a scent made from the combination of grandma's purse mints, lingering perfumes, and old book ink. I came here in the semi-dark whenever I needed to hear God through the noise pollution around me. I had found he often spoke in the lingering atmosphere of past prayers and yesterday's worship.

Okay, God, help me figure this puzzle out. As you know, to sabotage the success of their owners, two important Sulferson possessions have been stolen around the same time. Was it a coincidence? After all Zach wasn't technically a Sulferson. But some people would say there is no such thing as coincidence. What connected them, other than their tenuous family ties? Hmmm. People that were involved in both situations.

Let's start with Wendy. She was with Reginald when he was abducted. She claims she was knocked out before she saw anything. Her father is an old friend of Curtis. She seems to be everywhere at once, and is clearly a spy so she can dress like me. She works in our computer lab and hangs out with Jay and Kay. She gives everyone a different story. She lives in my house. Could she have vandalized my paintings? If so, that would connect her to Martin. And Martin is art faculty so he knows about the secret lab.

Of course, they both know me and I'm painting the dog and I've been to the secret lab. Judging by association I'm more likely the thief then either of them. God, I'm not proving to be much of a sleuth. A little help here.

The wail of sirens insisted on my attention as a herd of lumbering fire trucks screamed past the old church. I pushed off the floor by the altar as they vibrated the air inside the sanctuary. Running out the front door and jumping down the stone steps, I was in time to see the trucks tear into the campus parking lot of the fine art center. A few small black billows of smoke puffed into the air over the buildings blocking the center from my view.

I stuffed my list into a pocket and ran until a sharp pain split my side. Heaving for breath, I limped on past the last two structures blocking my view. And then I stopped dead in my tracks.

There was a mound of paintings on fire in the strip of lawn in front of the art building. A large sign posted next to it read, CLARE JAMES SAYS DOWN WITH MARTIN'S TYRANNY!

I turned and ran on the sidewalk back the way I had come. Away from the police cars blocking off the crowd of rubber-neckers. Away from the fire trucks drowning the pile of canvases. Away from the news truck pulling into the parking lot and spitting out crew like ants out of a hole next to corn bread.

This could NOT be happening. When I got inside our house, I swung the SPAM can door closed behind me and stood panting with my back pressed against it.

"Where's the fire?" Jackie yawned and stretched like a lazy

cat reading biology books.

"At the art center," I croaked out.

"No, Clare, I think she meant it like the expression you say when someone is in a hurry. It comes from being in a hurry to help put out a fire, but not literally anymore." Toby sat up off the floor from behind a bean bag and rubbed his head. "I must have fallen asleep while I was waiting for you to get back. Whew, late nights."

Jackie giggled. "You were snoring too."

I couldn't believe how nonchalant they were. "You guys, I know it's an expression. But there really is one. A fire. At the art center. With a sign that says something about Clare James is against Martin's tyranny. Huge stack of paintings burning. Fire trucks, police, news crews. First I wanted to see what was going on. Then I saw my name and I ran." I was out of breath. I slide my back down the door and sagged into a squat on my heels, deflated like a balloon.

"What? You're kidding," Jackie pushed her stack of books aside to look at me and Toby stood, frowning.

"No, I was at the church. I heard the trucks and I went to see what was going on. Oh my!" I gasped in a breathless wheeze as a flat brown face nosed out of our bathroom door and stood looking at me. "What in the world? Reginald! You found Reginald!"

"Oh, no, no, that's Rembrandt." Toby laughed and scooped the little pug off the floor and presented him to me with locked elbows.

All my weight was against the SPAM door as I tipped my head

back from where I was squatting and looked up at him.

"It's okay, Clare. This is Rembrandt. I adopted him from the shelter today for you to use in place of Reginald. I've been wanting to get one and I can keep a dog at the fraternity house. They've had an opening and I was next on the list for a room so I'm moving and I got him to celebrate!" Toby dropped the dog on my knees and sank onto the bed next to Jackie. They smiled at each other knowingly. I looked back down at the dog.

What on earth had made him think this was a good idea? And a frat house? What happened to surrounding yourself with like-minded friends? Is Jackie in favor of all this? The thoughts tumbling through my mind came to abrupt halt. At this vantage point I could see straight under my desk.

Is my carved box of notes from London missing? I glanced around the room. My closet door was a jar and I could see a lot of my clothes on the floor.

Has someone been searching my stuff? The same person who searched through Paul's paint cart? I sniffed the air, but I didn't smell any sour cut grass odor.

The dog growled and snipped at my fingers. His sharp little pinch made me yell as he half squirmed and I half tossed him from my lap the few inches to the floor. As he walked snootily back to Toby, I saw the dark brown fish shape on the inside of his back hind leg.

"That's Reginald, Toby. He's goldfish marked!" I jumped up excitedly from the floor forgetting my suspicions.

Toby scooped the dog up to the bed where he nestled onto Jackie's open book and turned to bark at me. They both laughed.

I was indignant. "Right there! There's no doubt in my mind that's Reginald. He doesn't like me, even though all cows, rabbits, cats, and other dogs I've *ever* met love me."

"No, Clare, he's a stray from the pound. They have papers documenting he's been there long enough to be in line to be euthanized, way before Reginald went missing." Jackie caressed the dog's ears and he quieted down.

"That's another reason I got him." Toby chimed in. "Seriously, though, Clare, not all animals on earth are going to like you. We're going to have to change your nickname from Wholesome to Noah, if you stick with that attitude." He extended a hand with a roll of round chalky candies laying across his palm. "Smartie?"

I shook my head. Something wasn't right here. I glanced down at the shadows under my desk. No, the note box was definitely missing. *One thing at a time*, I decided. I moved over to the dog and pulled his back leg out to see the birth mark. He nipped at me again, but I was quicker and his teeth snapped loudly on air. Jackie drew him up into her arms from her study book. "Clare! No wonder he doesn't like you. What are you looking for?"

"His real name is The Honorable Goldfish Marked Reginald

Winnyfeld Kampindiner Clarance Pepper the Third." I was madly digging through my stack of sketches on my desk. "Ah ha! Here it is! His goldfish mark. I sketched it for a reference. See, it's the same as what's on this dog's back leg! It's so unusual it's in his name, for crying out loud. Something is bogus. I'm calling the police."

"Don't be silly, Clare." Jackie nuzzled the dog in her arms. "Who do you think was running the adoptions today? The police were all over it helping dogs find homes. They would have noticed if a dog matched an APB or whatever it's called. Lots of dogs have stray spots on them."

"Not good, not good at all." I muttered as I swung the SPAM door open and stomped down the hall. Simone was studying to be a vet. She should know if there's a way to tell by dog DNA or something that we had found Reginald. And everyone in town was affected by the strike, so would police be helpful in this situation? A dirty cop wouldn't. Surely they all understood Mr. Sulferson needed the dog to complete the portrait to get the cash to meet the Union's demands to stop the scab riots. Adopting his dog out would be counterproductive to their relatives who worked at Sulferson's and was not what they were supposed to be doing as cops.

I didn't know why he was dumped at the pound with false papers, but I knew that was Reginald.

I pounded harder on Simone's door.

Glancing over my shoulder, I saw the front door pop open

and a flood of blue uniforms ringed the foyer. Rupert, Simone's boyfriend, stepped forward out of the blue swarm. *Ah, just who I need to check that dog out. Oh, and report my missing box. I know someone has been searching my room.* But before I could speak, Rupert's words chased every thought out of my head.

"Uh, Clare," He rested one hand on his hip and the other on his gun. The other men with him did the same. "Can you please come with me down to the station? We have some questions we'd like to ask you. You were seen fleeing from the scene of an arson today."

❦ Chapter Sixteen

"You can scan for the chip under their skin and it gives you basic information or the link to the information on a Veterinary database to locate where lost pets live. I would expect Sulferson to have that valuable of a dog chipped." Simone was eating an apple and swinging her feet off my desk.

"We can scan this dog and see if he has a chip. Just have Toby bring him over to the clinic when I'm in. I work with the scanner all the time. I've even been implanting some chips lately on my own." Her swinging slowed as she looked at me again. "In fact, a week or so ago a guy even stopped me in the parking lot and asked me to chip his pug."

She frowned at my sketch of Reginald's mark. "I wouldn't think they'd all have fish shaped marks on their back legs." She chewed on a bite of apple thoughtfully.

"What happened? Did you chip a dog with this mark?"

"Well, the guy had missed the free chipping event the clinic was offering. We were closed and I was heading to my car. He said he was just running late and he even had his own chip." She ducked her head. "I wasn't going to mention it to anyone because he offered me a thousand bucks to do it and I took it." She rolled her eyes and held out a hand in a defensive motion, even though neither Jackie nor I had responded. "I know, I know, I should have made him come back and had the vet do it. I should have at least refused the money, but times are hard and that kind of cash doesn't grow on trees. And I'd just been chipping all day under supervision. What could it hurt?"

"That's the real question. What could it hurt? Why offer you that much money for a chipping off the books? He could have come back and had it done for twenty bucks even without the free event, right?" Jackie tilted her head thoughtfully.

"Yah. He said he was leaving town the next day and he didn't want to have his dog at a kennel without a chip in case something happened. He was running late with all the travel arrangements and missed the chip event. It made sense at the time." Simone took another big bite of her apple with a sharp snapping noise. "And he didn't look like a shady character." She said with her mouth full. "He looked like that guy, Toby. You know, clean cut blonde, well-built. He was more glamorous, though, with a gold necklace, expensive sun glasses, and he was wearing a ball cap. And the dog had a fish spot like your sketch."

"But if it was Reginald, why was he being chipped at all? Like you said, he probably already had one." I picked up the receiver on the plastic cream phone standard to all the dorm rooms and punched the keys for Muriel's line at the Sulferson Mansion.

"Hello, Sulferson Hou – ah, ah, achoo! Oh, so sorry." Sniffle, sniffle. "Sulferson House, how may I help you?"

"Muriel? It's Clare. Is Reginald chipped?"

"Oh, Clare. So glad it's you. Sorry to blow your ear off! Oh, I'm trying to catch my breath. Chipped? Reginald? What's that?"

"You know, so when someone finds him, they know where to return him. A little piece like a chip is imbedded under his skin so the vet can scan it."

"I didn't know they even had such things. Well. Okay then. If it's cutting edge, then I'm sure Mr. Sulferson had it done, but I'm not privy to all those decisions. Sorry, have to go. Achhooo! Good-bye." The phone clicked in my ear. *That was a little odd. She only seemed to sneeze like that when she was near the —* my thoughts were interrupted by the anticipation in the room.

"Well?" Jackie bounced on her bed, sending a cascade of

books off on to the floor.

I frowned. "She didn't know, but someone else might be able to confirm it." I swung the SPAM door wide and marched across the hall to knock on Wendy's door. It cracked opened immediately and an eye stared at me.

"Ah, Hi, Wendy. I have a question for you."

The door opened to six inches, revealing enough of a slice of Wendy's body to verify she was wearing the same ripped jeans, Jesus' cruisers and shirt with an empty frame and words, "Baroque = Out of Monet" that I was.

"Weren't you taken out of here by a whole police force a few hours ago? Arson now. My, my, Clare, what next?" She asked with a smirk.

"Yeah, I'm fine, thanks for asking. Just highly irritated. I was NOT fleeing the scene of an arson. I was the VICTIM of an arsonist." I crossed my arms definitely. I had been so steamed, I hadn't even bothered to mention to Rupert that I'd probably found Reginald and someone had robbed me.

Who needed a bunch of bozos who thought I was the bad guy? I planned to figure this out and return him to Sulferson myself. As for my room being searched, I decided if I found the dognapper, I'd likely find the thief and maybe even the arsonist. He had to have been looking for my sketches to destroy any proof of the dog's identity. He must have been interrupted before he got through the piles on my desk and found the drawings I'd done of Reggie.

Jackie laughed from across the hall and called out to Wendy. "I'm sorry, Wendy, but that is rather comical. Clare, an arsonist? Seriously, Clare, do they have any real suspects? Obviously someone used your name on purpose."

"Look, I don't have all day. What was your question?" Wendy cut in.

"I have a question for both of you." Simone lounged out of our room and tossed her apple core in the trash can by the foyer's couch. "What's up with that shirt?"

I looked at Wendy, curious about her explanation for mimicking me. But she was not in a giving mood. "Look, I'm answering one question, so is it this the one? Or will it be yours?" She pointed at me.

I sighed. "We're trying to help find Reginald. Do you know if he was chipped?"

She looked sad. "I don't know. Sorry. I got the job when school started and I didn't have to do Vet visits or anything. I exercised him and helped with grooming stuff. I didn't even feed him." She clicked the door shut in my face.

I had my answer, but her behavior was not conducive to making friends. Was she really agoraphobic and it was torture for her to be social? I was trying to give her the benefit of the doubt, but it was getting harder by the minute.

I turned to Simone. "I don't know why she dresses like me."

"Oh, that," Simone laughed. "I thought you art guys had a dress code or something, like Greek rush. I assumed the shirt had your group name on it. I just couldn't figure it out. Barbecue equals out of Moe Net?"

I had to laugh at that. "No, No, No, Simone. There's no art major rush, she's just creepy. I got this shirt at a museum in Chicago. How'd she get the same shirt?" I shivered and Simone frowned. "Anyway, it's not Barbecue, it's pronounced Burr-Oak. Sounds like Broke. Baroque is a period in art history characterized by artwork for the masses, not just the wealthy. The last word is the name of a famous artist, Claude Monet, pronounced 'moan' with a long 'a'. It kind of sounds like Money with an accent. He was the father of Impressionism, an art movement that made things blurry and bright colored. So it's an art joke. A play on words. Broke equals out of Money."

"Awkwardddd." Simone drew the word out like she wasn't convinced this was a joke. I smiled. "We'll get Toby to bring Rembrandt by the clinic tomorrow when you're in. I'm positive it's Reginald."

"Okay. We'll know for sure once he's scanned." Simone rushed out the last words before she swung the front door open and threw her arms around a startled Rupert on the front steps.

"How'd you know I was here?" He sputtered.

She laughed. "I saw you out the window coming up the walk. We were in the hall already, Detective." Despite his dark skin, we could see he was blushing. It made him even more hunky.

"Hey, Clare," He turned to me after giving Simone a quick peck on the cheek. "I'm sorry about everything. We had to come with back up in case something had happened to you. It's protocol for anything involving anyone with special security clearance. I hated they were doing that, so I volunteered to drive you in. I know I already apologized, but I agree with you it was a lot of unnecessary force that created more attention. I know the rumors on campus are flying."

"Thanks, Rupert. You were just doing your job. And you didn't bring helicopters and swat, so there's that. But did they find out any more about it?" I asked.

"You mean no one from the department has called you?" He looked surprised.

"No," I frowned.

"Yeah, they apprehended a couple of campus potheads. That sign, an envelope of cash, and instructions printed from a computer were left at their door. It was probably there for several days because they had been on a bender and hadn't been to class for a week. There were no finger prints or any other usable evidence other then the note. The forensic lab is trying to track down if the printer used was from a lab on campus."

"Yeah, but hundreds of students use the printers on campus. How is that going to help?"

"Well, it narrows it to faculty, staff, or students first. Then from there, we can use the time code printed at the bottom of every page that comes out of the printer to determine who was logged on to computers feeding to that printer at that time."

"So, it's only a matter of time until someone's goose is cooked?" I finished for him.

He smiled. "Yes, and it's likely the same person responsible for the vandalism of your work."

"It will be great to stop whoever is harassing you before someone gets hurt. These things tend to escalate." Simone said it knowingly like she was in a late night police drama.

I grinned. "What about the dog, Rupert? Mr. Sulferson's missing pug? Any news on that front?"

"I can't talk about an ongoing investigat –"

"We don't want to keep you guys any longer then we already have!" Jackie leaned out the door, interrupting Rupert in midsentence.

"What she means is, we've found the dog." I leaned away from her attempt to pull me into the room.

"What?!" Rupert was startled.

"No, no, no," Simone butted in. "Clare's boyfriend or whatever he is, got her a dog and it looks like the missing pug. He thought it would help her finish that silly painting she's working on for Sulferson. Anyway, it came from an adoption drive and all those are police sponsored, you know?"

"Yeah, I was there when he got it. She's just being Clare. Flare for the dramatic." Jackie quickly added.

They all laughed and Simone shot me a stern look behind his back. They were up to something and even Wendy knew it. I saw the sliver that had reopened in her door disappear again with a click.

"Fine. So you can't tell me anything more, Rupert. It means I'm going to have to use Toby's stand in if Reginald isn't found. I've got to finish his portrait." I assumed Simone didn't want it coming out she had chipped a pug without supervision for money. Even if Rupert was her boyfriend, he was still a cop.

Rupert looked harassed. "Honestly, Clare, there is nothing to tell. After the first demand for ransom, the proof of life never came, so we had to assume the dognappers were bogus."

"Man-o-days! There was a ransom note? And none of us involved were told about it? They could have accidently killed the dog or the dog could have gotten away from them. There's a million reasons why proof of life never came. They should be found ASAP!" It was my turn to be surprised.

"Trust me, it's all being investigated and I've said way too much. Simone, shall we?" Rupert offered his arm to Simone, who giggled and rested her fingers lightly on it. With exaggerated pomp, they strolled down the hall to her room and disappeared inside.

I followed on Jackie's heals into our room and swung the SPAM door shut. "Rembrandt is Reginald, isn't he?" I could hardly get the words out of my throat fast enough.

"Look, I don't know who he is." Jackie said. "Getting him scanned tomorrow should go a long way in telling us. But I do know you need to cool it until we can find out what is going on. Toby didn't get that pug from the adoption clinic, okay?" She looked scared and her voice dropped to a whisper.

"You weren't home the other day when he came by. So he asked me if I wanted to go for a ride with him to get some country air. He wanted some company. He was supposed to pick up a dossier from one of his dad's clients who lives out there in the boondocks. I agreed before I knew what I was getting into. I mean, I like Toby. So if you're not going to date him, then set him free, alright, already." She held up a hand to fend off the onslaught of words that were about to explode out of my lips. I swallowed hard and gestured for her to continue.

"Maybe forget I said that, okay? Anyway, we left the city and drove forever. And then the client, or whatever he was, brings out this dog and he's a pug, like Reginald in your sketches. We just looked at each other and I nodded at him slightly to go along. I mean I'm scared 'cause this guy looks like he could kill us with his bare hands. So Toby acted all normal and took the dog.

"After we got out of there we agreed to tell no one, not even you, until he could get to the bottom of it. It was horrible lying to you when you were so flipping sure it was Reggie!" She giggled nervously. "But seriously, Clare, we were trying to protect you from being drug into it. The FBI would probably arrest *you* for stealing the dog."

✽ Chapter Seventeen

I couldn't sleep. Tomorrow, after our breakfast devotional, during which Toby had a lot of explaining to do, we were going to scan Rembrandt's body to see if he had a chip or two under his skin. And on top of that, I was meeting with Martin again.

I rolled out of bed and slipped my tennis shoes on by the moon light spilling into our room. The SPAM door slid silently open on its well-balanced hinges and I tiptoed down the hall in sweat pants and a t-shirt. I felt like a night run. I had to get my body too tired to listen to my mind's endless chatter.

I slipped out the front door of our house and avoided the

creaky porch board just before the steps. Pausing to look around me, I was amazed at the scene. Everything was starkly contrasted in black from the white blaze emitting out of the night sky. A full moon. The absence of color reminded me of an artist's work I'd seen recently, but I couldn't place the name. My crazy thoughts started bombarding me again and I forgot about the view and started down the sidewalk.

Why didn't Toby come clean about the dog? He said he wanted to be more then friends, didn't he? How could he trust Jackie more than me if that's what he really wanted? Why take anyone at all with him if it was such a big secret? And who was this guy with the dog? Was he really a client of Toby's dad? Maybe it's not so good for him to get into the underground lab after all. What was the connection? How does it all fit? Do I really know Toby that well at all?

My steps gained momentum as the questions continued to plague me. I could out run them! I sprinted further and further away from my own thoughts. Down sidewalks, up sidewalks. Passed the church, passed the dorms full of sleeping students, passed the dark cafeteria, passed the dark student center, passed the dark great hall where classes were held. Passed the softly glowing security station, passed more dorms, passed the library, over the hill by the gym, through the park and by more dorms.

And finally I stopped. I had to breathe. I bend over and clenched the stitch in my side, sucking in deep breaths of warm night air. I glanced up. I was in front of the fine art center. The black spot of grass where the paintings had burned still wafted smoky smells into the night air. It tickled my nose and I sneezed. The noise echoed off the surrounding buildings in the dead campus. The sound of a motor echoed down through the buildings and over the manicured lawns in a low, eerie hum. I hurriedly pulled my ring of keys from my sweat pants pocket and let myself into the center studio door.

A golf cart with two security guards cruised by slowly, swiping their flash lights over bushes and invading shadows cast by the moon. I slid away from the windowed doors and down the hall toward the painting studio. I didn't want to start another zoo with security.

I had expected the building to be quiet. After all, both computer labs humming far in the basement couldn't be heard from here. However someone was talking. Loud and angry. Was someone bothering Paul in his sleeping bag? I tiptoed toward the studio's huge swinging doors to listen. Someone might be in trouble and I could use the phone on the wall by the front doors to get security back here pronto.

"Shush! Keep your voice down. That was the front door. People are still using the lab downstairs."

Is that Martin's voice? I backed up a step.

"Like anyone is going to stop here, Dad. You've made them all hate you and hate painting. No one works all night in here anymore.

Not like when I was a kid. I used to come here and watch and listen to them. But even that creepy homeless guy, Paul, doesn't sleep in here anymore."

"He's only homeless when it suits him. But anyway, Zach offered him a real bed in the catacombs to be a guard. That kid is bright, I'll give him that. Too bad you didn't get any of those genes."

The conversation paused after the unflattering jab, but Martin being mean wasn't a surprise. No, I couldn't stop reeling from more than that.

DAD!?! Martin is a dad? And is he saying this girl is related to Zach Sulferson? Another almost heir? Whose voice is that? Do I know that voice? Come on, talk some more. I begged in my mind. The blood was pounding in my ears like a herd of elephants thundering by as I waited for another syllable. A dizzy feeling in the top of my head made me realize I was holding my breath. I exhaled and tiptoed closer to the studio door to hear their hushed tones better.

"Look, Dad, I want to come tomorrow. I want to know as soon as you do if I'm a match. And if I'm not, we'll make a public appeal. We'll ask people to be tested. There's a whole campus here of people. All your fans even. And we can talk to Curtis. He has money and power. We'll find you a donor if we have — "

"No, no, no!" He cut her off. "We'll do no such thing. I want no one to know. There's too much to risk in my personal life to open that can of worms. No. And I don't want their pity, either. I want to see admiration when I look in their eyes. No. They'll make me go home. I won't leave this place. I want to spend my last days doing what I love and I love this place." There was anguish in his voice. Martin's voice.

"But what about me, Dad? Won't you do this for me? Don't you love me?" I couldn't place the girl's emotional whisper to a face.

"Well, it would have been easier if you were a Stephanie or a Dirk or a Gladys. Ah, that takes me down memory lane. Those were the greats. They made my exhibits sparkle. I was somebody then. I need a comeback, a swan song. My last great show. My final body of work. I need a Clare James right now."

I was stunned, frozen in a crouch in the shadow of the wall.

"But, but," the girl's voice was rising again. "Mom told me about you. You're a fraud. You stole those kids' work and signed your name on it for all your exhibits. You ruined them, destroyed their reputations, and paid them off. You bullied them. You even got several of them hooked on drugs. They're dead now. How can you take pride in that? How can you love this place for that? How can you love them more then us? Then me?" Her speech had slowed down to a defeated croak. "Your own flesh and blood."

I knew it! I knew he was crookeder then a three dollar bill. There was less satisfaction then I'd imagined proving a worm was a worm. I caught myself before I sighed out loud.

"Look, you don't understand," Martin's voice had changed. I

could hear the click of his lighter. Cigar smoke wafted into the hall and I covered my mouth and nose, trying not to cough.

"I guess we better have this talk since my end is near." I could hear him exhale in a wheeze. He cleared his throat. "Your mother was disappointed in me. She didn't take the time to listen once she took up the cause of that brat from Iowa. That girl wanted money for her work and she was using a faux affair to blackmail me. If she'd exposed me for taking her paintings, I wouldn't have needed her to paint anymore. So she used an affair to try and force my hand. The hand that held my wallet, clever minx.

"When I tried to beat her to it and lay it all out honestly for your mother, she only heard the worst of it. She put two and two together and saw fourteen. Fourteen students I'd taken work from.

"But I never got to explain to her my success was an accident, the desperate act of a man about to lose his career which would mean his family too.

"The first time I took a promising piece of student work and signed my name to it was to keep my job. I didn't have any new ground breaking pieces and the University was demanding work to make them look good. It's the old publish or perish adage. I had to keep my job. I had to provide for you and your mother and I was in a slump. I knew I just needed one little painting to stall them. Keep them happy with a promise of more. I thought if I only took one painting it would hold them off until I could really do something.

"But it backfired. They went wild over the piece and demanded more immediately. While I was still in the room, they were scheduling interviews with the major players, the whole nine yards. Horrified, I saw the ground disappearing around me fast. I now had to produce a show.

So I invented the quantity and quality thing. The student whose painting I used in the first place painted a batch of new pieces and I declared their quality not good enough and took them. So he painted double, trying to get enough to pass the quality grade and still have enough to reach a decent quantity grade. It was brilliant.

"Eventually I got so famous he recognized his work. Of course I gave him an A and a generous share of the profits to keep quiet. And for him that was enough. When he graduated, I hired him in the print factory where they were mass producing the paintings for overseas living rooms. He was happy to paint new pieces and let me handle the publicity. He didn't want his personal life in the spotlight. He was one of those guys in the closet so it would have gone on indefinitely if he hadn't been killed in a car accident. This was all way back when you were in diapers. Your mother never knew him. What a gem."

Martin paused to cough again and I gasped for some fresh air in the hall filling with cigar smoke. *What a hypocrite. Accusing me of copying his chickens. He probably never even painted them! Well, he wasn't going to get away with it any longer. I wasn't going to be bought off or blackmailed or hooked on drugs.* My thoughts were as unforgiving as his wife's must have been. His story was trying to illicit pity, but it only emphasized I was as right as rain for disliking him.

"By the time my muse died, it was already too late for me." His raspy whisper continued in the darkened studio. "I'd been bitten by the fame bug. I was basking in the limelight and I was addicted. I couldn't get enough adoration. I was revered by fellow professors. I was worshipped by students. I was feared by art critics. There is *nothing* on earth like that kind of power. People will do anything for you. *Anything.*

"I *loved* hearing my name. I *loved* spending the money. I *loved* the feeling of pride I got whenever I walked down the street and people recognized me in hushed tones. It. Was. Amazing." Martin's voice had gained strength as the intoxication reignited him. "So yes, I hurt people. I lost your mother. You, my own daughter, grew up hardly knowing me. I manipulated and I stole. And I don't know if it makes it any worse or not, but I've enjoyed every minute of it."

There was a pause as Martin coughed again. His voice had grown tired. And sad. "Oh, what's the use? I can't keep pushing you away. Honestly, I agreed to send you away to school because I was protecting you. Don't you see? I loved you the most. I didn't want to hurt *you.* If you stayed around, you would have been hurt. That's why I needed students like Dirk and Stephanie, and yes, now Clare. But not you. Never you. Not then and not now. You've got to go back to your home. I don't want you here. I never have."

"That's not true! I can help you! If I'm not a match, I can at least keep up the Clare break down. I can help –"

"Don't be foolish." He cut her off. "I haven't had a student good enough to use in a number of years now. This has to be handled delicately. Her work is all religious funk. It's going to take more experience then what you've got to make this happen. If it even needs to happen."

"But that's just it. It does need to happen." The girl's voice rose above a whisper in triumph. "You reveal you're dying. You need a transplant and are seeking a donor. You have conveniently found religion at this last hour. Then her work will fit fine." Her voice was desperate and breathless.

"I see you've thought this all through for me." Martin coughed again. "So that vandal bit, that was you setting the stage?"

"Yes. I'm grown up now, Dad. I can help you. I've even got Sulferson's dog. I'm thinking ahead. If he doesn't help you, the dog gets it. Your life for Reginald's." She didn't sound so certain now.

"No, no, no!" Martin's voice was full of anguish again. "You love that silly dog, so stop it! You'll become what I was trying to avoid when I sent you away! When I belittle you and send you away from me, it's so you don't become like me. You're not making me happy." He seemed to be gasping for air and then he began speaking again in a low kind voice.

"I'm going to stop acting the part from this minute on with you. You don't see it yet, but I'm not fighting this. I'm making a death bed confession. I *did* discover I was a horrible person doing horrible things, when the doctor told me the news yesterday. It hit me so heavy, I went to that little church on the corner and the pastor was sitting there waiting for me. He knew. It chilled me to my toes that God knew it all and God had arranged for him to be there for me. God has forgiven me, Girl. And I realize I need Clare's help to explain that to everyone else. But if you keep mucking up the works with all this petty stuff, no one will believe me and you'll be right in it up to your neck. So stop it! I'm keeping up appearances until I know if we match or not and then I have a different agenda. One you don't need to be a part of. You need only to be my daughter and spend time with me. Can you do that?"

My leg was zinging to notify me it was falling asleep. I hadn't moved since Martin started confessing. And now I sagged in my stance. I was totally caught off guard by what he was saying. *Is it really true? He wants my help to change? If I believed with Christ all things are possible, then it was at least possible.*

"Wow, you really are a master con, Dad." The girl's voice dripped with scorn. "I could almost fall for that speech and think you did find God. You've perfected your craft when you can almost fool your own daughter! But I know you're lying again, since there is no such thing as God. You and Mom have always said it and I finally now believe it. Is Mom in on it too? I saw her on campus the other day."

"Your mother? What? No! She's not on campus. Look, honey. We were wrong. Your mother and I. And she's got no reason to see me anymore. Believe me, I've tried to talk to her, to apologize for all the things I did wrong. She won't have it. Although I will admit I keep smelling her perfume. You know, the first one she made when she started? The one out of corn hair, no what is that stringy yellow top called? Corn silk, that's it. I think it's hallucinations from the medication I'm on."

"You're so good at believing your own lies." The girl's whisper continued as if he hadn't interrupted her. "And it's a perfect angle to hook a goodie-two-shoes church girl's work this time. I should have known you'd think of it before I did. So stop acting with me and –." The fierce whisper was cut short by Martin's "Shush!"

A key was turning in the outside art center lock.

The door behind me swung open and several students burst into the hallway, laughing. I was caught in the flood of brightness from the motion activated entrance bulbs like a deer in the headlights.

"Hey, Clare! Just finishing a shift?" Kara was balancing a pizza box and Jay was carrying their back packs. *Shoot! Martin and his offspring had to hear Kara and know I've been in the hall. I have to play this cool.*

"Yes!" I quickly took Kara's unwitting cue. "Whew! Those

stairs seem steeper every time I come up." I grabbed my side and swung around toward the front doors, limping on my leg that had fallen asleep.

"Hey, don't go before the pizza! Double crust, double cheese, Canadian bacon."

"Oww. My favorite! Can I take a slice to go? I'm beat, you guys." The two in the studio remained silent. I tried to act normal, but my thoughts were racing again.

Hopefully Martin bought I'm passing through. I agree with his daughter, though, he's on his grand finale of a scheme. If he's even really terminal.

But I still didn't know who the girl was. She was the vandal and probably behind the arson. And the dognapping. She was accelerating with every act. There was no telling how far she'd go. I have to wait outside for her to leave and find out who she is. Thank the Lord Toby has Reginald safe and sound. Jackie didn't know the whole story. Toby must have paid off the guy she had holding him. They had gone on a rescue mission. That was it.

"Sure. Anything for you, Clare." Kara smiled and popped open the pizza box lid. I scooped out a big square slice and took a cheesy bite.

"Mmmm. Thank you, guys. Really. Isn't Kay with you?" I was trying to make standard small talk.

"No, he's with his girlfriend." Jay rolled his eyes and held the door open for me.

"Oh, the older woman?"

"Yah. I wish he'd never met her. She's, well, I'd better stop there since I've never actually met her." Jay backed out of his comment at Kara's raised hand.

"True, but easier said than done. I'll keep him in my prayers." I waved as I exited. The heavy door swung shut and their chatter disappeared behind me.

Rounding the side of the building, I dropped to a crouch and wiggled between two bushes, careful not to get leaves in my slice. I was settling in when a spot light blinded me. I paused in mid chew.

"Miss, I need you to come out of there, please. Come on."

No! Foiled by security! Kind of embarrassing. Hmm. Reason for being here? My mind was already on overload with all I'd learned.

"Can I see your student ID, please?"

I blinked hard and tilted my head from side to side to escape the glare of the golf cart's headlights and the two flashlights trained on me as I stood up.

"Awe, you know who this is, Bud. You don't need a student ID. Miss James, can we give you a ride home? It's late to be out without an escort."

"In the bushes no less. We're going to have to write this up, Bert. What are you doing here, Miss James?"

I looked down as I held my hand up in front of my face to

shield me from the blaring lights and my eyes focused on my salvation in the mulch.

"I dropped my keys trying to balance this slice of hot pizza some friends gave me going to the lab. Those keys skittered across the sidewalk faster than an eight legged mouse and I'm desperate to find them. Can you train that bright light over here, Bert, by the corner?" I waved at the ground and took another bite of my slice of pizza.

"Here they are, Miss James." Bud held up my key ring without a change of expression. It must have fallen out of my pocket when I was squirming around to hide. I'd have been in trouble when I got back to the house without them, but now they had made a perfect excuse for security why I was in the bushes with pizza at midnight.

The art center's door swung open and I held my breath as I tried to squint in the white light to see who it was. Bert jumped on the cart and pulled it up beside me. Two male students were walking the opposite way down the sidewalk. Not Martin's daughter.

"Sorry to blind you like that, Miss James. It's protocol. Hop on and we'll take you home. It's a might brisk for just sweat pants and a t-shirt."

"It's hot in the lab. All the equipment. And there's really no place to hang coats. We should talk to someone about that. Speaking of which, who do you have to notify about Picasso's daughter now?" They both actually chuckled as I cheerily swung onto the cart and angled the mirror on my side at the art center entrance. A figure was coming out as we sped away.

The mirror and the bright moonlight confirmed the niggling sensation that I knew the voice in the whispered conversation with Martin.

Wendy Gallonte.

✱ Chapter Eighteen

"What do you mean, Rembrandt is gone? Gone where?" I had been up the rest of the night wrestling with what I now knew and I was short on patience.

How could Toby lose a dog in one night? Just one night was all he needed to hang on to him for. Teriyaki Sauce, I'm going to blow a gasket!

If I could get Reginald safely back to Mr. Sulferson, I could finish the painting and life would be back to normal. For a lot of people. Whatever normal was here. Plus that would narrow my case load down to one missing movie. And exposing Martin as a fraud. Somehow. Unless he really did have a change of heart. Then he could confess himself. I shook my head. The Martin situation would have to work itself out. And probably sooner then later since I had my meeting with him today.

"I don't know where he is. Look, someone coming in let him out accidently. It's a frat house, for crying out loud." Toby was exasperated with me.

I brushed past him and marched across the hall. *Well, two can play at this game. If he doesn't have Rembrandt or Reginald or whatever his name is, then Wendy will know who does.* Balling up my fist, I pounded on her door with gusto. No one answered.

"Clare, what are you doing? You're going to wake the whole house. You've already said this girl has a few screws loose. Can't we leave her alone? Look, Brandt will come back when he's hungry. Or someone will bring him back to the frat. All the neighbors know him. Puzzle pieces! I didn't know you were taking this dog thing so seriously." Toby looked from left to right in the quiet hallway and changed his approach. "Look, one way or the other we need to eat. Let's go get breakfast. I can file a report with campus security on the way if that makes you feel any better."

"Why doesn't she answer her door? Even if Wendy is avoiding me, Sillo should be there. No one has seen Sillo in weeks. Wendy probably killed her so she could make this room her evil spy center headquarters." I was muttering under my breath as I pounded the side of my fist on the wooden door, making it rattle in its hinges.

"Hey, no one's home." Marcella breezed past us on her way

out. "I saw Wendy leave already. Out my window. Up there." She pointed upstairs while she shouldered the front door open. "And you know Sillo left for that aid thing with the earthquake, right? Nearly chatted my ear off at the bus stop, right after we'd had that whole talk about the Bible. Reminds me, have you got another one? Bible, I mean. I gave mine to her."

"Sure, want it now?" I was stunned a minute out of my rant. One brief conversation with Marcella had put a Bible in Sillo's hands. Someone I thought I'd never even get an opportunity with. It made me pause to think. *That's crazy good. Shows me again that you really are working it all out for us, Jesus. Help me chill out and think this through.*

"I'll grab it later, don't want to side track you. You look serious. Speaking of serious, have you guys noticed Sulferson's has stopped stinking up the place? Well, of course you have, you're Clare James. Ekkk, is that the time? Gotta go. See ya!"

Marcella dropped her skate board with a clunk and glided out the front door before ramping off the steps.

"Look, let's just go to breakfast, Toby." I headed out the front door after her, deep in thought. *She's right, it doesn't stink. Work must have stopped at the factory. This is getting ugly. Wendy has to have that dog! She overheard us talking with Rupert and stole him back from Toby. The question is, do I confront her, maybe even Martin, and give them the chance to come clean or should I go straight to Rupert?*

"Hey, remember me?" Toby stood next to me at the crosswalk

waving a hand in front of my face, baiting me. "What is going on in that head of yours? You think you know where my dog is, don't you?"

A slight edge of hardness had crept into his voice. It was times like this when he didn't feel like he was on my side anymore that made me doubt our connection. Doubt he was who I thought he was in London.

The light had changed and I started across the street. "Look, you don't need to come with me to my Martin meeting today. Paul will be in the studio and I think it's more important, with the town so on edge, to find this dog, whoever he is. I need to paint a dog and I need to paint it soon. You can pay a visit to each of your frat brothers and find out who saw the dog last." I delegated.

"Fine, but it's a waste of time. That's not how frat guys' brains work. Remembering clues and details. And are you sure you'll be okay with Martin? I don't mind saying I don't like that guy." Toby spoke calmly as he followed me up the sidewalk toward our breakfast spot, almost like he was rehearsing lines.

"You never know what you might find out and right now, it's the best direction for a lead we've got." I didn't have the patience to explain the whole Martin thing to him. He had an uncooperative air about him today anyway.

"I will need your help later, so let's meet up here again after lunch. I've got something cooking in my brain that's set to boil over."

How am I going to catch this little booger? He hates me. I should have gotten someone to come with me. Anyone, I thought desperately as I scampered across the wooden floor.

"Come back here, Reggie!" I panted.

Now I regretted not going to the police and blowing off meeting Toby at the house after talking with Martin. But really, I'd been afraid the police would blow me off unless I had evidence to go with the address and I didn't know if I could trust Toby or not. He'd lied about where he got the dog and then supposedly he'd lost the dog. Could he handle following a lead from Martin on the dognappers? When I had confronted Martin that morning he'd been all too willing to share everything with me.

"I suspected you'd been listening when we heard your friends come in and greet you last night." Martin had taken a puff on his cigar and collapsed on a stool next to a wet painting.

"Cursed corn stench!" He waved a hand in front of his face. "That's why I took up cigar smoking years ago, to hide that vile odor. Anyway, I don't know how much you heard, but Wendy did take Toby's dog last night before she came to our meeting. She believed you that he is Reginald. After you left last night she finally agreed to take him back to Sulferson house so he could be properly identified. She really does love the little guy, which is ironic considering who she is and how he plays into her life."

He was silent a long minute and I shifted from one foot to another in the uncomfortable pause before he continued. "And she's a match for my transplant, so there's no need to strong arm Curtis with the dog." He took another drag on the cigar.

"This is going to be my last one for a while." He held the cigar out in front of himself and surveyed it from different angles. I had waited impatiently for him to go on.

"I need a transplant or I'm dead. She's my daughter, you know? If they say her injuries aren't too serious for surgery, we'll be under the knife tonight."

"Injuries? I didn't hear about her injuries." I had slid onto a stool across the table from him, keeping my distance. He was docile today, but I still didn't trust him.

He looked old and tired. If he was trying to steal my work somehow, he should have a Grammy for this performance. "Some men attacked Wendy and took the dog this morning. She was devastated to lose him and have a bottle of her mother's perfume broken during the struggle. Julep's company doesn't sell her special scent. She only makes it for herself and she decided Wendy could wear it too. She'd just given her the bottle. Wendy hadn't even worn it yet.

"She's been trying to orchestrate a reconciliation between her mother and me. She seems to think this illness provides me with a free pass to do whatever is necessary to make things right for the people I've wronged. Someone should tell her it doesn't work like that because she won't listen to me." He barked out a series of gasping coughs and had to rest a minute before continuing.

"Unfortunately, Wendy got a concussion and she's in the hospital under observation to determine how soon the transplant can happen. And Clare." He paused like that was a sentence and I hesitated before standing up to bolt out. I'd gotten what I wanted and I didn't see how he was going to continue to be my advisor if he was terminally ill so I wasn't planning to show him my work. But something in his tone stopped me.

What if this is the last time I see Martin? What if he dies during the transplant surgery? Had he really talked to Pastor and changed his mind about God? Was I here to talk to him or was I here because of my own heart?

I had to blink hard to quiet my tumbling thoughts. I had licked my lips. "Martin –"

He had held up his hand. "Clare, I wanted to apologize to you. And ask your forgiveness. I've been more terrible then I can list in the next few minutes. I've done a lot of soul searching in the last week when I found out about my, well you know. I'm sorry. I don't know a lot about the Bible and stuff like that, but I know Jesus died so I could still get to heaven even with all the stuff I've wasted my life doing. Chasing fame and hurting people." He stabbed the cigar out on the easel tray of the wet painting next to him and fished a pencil and a piece of paper out of his pocket.

"Here's the address of a couple of guys who are for hire for things that you don't want to do yourself. I've had occasion to use their services, but they mainly work for the Union. Please give this to the police and tell them the dog could be there. A car is coming to take me to the hospital in a few minutes."

I nodded and took the piece of wrinkled cigar paper from where it had floated down and landed on the work table between us.

"Before I go, can I at least see what you put together for today? I've been trying to guess your next move. I never know what you'll do in response to the unpleasantness I toss at you. And I have to admit that's why I do it." His smile was sad. I hesitated. What could it hurt to show him the spliced drawings?

In my wildest dreams, I hadn't expected him to break down and weep at my work. He asked me to pray for him and Wendy. I decided that even if he was playing a game, I had been released from my hate of him. His tears had been salve on my wounds.

It had been powerful to pray with a foe who held such a piece of my heart in his influence. There aren't words in this world to quite describe how it feels to approach the throne of God with one you have feared and disliked and together ask for forgiveness and healing as you now agree on repentance and belief.

After I left the studio, feeling odd down to my toes, I'd

decided to follow Martin's hunch and case the address he'd given me before I called Rupert. Honestly, I was feeling a little bit invincible too.

And low and behold, as I walked by the house in the woods matching Martin's description and address, there was Reginald sitting on a window sill surveying the front yard like a tiny monarch.

There was no car in the driveway and the front door had been unlocked, so I tiptoed in. Reginald had yipped at me from the sill and jumped down. Misjudging his momentum, he had slid on the well-worn wood floor under a chair. Shooting out the other side, he look startled as I loomed over him. I was reaching down for him when a car door slammed outside. I froze and our eyes locked.

They were going to hear us and I had no idea how violent these people could get. If they hadn't come back when they did, I'd have been out of there with the little pain-in-the-neck and come back later with Toby and the cops. Instead, it was turning into a bigger rescue mission then I anticipated now that I was a damsel in distress.

Reginald took advantage of my pause and skittered under a cupboard beside us. I heard the second car door slam outside, so I gave one final grunt and stretched under the dusty armoire as far as I could. I caught him by a gold fish marked hind leg and pulled him out, squirming and snapping at me with a dust-bunny beard. Cradling him like a baby, I ran to the first place that offered shelter –

the coat closet across the hall. I could hear keys jingling in the front door. Two men were talking loudly as they entered or they would have heard Reginald's pouty whining.

I desperately clawed at my pocket for the treats I brought in case he gave me trouble, which was more than likely. He was a clean cut little pug with a creamy coat and a chocolate colored face that reeled you in with a blink of his big brown eyes. Before you could help yourself you were cooing and saying, what a big, stuffy name for such a teeny weeny sweetie.

And then it passed.

You realized you should have said, what a sweetie of a name for such a manipulative little barracuda. Snobby, mean-spirited, demanding, whatever you wanted to call it, he wouldn't cooperate. Ever.

How could I make him understand I needed him to behave or we were in serious trouble? I shoved all the treats in his mouth at once and his hot doggy breath, mixed with kibble, came back at me to tickle my nose. I swallowed a sneeze and gasped for air. At least his crunching and sniffling in the dark were quieter than his whining and sassing, but I still couldn't hear what the men who had come in were saying over his wheezing.

Knowing this wouldn't hold him for long, I shifted him to my left arm and patted around on the floor in dark where I was squatting while the voices in the hallway moved away from us. The unevenness beneath my sandals appeared to be a pile of shoes that had a unique odor about them and it wasn't pleasant. In fact it reminded me of the smell on the cartoon notes Paul had given me. I tugged on one, but it resisted. I grabbed another by the heel and pulled harder. In the dark, they seemed to be all tangled up. Reginald was shoving his nose insistently at my pocket attempting to squirm his entire body in after the smell of treats. Trying to balance his little twisting form in the dark, I desperately clamped onto the neck of a boot. I had to get one free for Reginald to wrestle with before he chewed my pants off.

The boot was upright and I slipped my fingers around its neck. But for some reason, it felt more solid than the others had. I slowly slid my fingers up its smooth length in the dark until I hit material. Also solid. The leg continued up and I patted at the knee in disbelief. I tipped my head back slowly, choking on the scream lodged in my throat. Reginald had frozen on my arm as well, as if he too had just noticed we weren't alone in the closet!

Oh God.

A gurgle erupted out of my throat, but a hand clamped over my mouth from behind me and an arm slipped over my head and brushed the door open a hair's width to allow a single sliver of light to spill in. Every muscle in my body tensed as I squeezed Reginald in terror.

And then my mind registered Key's tan Polynesian features

floating over me. He had a finger placed to his lips and I sagged back against his legs in relief. He took his hand off my mouth and leaned over closer to scoop Reginald out of my noodle arms. The tiny guy nestled against Key's broad chest and licked his face with sheer delight. Sheer *quiet* delight. Only Key could master that feat.

Outside the closet the gruff male voices had returned and they were still agitated.

"Don't tell me that rat has escaped again. He's got to be around here somewhere."

"It's *not* my fault this time, Red." A nasal voice whined. "I checked all the doors and windows before we left. He's hiding somewhere. It's a trick. He's trying to get me in trouble. He's not a nice little guy, you know. It's creepy. He's like an angry little old man. Just like the guy we rescued him from, Red."

"How many times do I have to tell you we didn't rescue him from anyone? Look, you knucklehead, just get his food out. He always comes running for that, greedy monkey."

In panic, I looked up at Key. His eyes met mine and he shook his head slightly. Reginald was sleeping like a baby in his arms. How had he managed that?

I tried not to chuckle. Relief was making me giddy. At least if the two guys out there found me now, I had a feisty guard pug and a connected Hawaiian tagger with me.

RATTLE, SHAKE, RATTLE.

The racket of the tin of dog food being vigorously shaken outside the door was like nails on a chalkboard. Up and down the hall the noise marched as the man tried to coax Reginald out with an awkward falsetto.

"Here Doggie, Doggie, Doggie. Nice Doggie. Come on Reggie. Here boy. Here Doggie, Doggie, Doggie. Time to eat."

I squinted up nervously at Reginald in the dark. He stretched and yawned in Key's arms and then settled back down with his chin on his paws in Key's elbow, his eyes closed the entire time. Then his hind leg twitched and a stink bomb enveloped the closet. Dog farts are the worst and in confined spaces, you can't get away from them fast enough.

Only we couldn't get away at all because the caterwauling was still going on in the hall.

"Come on little Reggie." RATTLE, SHAKE, RATTLE. "Don't get me in trouble with Red again." RATTLE, RATTLE. It's our little secret I fed you all them boiled eggs so you're not hungry now, Reg."

Reginald's hind leg twitched again in his sleep and a small tooting noise announced that it wasn't a secret anymore.

How many eggs did he eat anyway?

My eyes were watering and I buried my nose as deep as I could into the elbow of my sweater sleeve. I looked up at Key. He was a statue holding a dog. His eyes were closed and his lips were white as they stretched in a tight grimace. Reginald slept like a baby in his arms. His stub of a tail wagging every once in while with happy dreams.

Toot. Toot. Toot.

I gasped and hunkered lower to the floor, pressing my mouth against the crack the door was making into the hall. Air, fresh air. How was Reginald not hearing that man and all that food racket? It didn't matter, because things were changing in the hall. With one eye pressed to the crack I could see the two men facing each other by the front door.

"You let him out again, didn't you, Coop?"

"No, Red, honest. He must have slipped out when we left. Or maybe he's in our gear."

"Well, get out there and catch him. We can't let some college boy see him."

"I know, I know, Red. Just don't blame me, okay?"

"Blame you?" Red slapped him upside of the head with one hand. "Who should I blame then? It's either you or me."

Coop slumped toward the front door and Red turned around. He had a shot gun in his other hand. I involuntarily drew back in the dark.

"I'm waiting here till they call with instructions."

I heard the click of the front door as Coop went out to search for the pug.

How are we going to get out of here, Lord? And how long will it be before Reginald wakes up and gives us away with his noisy yipping?

I was going to die with a Polynesian gang member and a stolen dog in a closet full of methane. And I hadn't even gotten a chance to decide if I loved Toby yet. Well, if I was being honest, I think I already knew the answer to that one.

Toot. Toot. Toot.

❈ Chapter Ninteen

I turned my head to mouth at Key in the dark. Gun. I held up my hand and pointed the thumb and forefinger like a gun at my temple. He nodded and held up a hand with palm side out. Wait.

I like the expression hold your horses better than just plain old wait for situations like this, I thought, *because I'm about to crawl out of my skin and run like a wild horse!*

A phone jingled merrily somewhere in the bowels of the house. The man still inside answered it, but all we could hear was a murmur through the closet walls. Suddenly footsteps thundered passed us and we could hear the squeaky hinges of the front door.

"Coop, Coop, ya out here? Have you found that blasted dog?

Coop, answer me, will ya? We got instructions. Coop!"

The front door slammed and the screen door on the porch swatted itself shut too. We heard a yell for Coop in the distance.

"Now's our chance, move, Lily!" Key scooped me up off the floor and shoved the door open wide with his foot. My legs were asleep, but I slapped them with my palms as I staggered out of the dark closet and onto the braided rug in the hallway.

"This way, Lily. A back door goes out from the root cellar." Key flew past me with the sleeping pug nestled in one arm and flung open a basement door with the other.

I closed the closet door and then the basement door behind us and we paused a moment for our eyes to adjust to the dim light filtering through one small greasy window. The air was damp and cold and it smelled like dirt. Key begin to float down the steps in front of me, taking them two at a time in the near darkness.

Oh God, help us!

The old wood creaked and groaned as we descended. I clung to the rickety railing with one hand and the back of Key's shirt with the other as my feet found each step. Once on the dirt floor of the root cellar, I could see a rectangle outlined in light up ahead of us. We shuffled in the dark toward it.

"Look out and make sure one of them isn't standing right in front of the door when you wing it open." Key whispered as he rocked the dog gently in his arms.

I nodded and stretched up to a crack in the wood. Pressing my face against the rough planks, I peeked out. My eye watered at the bright light of the afternoon. The coast was clear. I nodded again at Key and grabbed the rusted handle on one side of the double doors. I bent my knees and then with all my might, I pushed up with my back. As bits of dirt and leaves rained in, I quickly closed my eyes. The door flopped to one side on the lawn like a beached dolphin. I stood upright in the hole it left and scanned the woods around the back of the house. I didn't see any movement.

Once we were both clear of the door, I flopped it back in place and brushed the leaves back over it.

"This way and talk to God for us," Key said in a low voice.

"I have been praying! And my car's that way," I pointed in the opposite direction and took a step away from him.

"Hey, what are you doing back here? Red! Red! We got trespassers!"

I ran after Key as fast as I could on the uneven ground between the tree trunks and away from the skinny man with the mullet. A shot rang out behind us and birds took flight from the bare bones of the tree skeletons all around. I flinched involuntarily and clapped my hands over my ears at the boom. Branches whipped my face and arms and I stumbled over rocks and small logs hidden under the blanket of leaves.

"That's right, run!" Red's deep rasp shouted after us. "We can track anything on four legs. We'll find you no matter where you go!" Another shot rang out and I heard the whistle of the bullet.

"Get the truck, Coop!"

Another blast from his shotgun cracked in the quiet afternoon air and Key hit the ground ahead of me, pulling me down beside him. We crouched behind a large tree stump. Despite our panting, we could hear them shouting at each other.

"Aw, Red, they're just college kids. Snooping. If they had the dog, he'd be barking by now. Forget them. Let's check the quarry."

Red growled something and fired again. We both flinched as the brittle branches crackled over head with the bullet's passage.

"For once you're right, you idiot. Quit wasting time. If that dumb mutt wondered down there, he's probably drowned and we're dead too. Get the truck."

They must not have seen the brown bundle tucked in Key's arms. Amazingly enough, Reginald was snoring softly as Key drew him in under his jacket. My chest had stopped heaving, but it ached. I took several deep breaths of the crisp fall air and licked my lips. The metallic flavor of blood I knew all too well took me straight back to the chase in London. I could smell the greasy restaurant floor I was laying on waiting for a bomb to explode on the sidewalk outside. I was helpless with crutches and a broken arm.

"Hey, Lily? You okay? Snap out of it." With his free hand, Key picked the twigs and leaves out of my hair and used a thumb to wipe the blood off my lip. "Looks like a branch gave your face a serious slap. It's going to sting for a bit, but you'll live." He squeezed my shoulder and our eyes locked. His irises were so dark brown they nearly disappeared into the black of his pupils. They were calm eyes. Filled with concern. Eyes that had seen far scarier things then two hillbillies with a shotgun. I gave him a small smile.

"That's better," he said. "We gotta motor now. Obviously, those guys are not going to find Reggie at the quarry and they'll be back. We can't risk hitch hiking to Sulferson's, so let's get to your car."

"You're right, but you've got some explaining to do. For now, though, I'll settle for the answer to one question. *How are you doing that?* Keeping Reginald from barking his fool head off. That's like trying to pierce a gorilla's ears without getting black eyes." I gestured toward the mute lump in his jacket. He laughed.

"I love you, Clare. You're the hilarious sister I never had! Trust me, it's no fancy trick. Just sleeping tablets rolled in bacon. Works every time. For dogs and people." Key's mischievous grin sagged slightly as Reginald tooted audibly inside his jacket.

It was my turn to laugh.

"Leave the keys in the ignition, the dog on the passenger side, and get out of the vehicle, slowly." The dispassionate voice said from the back seat. I'd never paid attention to the sound of a gun when it was slowly cocked, but that had to be what that clicking noise was. I glanced behind me and saw the glint of metal. *Yep, a gun. Twice in one day. Must be some kind of record.*

"Keep your eyes forward. No tricks or I'll shoot."

"Toby? That's not really you, is it? A gun? What's going on? Aren't we on the same side?"

"Clare, you're a bit stubborn, but I think your heart is in the right place. The gun's really for this guy. I don't know who he's working for." Out of the corner of my eye I could see the gun muzzle shove Key's shoulder.

I turned around in my seat. "Toby, what are you doing? This is crazy. You don't even believe me it's Reginald."

"Turn around, Clare, *please*. I know you think it's Reginald. But that doesn't matter now. I knew you'd rescue exactly the dog I need. Now do as I've asked and get out of the Jeep. Both of you."

"But if he's so dangerous you needed to use a gun to get your dog back, you can't be serious about leaving *me* with him! You're supposed to have my back. At least that's what you always said in London." My mind was reeling. *What is Toby doing? He's dressed up like a movie star. He looks great with that tan. So he's not under duress...*

The last time I was this close to gun point, someone almost died, Lord. Please help us. I don't want to do this again. Surely Toby knows this is not funny. Holding us at gun point over a dog he just got?

"Turn around, Clare, and face front. I can't look in your eyes anymore and do what needs to be done."

I gasped at the implication of his words. "Oh, God, you're not going to shoot us, are you?"

He cleared his throat. "Sorry, I was referring to simply completing my mission. I know you're still having nightmares about what you guys went through in London. Look, I don't want to hurt anybody, but if it has to go down like that, I will." His voice hardened and picked up speed. "Now you and Key are friends. He's not going to hurt you and without the dog, no one is going to hurt either of you. Keep your head and do what I ask." He adjusted the mirrored sunglasses he was wearing and made a circle motion with the gun barrel.

"What are you mixed up in?" I turned around and talked at the windshield. "We can help. You know us! And you know I need to finish my painting of him or the whole town is going to strike. People are going to get hurt! A lot more than just us. Please!" I looked over at Key helplessly. He nodded and took my hand.

There was silence from the back seat. Then a sigh.

"Just like everybody else, you've got the wrong dog."

"What? No, a fox doesn't lose the trail."

Another sigh. "I'm trying to tell you, not only do you have the wrong identity of the one dog you have, but you have the wrong dog for the identity you want."

"What?!" Key and I said in unison, our heads swiveling to look back at him. He leaned back in the seat and gestured at us with the gun again.

"Sure, go ahead and look. Reginald has a gold fish shaped patch on his hind leg, all right. But on the right one. The dog in his coat has the patch on his *left* leg. Go ahead. Look."

Key unzipped his jacket slowly and we looked the dog over. I couldn't remember for the life of me which leg had the mark.

We watched as Toby drove off with my loaner jeep and a blissfully sleeping pug supposedly named Rembrandt.

"Curtis Sulferson failed to mention this possibility to me when he called for help." Key raked his hand over his thick mane of black hair, dislodging his ball cap and then clamping it back on his head.

"Which possibility? My pseudo boyfriend is a loon, you might have to walk through a woods with men and shotguns, or there's two dogs with gold fish shaped markings on their hind legs?" I asked, exasperated.

Key busted out laughing. "I'm beginning to see what it means to be you, Lily. An ace detective has to rebound fast because you never know what to expect. No wonder you're so hard-boiled." I entertained a rubber band smile for a half second at his teasing, but I didn't feel hard-boiled. I felt like curling up in a ball and letting people with guns stay far away. Including Toby. *God, what is up with him?*

Key's concerned voice brought me back to attention. "I was only kidding about being hard-boiled. Maybe you'd better sit down. You've had a shock and you look abnormally white, even for someone whose nickname is Lily."

I steadied myself against a tree. "I'll be okay. He reminded me of the unpleasant parts of London, that's all. I guess there's more of a reason then I realized why I haven't been able to warm up to him since we returned." I absently twisted a hank of my bangs and chewed on my bottom lip. "He never has seemed like the same person I knew in London. And it still tries to come back and haunt me at times. Especially at unexpected gun welding times." I smiled at Key and felt better admitting it out loud.

"I'd think that was pretty normal. People aren't made to absorb trauma like a sponge. They need to be like a watering can and pour it back out so it doesn't become this stagnate goo inside. Sometimes they need help to pour themselves out. Do you have someone you can talk to?" Key spoke gently like a loving big brother.

"I do have Pastor and Edna. And I was "debriefed" in London. And I talked a lot to my parents over the summer traveling. But honestly now I'm back on familiar turf, I'm kind of miserable at times. I'm beginning to realize, though, that I was miserable before I left. Dodging Martin hasn't been a picnic. I did really enjoy London. Now that I'm back I'm seeing I had a big chip on my shoulder about Martin's behavior that I needed to deal with. And Toby! What's up with that? Seems like he's been trying too hard to be the perfect guy for me and I can't get into it and now he goes and does this?"

Key nodded. "Let's just say it wasn't what any of us expected, so I don't blame you for going white. I am a bit knock-kneed myself. But honestly, that goofy, playboy, Toby welding a gun at *us*?"

I grinned. *Toby. Toby wouldn't have actually shot us. Would he?* "Why did he want *that* dog so bad if he's only a relative of Reginald's? He said a mission. There's more to this then a lost pet. And that brings me back to you. The long walk ahead gives us time to catch up, doesn't it?"

We agreed it was closer to follow the twists and turns of the road along the thick ribbon of dark water to the Sulferson Mansion then to head in the opposite direction back to town. Someone at the corn palace could give us a phone or a ride.

"So, I assume you're looking for Reginald because somehow or other Curtis Sulferson is under the protection of the SPAM can tag." I relaxed into an easy stride with him on the quiet road. I noticed the wind was picking up and the overcast day looked like snow. I pulled my jacket around me closer and wrinkled my nose at the burned sweetness of the Sulferson Silk stench. At least the factory was working today and not barricaded behind bunkers of stubbornness. The white billows climbing across the grey sky between the naked tree branches meant gallons of the new sugar, high fructose corn syrup, were being funneled into tanker trucks. Drivers were maneuvering semis out of town and city crews were prepping snow plows for the upcoming weather to keep the route open and the trucks going. The factory's ripple could be applied toward every job in town, in fact in the region. Sulferson Silks was the hub of a lot of life.

Key had pulled his backwards ball cap down over his ears and jammed his hands deep into his pants pockets. His first words surprised me out of my bunny trail.

"I think I was a little bit in love with her myself. My brother's wife, that is." He kicked an acorn off the road and swung around in a circle to watch it skitter after a squirrel, not even breaking stride as he strode backwards. Before I could react, he started again and my mind painted it all in vivid pictures as he talked.

"My mom picked up and headed to Chicago when the community rejected her as a replacement for my brother, Tai. She was a witch and they wanted a Kahuna. I clearly did not have the gift. Pressure became intense. They were demanding my brother step up or we jump in the volcano and end our line so the spirits would select a new guide family. She was determined to drag my brother back, either to serve or to severe the line. Of course, as I'd told you, he had become a Christian. After school, he married his counselor's daughter. They had moved to Chicago to work in an intercity mission.

"When we got there, it became apparent Tai would never be a Kahuna. She and I basically squatted at the mission. We had nowhere to go. If we returned, we were dead. My mom never gave up hope, though. For years she put hexes and stuff on Tai and his wife, Ruth. And they proceeded to hold prayer vigils and stuff for us. And the whole time, Ruth was kindness itself to us. She helped me get a GED and bailed me out of jail when my brother was preaching.

"She told me these lines so many times, they echo in my head even now. She said, 'For you know that it was not with perishable things such as silver or gold that you were redeemed from the empty way of life handed down to you from your ancestors, but with the precious blood of Christ, a lamb without blemish or defect.' Now I know, thanks to the Bible I've been reading that's in 1 Peter 1:18 and 19." Key smiled at the memories.

"Ruth is so the opposite of my mother and all I'd ever known of the darkness and the emptiness. Her heart is light and graceful and she is full of peace and confidence. She never worries about anything or hoards her possessions or needs the best. I thought she was like that because she already was the best. And I dreamed of marrying a beautiful lily spirit like her." He paused a minute and kicked another nut. "Just like you."

"What?" I stopped dead in the middle of the road. I had been waiting for the part in his narrative when it connected why he was hiding in the same closet I was. But the last thing I expected him to say was *that*.

The reeve of a vehicle trying to crest the hill behind us made us both hit the ditch and lay quiet. Key had thrown his arm over me in a gesture of protection and it reminded me I was wearing the armor of God. I sometimes took it for granted that each morning now when I dressed my body I also prayed and dressed my spirit with the garments described in Ephesians.

The heavy snow clouds drooping almost to touch the earth made it overcast and dim. Headlights skimmed our stomachs as a pickup truck drove slowly past. I focused on the pieces of armor in my mind to keep from whimpering out loud as a man hanging out the passenger side window shouted nearly over our heads, "Here Poochie, Poochie, Poochie. Here, Boy."

Helmet of Salvation. Breastplate of Righteousness. Belt Buckle of Truth.

"Here Doggie, Doggie, Doggie. Nice Doggie. Come on Reggie."

Feet fitted with the readiness to spread the Gospel of peace. The Sword of the Spirit. The Shield of Faith to extinguish any flaming arrow of the enemy.

Red's mournful shouting was lost as the wind gusted up through the trees, shaking them until they roared. I closed my eyes and held my breath against the dust and terror that threatened to suffocate me.

What will they do if they find us, Lord? Please give me strength to face this. And forgive me for being so stubborn. I'm sorry about holding on to my hate for Martin. Please forgive me. I trust that you're with me. I know you've always loved me. I love you too.

I'm sorry I've been worried and yes, even angry, about what happened in London. I know you were able to use me to help others and I believe you when you tell me stuff like Jeremiah 29:11.

"For I know the plans I have for you," declares the Lord, "plans to prosper you and not harm you, plans to give you hope and a future."
For I know the plans I have for you," declares the Lord, "plans to prosper you and not harm you, plans to give you hope and a future." Jeremiah 29:11 For I know the plans I have for you," declares the Lord, "plans to prosper you and not harm you, plans to give you hope and a future." Jeremiah 29:11   *So now help me navigate through Protect us. Us. Wow, he's not proposing or asking me out or anything is he?*

I turned my head and peeked through my eyelashes at Key. His eyes were closed and he was mouthing something too. The head lights of the truck were gone. I sat up and saw its taillights pass over the distant hill. I looked over at Key as he sat up too and began dusting himself off.

I do love Key. Like a close friend, a brother. We laugh, we share things about hurts and our pasts. We understand each other and learn from each other. Like the connection I made with Penelope in London when she became my new sister in Christ. The wind had reminded me of her note fluttering on my curtain and what Jesus taught us about love. There were different definitions for the word love and humans were capable of loving in different ways. Like the differences between loving pizza, or a husband, or a child, or a sibling, or a friend.

I felt my heart beat slow and a sadness nestle on my brow as I realized that no matter what the reasons were behind what Toby was doing, I had to tell him we weren't an item.

He's got to have good reasons for what he's doing, Lord. I just know it. He will always be a brother in Christ. A dear friend who looked out for me and who I helped with our studies when we were in London, far from home. I blinked against the wind again and felt the cold drops of the first few flakes of snow on my face. *Nothing like gun welding to give a person clear perspective every time. Quit whining about your sorry senior year and get on with it, James.* I goaded myself.

Key had already begun talking into my thoughts. "Awkward place in a conversation for a pickup load of, what did you call them, mountain billies? To come driving through."

I busted out laughing. "*Hill*billies! Yes, it was spectacularly timed for me to think about my answer to your proposal."

"Wait, no, see, I knew it sounded wrong." It was the first time I'd ever seen Key look flustered. I laughed again. It felt good. I stood up out of the leaves giggling at his expression.

"Relax. I think you meant you wanted to marry a Christian girl, right?"

His shoulders sagged and his wide smile split his round face in half.

"Yes. When I met you the first time, you had what Ruth had and I knew my brother had not found the only girl in the world with such a beautiful spirit. There are more. There is a girl for me out there with the same love inside her heart." He hopped up straight off the ground and out of the ditch without using his hands or arms.

I followed him back onto the pavement and we began walking again along the yellow line at the edge of the road.

"Coop and Red would probably believe we are college kids left out here as some sort of initiation, especially since we don't have the dog anymore, but how do these guys figure into this anyway? Who are they and what instructions did they get on the phone? Do you know?" I asked.

"I don't know the instructions they got," he said, "but I do know they work for the factory union. I'm not entirely sure how Muriel's brother, Morty, ended up with him, because as far as I could trace it back, Muriel didn't take Reggie from the house in the first place. But I picked up the trail when Morty had Reggie and he sent a ransom note to Curtis Sulferson. Curtis called me for help.

"Apparently, one fine day at Sulferson Silks, Morty had been bragging around the water cooler about the money he was going to milk out of old man Sulferson. A lot of guys heard and that's when Red, who works at the factory too, got his bright idea and approached the Union. Some toughs decided strong arming Sulferson might be the only way to get their raises and improvements, so Red and Coop took Reggie from Morty. Since Morty had no proof of life, his ransom note was a dead end for the police. Every time I searched Red and Coop's house, though, Reggie was not there. Until today. Word on the street was they had lost him. And more than once too. Maybe he just wondered off, seeing as these guys are so bright."

"Do you think there are really two dogs or was Toby lying?"

"Oh, I didn't think of that," Key sat down on the side of the road. "I gotta think about that for a minute."

"Well, why would Toby want any other dog then Reginald so badly he would hold us at gun point? We would have found out it wasn't Reginald and returned him. It only makes since if he knew we would find out it was Reginald and he wouldn't get the dog back. For whatever reason, he's involved in the money to be made or the revenge to be had by dognapping Reginald."

"Or he's under a time restraint of some sort. Maybe he couldn't wait for us to contact the proper authorities and verify the dog isn't Reggie." Key suggested.

"That could be," I responded thoughtfully. "Especially if someone is forcing him take the dog. I can't see Toby doing this otherwise, but it puzzles me because in the car he was cool as a cucumber."

"That's how I would have judged it too." Key stood up and brushed off his pants before starting to walk again. "I don't think your Toby is who you think he is. And it probably has something to do with that lab break in."

"I would have said you were dead wrong before today, but I don't know what to think of his behavior. And he is trained on the computer and inheriting a big design company from his father. And I guess he could either be using my faith to manipulate me. I don't know."

We walked along in silence as the snow fell gently around us. The wind had died down and the big fluffy flakes made it look like we were in a snow globe someone had shaken up. My world was shaken up all right.

"Before I forget, can you tell me something?" Key nodded at my question. "When we first met, you encouraged me when you said you had been given something to say and even though you were frightened, you started out saying it small, then you were able to say more and more. Well, Martin burned your piece and you left. I never got to see what you had to say. What is it? What is the message you were given to say in your art, Key?"

He smiled and took my hand as we walked. His hand was warm and I pulled it in front of me and cupped it in both my frozen ones. He squeezed my fingers. The cold wind brought whiffs of the factory smoke to my nose. I wrinkled it, trying to shake the odor from my nostrils.

"That's an easy question. I always want people to focus on freedom. To do what you have to, to be set free from what's holding you back. For me it was my generations of family bondage. I found the same was true of the gang members who came into the mission. People were bound by so many serious things around me. Even when I met someone bound by a trivial thing, it didn't matter, because they still weren't free. It hurt me to see it.

"I know you didn't know this mantra of mine, so it excited me to the core of my spirit when you gave me a Bible last Monday Meal. Did you know you had opened it to the verse in John 8:32?

I smiled. "The truth will set you free! Yes. It seemed like a Word you would appreciate."

"I think it takes great faith to believe all the fantastical things religions require of a person." He kicked a rock off the road and pushed his sleeves up to his elbows as we walked. "But I believe the difference between them and God is you *get* great faith when you read the Bible." Key was talking faster as he grew more excited. "The Words in the Bible are alive. It says in Hebrews chapter four, about verse twelve, 'For the word of God is alive and active. Sharper than any double-edged sword, it penetrates even to dividing soul and spirit, joints and marrow; it judges the thoughts and attitudes of the heart.'

I could hear the blood pounding in my ears over the wind as he talked. I couldn't believe he was quoting back to me the verse I'd been using as my study theme since the beginning of the school year. It was so God to keep a lesson he was teaching me circling around and around my everyday world. I nodded as Key continued to share.

"It reminds me of a book we had as children. At night we had to shine a flashlight on the shapes in it and they made shadows on the wall that gave you hidden clues about the story.

"I think the Holy Spirit is the flashlight shining on the words in the Bible and the concepts reveal themselves more deeply to your spirit each time you read over them." He paused to choose his next words but his vivid explanation had already delighted my imagination.

"I totally know what you are talking about." I said. "Because it is living, it grows with you as you grow. It's like reading a preschool alphabet chart, a long division work book, and a biochemistry textbook all at the same time. I've noticed every time I read it, I understand something new. Not only with age, but with my heart changes too. Realizing God disciplines me to protect me because he loves me, I stop rebelling against him and submit to his guidance. Whenever this happens, the Bible reveals more to me."

We crested the last gentle hill before the Sulferson Mansion in the thoughtful silence of companionship.

Key sighed. "We're here. Before we go in, you need to know I owe Curtis Sulferson." We stopped at the foot of the driveway and leaned on the trunks of two oaks out of the wind. Key continued his story.

"While we lived in Chicago, I earned a name and chops among the mission's gang traffic as a graffiti artist. Even the blood thirsty ones who occasionally came out of the shadows to extract a pound of flesh or contract a tag, seriously respected me because my mother was such a powerful witch.

"She wrote letters impersonating my brother with news she claimed he gleaned from the spirit world for members of our community. They sent her money and wanted us to come home. As time passed, I realized this was all going to end badly and I needed another course. So I confided in Ruth. Like I said, I had a crush on her and my brother was always battling with my mother. Ruth used mission resources to hook me up with a scholarship fund for college. Despite Ruth's help, my mother loved this idea, so she left me alone.

"I submitted the SPAM sculpture you saw at Sulferson's to a foundation to match me with an education donor. Sulferson picked me to fund and brought me to this University. I later visited his home and saw he had hung my piece in his study. It was then I realized I had struck a deal with the devil, so to speak. He outlined that in return for my new life, gang activities would generally need to avoid his corn syrup distribution centers in Chicago. That was an easy exchange for me since there is no street value for the sludge they're shipping."

"But does he know what kind of grief Martin has given you?" I burst into his narrative, flinging my hands up into the cold wind. "Surely he wouldn't keep supporting the University if he knew his gang liaison was being harassed?"

Key shook his head. "Trust me, he knows. He was my biggest fan when I painted Martin's car. Eventually, he got tired of my superstitions about death and spelled out for me what he really wanted. He knew Martin would insult me from the beginning. That's what he wanted. He was planning on me taking a hit out on him. That's why I had to leave two years ago. Ruth hadn't gotten me freedom at all. The scholarship was Curtis's scheme to get rid of Martin. Martin is family. And family is the one thing Curtis Sulferson doesn't want for reasons beyond me. He's got buckets of money to go around."

A car was coming up the driveway. Key pushed himself off the tree trunk where he was lounging and waved his arms at the driver. His confession of debt to Curtis Sulferson had raised more questions than it answered. But they would have to wait.

The sporty red Nissan Pulsar stopped in the middle of the fancy pavers leading from the big house to the highway. A tinted window slide down.

"You two need a ride into town?"

Chapter Twenty

"It's freezing out here! Did you have car trouble? Why didn't you two come up to the house?" Muriel flipped the heater knob to high as we settled into the tiny car. I was sandwiched into a crawl space called the back seat, and Key's svelte frame was coiled on the passenger side. Muriel had furry boots under her business-like skirt and a soft wool scarf over her smart jacket. Her outfit did not fit the T-topped red rocket we were sliding toward town in.

I sighed. Maybe a shock would get some information out of her. "It's a long story but suffice it to say, Toby stole my car and left us."

"What?!" Muriel jerked the wheel so hard, she had to fight to bring us to a halt sideways on the slippery road. I braced my arms on the ceiling and my back against the seat, trying to steady my spinning head.

"Muriel! Chillax! You can't make sudden movements in this icy rain." Key whipped open his door and stuck his head out. "It looks like we are still on the road and no one is coming."

"So sorry. This car responds to the merest maneuver. I love it, but it's tricky in snow or ice." She unwound her scarf and tossed it in the back seat on me. I sluffed it off to the side. Muriel gripped the steering wheel with both hands, and eased the car back toward town. The sheeting ice had turned to falling snow fluff and it was hard to see out the front windshield.

"So why were you surprised at Toby stealing my car, Muriel?" I broke the tense silence as we all stared mesmerized at the white wall in front of us.

She laughed. "I guess I can spit it all out now. What difference does it make? I didn't do anything wrong. Key, you already know about my brother, so there's not much else to tell because what I did didn't affect the outcome anyway. But look, Clare, I'm sorry. I broke it off with him as soon as he came to the house with you that day to sketch. I didn't know he was seeing anyone else."

Now it was my turn to act surprised, only I wasn't driving a car, so the only thing to do was gasp. "Leaping lizards, Muriel, you're *dating Toby?*"

"I'm only a couple of years older than him," she said defensively. "And it's not like I work at the University or anything. I didn't even know he was going there when he asked me out last spring. Said his name was *Coby* not Toby and he worked for some big lab with computers. He was an artist and his project was secret. He told the most interesting yarns about his time in prison, which he was right up front about. A white collar crime, corporate espionage or something, so it wasn't like he was a murderer. Course, everything else he told me was a lie, so why should I believe he was ever in prison?" The car slide to the right and she turned into the slight spin to straighten us out. I pushed my hood off my head and peeled out of my mittens. It was getting way too hot in the sassy sports car for me.

"Did he tell you why he was lying to you?" Key's face was scrunched up in a thoughtful frown like a raisin.

"Yeah, and that's how my brother got Reginald." She paused to concentrate on the curvy road in the thickening snow. I didn't want to date Toby, but I was astonished by his lying. I thought he was my friend. *I've got your back, James.* His words in London echoed through my head.

"Well, what are you waiting for? Do tell!" I spoke louder then I intended and both driver and passenger jumped in their seats. She glanced at me in the rear view mirror and sighed.

"I'm so sorry, Clare. I guess I should have told you or the police or someone about what happened, but I felt so dumb." She blinked hard and we were so close in the compact car I could see her eyes were brimming with tears. "And hurt. I thought he was perfect and amazing and I was stunned when I saw him in your car and realized he was the boyfriend you'd asked permission to bring to the house. I wasn't supposed to be working that day, but the protestors had Mr. Sulferson rattled and he wanted me to come in. I came out to see if you had been harassed coming in too and there he was. With you. He acted like he didn't know me and you introduced him as Toby, so I thought maybe I was somehow mistaken. Maybe he had a brother or something. I mean, he wasn't wearing glasses and his hair was different." She reached over and turned the heat down without taking her eyes off the road.

"After you were settled in Reggie's room that day, I went to find him. I searched everywhere and was getting worried when I saw Wendy walking Reggie through the glass floor of the hall. None of us were supposed to be outside that day, remember? I hurried out to tell her to come in. She was obstructed from my view until I got to the outside garden door and when I opened it, Toby or Coby, whatever his name is, was there. Wendy was unconscious in the grass and Reggie was staggering around on the lawn. As he fell, Coby scooped him up into his backpack. I confronted him. And I was frightened."

"So wait," I said, "you're telling me that when I came across Toby or Coby, or whoever he is, eating a sandwich, he had just knocked out Wendy and drugged Reginald? So he got back into the jeep and we drove back to campus that day with Reginald sleeping in his backpack?"

"Yes. And I kept quiet because he told me he was undercover something or other and he was protecting Reggie from assassination. Even Wendy, the dog walker, was suspect. Her father was an unannounced heir to the Sulferson trust. He said that Curtis' sister, Santhe, which is short for Chrysanthemum, by the way, what a chore that name is! Anyway, she fell in love with her mother's boyfriend from the factory. If you ask me, that guy was a gold digger. Once he figured out Mrs. Sulferson wasn't leaving her husband, even with his illegitimate son, Humphrey, he moved on to the naïve daughter.

But anyway, according to Coby, they planned the factory explosion to fake her death and run away together. Unfortunately, or maybe on purpose, who knows? A lot of people died that day, including Santhe's sisters and her mother. Once evidence was found to prove this, Santhe and her lover became wanted felons. What could be pieced together over the years shows she had escaped the fire and she and Zac's grandfather had a son named Martin. So unlike Zac, who doesn't have any actual Sulferson blood in his line, Martin is Old Man Sulferson's grandson. And according to Coby, Martin came back to find out about his great uncle and his Sulferson family. But he's stayed at a distance all these years, sort of lurking. Maybe he was afraid to expose his mother. Or he was looking for a way to bump off Curtis and get the trust.

"Of course, Curtis has to know about him. He makes it his business to know about everybody. But it's not likely Martin knows he knows, as far as I know."

I tried not to giggle hysterically at the word 'know'. It was a lot to process. She was still chatting.

"Coby said that while the dog's death would cause a lot of problems for the town and a lot of people would get hurt, it would help other's claim the Sulferson trust faster since Curtis hasn't produced an heir yet and the trust is merely a matter of blood line. There's no will or excommunicating or anything. It boils down to either the people who have Sulferson blood or the dog."

I rolled my eyes in the back seat and she saw me in the mirror.

"Yes, the family is a fickle mess," she said defensively. "But look how popular that dog is now!" She lowered her voice. "Anyway, it doesn't matter. After I thought about it awhile, I decided he was lying. How ridiculous to be undercover to save a dog! You have to complete the painting somehow or the factory will implode anyway. And not only had Mr. Sulferson not briefed me on any of this, and I'm a trusted employee who would be on the lookout for foul play, but even if what he was saying was true, why couldn't he just guard the dog here, if he was protecting Reggie?

"And clearly our relationship was a sham. It hurt. He was playing every angle he could to make sure he got into that mansion. So I went to Coby's place in town and took Reggie at night when he was working at the lab. I was going to return him to Sulferson House the next day and let Mr. Sulferson decide whether or not to involve the police. He could find out if Coby was some sort of agent.

"But I have to say, my heroic plan didn't take into account I'm extremely allergic to dogs and pugs put me almost over the edge. So I asked my brother to come over and watch him for the night. He was thrilled. He's not the brightest crayon in the box and he was crushed when our dog died a few years back. It was the same litter as Zac's mixed pug, Jiggy Bites or whatever he calls it. The gold fish birthmark carries through their line. The little scamps.

"They were supposed to be euthanized, but the chauffer at the time pocketed the vet fee and tossed the lot, rather inhumanly, in the river. He was fired, of course, but the damage had already been done. The gardener had fished them out and given them away. Half the staff had pups. No one wanted to open that can of worms, so the family let it go.

"But, believe you me, every mark and distinction are carefully documented by a certified expert when a full blooded pug such as Reginald is born so there are no mix ups."

"So there could be other dogs with the goldfish mark on them?" Key asked calmly.

"There were. I would expect that Zac's is the last one left. But Morty thought I'd found another one for him. I realized I'd made a big mistake inviting him over so I had to tell him who the dog really was and that we couldn't keep it. When I woke up the next morning, they were both gone. He refused to tell me where he'd stashed Reggie and after a week he came by pretty beat up. He told me some guys from the factory took Reggie and he didn't have him anymore. What a mess it all turned into. I avoided Coby. I wasn't sure if he knew I'd taken Reggie from his place. Honestly, it's like holding my breath every day. I've been lying low and hoping you'd solve it, Clare, before one of us gets hurt."

❧ Chapter Twenty-One

Muriel dropped us outside the dark apartment complex where her boyfriend, Coby, lived. It had taken us several hours in the snow storm to get back into town and that, coupled with the walk to Sulferson Mansion from the woods behind Coop and Red's house, had given Toby a lengthy head start.

"If you see him, you tell him we're definitely over!" Muriel spun the tires in the snow as she gunned the engine and pulled away from the curb.

"Yeah, and if you never hear from us again, be sure and tell the police where you dropped us." I said calmly to her two red retreating tail lights.

Key snorted. "There's no way he's still here, dog or no dog. He'll know we're heading here first, if not with the police, then with some kind of justice and he won't be around."

"Yeah, speaking of that, what kind of justice are we packing? Cause we didn't have time to gather the police." I pulled my hood up against the cold wind and shucked my gloves out of my pocket. My stomach growled, reminding me we hadn't had any supper. I had to focus on mundane details like that since I didn't want to think about Toby's double life. About all the times we'd talked about the Bible. Was it all a lie? How could he love God and steal dogs and cheat on girls and have a seriously expensive computer in his secret apartment? I pushed the thoughts back.

Key made a gesture like a muscle man and I had to snicker. He was tiny, but he was strong. That was the only justice we had, but it was likely Toby wasn't here anyway.

The apartment windows were dark and no one came to the front door. I tried to see through the curtains, but all I could make out was the glow of a large computer screen. Key tried the door. It was locked.

"Reggie. Here boy. Reggie." Key called softly at the crack in the door.

The night was silent.

"Should I pick the lock?" He asked soberly.

"If he's not here, I'm not sure it's worth the breaking and entering charge we could get. Let's tell Rupert about it and see if he can search it. We can check the parking garage for anything, though." I paused on the balcony before turning around to go down the stairs. "There's one hole in your story, Key."

He stopped walking down the stairs and came back up to the outside landing where I'd lingered. "What did I miss, Lily?" He asked. It felt like he was using that name to find a soft spot and keep me open toward him. Or maybe he really did have great affection for me.

"You decided to leave the campus two year ago because you didn't want to order a hit on Martin and your funding depended on it. So how were you able to come back now? Are you working for Curtis Sulferson again?"

"Ah, you are quick, Little White Flower," Key chuckled in the night. His back was to the moon and I couldn't see his face.

"It was a difficult decision to leave school because I could have made one phone call and ended Martin. I would have had nothing to do with it directly. And, bonus, I hated the man.

"But I didn't like being used like that and it made me think about it long and hard. If I stayed in my mother's camp, I was not to take life without spirit guidance, which I didn't have. And if I stayed in my brother's camp, I was not to sin and take life or that God would be angry, which I didn't want since he was protecting me. Either way,

I was not in a good place, so I left.

"I did, however, have some outstanding warrants against me for vandalism and theft. When I returned to Chicago, the police picked me up and I too, like Coby, went to prison for a few years. I was told papers could get lost. I could be in there indefinitely, unless."

"Unless what?" I couldn't help myself. I had to jump into the gap of his silence like a cliff diver for a pool of water. He chuckled.

"The unless is implied. It means a deal for narking. My unless was unless I returned to this University and worked for Curtis Sulferson."

"That's what they wanted? Why on earth?"

"They couldn't pin the strongarm stuff in town on him. It was always a working stiff who took the wrap. They knew he was attempting to kill a remote family member, but they had no proof. They suspect he runs illegal things with his syrup tankers, and they also suspect he knows where his sister is, a federal fugitive on the most wanted list for the people killed in the terrorist act she participated in. They've been looking for a way for years to get in with him and they found me.

"So I got out of prison and turned up the gang targeting on Sulferson's trucks and distribution centers. Then I reached out to him. Told him prison had changed my mind and I wanted to come back and do whatever he wanted. He took the bait. I stopped the harassment of his trucks and came back to class.

"And now you know. I'm undercover FBI working for Sulferson to finish my degree and gather evidence against him in exchange for an expunged record. My quest for freedom is still ongoing."

And with that, he spun me into his arms. A car immerged over the hill and its headlights played over us before disappearing into the garage below. I giggled nervously as we pulled apart.

"This is just like being in a movie. But, hey, aren't you sworn to secrecy or something? You can't tell me you're really working for the FBI, can you? Anyway, in the movies they can't."

He chuckled. "I trust you, Lily and I trust our God too. No matter what happens now, I am already truly free. I am doing the right thing now to do the right thing. Come on, let's go talk to this person." He waved an arm at me and took the stairs two at a time. I made it to the bottom as a young woman was getting out of her car.

"Excuse me, we're friends of Coby in 4A and we wondered if you'd seen him around lately. He's been missing class and we wanted to make sure he was okay." Key was smooth and pleasant. I smiled through my nerves.

"Oh, Coby, yeah. I think he was coming in when I got home from work earlier. In a jeep or something he doesn't normally drive. Had the cutest little dickens of a dog with him." The woman scrunched her face in the look people get for babies and puppies and we smiled back.

"Oh, good. He must have been tied up with a new dog and taken a few days off. Thanks!" Key shook her hand and she draped herself across her hood as we walked away. He smiled and offered her a short wave.

"Yikes. She's scary."

"Yeah," I agreed, "but she's right. Here's the jeep Sulferson loaned me to drive." We had circled the garage and stopped behind the plum colored vehicle. It looked unharmed. Peering in the windows we confirmed no one was inside.

"Here's the valet key." I offered up the simpler version of the key fob for attendants to use when parking your car. Key swiped it from my palm.

"NOT shot gun!" He called as he unlocked the driver's door and flipped the automatic locks. Grumbling like a wet cat, I circled the SUV and crawled in the shot gun passenger seat. It was moist.

"Ewwww. I think Reggie peed on the seat."

"Or snow melted if the window was down or someone else got in covered in snow," Key said.

"Where are they now?" I asked God out my open window, looking up into the night sky dotted with a zillion stars. We pulled out of the garage and Key pointed the jeep toward campus.

"Sorry, Jackie. I gassed up the jeep and headed to Chicago before I thought too far ahead." I was shivering ankle deep in the snow at a pay phone outside of a deserted gas station in the suburbs of Chicago. "I should have taken someone with me or at least told you where I was going."

"You're sure as shootin' you should have. We've all been worried sick. When I got back from my practicum, that athletic little teddy bear, you know, the SPAM art guy, and Rupert, in uniform no less, were waiting for me. Scared me half to death. I'd been in a marathon of labs and up for seventy-two hours straight and I didn't even have a note from you! The way they talked, I thought Toby must have lured you out with the jeep and shot you before hiding your body somewhere."

"That's why I called. Well, that and directions. Look, I'm fine. After Key and I got back to campus I called Toby's old dorm and the frat house. No one's seen him or Rembrandt, aka, Reginald, since he held Key and me up at gunpoint. Which is totally not like him. I'm worried. He's not at the lab, either. He's nowhere.

"And it kept gnawing at me. What in the world is he doing? You were already gone to lab, so you didn't even know he was gone or dating Muriel this whole time, or whatever. Which makes no sense for a number of reasons, like she meet him last Spring, but we were in London then. Anyway, I mistakenly thought I'd be back before you got home. This weather is a bear to drive in."

"Clare," Jackie sounded concerned. "Clare, next week is Thanksgiving break. You've got a lot of school work to catch up on. Key has an ear to the underground network and in a few more hours, the police can file a missing person's report on Toby. He'll be listed as a person of interest in the dognapping. We don't know if he's dangerous or in danger."

"I know. That's the point. What if he's in trouble?" I hissed into the phone as some travelers passed me, slipping and sliding up to pound on the closed gas station door. I turned my back to them and ducked the frigid blast of air that pelted my face with hard little chunks of ice. "See, I figured Toby's dad might know something. And once that missing person's report hits, the police will be here to talk to him. He may or may not help them, but since I had met him in London and he knows I care about Toby, and for crying out loud, we're all supposed to be Christians, maybe he'll tell me what's going on."

Jackie's voice was gentle as she tried to coax me to change my mind. "Clare, it's too big for us to figure out without help. Come back to campus. Or go home. You could go home for break a little early. You can afford to skip class, you only have classes on Tuesday next week and then break starts anyway. You need a rest."

I shook my head to clear it of her siren song. I knew what it felt like to be alone on a roof top, with a gun pointed at your head, doing things you wouldn't normally do because your friend was bleeding to death beside you. I had to make sure Toby was all right. *God help me. Help Toby. I still don't believe he's who they are saying he is. Oh! And it's time for Martin and Wendy to be in surgery. Be with the doctors and be Lord over the situation. Thank you, God for forgiveness and your peace that passes all understanding.* I felt immensely relieved and a warmth spread through my body even though the temperature was dropping as I stood there. I remembered standing before Martin yesterday, guarded and hardened, braced for the arrows meant to lame me as I'd spread my drawings out. He had been eager to see them despite his apparent weakened physical state.

"Oh, Clare, you don't disappoint, whatever I've said in the past," he said immediately. "When you showed me your drawings last week, I was so jealous. They were executed with an absolutely masterful technique. Which was something I never had."

You could have knocked me over with a feather, I was so stunned at his words. He admitted being jealous? He couldn't draw as well as me? His voice had been sad and small as he'd gripped the edge of the work table with both hands and leaned over the drawings at me. "And I wanted it for myself. Just a few hours before my whole life changed, I wanted to destroy you and take your gift for myself."

His intensity caused him to dissolve in a coughing fit and I cringed, but started around the table to help his bent frame anyway.

He had raised a hand to stop me. He cleared his throat and straightened up, studying the curling scrolls pieced together before him.

His voice was weaker as he began again. "But even you have to admit such beautiful renderings did not make complete drawings. They were predictable portrayals of someone else's stories. I didn't know what you'd do when I destroyed them. I could hardly sleep until I could find out how your mind would attack the problem of my insolence and yet submit to my demands."

He was excited and it took his breath away. He stooped to cough and sputter. Part of me felt he deserved to be in such pain. Bent and wheezing before my youth and strength and talent. And then all of me was ashamed when he raised his head and his face was wet with tears.

"I am sorry for the way I pushed you, because it caused you pain. But I can't regret it because I'm so pleased with what you achieved." He sighed and smiled at me. Embarrassed by his unaccustomed praises, I ducked my head and raised my hand to a pretend itch on my cheek, only to feel my own face was wet with tears.

He continued his critique. "Each one holds intrigue, making them full of substance and questions for the viewer. They demand your eyes to look at them. Something down inside your body, maybe it's your heart, maybe it's your soul or spirit, I don't know about these things that well, but something inside responds to them. Please, please tell me what these drawings mean. Why have you chosen these people to deliver your message? Why have you chosen these pieces to put together in each one? And what is your message? Because you, you Clare James, always have a message."

"Clare? Clare, are you still there?"

I nodded, even though Jackie couldn't see me through the phone. A sprinkle of fine snow fell off the top of my hood into my eyes and I blinked as the cold revived me from my daydream. "I am here, Jack. And I'm free as a bird! I want to do this. I want to talk to Mr. Fir and try and help Toby.

"I only know the name of their design firm, but once I got near Chicago, I found the address in this booth's phone book. I need your help figuring out how to get there. Come on, Jack, you know Chicago better then a herd knows a watering hole."

The line crackled as the wind blew and I thought I'd been disconnected. Then her voice came from far away, "Maybe we don't need to know. Maybe we should remember Toby as we thought he was. You may not like what you find. I mean, for crying out loud," her voice rose again, "he asked *me* out before I went into labs!"

There it was. She felt guilty and she didn't want me to know she liked Toby. "Look, Jackie, I suspected as much. He's like a brother to me, not a boyfriend, so it's okay. We can figure all that out later. Once we know the truth about why he's acting the way he is and whatever he's mixed up in. And I think it has to do with the missing movie too, but what, I'm not sure. And it makes no sense why he's taken the dog. Everyone else had motives, but not him. And if he'd have wanted to kill me, I'd be dead in a ditch with Key. So I'm going to see if I can help him and then I'm coming back."

It was silent on the line again so I decided to bluff since she didn't know the station behind me was abandoned. "I'm going to ask directions in the gas station. I called to tell you where I'm at so goodbye and enjoy the Sulferson Silk corn steam smell for me. See you tonight."

"You win," she said drearily. "What's the address again? And can we pray about this? Maybe God can talk some sense into you."

When I walked into The FIRm, as the Fir family called their advertising and design agency, I wasn't sure what to expect. It looked like a typical office reception area with people coming and going like normal. I had to work to suppress the urge to scream, *your boss's son is a fugitive holed up somewhere with a stolen, annoying dog for no apparent reason. Any idea where he's at?*

But I smiled back at the receptionist and asked if Mr. Fir was in.

Her smile melted into a frown. "You don't have an

appointment. I'm sorry, but you'll have to leave."

"You didn't even ask my name." I hadn't expected outright snobbery.

She paused in her typing and folded her hands on the desk. "Mr. Fir has been in the hospital since last summer. You can't have an appointment with him, so you're obviously trying to get your foot in the door to ask for a job or sell Girl Scout cookies or whatever. Don't pretend outrage with me. And have a nice day." She went back to clicking the keys on her electric typewriter.

"Wait a minute, is he okay? I'm a friend of the family. Does Toby know?" *Hospital? Since summer. Must have gone in right after they got back from our spring semester in London. Why hadn't Toby mentioned it? He's got to be worried sick. Does he not know? Cause he should have been up here every weekend to see his dad.*

"Okay, I give. What is your name?"

I didn't mean to snap back at the sarcastic secretary. "Clare James."

"Oh." Her face paled and she picked up the telephone receiver off the bank of lights and switches in front of her. She turned her back to me and spoke low into the plastic banana shape. Swiveling her chair back around, she replaced the receiver in the cradle and took a deep breath.

"Miss James, my express apologies. Mr. Toby Fir has been running the FIRm since last summer when his father became ill. You are certainly on his guest list. I am so sorry I nearly turned you away. Please, take the elevator at the end of the hall all the way to the top."

Her eyes were large as she delivered her speech of impossibilities. Toby had been in school with me every day, not running his father's company and pining for letters from me. There was too much to process in what she'd said. I nodded at her and began shuffling toward the elevator. The answers were at the top of this building whether I liked them or not.

The walk to the elevator stretched out for an eternity. And then once inside the small box rising in slow motion, I found the air thick and hard to breath. I unwound my scarf and pulled my mittens off. My chest felt tight. I stared at the crack between the two doors. *How had he run a company here while attending classes and working in a secret lab in Sulfersonville? Who is going to be up here? Will Reginald be here? Will he shoot me?*

The bell chimed. The box I stood in ground to a halt. The doors slide silently open.

And there stood Trixie with her arms stretched out in a wide hug.

❦ Chapter Twenty-Two

"I hope you're not mad. I wanted to tell you I was back."

Trixie and I were sitting arm and arm on a sculpted bench in a glassed over patio off the executive board room watching the snow fall gently around us. It was designed to be a life size snow globe and despite the shock I'd just had, I was impressed with our surroundings. Serious props to the FIRm, whoever they really were, for design atmosphere.

She tossed a long hank of her flaming red hair over her shoulder and squeezed my elbow for the hundredth time. "It's so good to see you, Clare James! Too funny! Not a day goes by I don't hear your voice in my head telling me God loves me, even if I don't believe it."

I'd met Trixie in London. She was a theatre major and had gone abroad to intern in set design. We'd met off the plane at Heathrow Airport and the rest was history. When her semester internship was over, she'd decided to stay there rather then return for senior year. She had wanted to pursue her dream of working for the London theatre scene and she had a foot hold by the end of her internship. I had said a sad goodbye to her in a flat with two strange roommates. And she hadn't wanted a Bible I had brought her. I swallowed hard at the memory.

"I can't wrap my head around you being here. How long have you been here? What are you doing *here*?"

She whipped the conversation back to her earlier thought. "Don't be mad. Although you mad is something I don't think I've actually seen. Too funny. But really it was our decision together. Toby and I decided not to tell you about my work here until at least Christmas. I insisted on at least doing it then because I knew you'd probably invite me down to see the cows over the holidays. And I don't want to stay here. I'm sure it will continue to be morgue-like as long as Mr. Fir is in the hospital." She shivered. "I wanted you to come visit him like you did Simon. I bet you can get God to heal him, but Toby was too proud to ask you again, if you ask me. We know how seriously you take your art and school work. And since you wrote him and told him you didn't want to be distracted this semester with a long distance relationship –"

"What are talking about? I didn't write him. He's been in school all year with us. And where's Reggie?"

"*Clare!*"

My head pivoted toward the door and I fell back against the plush bench cushion as Toby's emotional voice hit the room like a sonic boom.

His face wore a smile that carried genuinely through his eyes, despite the dark circles under them. His hair was matted and his complexion was white as a sheet of paper. He looked super thin. I was taken aback by how fast his appearance had become so beaten. He held his arms out for a hug, but I remained in my seat.

"I don't know what is going on here with Trix, but why didn't you tell me about your dad? And why did you steal Reginald? And seriously, was that a real a gun, after all I've been through? And hitting on Jackie? My roommate of all people! You were supposed to have my back. How could you read the Bible with me every morning and pretend the whole time you didn't have an apartment on the side with a computer for movie making? You owe me some answers. And, like, *now*. Because in another hour it will have been long enough for the missing person's report to be filed and this is the first place the police are coming to start asking questions!" By the end of my outburst I was shaking.

Toby dropped his arms to his sides and looked seriously

confused.

"I don't know what you talking about. I was only following your directions, if this is about me not writing or calling. It's what you asked in your letter. If you wanted the opposite of what you said, you shouldn't play games like that. My dad is dying and this place takes everything I've got to keep it going *and* respect your wishes."

He looked hurt and exhausted. He slid on the bench across from us, his shoulders sagging, his head bent. The snow had stopped and the sunshine glowing through the thick clouds made his tallow skin look as if it had never been tanned. I wanted to slip an arm around his shoulders and tell him it was going to be okay. My heart was beating slowly in my chest. *Is this the same person I'd been talking to for months?*

"Toby, I never wrote a letter. You've been in school all year with me." I said gently.

"No, no, he's been here every hour of every day, working on the movie. It's an amazing thing, Clare. All done on computers. You should see it. He's got to get it done for the film festival reveal. In March. In Sarasota. You know, Florida. I've always wanted to go there. Too funny! Anyway, that's why I'm here. I'm working on set design in the old fashioned way to give a comparison demonstration. It's been so much fun, even if you weren't here to help." Trixie chattered nervously and squeezed my elbow again.

"How is that possible?" I asked, reeling. "He's had breakfast with me every morning since mid-term and I found out he's been dating a girl named Muriel and he has another apartment in town and like a double life as a guy named Coby." I had started out steamed as an oyster. But after seeing him looking like a lost little boy instead of that funny, carefree tease in London, I just wanted the answers. *Say something, anything! Explain yourself! What are you doing?*

"Did you say, *Coby?*" He looked up with a raised eye brow. "Hang on a minute, I think I may know what's going on here." Toby picked up a phone receiver from somewhere hidden in the bench and leaned forward to rest his elbows on his knees.

He could certainly have a minute to get his ducks in a row. I turned back to Trixie. "So spill it. *Why* on earth did you come back?"

She laughed, delighted at my attention. Giving her rust colored bangs a spunky toss out of her cerulean blue eyes, she stretched an arm and snuggled back on the bench. "I came back in September. The summer was kind of stinky. You were right, of course, about those wack-a-doodles I was rooming with. They got all obsessed and stockerish and I needed to leave. Not too funny. You're right about a lot of stuff, you know, Clare?" She asked rhetorically before plunging ahead in her characteristic style.

"So when Toby found out his dad was ill, he contacted me for help. I mean, since he was somehow led to believe you didn't want to be involved. At least for this semester. It really killed him, you know."

She lowered her voice and glanced at Toby rubbing his forehead on the phone. "To not be able to talk to you. You're all he talks about. And God." She rolled her eyes. "I can't get away from the Christians around here."

Despite my angst, I couldn't let that one pass. "Wait a minute, Trix. Doesn't that show you that God is trying to talk to *you*? You can't escape him. He loves you and he's trying to tell you. No matter what you've done, or what you are about to do, he'll still love and forgive you. Remember?"

Trixie nodded and smiled. "I know everything you told me by heart. Too funny." She said softly. "I can't talk about it, that's all. What I did. Not even to him, in my head."

I took her hand. It was like being smacked instantly back to England and all the other drama was somewhere else. I looked into her eyes and saw the shadow of hurt still lurking there. "Trixie, he already knows. Whatever happened, he was there. He doesn't want to make it hurt worse. He wants to heal you. I know. He worked a miracle for me and a professor I hated at school –"

Toby cleared his throat. We both jumped and looked at him. Trixie pulled her hand from mine and folded it with her other on her lap. I smiled. Whatever this all was, God had my back.

"Sorry to interrupt, but time is apparently of the essence." He paused, until we both nodded. "I think I have the answers to your questions, Clare. And I'm sorry I never told you more of my family history. Maybe this could have been avoided. I don't know." He raked his hand through his dry hair. It needed gel badly. I tried not to pity him. *This had better be good. He's got a lot of explaining to do.*

"It never seemed important in London and then once I got home, there was never time. I didn't even have time to come see you in person. By the time you had returned from Europe, my father was needing lots of care and the company was floundering. We have been working on this animation technology for several years now and with a real chance at making a name for ourselves in a film race, ah, are you familiar with what I'm talking about?"

I nodded.

"Ok, well, I had to keep it going for my dad. For all his hard work and what he believes in. What he wants to do for Christian filmmaking. For what he's done for me, for us." He paused and choked back tears. I looked at Trixie. She was uncomfortable.

"Should I go and let you two figure this out?" She asked.

"No!" We both said at the same time and she smiled. "K, what I wanted to hear."

Toby took a big breath. "My mother had been married before she married my father. She had told him her husband was a bad man and he was dead. His name was Martin something. Anyway, they had a daughter together, so I have a half-sister I've never met. She was kept in school somewhere. Anyway, when my brother and I were born –"

"Whoa, whoa, whoa, are you telling me *Wendy* is your sister?" I was startled.

"I'm sorry, I don't know her name or if she's involved in this."

Then the next part of what he was trying to tell us sunk in. "Time out, did you say you have a *brother*?"

"Yes, Clare. I'm sorry I didn't tell you sooner. His name is Coby. And we are identical twins. He's been in prison for corporate espionage so that's why he wasn't with me in London. Cody finished high school by fourteen and college by sixteen and was working for some heavy hitters before he could drive. He is an atheist and claims only now matters and for now he wants all the material goods he can get, even if that means illegal activities. I'm not making excuses for him. It's what he told us.

"When he was incarcerated, I started acting out and behaving ridiculously until I landed in London and met you, Clare. When Dad had business and came over, he was amazed at the choices I'd started making. We became close. Closer then I'd ever thought we'd be. He talked a lot about me coming to the FIRm when I graduated." He paused, choked up.

"Then he got sick. It came on suddenly. I'd been here working over the summer and so I stayed on. I guess I didn't think about my registration at school. They never contacted me or anything. That should have seemed strange, but I've been trying so hard to make this movie perfect by the deadline. I didn't even have time to come see you when you got back. I tried calling, but the FBI had you on some kind of call screen list and I decided it was easier to write." He stopped again and ran his hands through his hair.

"I honestly thought you'd come to Chicago and help me when you heard what had happened. I was embarrassed I'd overstepped and thought our relationship was more than it was." He looked at the ground. Then his head bobbed up and our eyes met.

"It makes more sense knowing that you never wrote the letter I got. It had to be Coby. I had no idea he was out or pretending to be me. We thought he still had five years to serve, but our attorney just confirmed for me he's out on good behavior. Since Dad and I were overseas in London when he was released, we weren't notified. He knew about Dad, though. I sent letters to the prison constantly, but they were never answered."

Toby held out a frame with a photo of a foursome. I recognized his dad, assumed the lady was his mother and then focused on the two young men. Two replicas of Toby, smiling. I felt like a balloon letting out all its air. Relieved and relaxing. There was an explanation for his behavior. *It's not him!*

Toby spoke again. "He had to have waylaid the letter I wrote you and written me a bogus one from you to keep us from communicating. And he took my place at University. So he's been hanging out with you and …?"

"I've been avoiding you, frankly." I said with a twinkle in my eye. "Certainly no hanky-panky." I tried not to blush at the silly term. "It probably made it easier for him to keep up the charade since I was the only one who knew you at this new University. But he did ask my roommate out and he was dating a girl that worked for Curtis Sulferson, you know, of Sulferson Silks."

"Being a cad was never his MO. That was more me, so I suppose he thought that's what you'd expect. It sounds like he's been up to no good, though. But are we okay now? I could sure use a tall glass of your encouragement."

I smiled. "I think so."

"Good," he smiled uncertainly. "So what do I need to do to stop the police from hauling me away?" He looked tired again. The strain of this new facet of life was not going to be easy to deal with.

We were interrupted by screams somewhere far away.

"Do you guys hear that?" I asked, standing to my feet.

The door to Toby's office slammed against the wall and I ducked involuntarily. Men clad in black with guns crossing their bodies swarmed the room and threw us to the ground.

With my face crushed into the soft pile carpet, I couldn't see anything. I didn't have any breath to yell with anyway. I hadn't expected Rupert to muster this kind of force for a dognapper.

✣ Chapter Twenty-Three

"I'm back to square one and that's with knowing everything that's happened so far. I mean I know what's happened, I just don't know why." I straightened up to survey the paper in front of me. I liked where this drawing was going. It felt like surprised anger and that's what I wanted to put in it. Hurt. Betrayal. All the things that people disappoint you with and all the things holding you captive from being all you could truly be. *Until Jesus sets you free right where you're at. Perfect for white lilies to litter the grass all around her body.*

My hands were slick and black with graphite. I padded into the adjoining bathroom and watched the soap turn grey and bubbly as I lathered up under the warm water. The clean smell helped alleviate the high pitched baking smell of the Sulferson factory. I buried my face in the fresh towel I was wiping my hands on and inhaled the comforting scent of laundry.

Jackie stretched and yawned under a quilt on the bed where she was reading and high-lighting textbooks. "I can't believe what a tangled tale you can weave. Literally! I think I should get my PhD for just keeping it all straight." She ticked off the events on her fingers. "Toby took Reginald from the mansion first, then Muriel took Reginald from Toby's place in town, then Morty took Reginald from Muriel's place, then Red and Coop beat up Morty and took Reginald, then Toby got him back from Red and Coop somehow and brought him to the frat house here on campus. Or at least a dog very similar to Reggie. We're operating under the assumption that there is only one dog. So after that, Wendy coaxed him out of the frat house and Red and Coop bashed her on the head and took him to Red's sister's house where you and Key converged. As you two jumped in your loaner car from Sulferson, Toby held you guys up and voila, drove off with one pug having a gold fish shaped marking on his back leg. Oh and replace all the times I said Toby with Coby. Am I right, or am I right? What is up with this dog?"

I had returned to my easel by the windows and began shading the soft curves of the white flower petals with a 9H pencil. The H stood for hardness and the graphite was diluted down to almost nothing in the clay mix that suspended it and kept the strokes pale and scratchy on the paper. With a gentle nudge of a blending stump I caressed the vague graphite into a soft grey blush coming from the center of the flower. Key could master a lily in spray paint the size of your car, but I could form one with dust and smudge and the blowing of soft breath across the paper. I was in love with how it looked. Moving up to the next one peeking out from under her wing, I began the process again, thinking about Jackie's summation of the case.

Trixie and I had been released from the Chicago PD, almost before we'd entered the building, but it had taken longer to untangle Toby. The lab tech who had been injured in the robbery had died. Once the missing person's report had been issued, Rupert had been able to get a search warrant for Coby's apartment and the computer inside had been stolen during the lab break in. An arrest warrant was issued for Toby for murder and before it could all be sorted, Toby had spent a night in jail. Proof of his identical twin, witnesses, and finger print evidence got him cleared and he had spent Thanksgiving with Trixie at my parent's house. Now they were both back at the FIRm, working on their movie. I planned to join him and Trixie in Chicago over Christmas break, but first I had to finish half my exhibit pieces and Reginald's portrait commission. Coby and Reginald and the missing movie file had not turned up. I eased the pencil off the paper with a delicate hand and realized I'd been holding my breath. Exhaling, I turned toward Jackie.

"You're right. I actually feel sorry for the little rascal. The factory workers and Morty and Muriel, all that makes sense. Even crazy Wendy wanting to help her dad find a donor kind of works, but what about Coby? Why did he take Reginald and keep taking him? And he's the one that started it all in the first place. I don't get it. Arggghh!"

I tossed my pencil at my drawing and stretched my arms up over my head. At least this piece was coming along great for my exhibit and I'd be able to show it to Martin this weekend when he came home from the hospital. I was eager to see if the new Martin was still kicking or if he'd reverted to evil Martin.

Either way, this piece was for him. It was deeper and darker than anything else I'd ever drawn. But like Key said, there were many false paths to freedom and things that can derail us from attaining it and this was my depiction of freedom failure.

She was breath-taking. I sighed and crossed my arms in front of me. I couldn't draw anyone more beautiful and more lost. I studied the pale fan of feathers as it cascaded down from her outstretched arm and nestled against the thick coarse grass and lilies she'd landed on. Stray feathers gracefully scattered on the grass down from her wing and across her stomach. The drawing only showed her from waist up, her left side cropped off by the page, her hair splayed out from the right side of her head and entangled in the grass. A tickle of blood from her mouth was the only thing to mar her perfect skin and spot the front of her white lace tunic. Her eyes were glass-like as they stared straight into your soul, locked in the moment when she tasted pride's full flavors and it took the breath from her body.

I wasn't one for Greek mythology, but stories made by the conspiring of man and demon seemed appropriate to illustrate Martin's life. The piece was a portrait of him and the ugliness in my own heart I had nearly been trapped by.

The lovely maiden in the drawing was like Icarus. He had wings made of wax and feathers and he was warned not to fly too close to the sun as he escaped the Labyrinth he was trapped in. Once he started flying, though, he was intoxicated by hubris and flew higher and higher and higher. When the sun's heat melted the wax holding the feathers together, his wings disintegrated. He fell to his death. I planned to tint her eyes with the faintest hints of golden brown and the blood droplets with the ripe blush of red colored pencil. The Bible warns us that pride goes before a fall.

I swiveled my chair from side-to-side with my hips, expelling adrenalized energy from creating. My mind drifted from the drawing to Martin to Sulferson to gnawing at the dog problem again.

What am I missing?

The deadline for Reginald's painting was looming dangerously close. Muriel had given me an appointment tomorrow on Curtis Sulferson's packed docket to show him the painting I'd been working on with Zac's dog as a stand in. But I didn't have much hope he'd go for it. He was being so stubborn. If I made the markings according to the documentation of Reginald, the judges wouldn't, they couldn't, actually know the difference. It was as if he wanted the painting to *not* get painted.

I mean, come on, what a joke to hire poor Sammy in the first place. Then when her mom got burned so badly in the car accident she had to return to help her family and was unable to paint it . . . *Wait a minute. Could Sammy's mom's accident have been orchestrated by Curtis Sulferson? According to Key, the FBI is trying to pin things like that on him...*

He had put almost impossible demands on Sammy to find a replacement, which against all odds, she had. Then he brought in Wendy, a daughter of a 'friend' to be the dog walker. Not only did she kept getting bonked on the head, which was helpful to eliminating an heir, but she began to sabotage my work. Did Sulferson know Martin's secret inability to paint? Clearly I could accomplish the painting.

So when Wendy and Martin failed to stop my work, did Sulferson hire Coby to take Reginald? But that's crazy. Why wouldn't he want the trust to dole out the funds to fix the factory and stop the riots?

What would happen if the fund was held up? The factory would destroy itself with riots and the town would fold. People would move. Would the University move? Would Martin move? Martin was supposed to die from a terminal illness. His daughter could be arrested for vandalism and theft and who knows what else Sulferson could drum up. She could be killed in prison. And the trust? Well, what would happen if no dogs inherited? As long as there were people to, they should, right? Santhe, Martin, and Wendy people, that's who. But if they were all dead, then where did all the money go?

I dropped my arms from behind my head and spun my stool around to face Jackie's study nook.

Jackie looked up from her book and noticed my stricken face.

"You should be used to the smell by now," she said with a giggle.

"Oh, no, I was thinking about something. But now that you mention it, Sulferson Silks is sure putting out the smell like a toaster burning bread, aren't they?"

"Yah, sometimes it makes it hard to concentrate." She shifted and looked at her watch. "Hey, shouldn't you be leaving to babysit Prof Bob's kids?" she asked. I blinked.

"Oh, yeah. Whoops! I spaced that like a chicken wanting a banana!" I bolted from my stool as I noted the time.

"Stop! Wait a minute!" She sat up from her books wagging a hand toward my drawing board. "Don't leave her to stare at me all night."

"Sorry." I grabbed a sheet on the floor next to the easel with two hands and billowed it up and over my work area. "I think I figured out why Coby took the dog, but I need to work it out in my head again to make sure it makes sense and I need to find out what happens to the money in the Sulferson Trust if there's no dog *or* people to inherit it. Tell you when I get back." I yelled down the hall as I sprinted for the back door, wiping graphite on my jeans and dragging on my coat.

Prof Bob lived across town in a quaint cottage for University staff and students with children. I had baby sat for them a dozen or so times since school had started. It gave me a little cash and them a reliable sitter since the only family near them was Prof Bob's aging parents.

The little multicolored picket fence he'd painted with his girls last year peeked timidly out of the deep snow surrounding the squat bungalow. As night set in, the side windows spilled a glow out onto the high white banks on either side of the house as if it couldn't contain the warmth and love within. The lights of a Christmas tree winked at me in the front picture window like something out of a Thomas Kincaid painting.

"Clarey Bear! Clarey Bear!" Two waist high heads bobbed in and out of the front door, jumping excitedly to see me and expelling breath clouds into the crisp evening air. I slammed the door of the jeep and waded through the thigh high white powder to the steps.

"Oh, sorry, Clare. Our guy is buried and didn't make it by to shovel out the walk." Mrs. Bob's flat face and slanted eyes always looked happy, even when she was apologizing. Maybe it was the way she tilted her sheaf of iron black hair from side to side, or fluttered her dainty hands, that made her appear perpetually celebrating. Whatever it was, I liked her. Her daughters were swinging on my scarf, and tugging at my jacket and mittens, with the dozen hands two anxious toddlers seem to possess.

I laughed, stomping my boots off on the welcome mat to dislodge the clumped snow. The room was toasty. The occupants had made it homey with colorful furniture and framed works of art by both daughters' crayons and daddy's computer mouse.

"It's fine, Mrs. Bob. I made it! Are you sure you want to go out tonight in this weather?" I glanced out the picture window at the sudden snow shower illuminated by the street light out front. A girl, who had been walking by the house when I pulled up, was walking by again the other way. She looked familiar. *Could she be that Kelly Splint chick I met in Zac's lab with the twins? I guess she has to live somewhere, but why is she pacing out there?*

"Originally it was going to be a girl's night out, Clare, but we cancelled that. Now, with Bob away at conference and his mother so ill, I wanted to use the time to run her and his father over a meal and tidy up their house. I don't know how bad she is, you know? If she needs to be coaxed to go to the clinic, I want to go sooner than later."

"Oh, sure, no problem. We'll be fine here. Everything the same as usual?" She nodded. "Then take as long as you need." I waved from the living room where I was already being pressed into service as a Lego-balancer, purse stand, ball bouncer, artist outlining their hands, and fellow princess with crown. She smiled and left through the still open door, closing it gently behind her.

Lights from her car had no more then shot across the ceiling as she backed out to leave then the doorbell rang.

"Hang on girls, your mommy must have forgotten something."

"Clarey Bear! Clarey Bear!" They chanted, running off to their room.

I swung the door wide and the smile froze on my lips. "Can I help you? Kelly Splint, right?"

She smiled. "It's freezing out here, can I come in?"

"This isn't my home, so I'm sorry, no." I slightly closed the door and squared my body across the opening. "Are you having car trouble?"

"No." She tossed her blond hair to dislodge the clinging snowflakes and jammed her hands deeper in her pockets.

"Look, Clare, I'll be honest with you. I need to check something for Prof Bob."

"That seems a little far-fetched since he's out of town and that's why I'm here babysitting, which you seemed to be waiting for."

"Look, he'll be back when he figures out the conference material he was sent all contain the wrong dates and his mother isn't sick, just sedated, get the picture? I need to get into his office for four minutes tops and then you'll probably never see me again." She pranced from one foot to the other on feet that must have been freezing in snow crusted ballet flats.

"You'll have to bring me permission from the Bobs or evidence showing they're super villains if you want in this house." I had slammed the door and flipped the bolt before I finished talking and she could launch herself inside. The phone was ringing. I glanced out the window as I went to check on the girls. She was still standing on the front step shivering.

The girls were nestled in their canopy slash life-size doll house cooing to each other with their books and dollies and blankets. The phone was still ringing. Apparently the Bobs didn't have an answering machine, which I'd never noticed before. But I guess the phone never ran when I was there before. I picked up the receiver in the living room.

"Hello, Bob's residence, this is the sitter speaking."

"Very professional sounding, but it tells the caller the Bobs aren't home and a person unfamiliar with the house is in charge. Not safe, Clare." A stern voice admonished me from the other end of the line.

"Well as soon as you ask for Prof Bob or Mrs. Bob and I ask if I can take a message, you'll know the same thing, Director Pierce."

"Not necessarily. They could be in the shower or the attic and can't come to the phone. You could be a mistress or an adult child visiting. Either way, it's not as safe a bet as a young female baby sitter."

"You've seen too many movies." I said. She laughed.

"They'd keep you on the phone until they got all the information they needed, but since we already have almost all we need, I have only one thing to ask of you, Clare."

"Is this about Kelly Splint?" I lifted the curtain away and peeked out the front window. She was clapping her hands and hopping in the snow under the little front stoop.

"Yes. We are systematically clearing people for the tech murder who have access to any sort of computer lab. We have to make sure Prof Bob isn't a super villain, as you put it. Kelly needs to check his home office."

"We artists call it a studio, but does Kelly work for you or Zac Sulferson?" I asked.

"Both," she said evenly. "But me more."

"Have I been cleared?"

"Yes. And so has Toby. He has his own version of a movie going that's nothing like the stolen one, not to mention a solid alibi and all that good stuff."

"But his brother's in trouble."

"I can't discuss an open case with you, Clare. Let Kelly do her job and enjoy those two sweet little girls for me. They grow up all too soon." She sighed on the other end of the crackling line. "I hope Kelly doesn't find anything there."

"Me too." I hung up and flipped the bolt on the front door.

❧ Chapter Twenty-Four

"That ridiculous blanket! I always forget to tie it down and it sails off my lap every time. No matter how many times it happens, I always start out of my room lickety-split, enjoying the wind in my hair, and then I have to face the consequences. We're all like that, aren't we, Miss James?"

I stood up and handed him the blanket from the foot of his wheelchair.

"Sir?"

"You know, headlong into bad behavior, loving every minute of it and then we have to face the consequences? Man is a sinful being by nature. Our savior is the only get out of jail free card we get and if we don't accept him, the consequences will be long and lean in hell." He flipped his chair around and looked out the window.

"What about you, Miss James? Are you getting out of jail free?"

"Yes, Mr. Sulferson. I am." I shifted nervously from one foot to the other, surprised by the turn the conversation had taken. I was there to present the work on the painting I had done with Gigabit as my model. Did Muriel tell him why I had made this appointment?

He spun his chair back at me and his wrinkled, weathered face broke into a smile. "Glad to hear it, I am. That puts us on the same page. A standard, so I know what you mean and you know what I mean.

"I know there's a lot of misconceptions about me floating about out there. A lot of rumors. A lot of conjuncture and speculation. But one thing I can tell you, Miss James, is that the Bible is my Golden Standard. So whatever you hear, if it doesn't measure up, then it's not true. And you can always come to the source and ask me and I'll tell you the truth about any of it."

He stopped talking and looked at me.

"Okay. If you're really serious, Sir. Did you hire Coby Fir to take Reginald?"

He busted out laughing. "That's what the police think? What is my motive, pray tell, Young Lady?"

"Well, I don't know about the police. I've traced Reginald's dognapping through a number of people, but I know Coby took him first and I don't know why. He's gone missing and I can't ask him."

"Convenient for somebody." The old man looked ancient in the morning sunlight as he leaned his head back on the motorized chair.

"It kind of looks like for you, Sir. I mean. You hired Sammy in the first place when she couldn't paint the last stripe on a zebra. Then she starts to pick it up in Italy and her mom coincidently gets hurt. Accidents can be faked." He had closed his eyes and wasn't moving, but I hurried on nervously. "Just saying. If we're talking supposition. It made it impossible for her to come back and paint. And you also put impossible demands on her replacement, but she managed to find me. Now, you also hired Wendy to work for you and Wendy is sabotaging my work on campus. Which could get me expelled or at least run off to another school. But here's me, still working on the painting. So if the painters won't stop painting, what if the subject is taken away?"

I paused and took a deep breath.

"Is that all?" He asked quietly.

"Is it because of the Trust terms, Sir? You know, on second thought, if it's going to endanger me, I don't think I want to know." I sagged down in a leather chair and looked at my feet. *What was I doing? Sealing my own death warrant?*

At his chuckle, I raised my head and looked at his jolly face.

"Clare James, what an imagination you have! Be reassured, I'm not going to hurt you, or anyone for that matter. Sammy was selected by the Commission Club for me. I didn't know her before she came the first day to start.

"I tried to help her, but when her mom was hurt, I had to make sure my investment was covered. I would have still covered her expenses, I only wanted to motivate her to find you. I'd heard about you through the grapevine and I wanted to have you back and working on the painting for me. I knew you could do it and I also knew some things weren't right around here that a good sleuth could uncover.

"I didn't have Sammy's mom hurt. I didn't have Wendy vandalize your paintings. She's a relative I've done a favor for giving her a job. And she loves Reginald. I'm sorry she's been harassing you and I can try and get to the bottom of it, but you strike me as a perfectly capable woman to do so yourself.

"Hmmm. Oh, yes, and to answer your biggest question – I did not have Reggie stolen." He stroked his blanket absently and looked out the window at the river again. "I know he's a means to an end for this family, but I miss the little guy. I've had private investigators and the like trying to track him down and I can only pray he's okay."

"I wish I could help," I said. "I only know Coby took him last from Key and me at gun point and disappeared."

"You think he's in the catacombs?" Curtis offered.

"You mean under the theatre?" I hadn't thought of that. I had expected him to run far and wide, not stick around. Hiding in plain sight?

"Look, Clare, I know you're here to show me the painting. But part of integrity is not lying. Even if the judges can't tell the picture isn't Reggie and they pass the painting, we'll know. God will know."

He stopped talking and looked at me again.

"You are right, of course, Sir. It's your call. You know what's at stake and what we can do with what we have."

"Let me see it." He waved a hand at the covered canvas I had leaning on my leg.

I pulled the sheet off and spun the piece around to face him in the light from the open window. I was looking down at it and I quickly looked up at him when I heard his gasp.

"It's perfect." He breathed, his face pale in the morning sunlight. "I hadn't expected it to be so good, Clare."

"Well, thank you, Sir." I prayed a moment in my head before I spoke again.

"I understand what you're saying, so if you don't want the painting, I can start again when we find Reggie. This painting is Reggie, though, Sir. I may have looked at another source for exact color and texture references but I was painting him. I had him in my mind's eye and I had sketches I'd done of him. This is a painting of him. I mean, just because he didn't sit for me clear to the end of it, I'm not sure there is an integrity issue here."

Curtis Sulferson hadn't spoken, but was still frozen in his chair, clenching at his chest.

"Sir? Mr. Sulferson, are you okay?"

I touched his elbow.

"Sir? Can you hear me?"

When he didn't move, I dropped the painting, and ran into the hall screaming for help.

✤ Chapter Twenty-Five

"So did you do it?" Jackie was wrapped up in a blanket, her perpetual book attached to an arm, fingers made of highlighters. "Did you turn the painting over to his solicitor?"

"I had to." I tucked my flash cards for art history away and settled on my stool in front of my drawing easel. We had eight hundred pieces up to now that we'd studied over the last three years and my handmade flash card set refreshed my memory weekly. By the end of senior year, we'd have memorized the period, artist, title, and media of one thousand ancient or past artworks. And any one of those pieces were fair game in our weekly tests. Tests in the dark looking at only a four inch piece of each painting.

The slivers were enough to identify or make an educated guess from. At random we had to give either the period, the artist, the title, or the media. It made it impossible to cheat and nearly impossible to best.

I loved it. It was the ultimate challenge for me. A game I only got better and better at, but told no one about. Instinctively I knew I'd be hated and envied if it got out I hadn't missed a single answer since my first test freshmen year. I also suspected the prof added curve balls here and there to try and stump me. I assumed I was the only one with the current record. My mother had warned me what to expect from her college classes years ago. I had practiced in high school and I was raring and ready to go when the room darkened the first time. A collective flabbergasted exclamation had blossomed in the air as only a ring, a scarf, a pair of shoes, a horse's eye, and a parade of other items flashed before us with the monotone voice never wavering. "Number one, period. Number two, artist, Number three, period. Number one again for number four, title..."

Jackie said my flashcard set would be worth hundreds of dollars on the student note taking black market when we graduated. I didn't think I'd sell it. Its corners were worn and smooth from use. Its layers were crafted by my own shorthand. It was a work of art. *Maybe it could be in my show? Humph. Kind of cool. It would need some heavy insurance because it would more than likely get stolen. But speaking of shows, let's get cracking on this piece.*

I broke out of my day dream to find where I'd last left off caressing stroke after graphite stroke of grass on the paper before me. Martin had praised my drawing of Miss Icarus, but he wanted something to make her feel like she was laying down and we were standing over her. Right now she looked like she was standing in front of us the way the drawing was hung on the wall. I was adding more thick grass and rocks and items to ground it. I liked all the texture it was adding to it.

I rubbed over the graphite strokes I'd applied with a tissue and watched them defuse slightly into the paper and each other. Art supply companies sold you a drawing hide made from calf or lamb skin to do the same thing, but I thought they felt gross. Kind of slimy, they were so soft. And they gathered graphite so fast one had to constantly clean them and work the stiffness out. It was all a pain. I opted to use a tissue I could toss when I was done. One of my drawing teachers had shared her secret with me years ago and I'd never looked back like Paul Revere.

"Well, you could have said it wasn't done or it wasn't him." I jumped at Jackie's voice as she stretched and her blanket slid off onto the floor.

"Oh, the painting. I tried to explain. He didn't care. Curtis is still in a coma, not likely to come out of it. The heart attack was bad. The lawyer said my contract was to produce a painting by the deadline or be sued by Curtis Sulferson's private estate and probably the Worker's Union too. I handed him the painting and he left. He's apparently employed by the trust, but clearly thinks it's silly. It's in the hands of the judges now. I did what I was hired to do."

"I guess it solved the argument you were set to have with Sulferson about whether the painting was genuine or not. Of course, I can't imagine the judges stymieing the verdict and holding up the funds. The factory will get its repairs, the workers will get their raises, and the world will continue to get things sweetened by something other than cane sugar. All will be well." Jackie highlighted something in her book while she spoke.

"How do you do that?" I asked her admiringly.

"Do what?" She looked up, confused.

"Talk and read at the same time." She'd done it for years.

"I don't know." She laughed. "Any word on Coby?" I knew she was slipping it in there casually because she was dying to ask, but didn't want to appear interested in a double agent.

"No, none yet." I looked at her slyly over my shoulder. "I'm glad it turned out there was a brother for each of us."

I ducked the pillow she threw at me. "I'm not saying I want to see him after all he's done!"

"You can be one of those prison groupies or what are they called?" I didn't duck in time and the second pillow winged off the side of my head and brushed through the graphite on my drawing, making a smooth patch.

"Oh, sorry, did I ruin something?" She sat up quickly and bumped her head on the top bunk above her. "Owww. Oh, I've got to get used to these beds again." She cried out, rubbing her scalp. "Seriously, did I maim your senior project?"

"No, No, it's fine. I like what it's doing." I drifted into the soft texture and was lost in the graphite, pushing and pulling, laying it on and erasing it back off. I was quickly unaware of anyone else in the room or of any troubles in the world around me.

The phone jangled on the desk beside me, but I barely noticed as I muttered to myself and gauged how a darker shadow here would pop the feathers off the dirt area there. Jackie answered the phone and said something to me and left the room. I slowly lost concept of time and didn't even have a pang of hunger as the supper hour came and went. I drew deeper and deeper into the night, guided only by the circle of light cast from a reading lamp over my easel.

Hours later, the soft rays of dawn licking at the edge of my paper through the frosty window pulled me from my concentration. My neck was stiff and my back ached. My hands and forearms itched from the graphite dust. My nose was itchy too. I pulled a tissue from the box on Jackie's desk and blew. The snot was dark gray. Graphite dust.

I noticed Jackie was snoring softly. She had returned some time during the night and was sleeping peacefully on the bottom bunk. She must have changed into her p.j.'s without my notice.

I stretched stiffly and wandered into our bathroom to wash my hands and shuck my contacts. The chill in the room made my breath into a steamy coating on the mirror in front of me. I blinked at my elongated nose and neck, distorted by the mist in a Modigliani like stretch. Poor man, I knew nothing of him but that he painted and drew portraits in a long and stretched out way. And his name was fun to say. Mawd igg le on e. Miss Burke in the sixth grade said it like so, but was she even right?

People can at least pronounce my name without question. Clare James. But is that all they will remember of who I am? Her name was simple, oh and she drew pictures of things which didn't coexist, making them appear to belong to each other. I leaned on the sink and locked my elbows, peering into the depths of my brown eyes. There were flecks of yellow and green in them. I had long lashes and dark eyebrows. Was that a good thing? Was I pretty? Was I memorable?

Ah, my art is, one way or the other. The coexistence is the key. Saint can live with sinner because we are all sinners. Wings on a girl because while we will crash and die on our own, with Jesus, we can all be free to fly. For the wages of sin is death, but the gift of God is eternal life in Christ Jesus our Lord. Romans 6:23.

Be careful to depict a message people need, so when they remember it, it will help them. For what good do elongated faces do me? A wasted opportunity to express the gift of God. I shook my head.

Sliding under the covers in the top bunk, I was satisfied. Half my show was done and it was time to pack my bags for Christmas vacation. Christmas Eve and Christmas Day at home and then on to Chicago. When I returned from helping Toby and Trixie, I'd have four or five uninterrupted months to finish my show pieces before it went up and I graduated.

Graduated. Graduated. Graduated. The word echoed in my tired brain.

What is going to happen after that? Originally Toby and I were going to work together at the FIRm. But now I'm not so sure. Do I want to work with Toby after all the confusion with Coby? I yawned and rolled over to snuggle into the covers deeper. My last thoughts drifted hazily away on a cloud of sleep. *Can I fall in love with him now, Lord?*

❧ Chapter Twenty-Six

"Would you like a hors d'oeuvre?" I tried not to laugh as Kay, who had stuffed five of the little shrimp and cracker works-of-art on his tray into his mouth, before flourishing the tray at me with a muffled offer. He was sporting a tux and pedaling a silver platter of delicacies with white gloves. Clearly he was also eating more then he was serving to guests.

"Why is it you're always around when there's some kind of food available?" I teased him.

He grinned at me and popped several more into his mouth so fast I almost didn't notice.

"Is he giving you trouble, Miss?" I turned at Jay's voice and saw him in a matching penguin suit brandishing a tray of chocolates. I gave up trying not to chuckle at seeing double as I sampled his wares.

"How do you guys get to work here? I mean, I see the symmetrical room design and your outfits make it feel like Sol LeWitt and Rene Magritte's paintings had a baby, but I thought only work-study students got to fleece the posh parties and collect the big tips."

Work-study students came from low income families and this guaranteed them wage paying jobs on campus. The best jobs on campus, like this one at the art center, were ear marked for work-study employees only.

"Nah. Since Martin saw you in the lab with us at the beginning of the year, he offered us jobs during his gallery openings." Kay said around bulging checks.

Jay chimed in. "We work all his shows, even the ones downtown or in Chicago. And he always uses our twin-ness to make a statement of some sort."

Kay finished his thought. "But it's great tips, so we don't mind. We haven't seen him the last few shows, anyway."

"Which has been a relief," Jay continued, "because he only hangs around and asks us about students."

"And you," Kay said.

"Mostly you," Jay finished.

I rolled my eyes. "He's in the hospital now, recovering from an organ transplant. It went well. Praise God."

"Forget about that. Aren't you going to ask us what he wanted to know?" Kay looked crest fallen I hadn't taken their bait. They were acting like two little boys trying to catch a lizard.

"Or more importantly, what we *told* him?" Jay narrowed his eyes and tried to look mysterious. I had to laugh again.

"I have a pretty good idea what he wanted to know, but it's all water under the bridge anymore. Sorry guys, I gotta mingle." They both looked disappointed as I turned away with a swish of my deep burgundy evening gown.

I turned back just as fast when I caught a whiff of the smell on Paul's comic notes. But the brothers had dissolved into the crowd and there were so many people around me gussied up in finery I couldn't tell where the odor was coming from. Who had searched Paul's things and was it the same person who had stolen my box of notes from England? Thinking of Paul reminded me why I'd come tonight and I began to make my way across the crowded room.

Martin didn't want to steal any more work, but he had been too sick to stop this exhibit opening. Per his usual M.O. it was all taken from one particular student. And it was all branded with six letters M-A-R-T-I-N. No matter what style of work he was exploring, or exploiting as I liked to think in my head, the critics adored the way

Martin used a branding iron to leave his name seared dark brown into the surface of the paint.

I thought it was tacky. Especially since I knew none of the cattle were his to claim.

But the new Martin had begged me to find Paul and make sure he was all right. I was to express Martin's apologies and offer to make a public statement when he was well enough. I wondered if Martin would ever admit in public he had stolen all his famous works. I was skeptical. He'd get out of it somehow, even if he had to die to do it.

I spied Paul, looking uncomfortable in his monkey suit, surrounded by a gaggle of freshmen sorority girls. I shooed them away like flies, offering him one of the champagne flutes I'd taken from a tray held by a man who looked too old to be a student, or at least a work-study student. I clinked the edge of his glass and took a sip before linking my arm through his and pulling him out into the middle of the gallery. We sat on a bench facing a wall of his pieces and surveyed the splendor in silence. His work was abstract. A bit like if candle wax had dripped on the canvas in different colors. The longer I looked, though, the more I saw in each piece. A face, a hand, a light bulb. They were hidden object puzzles with a sense of humor. And with Martin's famous name on them, they were selling for thousands of dollars as red dots blossomed across the wall on each name plate.

I squeezed his arm through his jacket sleeve. "You're going to have a sold out show at this rate. Each dot shows a piece someone has bought."

He looked melancholy. "What difference does it make? They don't know it's my work. *Martin* will have a sold out show." He sighed. "I thought I could handle it. I thought it might even be fun. But I realize now I can never get back these parts of me on the wall people are going to take away. Only it won't be me they think they are holding.

"I wasn't prepared, Clare, for how sick it makes me feel. Like a part of me has been betrayed. Violated. Like after I took the movie file and then it was all over the news the next day." He stopped talking, but my heart was in my throat. *Did he say movie file?*

"Okay, up on your feet, you big ox. March. Into the studio right now, Mister. We need to talk."

Chapter Twenty-Seven

"I can't believe you stole the movie file from the Sulferson lab!" I sank onto the linoleum floor and looked at the dust bunnies under his paint cart. A small scrap of paper was under one wheel. My mind didn't want to accept what he was telling me, so I shoved the cart over a smidge and dislodged the four inch by three inch piece of wrinkled and stained paper. It was one of Paul's little drawings. My heart sank further down in my body, seeming to touch the bottom of my stomach and thus the floor.

"Why couldn't I steal it?" Paul's anger ignited to red hot instantly. "Because like all your other friends, you think I'm an ignorant fine art major who isn't smart enough to turn on a computer, let alone steal its contents? A crazy painter who turns his underwear inside out to wear it longer! A vagrant who lives in the studios! I know the rumors. I'm not deaf or dumb!" He threw his jar of brushes across the room and the glass bottle shattered against the wall sending glinting shards and stick handles in every direction.

I cringed and I held up the scrap of paper for him to see. My eyes looking at him over the top of it were hot as I blinked hard to keep the tears from brimming over. "Because I didn't want it to be *you* in trouble."

He was frozen by the image on the paper. His shoulders sagged and his head bowed. He sank to the floor on his knees and then slide over beside me. We magnetized toward each other until the tops of our heads rested together, making a teepee shape with our bodies. Not speaking. Just hurting.

And then sobbing.

I wasn't sure why I was crying with him, except that his hurt was so strong I could feel it too. Empathy, I suppose, for the pain his spirit was going through. The grief racked our bodies so hard it made little pools of tears on the floor under our chins.

I had never seen a wound deep enough to create a puddle of tears before. As we came to the end of the water our bodies could spare for such activity, we both sputtered and coughed, gasping for breath in the thick air polluted with the smell of Sulferson Silk.

Paul's head was warm where it touched the top of mine and I

looked down at my hands. His tiny cartoon was crumpled in my clenched fist in the folds of my dress spread out around me like a flower where I knelt on the floor. I unwound my fingers and smoothed the wrinkled paper out on the lush, velvety material covering my knee.

Paul's typical sketch of Martin with Einstein hair and a big nose was featured here. But instead of setting students on fire with his breath or beating someone with a paint brush, he was doing something entirely different. He was holding a little boy's hand.

Sniffling, Paul sat up. I caught my balance and sat up straight too. I pulled some clean paint rags from off the cart behind me and passed him one. We wiped our faces and blew our noses and sat quietly. He loosened the collar of his tux shirt buttons and I pulled off my uncomfortable strappy shoes. The old metal clock on the studio wall knew all the secrets of the people who had come and gone and it seemed to roar at us in the silence. TICK. TOCK. I. KNOW. ALL.YOU. GOT.TICK. TOCK.

I jumped when Paul spoke next.

"She was my mom, you know. The first student whose work he passed off as his own to the University board." His voice was empty of emotion. Monotone and impersonal. "Martin tells the story of a male student artist whose work he used with mutual satisfaction to them both, but he's lying. I don't know why. I used to like to think it was because he couldn't bear to think about my mom.

She was one of his freshmen art students. Her name was Margaret Vales. She was in love with him and maybe he loved her as much as he could love anyone. She wrote me letters and drew me pictures in her journal before I was born. Little sketches like I do. That's why I do them. It's all I have left of her.

"They started his art empire together with her work and his connections. She eventually graduated and moved into a river cottage. The one that's a guest house for his current estate. She had me in the summer and his wife had Wendy the following fall.

"Martin was arrogant and self-centered. He lived a double life in the same town. Two families, two miles apart. Margret knew he was married, but I don't think his wife knew about her, at least at first.

"As his career was hitting the pinnacle of perfection, Margaret was killed in a car accident. Burned. Like Sammy's mother. Mrs. Sullivan's accident looked like someone was trying to sabotage the dog painting to me. I got to thinking about my own mother's death and it occurred to me Margaret might have been murdered. I got the accident reports on both incidents and I was right. Fuel lines cut, brakes cut, but no suspects. Unsolved cases slanted as tragic car accidents in the media.

"I suspected my dad for a while. But Martin was in anguish whenever he appeared in the papers. He suffered from depression and had stopped working according to the official statements. And from anyone I've tracked down who was a past student of his after the year my mother died, he was nothing but horrible to everyone. He didn't act like someone who had eliminated a problem. It nearly destroyed him, deforming his greedy and manipulative tendencies into the guise of a cruel task master.

"I decided if I wasn't going to accuse him, then the next place to look was means. I turned my investigation to Curtis Sulferson, my great uncle and the reigning patriarch of the family. He certainly had the money and the reach. He could have been trying to clean up the family skeletons or manipulate the release of funds from their stupid dog trust." His voice choked with emotion.

"I'm so sorry, Paul." I laid a comforting hand on his shoulder and choked on a sneeze. The ethanol odor from the factory was particularly strong today. I blinked hard as I finished my thoughts out loud. "From what you've said, your mother must have loved you very much. Who took care of you after that? Do you think Curtis will try to hurt *you*?"

Paul shook his head. "He hasn't so far, which is strange if it has something to do with the family. But anyway, everyone conveniently forgot me in foster care. I was four or five. I had my mother's journal and the clothes on my back. As I got older, I understood my mother was gone, but I dreamed of the day my father would come to get me.

"And finally, *finally*, Martin's well of student's to poach ran dry. And he remembered his first cash cow's son. His son. Hoping I had some talent, he found me in a group home, ready to age out of the system. He got me into this University and enrolled in the art department. I had enough clues from Margaret's journal to know who he was and what he probably wanted. It hurt like hell to know he didn't want to know me. I mean literally like the fires of hell burning my skin. He and God had forgotten me. Didn't want me. Didn't care. Until they needed something." He gasped as if he were choking and I grabbed his hand and squeezed. His eyes locked with mine and he nodded he was okay.

"I chose to come because I had no other options to get out of where I was at, but I only took from him what I had to. I got a job to pay for my own tuition, books, and food. I do sleep here occasionally because I like it here. Even though my father isn't keen on a family relationship, I like to be near him and he's here a lot. But I shower and wash my clothes at the river cottage he still calls his. Technically, the wedge of property it's on is mine. I inherited it from my mother, who had bought it with her share of the art empire. She left me a small trust that has paid the taxes and kept it intact for me. I had access to the bank account tied to it when I turned twenty-one last year.

"I found Wendy, my half-sister, in Washington State. I invited her to come to town and spend some time with our father. We didn't know he was sick yet. She's kind of off the wall and I figured she'd drive him nuts. And I wanted family around. She already had a degree since she's a bit older. Instead of taking classes, she opted to see how long she could be a squatter. She moved in with a friend she'd met on a tree hugger retreat – Silage or Silo or something."

"Seal-o," I annunciated for him

"Yah, her. I found Martin's wife, Julep, had remarried and had twin genius sons a bit younger then Wendy and I. One was in London, and the other was getting out of prison. I met with Coby, the evil twin, and a plan to plague Martin and investigate Uncle Curtis began to unfold. It all would have gone off without a hitch too, if Coby hadn't decided God existed while he was playing the part of his goodie-two-shoes brother and hanging out with you, little Clare." He reached out a hand and caressed my cheek.

"I have that effect on people, or so I've been told." I smiled sadly at him.

"I know," he whispered. "I can't blame him when it feels like more and more I'm going to be one of them. I've got no other options to get out of where I'm at."

"God never forgot you, Paul."

"I know. I've turned my energy to studying Christianity since we saw the food materialize out of nowhere one Monday night a few months ago." His thick lips stretched in a shy smile. It struck me how much he looked like Martin. I shivered involuntarily. I was at peace about working with the new and improved Martin, but old cringes died hard.

"I've learned while she was living a lie, her sin allowed a door to be open for evil to come and go in our lives as it wanted. We live in a world ruled by sin so we have to keep asking for God's protection and help to live righteous lives. She wasn't doing any of that which gave her no protection and no way to protect me. She was killed and I was tossed a drift, helpless. I had Godly people take me in, but I rebelled and my heritage of generational issues prodded me to reject God and misbehave. And I listened to them instead of love. Bad got worse and grief turned to hate. Until it's nearly consumed me."

I was floored by his shrewd summation of the pain in his life. It didn't make it any easier to feel, but he knew what was causing it and what he had to do to stop it.

Paul does know a lot more than anyone gives him credit for. Including me.

"But I still don't understand why you wanted to steal the movie file so bad from Zac you'd hurt someone at the lab to do it."

"That's the thing, Clare, I didn't hurt anyone. There was no one around when I was there. If they hadn't said that was part of the heist, I'd have come forward with the movie a long time ago." His voice gathered strength as he warmed to his explanation.

"See, one of the opportunities I got when I tracked down my great uncle was a position for a security management company he put me in touch with. Companies hire me without knowing who I am so they can't watch for me. I break in and take whatever item they are trying to protect. I was hired anonymously to pinpoint the protection issues for the movie file. I didn't know Zac owned the lab nor what the file was even about until later. I only focus on getting in, getting the item, and getting out undetected.

"After I take the item, I return it with a password so they know I'm their consultant and it's not a forgery. I give them a professional evaluation on how to heighten their security. It's all in-house and never reported to the police or the media for any reason.

"When I saw all over the news the lab had been destroyed, I knew someone else had come after me trying to find the file. And it was someone dangerous since they'd hurt a lab worker. We've been trying to find out who it was so I could take the file and the evidence to the police, but we haven't had much success."

"Who's 'we'?" I asked, rubbing the tickle in my nose from the factory smell crowding the air in the studio.

"I went to Jay and Kay for help. They had more knowledge about the graphic design world then I did. Only they were as clueless as I was as to who had planned a heist on the same night I was testing the security. They got cleared to work in the underground lab here and brought you in for ideas.

"Personally, I suspected Curtis Sulferson since he had gotten me the job and Zac was a part of the family tree he'd just as soon not have in the spotlight. Plus everyone knows he has his hands in some shady stuff."

"Uh, Uh," I said and held up my hand. "He claims he is not involved in shady things and has been made notorious by rumors. He professes to be a Christian. Don't know for sure, just saying," I ducked my head, "that's what he said."

"If he's not involved like we think he is, then that could very well be the case. But I'm skeptical." Paul scratched his head and doodled in the dust on the floor with his fingers for a moment. "Anyway," he continued, "Before all that lab stuff went down, Coby and I were trying to figure out the undercurrents around here. Coby moved to the area last spring while you were gone. He couldn't get a job at the lab because of his record and his dad's firm, so he took Toby's spot in school and worked an angle with Sulferson's PA."

"Yes, I know, Muriel. So you knew Toby was really Coby the whole semester?" My eyes had narrowed despite my best efforts to remain an impartial listener.

He nodded, miserable. "I'm sorry, Clare. I hated fooling you, but I knew Coby was harmless." He cleared his throat. "And I've always hoped deep down inside you'd fall for me."

"Awww, Paul. I thought it was an infatuation freshmen year. I didn't know you still wanted to go out."

"That will be enough. Thank you, Miss James, we can take it from here." Director Pierce stepped forward out of the shadows and we were surrounded by agents.

Not being alone when you think you are is an unpleasant experience. We both leapt from the floor with a yell and Paul stepped in front of me shielding me with his body.

"It's okay, Paul, I'm Director Pierce from the FBI. Clare can verify my ID. We've been shadowing her all semester. She keeps crossing back and forth through this case like a drunken sailor on furlough." She held her hand out for a shake. Paul held his hands up on each side like a man under arrest in a movie. We waited for her to go on. She relaxed her arm back to her side.

"I didn't know they were here, Paul," I said, unclamping my hands from his shoulders where I'd clung to him when they barged in on us. "How long have you been listening?" I asked.

Director Pierce was all business. "We need your statement, Paul, and the movie file. Once we find the real killer, the most you would be looking at would be obstructing an investigation because you didn't come forward with the information you had. But I'm going to recommend no charges with your cooperation."

"But I don't have the movie file now." Paul's hands in the air drooped and his shoulders sagged in defeat.

"Do you know where it is at?" The Director was doing all the talking. The rest of the agents watched us silently.

"I gave it to Coby for safe keeping since it was so small. I'm clumsy with stuff and he's precise. He had it injected in the pug he took from Sulferson. Like a microchip. We thought it would be well hidden and safe in such a high profile dog until we could figure out who had raided the lab after me. Coby had taken the dog in the first place so we could get Sulferson to talk. We thought he was behind the lab job and we thought he'd talk to get the dog back. At least a name if not a confession.

"Only Reginald has been a nightmare to keep a hold of. He's been in and out of our hands so fast and so many times I never got to confront Uncle Curtis. And now I don't know where he or Coby are at."

"*That's* where the movie file has been this whole time? *Inside* the dog?" I was flabbergasted. "How is it possible for a whole movie to be inside a dog?"

"Let's sort this all out back at the farm. It's better you come with us then wait for the local PD to piece this together and pick you up." The Director rotated her arm over her head and the agents seized Paul and headed off through the center of the building.

"Where are you going? Aren't you taking me too?" I ran after them.

Director Pierce held back and fell into step with me. "It's okay, Clare. We'll take care of him. If his story checks out, we'll keep him safe while we look for Coby. We're going out through the catacombs in the basement to keep a low profile. Go back to your room and finish packing for Christmas break. There are agents still keeping an eye on you so you'll be fine."

My steps slowed until I stopped on the darkened stage in the middle of the arts building. Paul looked back at me as they pulled him down the stairs at the back. His eyes were red-rimmed from crying but his square jaw was slack with relief. He didn't have to keep any of his secrets anymore. I waved uncertainly. Then I was standing alone on the stage. It was cold and deathly quiet in the giant black auditorium.

It occurred to me that I now knew where the movie film was and they still hadn't caught the person who destroyed a lab and tortured a technician trying to locate it.

And then the bag went over my head and the dark auditorium got a whole lot blacker.

❧ Chapter Twenty-Eight

I couldn't remember the way the saying went exactly. Something about as dark as a blind man looking for a black dog in a room with no lights. *Is that how that saying goes or am getting disoriented in the dark?* I thought with irony as I squinted to see through the bag's material.

We hadn't gotten very far. My captor and I had waited for a bit, me hanging like a sack of potatoes over his shoulder, him panting under my weight. And then when he finally began to descend the stairs the FBI had used moments before, he staggered and swayed.

Oh, God, don't let him trip! I thought in a moment of panic. *We'll be sausage by the time we reach the bottom of all these stairs. Help me get out of this whole mess in one piece.*

Even through the bag over my head, the damp, stale, burnt-corn smell of the underground tunnels was overwhelming. I switched to breathing through my mouth. My wrists were chaffing where they'd been bound behind me with zip ties. I wondered how far ahead of us the FBI agents were with Paul. *Could they hear me if I yelled?*

My kidnapper staggered and clenched at the hand rail and I instinctively curled my body tighter around his shoulder. He paused, grunting. *This guy is going to kill us if I don't say something. And besides, he's wearing some super nice cologne. Anyone who wakes up and puts on that cologne is not a devious person. It's such a pleasant smell. He isn't going to stab me yet anyway, I haven't told him what he wants to know. I do like that cologne, though. In fact, he wears the same kind of cologne as . . .*

My thoughts were interrupted as my kidnapper leaned against the wall next to us, smashing my leg at a painful angle under his weight.

"Look," I started. Inside the bag, my voice sounded muffled to my own ears. "If I'd have known you were going to go to these lengths to talk to me, I'd have skipped the piece of cake after lunch. Can't you set me down and let me walk down the stairs with you? You should be wearing a mask like the lone ranger or something, then I wouldn't have to have this bag over my head and I could see where I'm going."

He busted out laughing and then bit the echoing noise off as quickly as it had burst from his body. He turned his head and whispered in my ear. "Clearly you're a better kidnapper then me." I felt him tilt to the side and I slid off his back, feeling for a step with my toes, my party gown swirling around my ankles. Once I was balanced on a stair, the bag was shucked off my head and I was looking up into Toby's dark blue eyes in the dim light.

He cupped my face in his hands and bent his head to kiss me. His mouth tasted salty with sweat and I could feel myself melting from the inside out in my first real kiss.

Wait a minute. Toby's in Chicago and his eyes are light blue. This is Coby!

I shook my head against his hands and felt with my toe for the next step down. "Stop, please!" I whispered fiercely into the dark.

He released me as I stepped down and away from his embrace.

"I don't even know who you are *and* you're kidnapping me. It's a little early to claim Stockholm syndrome."

"Clare, Clare, it's me. You do know me." He grasped my shoulders and bent down to speak inches from my face. "I heard you figured out Toby had a twin. Well, you and I have spent the same amount of time going to school together that you and my brother did in London. I know all about it because he wrote me every detail in his letters. And I've changed the same way he has. Thanks to you, I understand God in a way I never did before.

"Since I've had to stay out of sight, I've missed you, Clare. Not being able to ask you what I should do next has been killing me this whole time." He ran a hand through his hair and looked down at the stairs under our feet. "Look, I have to confess, I'm the one who took your box of notes from London. I couldn't risk you comparing my handwriting to Toby's and exposing me until we got this whole thing figured out. But I still have them all for you." He looked up quickly and took my hand. "I've been so torn up doing stuff like that. I hated it. I wanted to tell you everything. I needed you to pray for me. The Bible has made me feel alive. More than all the thrills I sought before," he paused and kicked at the step he was on. "Well you know, jail."

"Well, that explains a lot." I sighed. "Did you search Paul's things too?"

He looked up startled. "No. No, Paul and I are working together. I didn't go through his stuff."

"Hmmm." I stared at him, not seeing him. I almost remembered something, but I couldn't quite recall what was important about what he had just said.

"Clare? Clare, don't leave me hanging. What are you thinking?" Coby's uncertain words snapped me out of my puzzling.

"Sorry. Look, I'm so thrilled you have come to know and love God as much as I do. Really. But I didn't do that for you. God's been working in your life. The fact that you hated deceiving me shows you have been listening to his voice. He's the one changing your heart, not me or anything I can do or did. Coby," I hesitated over saying his name. It was disconcerting. "You don't want your salvation or reasons for it to be tied to a person. It should be for you and about you. Only." I swung my bound hands out from behind me in the dim light. "And there's something creepy about tying me up and holding a knife to my back to tell me."

"Oh, no, I'm so sorry. I forgot about that." He quickly moved down on the step where I was balanced in my strappy shoes and slit through the zip tie with his knife. I brought my hands around in front of me and rubbed my wrists.

He smelled and sounded so much like Toby, I wanted to hug him and tell him it was all going to be all right. But that wouldn't be fair to him since I was planning to tell him I wasn't attracted to him. Just his brother who looked exactly like him.

This is so confusing. I shook my head as if that would help clear it. *If life ever gets back to normal, I'm not sure I want to get involved with a twin, even if it is Toby. I feel like I'm talking to Toby, but then whenever I remember I'm not, I feel like I was tricked. Well, I was.*

Coby was whispering by my ear again. "I didn't mean to scare you, Clare. I needed to talk to you without the FBI arresting me immediately. I didn't hurt anyone and I've been keeping Reginald and the movie file safe down here in the locker room next to the brown living room. I saw them take Paul away and your guards were outside, so I jumped at a chance to give you the movie chip and slip away. But I've obviously messed this all up. It was a spur of the moment thing. I didn't even think about how it would look. The bag and ties were in a maintenance box back stage and I have a pocket knife because no real artist should-"

"-ever be without a knife." I cut him off to finish the familiar phrases.

He was grinning at me, leaning back against the hand rail. "My mom says that all the time."

"Well, that would make sense, I guess, since she's Martin's ex and he used to drill us with stuff like that in class. I'm still trying to wrap my head around Wendy, your half-sister, and Paul, who isn't really any of your relation, but he's Wendy's half-brother."

"Yah, crazy how people mess up their lives and their sins hurt their children with dysfunctional relationships. Since I met Paul and learned from you about God, I've been looking at relationships in the Bible. It fascinates me how families interact.

"I mean, look at Paul. He had a rough time of it. Then there's Sammy. Her stepdad adopted her and raised her like his own. They had the same philandering father, but their mother's choices –"

I cut him off. "Wait, did you say, Sammy? As in Samantha

Sullivan? Who I'm doing the painting for?"

"Yah. Her mom was one of Martin's conquests. My mom, Julep, told us all about what a bad guy he was. Which was a little like the pot calling the kettle black, as you'd say, since she lied about being a Christian so my dad would marry her. She told me she did it because she loved his loyalty and the good morals he got from being a Christian and even though she'd never be one, she knew he wouldn't act like Martin. Martin is bad news. He drove several of his students to suicide.

"Sammy came here at Martin's invitation, like Paul, to get to know her father. But Martin was looking for the next big artist to steal work from, like he did with Sammy's mother when she was a student here. Only Sammy can't paint her way out of a paper bag. You told us so. So Martin revoked her scholarship. That's why she took the dog commission, you know?"

What he was saying tied up a lot of loose ends. If Sammy was Martin's daughter and Santhe's granddaughter, then the Sulferson trust would provide for her when she completed the painting. She needed me to rescue her from financial ruin all right, by completing the painting of Reginald.

And I'd heard somewhere else about Martin's students killing themselves. It was Wendy the night I overheard her confronting Martin in the studio. She said her mother told her about it. Her mother, Julep Gallonte Fir.

I turned and ran down the stairs in the dark, clenching my skirt up around my waist and screaming, "Director Pierce, Director PIERCE, STOP! HELP! I KNOW WHERE REGGIE IS! STOP! WAIT FOR ME! I KNOW WHO DESTROYED THE LAB AND KILLED THAT GUY! Or at least I have a pretty good idea." I muttered under my breath as I reached the last step and hit the floor running.

❧ Chapter Twenty-Nine

"Can you pass the gravy, please?"

I leaned carefully over my plate to hand the antique gravy boat across the table to Trixie. She was framed by a large painting of fruit in oils hanging behind her that I'd done my freshman year. Her cheeks were flushed and her eyes were big and starry. The room was toasty, what with the swirl of Christmas dinner smells, the number of happy people packed in the old farm house, and the roaring fires in the coal stoves heating the rooms. I shrugged out of my sweater and draped it over the back of my hard wooden chair. When I turned to hang it better, I could see snow falling outside through the large white paned windows framed in Christmas garlands. Dusk was creeping over the landscape and making the lights in them twinkle.

I could glimpse the big spruce standing guard out in the living room where it was decorated to the nines with a collection of handmade ornaments that took years to assemble. Strings of popcorn and dried berries looped the branches. When the festivities were over we'd hang the lines on trees outside and the birds would have a holiday feast of their own.

I turned back to the room and looked from table to table. They were pieced together in a long snake for all the revelers I'd invited home to belly up to. Martin sat, pale and smiling, hanging on Wendy's every word as she told a funny story. Paul and my dad laughed heartily at the punch line and slapped Jay and Kay on the back. I smiled at Kara as our eyes met and she shook her head in a knowing gesture as she took Jay's hand. Trixie was across from me listening to my Grandmother talk about country Christmas's she remembered and my Grandfather was next to Key and my youngest brother, John, listening to stories of Hawaii. Toby and Coby were sampling stuffing as my mom shared what she's put in it and my middle brother, Eugene, punched my arm from where he sat next to me.

"Pass the dirt." He snickered. I handed him the pepper and punched him back. We both sneezed as my jab jostled his arm and sent a small cloud of black spice into the air.

"Toss me a roll, will you, Clare?" I heard my dad through the buzz of voices and automatically launched a homemade dinner roll over the diners' heads. He snagged it out of the air.

"You just threw a roll! Too funny!" Trixie was delighted.

"I certainly did. Doesn't everybody?" I raised my eyebrows and shoveled a big bite of turkey into my mouth. She laughed and stuffed her mouth with ham.

"Hey, you can swallow, but you can't take any more bites until you finish the story of why all these people are crashing our Christmas Eve." Eugene waved his fork at me.

"Shhh! Keep it down. No need to be rude." I nearly choked, shushing him. I speared some green beans my mom and I had canned last August after we got home from back-packing across Europe. It felt like years had passed since then. It had only been four months. I waved the beans at him.

"So where was I? Oh yeah. So Curtis Sulferson, the guy who owns the big factory in town, you know, the one we always pass on the way to my school?" He nodded. "He thought Martin, the professor over there, was a serial killer. Martin is his nephew and for decades, his students have ended up dead. Granted some were suicides and some were accidents. And they were all over the country." I paused to eat my green beans. Eugene waved his fork at me impatiently. I swallowed hard and laughed.

"Ok, Curtis' sister had run off with his mother's boyfriend after they blew up his mother and other sisters at the factory years ago. She has remained in hiding her whole life, but she told her son, Martin over there, everything about her family and what happened. Martin came back to Sulfersonville and began teaching at the University with a young wife and a new art career. Curtis knew about them immediately and kept an eye on Martin. His investigators easily unearthed Martin's mistress and son, that's Paul we're talking about, several miles from his wife and daughter, who is Wendy there." I pointed again down the crowded table. Eugene nodded.

"So, Curtis suspected that Martin hadn't painted or drawn anything of his own in his art shows, which he hadn't, but Martin was savvy and left no trace. His students denied doing anything for him and eventually ended up dead somewhere under no suspicious circumstances. Just that they *all* ended up dead. Since Sulferson couldn't find any evidence to turn over to the police, he tried to manipulate Key here next to you, into putting a hit out on Martin through his gang tagging connections. We can give him points for vigilante creativity. He planned to stop a predator and turn Key in to the police tied with a bow."

Eugene nodded, but I waved a finger, no, at him. "But he had the wrong people. Martin and Key weren't killing anyone. And his behavior was so suspicious he got himself put under investigation. Key went undercover with an FBI deal and cleared Curtis, as well as Martin. Only Martin was still losing students." Eugene's eyebrows went up.

"And then it clicked for me when I was on the catacomb staircase with Toby. I mean Coby. He told me Sammy was Martin's daughter too, which I hadn't known. And his mother had told him about other students hurting themselves because of Martin. I remembered Wendy had mentioned Julep told her the exact same things.

"Someone other than Martin was destroying his prize students so I surmised it had to be someone he hurt. But it wasn't a student because anyone who had done at least a show's worth of art for Martin was dead. Except Paul, but he wasn't old enough to hurt his own mother or the first few students, so it couldn't be him."

"Okay, it's time for pie and presents!" My mom clapped her hands and stood up from the table. She began bustling about clearing away the empty platters and bowls where hot food had been heaped only an hour ago.

The room burst into one big protest.

"You said no gifts."

"You threatened not to let us come if we brought presents."

"Hey, we didn't get you anything."

"Oh no, so sorry."

I held up my hands for silence. "Whoa, Whoa, you are all correct." The room quieted. "However, these gifts are not from us. We offered to give them to you, though, since you would all be here at the same time."

My parents were nodding agreement and the guests settled down but they were clearly mystified. I disappeared into the next room and pulled the rectangular, brightly wrapped boxes out from under the tree. Passing one to each guest, I helped my mom finish clearing the china place settings. We circulated through the room refilling punch goblets and passing out thick wedges of pumpkin and pecan pie with dollops of ice cream or hand-whipped cream. Coffee, tea, and peppermint hot chocolate brewed in the kitchen, perfuming the house for the evening of games to come.

Soft Christmas carols played in the background and the conversation swelled again as the guests tore at the traditional paper wrappings.

"I knew it! It's a study Bible. I love it!" Coby (or was it Toby?) burst out first. Martin was caressing the cover of his copy with a far off look in his eyes. Wendy and Paul had flipped theirs open without a word and were lost among the pages of footnotes and study maps. Kara and Jay were filling out the name cards on the front page. Kay's package was unopened on the table in front of his empty seat, his untouched slice of pie balanced on top. He had excused himself to go to the restroom just as we had started passing out the goods.

I sat back down at my seat with a dessert plate and glass of punch. Key and my brother were laughing over something the neighbor had done and Trixie was listening politely, but her gift remained unopened on the table next to her empty plate. I leaned forward and nudged her with my foot under the table.

"You've got to be kidding me, Girl. Who doesn't take something free?"

"But it's not free, Clare." She was seriously uncomfortable.

"Oh, that's right, you have to turn over your pain, your bad relationships, and all your unhappiness. Man, you've worked hard for a long time acquiring that mound of goodies. I can see where it would be hard to let such precious, fun stuff go." The sarcasm in my voice stopped my brother's conversation. My Grandmother put an arm around Trixie's shoulders and Key put his hand over mine on the table. His voice was gentle as he spoke for me.

"She loves you, you know, Trixie. She wants the best for you, and she's getting frustrated 'cause she can't understand what you're doing. You on the other hand, think you're okay. But here's the deal. It's a mirage. It feels easier to hurt 'cause it's what you know. All you've ever known." His voice was like salve soothing a sunburn. "You're with friends here, Trix. I don't have to know what you did. I already did it before you." Trixie had been staring at her hands until he said that, then she looked up at him, startled. Key seemed not to notice as he continued, "Sin is sin in God's eyes. No matter what it is we did, it all separates us from him and looks like black goo on us when he sees us.

"I've been in your mirage too. And I chose to take Christ's

hand and walk out of it. I chose to trust him. And I can tell you from experience, I found out his helping me was a lot less work then nursing the hurt and running scared. So how about it? Be free, Trixie. Be free." He held out his hand to her across the table. His other hand was holding mine and I grabbed my brother's hand. He grabbed my Grandfather's hand and so the chain went around the table. Conversation had stopped as the life line to pull her out of the mire linked like quicksilver. Every one sitting at the table was looking at her.

She studied Key for a long moment without looking around the room and I realized I was holding my breath. When she slipped from her chair to return the unopened gift to the base of the Christmas tree I exhaled in a long sigh and the room murmured in disappointment.

"What do I do, guys?

Key and my brother looked at each other.

"Keep praying," Key offered. "Don't ever stop. It's not too late yet. In fact, while we are all here and holding hands..."

"There's no time like the present, let's pray now while we are all together," my dad suggested as Kay slipped back into his seat and Paul and Wendy parted hands to bring him into the circle. The room was quiet as we bowed our heads.

"Dear Jesus," my dad paused to gather his thoughts and I took a deep breath before he continued. "We open our hearts to listen to your words in John 3:16. *For God so loved the world that he gave his only begotten son that whosoever believes in him will not perish but have everlasting life.*

"Please forgive us for our sin and our wrong choices and the things we've done to hurt each other and you. We know we are bad and we need you. We believe you are God's Son and you died in our place for our sin so we could have fellowship with God. Thank you, Jesus. We ask you to soften the hearts of those we love, such as dear Trixie. Break down the barriers holding her back in Jesus' name and release her, God. We lift her family and all the families of those here tonight up to you wherever they are at. Be with them, encourage them, love them, and bless them. Thank you, God, in Jesus' name we pray, Amen."

Amens echoed around the room.

My brother nodded. "Yah, and be thankful, Clare, for all these other friends you've got who opened their gifts from Jesus. Merry Christmas, Sis."

"Merry Christmas, Lily." Key squeezed my hand.

"Merry Christmas, Guys." I choked back tears of emotion as my heart swelled. I was vaguely distracted by the faint smell of sour grass.

Martin stood up, knocking over the dining room chair he was sitting on and called out in panic, "There's something wrong with Paul. Oh God, help him."

The room erupted in chaos as Paul clenched his throat and grew pale. It felt like I was frozen in time after I leapt up from my seat. I could hear the other guests yelling as chairs toppled over and glasses bounced on the table cloth, spilling their bright contents among the shreds of Christmas paper and pie crust crumbs. Paul sank to the floor and I lost his face behind the crowd of backsides.

"STOP, JUST STOP, OKAY?" Kay leapt up on a chair and clenched at his short hair, his face contorted in the misery of the figure in Munch's painting 'The Scream'.

"Get back! Give him air! Let him breath! I know what's wrong with him," he said.

"What?! *You* do!? No! No, you don't have anything to do with it." Jay grabbed at his brother's arm, trying to pull him back down to his seat.

Kay brushed his brother's arm off and waved everyone back. He pointed at Paul, wreathing on the floor. "Call an ambulance. I poisoned him. It was my girlfriend's idea. She got me the stuff and told me how to do it. I left the room because I didn't want my brother's God, but I saw my chance to prick him with my ring when you were joining hands to pray, so I joined back in. But then you all accepted me, unconditionally, no questions asked. You prayed, Sir, and frankly I, I don't know what happened. I changed my mind. My heart felt full or something. Full of sludge. I don't know what happened, but I want to know Jesus. I don't want to hurt Paul. I don't want to do bad things anymore just to get someone else to like me. Is it's too late for me? Is it too late to save Paul? My ring has already pricked him. He's going to die! I'm so sorry. Help him. Help him."

The frozen breath from outside filled the room as the side entrance to the house popped open, letting snow and a flood of people in through the front hall. No one flinched as the cold licked our ankles and our bare arms. The entire room was already frozen by Kay's declaration. I looked up and noticed the room's two small chandeliers swaying in unison on either side of his head.

"Son, what did you give him?" The stern voice of a man in black with a big gun slapped Kay from across the room. He shook his head and stopped crying long enough to stutter out the poison his girlfriend had distilled at her perfumery for his ring dispenser.

Two swat members drug Kay out of the room clenching the still wrapped Bible.

Paul had stopped moving and the paramedics worked quickly to give him several shots. Martin was moaning softly from the floor where he knelt, holding his son's lifeless hand. Wendy was stroking her father's head as she stood beside him. Paul's eyes blinked and he sputtered to life again, gasping for breath and waving his free arm. The paramedics quickly took his vitals and signaled he was ready to move. Unable to speak yet, Paul clenched Martin's hand and winked at Wendy, reaching across the paramedic's back to squeeze her arm with his free hand.

"Folks, he's going to be fine." One of the paramedics stood to address the room. "Thanks to the quick poison identification, we were able to administer the proper antidote and he's going to be just fine. We'll take him in for observation tonight, but he'll be back before Christmas dinner tomorrow."

The room erupted in applause as a stretcher was brought in to load Paul out to a waiting ambulance. They had shucked his holiday sweater and undershirt and Martin gathered them into his arms. Through the door standing open I could smell the vehicle's diesel fumes and the coal smoke pouring out of our chimney. Trixie was standing in the arch way from the living room, blocking the cheery view of the Christmas tree with her body so the tree's blinking lights made her glow.

One of the guys with a jacket emblazoned with FBI paused in the door on the way out. "They'll keep him for observation overnight at Goshen Hospital and then he'll be back here right as rain tomorrow for Christmas. No need to try and visit him tonight. Everyone should rest. We'll let you know more after the holidays, but we have all we need to stop a dangerous serial killer." He glanced around the room in shambles. "Sorry for disrupting your meal, folks. But at least it's going to be a Merry Christmas!" He closed the door tight behind him.

The room was quiet except for the soft music still playing in the background as if nothing had happened.

"Well, knowing it was going to happen didn't make it any less terrifying." I said, sinking into the seat Key had up-righted for me.

"Wait a minute," Wendy said with a sniffle. "You *knew* this was going to happen?"

"How'd you know?"

"Not too funny, Clare."

"What just happened?"

The questions came at me like a swarm of angry bees and stopped with one louder than the rest.

"You *knew* my brother was going to do that? Why didn't you tell me? I could have stopped him!"

I wiped my hand across my eyes and looked at Jay.

"I didn't know who the accomplice was, Jay. Or even if there was one, you guys. She could have had a slow delivery system set up somehow in his clothes or his food. Look, let me start from where pie interrupted the story I was telling." I pleaded. The room was full of shock and grumbling as chairs scrapped and glass tinkled. Everyone was seated again and all eyes were on me. Trixie had rejoined the table and was leaning into my Grandmother's arm. My mom was hugging Wendy and Martin was sitting wedged between Toby and Coby, still clenching Paul's sweater. My brothers and dad sat near the windows glancing suspiciously into the night.

"What happened here tonight involves people some of you know and even love. I'm sorry if what I have to share causes you pain, but it proves guilt beyond a shadow of a doubt." I paused to take a drink of punch from my still standing glass.

"As you all know, the authorities have been investigating a break in at a computer lab where a valuable movie file was stolen and one man was killed. At a dead end for suspects, the police agreed to look at the heist from a different angle, especially when they learned Paul had taken the movie file as part of a security test and there was no robbery.

"I suggested the heist was to hurt or defame Paul, rather than to steal the movie rights or harm the lab's owners. With that in mind, the investigation focused on Paul's history — his mother's accidental death and what he had in common with a lot of other students who were now dead."

I hesitated and glanced at Martin. He nodded. "They were all art students. They had all helped Martin with his art exhibits over the years. Just like Paul had with the last exhibit Martin launched before his surgery and treatments.

"We knew from Sulferson's investigations Martin was only the common denominator, not the killer. So we went back to the beginning and traced who had died and who had lived in his inner circle.

"Process of elimination highlighted Martin's first wife, Julep Gallonte, who later became Julep Gallonte Fir. She's both Wendy Gallonte and Toby and Coby Fir's mother, but unfortunately she's

...an a skunk with rabies.

Clearly she figured out Margaret Vales was Martin's student ...ss, art creator, and Paul's mother. She killed her in a car ...ent, but that didn't solve her jealous problem. Martin continued ...eek help from students, both men and women, to be successful ...d famous. And it didn't stop Martin's affairs. Julep left him. Martin ...ent through a dry spell of depression and exhaustion and the exhibits and deaths both stopped.

"After she remarried," I gestured toward the twins, "and had other children, Julep still kept tabs on Martin's activities, according to evidence the FBI has gathered. She didn't approach any of his art liaisons however, until she found out her husband was sick and possibly dying. I'm so sorry, Guys," I licked on my lips and tilted my head at Toby and Coby. They sat expressionless, listening.

"The timeline fits." I continued. "Sammy's mom was attacked this summer when the Fir brother's dad went into the hospital. The FBI profiler believes his sudden illness unleashed whatever helpless feelings she had used in the past as motivation to attack the other people in Martin's life. She felt as helpless to stop her current husband's illness as she had to stop her first husband's affairs. Since art is so personal, she lumped it all together and went after anyone Martin used for anything she couldn't do."

"She finally came full circle back to Paul, the son of Martin's first mistress. The FBI profiler believed she didn't bother with him in the first place, because Martin didn't want him. Abandoned in foster care, Paul was safe as long as he stayed away. It's not logical, but taking human life isn't logical." I took another sip of punch and avoided Jay's eyes.

"So, with a son here on campus. Sorry, Coby. And Toby too actually. She manipulated both of you to make sure she had one person on this campus to report back to her what was happening. In fact, Toby, it was not accident you transferred to our campus after London. When you think about it, you could have transferred anywhere. And when you decided to stay home and help your dad's company, it's no surprise Coby and Paul met. Even better for her, they became friends. She could stop snooping around campus and spreading her famous corn silk perfume all over the place. I knew that smell wasn't my imagination. Anyhow, she got firsthand information Paul was painting Martin's next show from Coby."

"Actually, that part's not right." Coby spoke up in the middle of my narrative. "It wasn't me. I didn't want Toby to know I was down here until I got a square shot at winning you over Clare, so I stopped talking to her about what I was doing. I'm still sorry for deceiving you guys." Toby doffed him on the shoulder and he grinned. They had made amends after years of strife. I just wasn't sure how I felt about either of them. Coby's smile faded as his eyes met mine across the room. I had to invite them to this trap to catch who was helping Julep, but I had told them both I wasn't dating them. Coby had taken hen Toby. I wasn't surprised. Toby had a lot on his plate.

Mom must have gotten most of her information from Kay." ontinued. "I had my suspicions she was seeing someone, but I want to face it. I mean, our dad could still pull through and s dating a guy our age. How could she do that? It's gross."

Martin groaned and rocked gently, hugging Paul's sweater. he twins on either side of him put their arms around him and whispered comfort in his ears. Wendy was still sniffling. I sighed. None of this was easy. I better just get it over with as quickly as possible. I picked up with what Director Pierce's team and I had pieced together.

"The only thing that saved Paul that night at the lab was the weather report. He thought a bad storm was coming during the night he'd scheduled to do the security heist of the movie file so he went earlier than originally planned. He had come and gone by the time Julep arrived to destroy the lab and set a trap to attack him. She mistook an artist, who came back to download some images he forgot, for Paul."

"The profiler believed she had cultivated a new romantic interest to replace Mr. Fir and even help her with her revenge. We were looking for a male student without moral or religious inhibitions who had ties to the art department or Martin. Someone left out or not as successful as the other students."

I looked at Jay.

"They didn't even have you guys on my list to come this weekend. You weren't suspects. I knew you were a Christian and I thought Kay wasn't far behind. And you were graphic artists, not fine artists. Kay asked to come. He said he wanted you to be able to celebrate a real Christmas since your parents would forbid it. I'm so sorry, Jay."

My dad came around the long table and put his arm around me. "None of us can control each other's actions or make choices for each other. God gave us free will so even he couldn't force us to choose salvation. Thank God, he was able to use this situation to break Kay's heart and help him see the salvation he desperately craved during the very prayer he was using to harm someone and damn himself. How amazing is that?"

Jay flung his arms around the two of us, sobbing. We group hugged, pulling in Kara.

Toby placed a warm hand on my back and I turned and gave him a hug too. "Why didn't they just arrest mom. Ugh, I can't hardly call her that now." He paused to collect himself. "But you know, why risk Paul's life? I mean, how did they know Kay was going to hurt him here?" He asked in a low voice. The group hug broke apart and everyone turned to listen.

"There was a ton of circumstantial evidence." I swallowed on a dry throat. "But there was nothing to physically connect her or her accomplice to the crimes. They couldn't arrest her.

Paul suggested being the bait. He wasn't fazed by the risk
 he does it all the time with the faux break-ins. The FBI had a
 ction detail on him. They asked me to host an event they could
 itor. They needed to draw out her sidekick and make sure they
 d an airtight case against her. Now they can use Kay's testimony
 nd the evidence they obtained during her attempts on Paul's life.

"I do love having you all here for Christmas, though, don't get me wrong." There was nervous laughter around the tables.

"Attempts?" Wendy spoke up. "Did you say *attempts*, plural, on Paul's life?"

"Well, yes." I ticked them off on my fingers. "There was the lab attack, this poisoning, and when she came down to see you in the hospital. Some medical items went missing from your room and it's likely she took them. She spent some time in the art studio and around Paul's cottage, but nothing happened."

Wendy gasped. "I thought she was truly sad about Martin, I mean dad's, illness and the transplant. I thought she really wanted to see me in case something went wrong. She was only here to kill Paul? She's a monster!"

The people in the room murmured agreement as Wendy paced back and forth across the room hugging herself.

"This is a lot to process and a lot of hurt too." My mom stood up from her seat and gathered Wendy into a one armed hug. "I'm going to invite our pastor and his wife over tomorrow for anyone who wants to talk. And you're all invited to stay the night. I'll start getting sleeping bags and pillows around."

"Let's get this place cleaned up and play some games or something." Trixie jumped up and began setting up glasses and stacking pie dishes.

"Yah, Paul wouldn't want us to sit around sad. None of us can change Julep's actions, and Kay is going to get help." Key gripped Jay's shoulder and squeezed it. "In the meantime, we can enjoy each other's company and the time we have together."

"And that mint cocoa and coffee smell great!" Kara chimed in.

"I agree." The room paused as Martin spoke for the first time. "There's plenty of guilt trying to weigh me down and I have to keep asking God to forgive my actions and free me from it. What I did in the past was wrong. And it may have incited Julep to hurt people. But I didn't make her do it. Paul did a brave thing, volunteering to stop someone from hurting more people. I thank God he'll be back with us tomorrow and I don't want any of you kids to blame yourselves for anything that has happened. Whether good or bad, we can chose what we do. For now I choose to trust God to take care of all of us and I'd love to play some games."

Everyone cheered. His speech summed up the evening nicely. Martin pulled his walking cane up from where it rested alongside the wall and hobbled into the living room. Everyone pitched in to make quick work of the cleanup and join him. While they bustled around, I slipped out and sat on the floor across from where Martin had positioned himself on the couch to see the tree lights.

"How are you doing, Sir?" I asked timidly.

"With my insane ex-wife, my health, or my dozen children?" He coughed a little.

"I didn't know you had a dozen children!"

He laughed and pretended to smoke a cigar. "Old habits. Air cigar they call it." He took a fake drag and looked at me over the top of his glasses.

"I might have more children. I don't know what was happening out there beyond the walls of my little kingdom. But I can say, with healthier living and the Lord's blessing, I can maybe make it another ten years. Time to get to know my children the right way. Time to find the families of the art students whose work I used and divide up my personal fortune between them.

"And time to make sure the Sulferson Silk Trust has all my offspring properly documented so that every time it releases money for meeting one of its daffy demands, they get what they need. One thing I've learned, desperation and hopelessness make people do ugly things. I want my kids to have options. The trust releases an amount proportionate to the number of heirs documented so no matter how many there are, they all always get the same funds. When you completed Reginald's portrait, you helped release funds again. We have thirty days to offer proof before the vault closes until next time."

"So it benefits none of you to produce more or less heirs?" I asked.

"Bingo, my girl." He puffed away on his air cigar. "Everyone is equal. Old granddad was a smart guy. He protected the family fortune and the family."

I considered what he said. Protecting the family fortune and the family. It was easy to see who was in God's family, but it was not so easy to protect what was God's family fortune. His fortune was made from moments like this. Sitting across from my most feared and hated professor at the base of my family Christmas tree. Because of God's forgiveness.

"So are we all good, Sir? Is it all over?" I leaned my head sideways and laid my cheek over on the seat of the couch across from him where I was leaning my back.

He smiled. "On the contrary, Miss James, it's just beginning. My life is just beginning as a new creation in Christ." He ground out his air cigar on the sofa arm next to him and smiled at me.

"Merry Christmas, Clare."

I smiled back. "Merry Christmas to you too, Martin."

If you enjoyed Soul Stain, like charleneyoder on facebook,
write a review on Amazon,
or better yet, give it to a friend to read.
You know Clare would!

And join Clare in 2016 for her next art adventure:

SOUL CHARADE

Be self-controlled and alert. Your enemy the devil prowls around like a roaring lion looking for someone to devour. 1 Peter 5:8

The devil doesn't come to you with his red face and horns, he comes to you disguised as everything you've ever wanted.

Clare is thrilled to take a vacation and monitor Toby Fir's movie for him at the Sarasota Film Festival in Florida. Famous white sandy beaches and cookouts by day, infamous Hollywood actors and red carpet soirées by night. What could be more exciting then Spring Break in paradise?

Certainly the handsome stranger she keeps running into without getting his name has some possibilities.

Or finding the identity of a helpless girl with amnesia who was roofied at a wild party.

And it's dazzling to think of working for a wealthy art patron who's offering her a job restoring the masterpieces in a sea side mansion.

But perhaps the best adventure of all is locating the owner of a ring embedded in stone on the finger of a statue that a circus performer slipped in her pocket when she was visiting the run down Ringling Museum...

Who is not what they seem? Can Clare let down her own guard long enough to catch who is masquerading before it's too late and she's tricked into selling her soul to the devil?

Discussion Questions

Topic One

Have you ever given up something you thought was distracting you from God? If not, would you be willing to do it?

What Clare experienced abroad left her aware of a supernatural world existing alongside our natural world. She is convicted to examine magic as evidence of Satan's side of that world and decides to try and eliminate her casual use of it in acceptable social contexts. When she doesn't eat her fortune cookie after a meal with friends, they laugh at her.

Read Matthew 9: 18-26
Have you been laughed at or teased for what you believe? Or perhaps you've laughed at someone else? Maybe not to their face, but you were thinking they were crazy as you listened to them. The people in the house laughed at Jesus when he told them the girl was only sleeping. They knew beyond a doubt she was dead, and yet she wasn't. It's important to check what others tell us with what the Bible says, and we also need to recognize that God is not limited to our earthly understanding of things .

Bunny Trail

Read Acts 19:11-20
Do you think magic is used the same way in our world today as it was in Bible times or are we more educated and in less need of it? What do you think God's reasons are for commanding his people to avoid sorcery and witchcraft? What do you think would happen if you decided to eliminate magic from your vocabulary and entertainment?

Topic Two

Browse the story of Joseph in Genesis 37-45
Read Colossians 3: 12-14
Clare struggles with forgiveness in the story. She deals with how she feels about the way her professor treated her by ignoring him. She relishes her bitterness and enjoys when other students retaliate against him. Eventually she realizes she must make amends with him, but is further hurt by the way he takes her olive branch offer. Over time Martin actually becomes repentant over his behavior and they are able to work on healing together. This isn't always the case with forgiveness.

Have you ever tried to avoid forgiving someone? How does it feel? What should we do if the person we need to forgive doesn't change toward us? Are some actions too bad to forgive? How do we feel until we actually forgive someone?

Topic Three

Romans 12:19
Is seeking our own justice or revenge ever warranted? Key painted Martin's car rather then physically harming him for destroying his work and insulting him. According to the code he lived by, this was mercy. What is mercy? Was this real mercy?

Curtis Sulferson thought Martin was a serial killer but he had no proof. He tried to orchestrate his death to protect others by manipulating a thug he thought should be imprisoned anyway. He planned to turn Key in after it was done and thus create a punishment for both men. Was he right in acting out this justice if Martin had been the real killer?

As it was, Martin was not the killer, and Key was on a path to get out of his entangling life. God can see the bigger picture. Is this why he asks us not to take revenge? Have you ever taken your revenge on someone and felt better? What could you have done instead?

CPSIA information can be obtained at www.ICGtesting.com
Printed in the USA
LVOW11s0954310116

472840LV00005B/15/P